FRIENDS AND ENEMIES

FRIENDS
AND
ENEMIES

Also by Kate Alexander

FIELDS OF BATTLE

FRIENDS AND ENEMIES

Kate Alexander

ST. MARTIN'S PRESS
NEW YORK

Library of Congress Cataloging in Publication Data

Alexander, Kate.
    Friends and enemies.

    I. Title.
PR6051.L363F7   1983   823'.914   83-2890
ISBN 0-312-30545-1

First published in Great Britain by Macdonald & Co Ltd.

First U.S. Edition

10 9 8 7 6 5 4 3 2 1

Chapter One

The snow was good in Kitzbühel in January 1938. On the first morning of her holiday Christine Brookfield was awakened early by the brightness of the sunshine reflected on snow. She had folded back the long wooden shutters of her bedroom window the night before and now she turned over and blinked in the clear morning light. She threw back the billowing *Federbett* under which she had slept and got out of bed, feeling with her feet for her slippers.

Pulling her dressing gown round her, she opened the windows and stepped out on to the balcony. The air was bitingly cold. She tucked her hands into her sleeves and stood hugging her arms to her, knowing that it was silly to stand there and freeze and yet unable to tear herself away.

Her room was at the back of the hotel. Immediately in front of her there was a wide field newly covered with untrodden snow; beyond that a low, undulating hill, a scattering of dark fir trees, and then the mountains, stabbing upwards into the clear blue sky.

She yawned and took a deep breath of the crisp air, and was just beginning to turn away when a movement on the higher slopes caught her eye. She paused and waited. Someone was ski-ing down with effortless ease, a young man, wearing trousers and a sweater of vivid blue. All alone, he swept over the powdery snow, bending and twisting, absorbed and expert. There was something particularly appealing about that solitary figure making its brilliant, swift descent. Christine could not take her eyes from him.

He reached the nursery slopes and gave a vigorous push with his ski-sticks to take him across the almost level field behind the hotel. Christine leaned over the balcony, forgetful of the cold. As he drew near he seemed to sense that someone was watching him. He looked up and saw her. Slowing down, he shifted both sticks to one hand, pushed his goggles back on top of his head, pulled off his blue knitted hat with his free hand and waved it in the air, laughing up at her. He was very tall and very fair, with smooth golden hair falling forward over his forehead. She wasn't near enough to see his eyes, but she was sure that they would be blue. His face was tanned, and he had sharp, clear-cut features. Christine made a little movement of her hands applauding him. He laughed and flourished his hat again and then disappeared from sight round the side of the hotel.

She realized that she was shivering with cold and turned back into the warmth of her bedroom. There was a knock on her door and her brother's voice called: 'Chris, are you awake?'

'Awake and out of bed,' she said. 'Come in.'

She sat down on the bed and pulled the *Federbett* round her.

'I've been out on the balcony and I'm frozen,' she said as Michael came into the room.

'Daft.'

'It was worth it. There was someone ski-ing down the mountain. He was marvellous.'

Michael glanced out of the window. 'He must have been good,' he said. 'That's not a regular *Piste* and ski-ing over virgin snow isn't for beginners. Are you going to sit there all day huddled up in a quilt or has he inspired you to get up and take your first lesson?'

'I long to get started. It looks wonderful.'

'Don't imagine you're going to find it easy, just because you've seen what an expert can do,' he warned her. 'You're in for a few spills in the snow before you get within spitting distance of that standard. Still, you're fairly athletic and reasonably fit. You shouldn't do too badly.'

'What's the day's programme?'

'We'll talk over breakfast. Get dressed and I'll see you downstairs.'

Over their coffee and rolls in the dining room he said: 'First, we must get you fitted out with some decent skis, then I'll find you a beginners' class and one more advanced for myself.'

6

'Do you still have to go to a class, even though you've been coming for five years?'

'Yes, unfortunately,' Michael said with a rueful grimace. 'Two weeks a year doesn't turn you into an expert. I need some tuition just to bring me back to the point I reached last year. I'll join you again at lunchtime and if you're not too worn out I'll take you out for some practice this afternoon.'

They walked down the street together after breakfast, between the wooden houses with their balconies and overhanging eaves.

'Just like all the photographs,' Christine said contentedly. 'Oh, Mike, isn't it beautiful?'

'It does get you, doesn't it?' he agreed. 'That's one of the joys of ski-ing, the scenery is so grand.'

They were early arrivals at the ski hire shop and Christine was soon fitted with skis of a suitable length. She was a tall girl, nearly as tall as her brother, and from being a pretty child she had begun to turn into a striking young woman. It made Michael uneasy, the realization that if she hadn't been his sister the only way he would have been able to describe young Chris was 'gorgeous'. She had everything: a lovely face, a mass of ash blonde hair with a natural curl, a tall, slim figure with all the right curves and, above all, the thing which made her vitally attractive, a look of glowing health and the enjoyment of being alive.

Michael was built on stockier lines than his sister, darker and less strikingly good looking. He was four years her elder and until recently had treated her patronizingly as his kid sister. Now she suddenly seemed to have grown up and a new companionship had sprung up between them. When she had begged to be allowed to have a ski-ing holiday he had agreed to take her along with him.

'I suppose it will be all right,' Barbara Brookfield had said doubtfully.

'I think they'll be safe enough in Austria,' Harry Brookfield had replied. 'There's been a bit of Nazi activity, but they shouldn't run into any real unpleasantness.'

'That wasn't what I was worrying about. Christine is only

seventeen. I suppose Michael will know how to look after her? I mean, all those dashing ski instructors . . .'

'Don't be silly,' her husband had replied from behind his newspaper. After a brief pause he had added: 'I'll have a word with Michael.'

'Thank you, darling.' Barbara touched him lightly on the head as she went past.

She might have been less reassured if she had known that the extent of her husband's warning had consisted of one laconic sentence.

'Keep young Christine out of mischief,' he had said. 'I suppose it's a bit too late to tell you not to do anything you shouldn't?'

Michael grinned at him. 'I can look after myself, you ought to know that by now. As for Chris, I'll keep an eye on her.'

He remembered this brief conversation with his father when he noticed the ski hire man's quick admiring glance at Christine's long legs and taut behind as she bent over to try the fastenings on her skis. Randy old devil. Michael gave him a frosty look and hurried his sister out of the shop.

He recalled it even more vividly when he met her ski instructor. He had just seen her put into the care of a dependable-looking man in his thirties when a young blond giant came up and joined the group.

'This week I will take the Novices Class,' he announced in English. 'Hans . . .' He spoke rapidly in German to the other man, far too quickly for Michael to be able to pick out a word of what he said, but he put his own interpretation on the other ski instructor's surprise, his smile, the quick, understanding glance he gave Christine. A bit of fixing was going on, a change in classes was being made, and the reason for it was young Chris, grinning all over her face and trying to pretend she didn't know what was happening, and looking, Michael had to admit, good enough to eat.

'I am Gunther Hofmeyer,' the young man said.

'I saw you earlier this morning,' Christine said with an eagerness and a naivety that gave away her youth. 'It was you, wasn't it, ski-ing down the mountainside?'

She tried to sound nonchalant, but this really was the most

thrilling thing that had ever happened to her, to be picked out by such a fascinating man on her very first morning. She had been right about his eyes; they were the bluest she had ever seen.

'I have seen you also. You stood on the balcony in the cold and clapped your hands.'

Christine's smile was radiant. 'I enjoyed watching you.'

'It is my great pleasure. There is a restaurant at the top of the ski tow. Every morning I go up with the new bread and ski down with no . . .'

'Tiresome pupils.'

'Not all pupils are tiresome. You, I think, will learn quickly. You look fit, probably you play games. I think it will be easy for you.'

'She's not long left school,' Michael said.

Christine gave him a furious look. 'Go and find your own ski class,' she said. 'I'll see you later.'

'All right, but watch your step.'

'I'll take great care of her,' Gunther promised. 'No bones will be broken.'

As Michael left them he said: 'He is your boy friend?'

'My brother.'

'Ah, yes. I see now the likeness.' He looked at her thoughtfully with a smile in his vivid blue eyes. 'Some likeness.'

Christine struggled to appear unconscious of his meaning. Falling for the ski instructor was the oldest cliché in the book, but a girl had to be allowed to feel flattered when someone who looked as if he had just stepped down from Valhalla hinted that he thought her attractive, so she smiled and coloured up and looked very pretty and very young and Gunther was amused and intrigued by her confusion. She was easily the best looking girl of the season so far, with just the sort of looks that appealed to him: long legs and strong, slim body, charming colouring, and above all a laughing vitality, an air of being eager for life, that made her more exciting than the usual run of pretty little girls who passed through his hands.

'To work!' he said. 'Come. I will give you your first lesson.'

During the morning Christine learnt to sidestep up a slope,

to ski down it, although in a wobbly fashion, and how to adopt the inelegant plough position which helped to check her speed of descent. She fell in every conceivable position and Gunther laughed and made her struggle up out of the snow on her own.

'I am very hardhearted, but it is better that you learn,' he said.

'I'm hopeless. I shall never be any good at this.'

'Not so! This afternoon you must practise what I have taught you. Perhaps the brother will help you.' He hesitated. 'Unfortunately, I am not free.'

Christine struggled not to look too gratified at the implication that he would have liked to have spent more time with her. Pushing her straggling hair back under her woolly hat she said: 'I'll be too stiff to move tomorrow.'

'No, I think you will not feel it as some of the other beginners will. A long hot bath when you go back to your hotel and perhaps this evening a glass of *Glühwein* at the Glockenspiel Bar. That will revive you.'

It was not a date, but when Michael said later: 'What about this evening? Do you want an early night?' Christine said: 'I heard that the Glockenspiel was a good place to go. Don't let's miss out on anything. We're only here for two weeks.'

Michael agreed readily, not minding where they spent the evening, but by the time they arrived, the Glockenspiel was crowded, hot and noisy.

'Not much room,' Michael said, looking round. 'Do you want to stay?'

'Oh, do let's. Look, some people are going over there. If we hurry we can get their table.'

It was a heavy wooden table set against the wall, with benches on either side and room to seat four. They slid in opposite one another and sat watching the shifting crowd of people. A group of musicians in leather shorts and embroidered braces began playing a jolly, thumping tune on accordions. A waitress came over to them and wiped the table with a quick, professional flick of the cloth. Michael ordered *Glühwein* and watched a little regretfully as the girl went away to fetch it. A nice, buxom wench, but having a sister along was going to cramp his style on this holiday.

Christine was just taking her first tentative sip of the hot, spiced wine when a tall figure moved away from the bar at the other end of the room and stopped at their table. It was Gunther, carrying a large mug of beer in one hand. Instead of his ski clothes he was wearing a *loden* jacket of dark green with lighter green facings and a fine lawn shirt tied at the throat with a green cord. His bright hair lay smooth against his head like a layer of golden paint.

'So, you are still able to walk?' he asked.

Watching his sister's flushed cheeks and pleased smile, Michael was filled with gloom. So that's why she had been so keen to come to this particular café. Little minx. A fine holiday this was going to be if he'd got to sit around playing chaperone to young Chris the whole time.

'Would you like to join us?' he asked Gunther reluctantly. Better for it to come from him than from Chris, who was obviously going to invite him to stay anyway.

'Thank you.'

Gunther sat down beside Michael and opposite Christine. 'Have you enjoyed your day?'

'Oh, yes!' Christine said. 'I've been practising like mad this afternoon, haven't I, Mike?'

'You've been very conscientious,' he replied with a dryness in his voice which was not lost on Christine. She gave him a quick look, conscious and apologetic, and he shrugged slightly. The child had got to grow up some time.

'Do you live in the village?' he asked Gunther.

'No. I am here every winter since many years because my cousin is married to the man who owns the ski school. It is a very good opportunity for me to make sport and also, since I am become proficient, to earn money. I myself am from Berlin.'

'Then you're German, not Austrian,' Michael said slowly.

'Yes, I am German.' He glanced from one to the other of them. 'This makes a difference to you?'

'Of course not!' Christine spoke quickly before Michael had had a chance to think of a reply. 'I mean, I think it's terribly important for ordinary people like us to be friends and understand one another.'

11

'I am glad to hear you say that. In Germany there is much goodwill towards England. It is not natural for us to be against one another. We should be allies.'

'Germany has made that rather difficult,' Michael said. 'The regime in power at present . . .'

'Oh, you must not say things against Hitler! Truly, he is a great man. He has done wonders for our poor country.'

'Are you a Nazi?' Christine asked. She looked troubled. He was not at all like her idea of one of Hitler's supporters.

'I have never joined the Party,' Gunther admitted. 'But that is not because I do not support what has been done. I am not quite old enough to remember the years that are past, but my mother has often spoken of the times when it was necessary to go shopping with a suitcase full of marks because of the terrible inflation. Our unemployment rose to six million. All this has been changed. Our economy has been transformed.'

He hesitated and then he said: 'There are things which have happened which we must all regret, but you must understand that it has been a time of revolution for us and revolutions do not happen without bloodshed.'

'What about the Jews?' Michael asked in a low voice.

Christine looked from one to the other of them, out of her depth. She was scarcely given a thought to the people behind the newspaper stories she had skimmed through. Now, because of Gunther, they became real to her. Gunther was very real, and he was a German.

'Oh, yes, the poor Jews!' There was a touch of sarcasm in Gunther's voice which made Michael look at him sharply. 'That question, too, must be seen in the proper context. All over Eastern Europe there have been pogroms against the Jews. They have fled – where to? To Germany. We have been flooded with them and we cannot afford them. How many, I ask, have you taken into England?'

'I don't know,' Michael admitted. 'But we have heard some nasty stories about the way they have been treated in Germany.'

'I too have heard these stories. To my great regret, I have to say that I believe that some of them are true. There has been perhaps some exaggeration, but also there have been cases of

injustice and even hardship. What can I say? There are good
men and bad men in all countries. There are even, if I may be
allowed to hint at such a thing, both good and bad Jews. Some
of them aroused anger by their money-grubbing ways. You see
how good my English is? "Money-grubbing", that is very
idiomatic, is it not?'

Michael suspected him of trying to change the subject.
What Gunther was saying went against everything he had
believed, but it was very persuasive, especially when he went
on with real earnestness: 'I can only say to you that never have
I lifted a hand in violence against any man, woman or child of
any nationality or religion. We are here together for this short
time. Can we not set an example and show that it is possible
for us to be friends?'

'Yes, we can,' Christine said.

She held out her hand and Gunther took it in his. 'Do you
permit that I ask your sister to dance?' he asked Michael, but
his eyes were fixed on Christine's face and her hand was held
fast in his.

'I suppose so,' Michael said. It was a grudging consent, but
Christine's enthusiastic acceptance more than made up for it.

Dancing with Gunther was a delight. He was taller than she
was, for one thing. She had to tip back her head to look up at
him. He had natural grace and a strong sense of rhythm and
even though the dance was an unfamiliar Austrian one with a
lot of stamping of feet and twirling round he guided her so
strongly that she had no difficulty in following him.

They returned to their seats laughing and very pleased with
themselves. Michael was still sitting alone, staring down into
his almost empty glass. Gunther gave him a quick thoughtful
look and then glanced round the room.

He lifted his hand and a girl detached herself from another
group and came to join them.

'This is my cousin's eldest daughter, Mitzi,' Gunther said.
'Perhaps for this evening we four can join up together?'

Michael opened his mouth to say he would find his own
girls, thank you, then he took another look at Mitzi and
changed his mind. She was small, dark and plump, with a
delightful, mischievous smile.

'You are English?' she asked. 'I am so happy! In other years we have had many English for the ski-ing. Now, they are few.'

'Therefore we must be particularly welcoming to them,' Gunther said.

'That is true,' Mitzi agreed.

In the face of so much goodwill, and of the saucy look she was giving him, Michael's animosity weakened. They were, after all, in Kitzbühel to enjoy themselves, not to put right the wrongs of the world. Whatever the shortcomings of his nation, Gunther himself seemed a decent chap and Mitzi, of course, was Austrian, which made a subtle difference.

By the end of the evening they were all firm friends. They parted at the café and Christine and Michael walked back to their hotel together. No arrangements had been made, but there was a vague feeling that the next evening would probably be spent in much the same way.

'You do like him, don't you?' Christine asked anxiously.

'He seems all right. And he can't help being German,' Michael said tolerantly. 'Don't let him sweep you right off your feet, will you?'

'Certainly not. For Pete's sake, it's just a holiday friendship. But I must say I think I'm terribly lucky to have the most glamorous man in the place interested in me.'

In the face of that simple expression of self-satisfaction Michael didn't feel called upon to utter any of the more serious warnings that had been passing through his mind. After all, how did one set about telling one's sister not to get herself seduced? It was impossible. Young Christine was no fool and she had been sensibly brought up. She would be all right.

By the third evening Michael was too heavily involved with Mitzi to care that it was Christine and Gunther who walked home alone under the dark, starry sky with the frozen snow crackling under their feet. They walked slowly, arm in arm, tired from a day spent in the open and an evening of vigorous dancing, heads a little hazy from the hot wine they had been drinking, conscious of the harmonious movement of their bodies as they walked in step.

Before they reached the hotel, Gunther stopped and turned Christine to face him. She lifted her face and he kissed her.

14

When they separated she leaned against him, her face buried against his shoulder.

'M-my hat fell off,' she said in a muffled whisper.

He bent down and felt on the ground for the little red knitted hat which had fallen from her head when she tilted it back. He slapped it against his thigh to get rid of a sprinkling of snow and then fitted it back on top of her head.

'This is because I am so good at kissing,' he explained. 'It popped right off your head in surprise.'

There was a teasing, laughing note in his voice which gave her a strange sensation in the pit of her stomach.

'I think perhaps that's true,' she said. 'Oh, Gunther!'

They clung together again and this time he held her tightly against him and did not let her go until she began to struggle to free herself.

'So, now I know all about you,' he said.

'What do you know?'

'That you are very young, very sweet. That you have not made love . . .'

'How could you possibly . . . I mean, of *course* I haven't . . .'

'I have embarrassed you,' he said, laughing at her. 'Always I have heard this expression "an English rose" and now I know just what it is. A girl as soft as a rose petal, cool and fragrant and, deep inside, a heart of fire. That is my English rose.'

There was nothing Christine could say in reply to that. She stood with her arms round him, her head turned against his chest.

'I can't think of anything to say,' she whispered. 'I feel . . . inadequate.'

'So? There is no need. You are very adequate. Come, you will catch cold. We must not stand here any longer. I must take you to your hotel and go to my own lonely room and try to sleep, which will not be easy because I shall be thinking all the time of my English rose.'

'Me too,' Christine said. 'I'll be thinking about you, I mean.'

She spoke fervently, and a wry little smile twisted his mouth as he realized that it had not even entered her head that he could be hinting that they might spend the night together. A very proper little girl, very nicely brought up and, in spite of a capacity for passion which he detected in her, likely to go home from her holiday the same pure virgin she had been when she came.

It occurred to him in the days that followed that it was a pity he had come to like Christine and her brother so much. He ought to drop her and find someone with a better understanding of the game he was playing. Not that it was really so important. She would be gone at the end of two weeks and there would be other girls, new arrivals, someone who would take his mind off an unfortunate weakness for a mere babe. The trouble was, she so exactly suited him. She learned to ski quickly and easily, spurred on by her desire to please him. At the beginning of the second week he was able to take her on her first long downhill run. He was surprised how anxious he was for her. When she fell halfway down the slope he felt his heart give a lurch of alarm and it was not until he reached her side and saw her lying in the snow laughing helplessly that his breathing righted itself.

When they danced together it felt exactly right. The top of her head was just on a level with his mouth. He loved the soft brush of her hair against his lips and leaning his cheek against her smooth forehead. She was eager and intelligent and quick to laugh.

Towards the end of the second week they grew silent with one another, unwilling to speak of the thing that was uppermost in both their minds, that in a day or two they would have to part. His kisses were more urgent now, and he handled her body in a way that made Christine gasp in a shock of pleasure and alarm. He knew that he had gone too far when she drew away from him and said in a whisper he could only just hear: 'It's too much, Gunther. Please, I can't bear it. And I can't . . . I mustn't . . . you do see that it isn't possible . . .'

'Yes, yes, *Liebchen*, I know.' He took her back in his arms, but gently this time. He heard her agitated breathing and felt the way her heart was beating against his chest. He put his head against hers and closed his eyes in an agony of frustrated desire. 'I would be very good and gentle, and very careful with you, if you would let me love you,' he said, but with little hope that she would agree.

'No, I can't. We've known one another such a little time. Please, we mustn't do anything foolish. It would be sordid and horrible, and I'd feel people knew.'

He did not reply, but his arms slackened and they began their slow, reluctant walk back to the hotel. He felt angry with her, but when she asked him he denied it.

'Oh, no! I am a little hurt because you will not trust me. And it is hard – I think perhaps you do not realize how hard it is – for a man to want a girl as much as I want you and to be refused.'

They reached the lights of the hotel and he added: 'Now, go quickly, before I forget all my good resolutions and pick you up and carry you off and make you forget that you are a good little English miss.'

He turned away and left her and Christine went into the hotel and up to her room and undressed with hands that shook and limbs that felt as if they were on fire.

They were a little strained with one another when they met the next day, but the coolness between them did not survive their nightly walk to the hotel. They clung together as urgently as ever, until Christine drew away and whispered: 'Gunther, do you get a holiday this year? A summer holiday, I mean?'

'Yes, I shall have several weeks,' he said. 'Why do you ask, *Liebling*?'

'I wondered if you would come to England. You could come and stay with us. I can't bear to think of going away tomorrow and never seeing you again.'

'Your father and mother . . .'

'They'd be pleased to have you. Do say you'll come.'

'I will certainly think about it,' he said slowly. 'While I am still training to be an architect I don't have much money. I must consider whether I can save up the fare.'

'Can we write to one another in between? I'll start learning German.'

There was something about the earnest way she said that which touched him. 'I would like that. Yes, we will write and if your parents truly invite me I will do my very best to visit you this summer.'

It was the only thing that kept Christine going during the long journey home. All the way across France in the train, all the time they were heaving around on the ship in the cold English Channel she felt desperately miserable. It was still a very new experience, being in love. She had been pleased and excited when Gunther had singled her out, but the kisses she had given him had been even more experimental than he had realized. She had not been prepared for the passion in his response nor for the way she had so nearly been swept away by it. Above all, she had not expected it to hurt so much when she had leaned out of the train window and seen Gunther, playing truant from his ski class, turn and walk abruptly away from the station.

She did her best to conceal her state of mind from her mother, chatting gaily about her wonderful holiday and her enjoyment of ski-ing, but inevitably Gunther's name began to creep into the conversation and her voice changed when she spoke of him.

'We liked him very much,' she said with a false brightness which made her mother look at her carefully. 'We became real friends, didn't we, Michael? As a matter of fact, Mum, I've suggested he might come and visit us this summer.'

Mrs Brookfield saw the look of dismay which appeared for a moment on Michael's face and drew her own conclusions, but all she said was: 'A German, darling? Do you think that's wise with all that's going on over there?'

'He's not a Nazi,' Christine said quickly. 'He's really . . . very nice.'

She looked at her mother with desperate eyes and Mrs Brookfield took pity on her. 'You know your friends are always welcome,' she said. 'It's a long time until the summer, but if he still wants to come I am sure we can make arrangements.'

'We're going to write to one another,' Christine said. 'As a matter of fact, I've been thinking of adding German to my secretarial course. You know they said I'd stand a much better chance of a really good job if I had a second foreign language besides French.'

At the secretarial college which Christine had attended since leaving school the previous summer the pupils were encouraged to discuss what they read in the newspapers. Christine, scanning the papers with an attention she had never shown before, tried to defend the German position, but she did not find it easy. Nor was the remainder of the news very cheering. The war in Spain continued and in Moscow the trials of dissidents were being held with a cynical disregard for truth and justice.

At the beginning of March she read that Pastor Niemöller, an outspoken, courageous opponent of the National Socialist regime, had been tried and sentenced to seven months imprisonment. Since he had already served eight months in prison awaiting trial he should by rights have been released immediately. Instead, he was taken into 'protective custody' by the *Schutzstaffel* and disappeared into a concentration camp.

'A good man,' Harry Brookfield remarked. 'I'll be interested to hear what your German friend has to say about that trial, Christine.'

'He doesn't mention it,' Christine said.

She was troubled by a new constraint she detected in Gunther's letters. She had asked him what he thought of the outbreaks of pro- and anti-Nazi demonstrations in Austria and he had simply not replied.

The trouble in Austria grew more intense and Christine struggled to understand the complex issues involved. Chancellor von Schusnigg called for a 'free and independent Austria' and arranged for a plebiscite to be held to determine the will of the Austrian people. The Nazis riposted with the slogan 'One people, one Reich'. On the day before the voting was to have taken place German troops massed on the border. Under threat of invasion the Chancellor abandoned the plebiscite and resigned his office. After the Austrian President Miklas had refused to nominate as the new Chancellor Dr von Seyss-Inquart, who had been appointed Home Minister at Hitler's request, the German troops crossed the border. The President was forced to yield, Seyss-Inquart became Chancellor and an all-Nazi Cabinet was announced in Vienna.

Gunther's reaction was contained in a few guarded sentences in his next letter to Christine: 'You will, I am sure, have been anxious for Mitzi in the last few weeks. She and her family are well, but I grieve for them in their affliction.'

'It seems a funny way of putting it,' Christine said when she read this portion of the letter out to Michael.

'My guess is that he suspects his letters are being censored. He doesn't sound quite so cocky about his friend Hitler now, does he?'

'He says something else a bit further on about his visit to England. Listen: "I would ask you to let me know if my visit to you would still be welcome. I wish very much to come and I think it will still be possible, but only if you wish it." Well, of course, I do want him to come. Have Mum and Dad said anything to you about it?'

'Dad isn't keen. Mum's main worry is that he'll be here at the same time as the Jardines.'

'They're not going to stay with us,' Christine pointed out. 'I know Mum's all worked up at the thought of seeing her long-lost friend from America, but surely that needn't stop me having one of my friends to stay?'

She tackled her mother that evening. 'I can still have Gunther over this summer, can't I, in spite of Austria and everything? I mean, politics really have nothing to do with the way we feel about one another.'

'How do you feel about one another?' her mother asked quietly. 'Do you imagine you are in love after a two-week holiday and a few letters?'

Christine's face flamed at the way she had given herself away. 'When you meet him you'll understand,' she said. 'Dad won't stop him coming, will he?'

'I'll talk to him,' Barbara promised. She explained to her husband when they were in bed that night. 'Don't put your foot down and say he's not to come,' she advised. 'Christine has worked herself up into such a state that she'll see the pair of them as a couple of martyrs if you forbid it. Quite honestly, darling, I think a second meeting may disillusion her. Let him come and this silly infatuation will work itself out.'

'I don't like it,' Harry said. 'I came home on the train with

Rosen tonight. You know, Mark Rosen, the accountant. He's a Jew, of course. His sister is married to an Austrian and living in Vienna and he's had no news of her since the *Anschluss*. He's sick with worry, talking of going over and trying to get her and her husband out of the country to join him here. When I talk to someone like that I'm uneasy, to say the least, about having a German to stay in my own house.'

'I could make the excuse that it's not convenient with Connie and Bob and Lucy coming over from America.'

'Not much of an excuse considering they'll be staying with Connie's mother,' Harry said, echoing his daughter. 'No, I'll bite on the bullet and accept this young chap for a week or two. He can't be all bad if Michael and Christine like him.'

He was not pleased when he learned that Christine, without consulting her parents, had invited Gunther to stay for three whole weeks, but he confined himself to a few pointed remarks about lack of consideration and treating the house like a hotel which Christine recognized as no more than a token grumble.

The other friends they were expecting to see that summer were Connie Jardine, who had been a friend of Barbara Brookfield's ever since the days when they started school together, and her American husband and young daughter, who was Barbara's godchild. Connie's husband was a lawyer living in Minneapolis, with an extensive practice which made it financially easy for him to bring his English wife over to visit her family from time to time, but it was five years since Barbara and Connie had last met and the letters which had been crossing the Atlantic between them were full of plans for the visit. One of the first things that Connie did on arrival at her old home was to telephone Barbara.

'Hi, there!' she said. 'Guess who?'

'Connie! Wonderful to hear your voice. You sound so American, much more than you did last time you were over. Did you have a good voyage?'

'Just great. I sound American? Bob is always telling me I'm so British!'

'When are we going to meet?'

'I'll come over to see you tomorrow.'

'By that time Christine's German boyfriend will be with us.'

'I certainly sympathize with you about that. Never mind, Babs, I'm sure you're terribly wise not to turn it into a Romeo and Juliet affair. They're just a couple of kids who'll fall in love half a dozen times before they finally settle down.'

'Christine had her eighteenth birthday last month and Gunther is nearly twenty-two. Hardly children. Still, I'm cheered to know you think I'm doing the right thing. Oh, I am so looking forward to seeing you, Con.'

It occurred to none of them that Gunther, too, might be encountering opposition to his visit to England. His sister disapproved and said so.

'An English girl! Are there no suitable girls amongst our own people for you to marry?'

'We are not speaking of marriage. It is a friendship.'

'So I should hope! You have good Aryan blood in your veins, you should perpetuate it.'

'Really, Frieda, that is no way to talk,' Frau Hofmeyer intervened. She was a thin, grey-haired woman with an anxious expression, a silent person who kept her thoughts to herself except when, as now, she was trying to keep the peace between her two children.

'One is able to speak frankly of these things in the new Germany. The Führer wishes good Nordic types like Gunther to marry young and have plenty of strong, healthy children.'

'Gunther is not yet established in his profession. Time enough for him to have a family when he can support them.'

'I accept that, but I can't approve of these English friends. The British are against us . . .'

'Perhaps I can persuade at least one or two of them that we're not their enemy,' Gunther said.

It made his sister stop to think. 'There's something in that,' she said. 'I'll talk it over at the next meeting. Why don't you join the Party, Gunther? It would be easier then for you to understand where you may be going wrong. You would be given guidance.'

'Suppose they turned me down for being too frivolous? Think how humiliated you'd be!'

It did not please her, but not for the first time he had succeeded in avoiding an issue which was a bone of contention between them. Frieda was a dedicated Nazi, unquestioning, full of devotion. Gunther had doubts, doubts which had been unformed, almost unacknowledged, at first, but which had grown stronger and now, with the annexation of Austria, had become a source of profound anxiety to him. He looked forward to his visit to England not only because he wanted to see Christine again, but also because he thought of it as a respite from the questions which haunted him. If Germany had been wrong over the Austrian question, was it possible that there were other things which he had accepted in the past which might have been equally wrong? There was no-one with whom Gunther could discuss such thoughts and it was gradually borne in on him that the fact that he did not dare to voice them outright, even to his most intimate friends, was the most damning indictment he could have made of a regime which had seemed to him so recently to promise new hope to his troubled country.

His fears were reinforced by a visit from one of Frieda's co-workers after her Party meeting. Ulrich was not a man Gunther liked. There was something secretive about him, though on the surface he appeared open, even brash, in his wholehearted support of the Nazi Party. Frieda was devoted to him, in her eyes he seemed to come second only to the Führer himself, and Gunther guessed that she cherished a painful and probably hopeless love for him.

Gunther stiffened when Ulrich spoke of his visit to England, anticipating that he would have to justify himself, but the Nazi appeared to be in favour of the idea.

'You're just the type the British like,' Ulrich said. 'They'll treat you as a friend because you are good at sport. You can do a service to the Fatherland by explaining our policy to them, making them see how necessary the *Anschluss* was, how ardently the Austrian people themselves desired it. If it's put to them properly they must understand the plight of the Germans in Czechoslovakia, too. They've been separated from their homeland long enough.'

23

'It's a difficult question. I'm not sure I've studied it deeply enough to call myself an expert,' Gunther said.

'There's time enough for you to master it before you go. There's another thing. Frieda tells me you have no camera.'

'No.'

Ulrich smiled and held out the leather case he had been carrying over his shoulder.

'This is an excellent one. Made in Germany, of course. No-one can rival us in the production of high-class lenses.'

'For me?' Gunther said in bewilderment.

'We'll call it a loan, but if you make good use of it then I think you can look upon it as your own on your return.'

'I don't understand.' He said it with quiet determination, but in his heart he knew and feared what was coming.

'Take as many pictures as you can. Snapshots of your friends, of course, but other points of interest as well. The port when you arrive, railway lines, factories, military establishments if you have the chance – and the British are so careless, so stupid, that it's quite likely you will find many opportunities.'

'I'm not a spy.'

'You're a German. Do as you're told.'

'I'm going to stay for a short time with some people who live in a suburb outside London. I can't believe that any opportunities such as you speak of, will come my way. And what is the purpose of it? We aren't at war with Britain and we've been told war is not our aim.'

'It's as well to be prepared. The British are a treacherous race. Who knows what they may spring on us. Surely you wouldn't refuse to defend your country if it were attacked?'

'No.'

'Then look upon this as a form of defence. Take the camera and use it well. We'll meet again on your return.'

Gunther glanced at his sister. She was smiling, her face flushed with pride. Gunther felt a surge of disgust. It was wrong that she should look pleased because he was being asked to do something so repugnant. But he took the camera without any further protest and included it amongst his belongings when he packed.

It swung over his shoulder during his journey, a heavy reminder of the unexpressed fears in his mind. As the cross-Channel steamer approached the English coast Gunther slipped the camera from his shoulder and stood holding it in his hand, dangling from the strap. The ship lurched and the camera banged against the rail. Gunther opened his fingers and let the strap slip through his hand. There was a splash and the camera disappeared beneath the water.

It was his first visit to England, even though he had studied the language so successfully, and everything about it confused and surprised him. The greenness, the tidy gardens full of flowers, the bustling life of London when he passed through it, the unintelligible Cockney voices when he asked for directions, and the friendliness of the people. He managed to put through a telephone call to announce his safe arrival, found his way to Victoria Station and caught the train to Eveleigh. It was further from London than he had expected and the size of the Brookfields' house, with its large garden and swimming pool, surprised him.

Connie Jardine also remarked on the swimming pool. 'That's new,' she said. 'How come you decided to indulge in such a luxury?'

'I had a legacy from an uncle,' Barbara said. 'And you'll probably remember that there was a piece of waste ground next to this house which had always worried us. It would have been a disaster if someone had bought it and put up a house which overlooked us – we've grown so used to our lovely secluded garden. Harry was enthusiastic when I suggested buying the plot and adding it to the garden, but not so keen on the extra work, and it was the children who thought of the swimming pool. It cost quite a bit to install, but they've had so much pleasure out of it that it has really been worthwhile. Our climate is the only drawback. You can never count on having sufficient sun to make it worthwhile. On a day like this, of course, it's wonderful.'

They were sitting by the pool a few days after Gunther's arrival, watching their children splashing around in the water.

There was Michael, enjoying his long vacation and for the time being putting to the back of his mind the reading he ought to be doing; Christine, a little too conscious of looking her best in a tight green swimsuit; Jimmy, the youngest of the Brookfield children, just fourteen and already taller than his elder brother; Lucy, Connie's only child, a year older than Jimmy, thin, dark and intense and, when she thought she was unobserved, with eyes for no-one but Michael; and Gunther, suntanned, muscular, and sleek as an otter as he moved through the water.

'That is a very beautiful young animal,' Connie remarked, watching him as he climbed out of the water, stood for a moment poised on the side, pulled all his muscles taut and dived back in again with scarcely a ripple to disturb the surface of the pool. 'Are you keeping Christine under lock and key?'

'Oh, my dear, what is one to do? I've given her all the usual warnings, but if you were eighteen years old and being pursued by a young god would you be held back by the thought that "Mummy says I mustn't"? Since I've seen him I've been quite sick with worry.'

'She's a sensible girl at heart.'

'I hope so, but my idea that when she saw him against the background of her own home some of the glamour might fade hasn't worked out at all well. The trouble is, he really is a perfectly delightful boy.'

'If he weren't German . . .'

'Oh, absolutely! If it weren't for that I'd be clapping my hands at the idea of a charming son-in-law – though I still think Christine is far too young to tie herself down. He's fitted in here perfectly. He's polite and considerate and Harry thinks he's clever into the bargain.'

'Hasn't Christine any other boyfriends?'

'No-one she's ever taken seriously. And I'd hope not, at her age. She *is* pretty, I suppose, and has always been popular. I'd resigned myself to a few years of changing faces and emotional ups and downs. I never dreamed she'd fall so hard and so early. And for a *German*!'

'Has she faced up to the fact that it's going to come to nothing?'

'I think not. Just look at her! She's living in a world of her own, a soap bubble, all shining walls and lovely colours.'

'And when the bubble bursts . . .'

'She'll break her heart. Oh, these wretched politicians. I can't forgive them for what they're doing to my little girl.'

'Since we've been here Bob has come to feel that war is inevitable.'

'Harry thinks the same. We keep hoping against hope that something may happen to avert it, but Hitler seems determined to keep making trouble.'

A silence fell between them which Connie broke by saying: 'Babs, if war breaks out would you consider evacuating Jimmy and Christine to us in the United States?'

Barbara looked startled, 'How horrible even to have to consider such a thing. I doubt whether Christine would be able to go – I imagine she'd be expected to do some sort of service – but Jimmy . . . I'd hate to part with him, but yes, we'd think about it.'

In the background there were shrieks from the two younger children as Michael came up behind them and tipped them both into the water.

'It's angelically kind of you,' Barbara said. 'It will be a relief to know that at least one of them is safe. Michael, of course, will be called up.'

Connie knew her friend too well to be deceived by these quiet, sensible words. Barbara's hands were gripped together in her lap so tightly that the knuckles showed white.

'What a nice creature he's grown into,' Connie said gently.

'Michael? Yes, he's turned out rather well. He favours the RAF if it comes to a fight. I do think there's something *particularly* dangerous about flying, but of course they're all wild about aeroplanes.'

'You may have noticed that I, too, have daughter problems. Lucy thinks the sun and moon shine out of him.'

'Poor little duck. I dare say he'll be kind if he notices, but of course she's far too young for him.'

'Too young to be taken seriously and old enough for it to

27

hurt. And Lucy takes everything so hard. I would have bet on Lucy being the one to indulge in an unhappy love affair, not a sunny-natured girl like your Christine.'

'Here we are, back at the same problem again! Let's have some tea. I know it doesn't really help, but I find myself clinging to minor comforts in times like these.'

Chapter Two

It sometimes seemed to Barbara as the golden days went by that her daughter's love affair might have been easier to control if the weather hadn't been so fine. If the children had been kept indoors by rain she could have kept an eye on them. As it was, they were out all day and every day, disappearing into the country in Michael's little car, visiting London, swimming, playing tennis – which Gunther, to their astonishment, had never played but which, with his fine co-ordination and long reach, he soon picked up. It was not long before he and Christine were a match for Michael and Lucy. It amused Michael that Lucy was upset when they were beaten by the other two.

'It's only a game,' he pointed out. 'Cheer up!'

'I let you down,' she said, with her eyes on the ground.

'Nonsense! Christine is a demon player and she's used to playing against me and, of course, Gunther is a natural, not to mention being nine feet tall. They're just too good for us.'

'Don't you mind?'

'Not a bit. If you only play games in order to win you don't get any fun out of them.'

'I have heard of this English attitude,' Gunther remarked, coming up behind them. 'I did not believe it. To me it seems – forgive me, Michael – hypocritical to say that you do not play in order to win.'

'It's a different way of looking at things, I suppose,' Michael said.

He did not want to admit it, but in his heart he did slightly resent Gunther's effortless superiority in a game he had only begun to play in the last two weeks. 'There's a dance at the

29

Tennis Club on Saturday,' he said, changing the subject. 'Are we going?'

'Yes, rather!' Christine said. She was flushed from her exertions, her hair clinging to her forehead in damp tendrils. 'You'd like to go, wouldn't you, Gunther? It's quite informal, no need for a dinner jacket or anything like that. Will you take anyone, Michael? Angela's still away on holiday, isn't she?'

'I'll find someone,' he said carelessly, but as he spoke he caught a look of wistful longing on Lucy's face. 'What about you, scrap?' he asked. 'Will you be my partner? I bet we can wipe the dance floor with these two, even if we can't beat them on the tennis court.'

He was rewarded by the way her face lit up. Flushed and incoherent, she could only nod vigorously.

Lucy rushed to find her mother as soon as she reached her grandmother's house.

'M-Michael's asked me to go to the Tennis Club dance with him and Christine and Gunther on Saturday,' she said, the words tumbling out of her mouth in a torrent of delight and anxiety. 'What am I going to wear?'

Connie was in her mother's kitchen, making a cake for tea. She paused with her floury hands in the mixing bowl and looked at her agitated daughter in mingled amusement and dismay.

'Every woman who was ever born has said that when a man asked her out,' she said. 'And, do you know, the beasts don't actually notice what we wear at all.'

The look of anxiety in Lucy's dark eyes intensified and Connie took pity on her. 'Well, you can't wear shorts or a cotton frock, I quite see that. We'll just have to go and look round the shops and see if we can find you something suitable.'

'Not too *young*,' Lucy urged.

'Something suitable, I said.'

It took a visit to London to find the sort of dress they both had in mind, but in the end Lucy was satisfied with the pale green voile they bought for her.

'All of a sudden I feel old,' Connie informed her husband that Saturday night. 'Didn't she look sweet?'

'Growing up, isn't she? She's not exactly pretty, but she's a nice kid,' Bob said.

'You wait! Lucy is one of those deceptive ugly ducklings who amaze everyone by turning into swans.'

'My idea of a beautiful girl is young Christine.'

'Yes, there was never any doubt about Christine. She was a pretty baby, a sweet little girl and she's certainly lovely now, poor child.'

Christine herself knew that she was looking her best on the night of the Tennis Club dance. With her hair newly washed and curling round her face, her eyes shining, lit up with love and laughter, she was unquestionably the loveliest girl in the hall. She was wearing a dress with a bodice shirred with elastic and small puffed sleeves which could be worn either on or off the shoulders. In response to her mother's raised eyebrows Christine had moved the neckline upwards, but she pushed it down again as soon as she was safely out of the house, revealing as much of her shoulders and breasts as she could without complete disaster. In spite of her fairness she tanned easily and the golden glow to her skin and her look of sparkling, radiant health added to her attraction.

She was in a strange mood, very conscious of the admiration she excited, a little conceited about it, pleased with herself not only because of her own attractions, but also because she was accompanied by an outstandingly good-looking man. She flaunted her ownership of Gunther, tilting her head to look up provocatively into his face as they danced, clinging to his hand and refusing to let him go when the music stopped. She would have danced every dance with him, careless of the comment she was causing, if Gunther himself had not protested.

'I think some of your friends are feeling displeased,' he said. 'It is not well to neglect them. They will be here when I am gone.'

He said it deliberately and for one moment it quenched the brilliant excitement in Christine's eyes, but she only tossed her head and turned away from him into the arms of another of her eager admirers. He watched the reckless way she swirled around the floor, knowing that the flirtation she was conducting was entirely for his benefit, and a look of pain came over his face.

'She does like you best really,' a voice said from beside him. He looked down and saw Lucy watching him anxiously.

'Yes, I know,' he said and smiled, even though the assurance did nothing to ease his hurt. 'That is why it is so sad,' he added, almost under his breath, not thinking she would understand him.

'If she didn't love you it wouldn't matter so much that you will soon have to say goodbye, you mean?' Lucy asked.

'You are too old for your years! Yes, that is exactly what I mean. Don't look so worried, little Lucy, it is not your problem.'

'I do worry about people,' Lucy admitted. 'I feel responsible for them.'

'You are an unusual person. Not at all like my idea of an American child.'

'I know. We're all supposed to be outgoing and cheerful and thinking about nothing but dates and ball games and icecream sodas. There are kids like that back home, but I'm one of the serious ones. I guess it must be my European blood.'

'I hope you will never lose your kind concern for other people,' Gunther said, smiling slightly. 'But you must leave Christine and me to work out our own problem. If it is not treated as being too serious it will in the end be better for both of us.'

He moved away, but something about the way he had spoken made Lucy very thoughtful. 'Shall I tell you a funny thing?' she said to Michael when he remembered that he ought to be looking after her and asked her to dance. 'Funny in a peculiar way, I mean. I think Gunther is much more in love with Christine than Christine is with Gunther.'

'How can you know a thing like that?'

'Don't say I'm too young! I was *born* knowing about the way people feel. It's real uncomfortable, but I can't help it. I think Gunther loves Christine herself, but Christine loves the idea of being in love with Gunther.'

'That's much too profound for me,' Michael said firmly.

32

'Stop worrying about Chris and concentrate on your dancing. That's the second time you've trodden on my toes.'

He was thankful that he had succeeded in silencing her since he suspected that she had hit on an uncomfortable truth. He had tried not to let his sister's involvement with Gunther trouble his mind too much. He had thought that it was a pity that she had allowed herself to be so violently attracted to him, but had had a vague feeling that it was something his mother would cope with if necessary. Now he considered the matter from Gunther's point of view and he saw that Lucy could very easily be right. What young Christine needed was a good spanking.

He thought so even more strongly when, at the end of the evening, Christine said to him in the most offhand way in the world: 'You'll drop Gunther and me off first, won't you, and then run Lucy home?'

They had gone to the dance in Michael's car and the most logical thing would have been for them all to go with Lucy and then drive home together. What Christine was asking for, with a lack of subtlety that grated on her brother, was a chance to be alone with Gunther. He almost refused, but that would have made his understanding of her motive too obvious and he couldn't bring himself to do it. He dropped the pair of them off at the gate of their home and drove away again in a silence which made Lucy turn her head to look at him, trying in vain to read his expression in the dim light inside the car.

Her grandmother's house was in darkness except for a light in the porch and in one downstairs room.

'Mom said I was to let myself in quietly and not ask anyone in because of waking up Granny,' she said apologetically.

'I'll just see you safely indoors,' he said. 'Got your key?'

He opened the door for her and she turned to face him with the light shining on her earnest young face. Standing on the doorstep her head was almost on a level with his.

'It was just the most marvellous evening of my life,' she said. 'Thank you. Thank you for taking me.'

'It was just a Tennis Club hop, but I'm glad you enjoyed it,' Michael said.

He gave her a playful little punch on the chin with his fist

33

and then, without really thinking about what he was doing, opened his hand and cupped it round her cheek, bent forward and very gently kissed her on the lips.

He drew back almost immediately, it was the merest fleeting touch of a kiss. 'You'd better leave that out when you tell Aunt Connie what you've been up to tonight,' he said. 'You're much too young for such larks. Run along in, scrap, and sleep well.'

Lucy put out the lights and climbed up the stairs to her room in a dream. Once inside she stepped out of her shoes and left them carelessly in the middle of the room. Her short woollen jacket was dropped on to a chair. Lucy went down on her knees by the side of her bed, her eyes closed, a fierce frown of concentration on her face.

'Please, God,' she said. 'Please don't let Michael marry anyone else until I'm old enough to make him want to marry me.'

After Michael had dropped Christine and Gunther and had driven away Christine caught Gunther's hand in hers and turned him towards the garden.

'No need to go in yet,' she said. 'It's a lovely night and quite warm. Pity there's no moon. We can sit on the garden seat for a few minutes.'

He let her lead him across the grass to the wooden seat which stood on a small paved area at the far end of the garden. It was a place Barbara had created as somewhere to sit and sew or write letters in the afternoon sun before everyone came home and disturbed her. She had planted rose bushes all round it and the scent came to them in the darkness.

Christine sat down and pulled Gunther down beside her and snuggled up against him. She was surprised when he did not put his arm around her, and also a little disturbed, with an uneasiness which had been growing inside her ever since he had arrived in England. There was something different about him. He was not the same lighthearted companion he had been in the snow in Austria, nor was his lovemaking as insistent as it had been then. He seemed older, more serious, which was ridiculous because it was only seven months since he had almost overwhelmed her by the ardour of his kisses. Christine shivered as she remembered how near she had been to giving in to his whispered demands to be allowed to love her, love her, love her to death.

'You are cold,' Gunther said.

'No, I'm not cold in the least.' She pulled the thin woollen stole she had worn closer about her bare shoulders. 'It was a good dance, wasn't it? You did enjoy it, didn't you? Say you liked it, Gunther.'

He did not answer and she began to feel uncomfortable and slightly offended. 'There's nothing wrong, is there? You did enjoy it? People were friendly to you, weren't they?'

'Everyone was most kind. Except you.'

'I was kind! I danced with you, spent almost the entire evening with you. What more do you want?'

'I want, I think, that you should mean it when you look at me with great big shining eyes as if I were the only man in the entire world. I do not like it that you pretend to feel more than is true because you are making an exhibition for your friends. And I do not like to be like an animal in the zoo.'

'I don't understand. I'm not pretending. You know how I feel about you.'

'Yes, I know very well how you feel about me. You feel very proud. "Look," you say, "look what I have got – a German lover. How exotic, how strange!" To you, I am like a . . . a hippopotamus.'

'That's not true.' Christine disputed it hotly, but there was a tiny spark of shame at the back of her mind. She had exulted in showing Gunther off to her friends, but surely he could understand that her pride was part of her love for him?

'When I knew you in Kitzbühel you wouldn't have thought like this,' she said slowly.

'Perhaps I have changed a little.'

'Yes, you have. I've noticed it. Are you sorry you came?'

'I see that it was a mistake, and yet I am not sorry.'

'I don't understand. Do explain. We aren't going to quarrel, are we?'

'No, we will not quarrel. Perhaps I can make it clear. When we were in Kitzbühel I thought you were a very beautiful girl and it was interesting that you were English. Yes, I understand very well how you feel when you show me to your friends! I, too, felt the excitement of having an English girl to make love to. And that was all I wanted, just have the pleasure of your company, to laugh, and dance, and ski and kiss and perhaps persuade you to get into bed with me. I did not succeed, but it did not matter too much, because the next week there would be another girl and then another.'

'And was there?' Christine's question was a very small hurt whisper.

'Yes. And it was not at all a success because all the time I thought of you. This I am not used to. In the past I have forgotten very easily. The girls who came before you, I do not even remember their names. You I did not forget. And then we began to write to one another and I saw that you had been serious when you asked me to visit your home and I wished to come – how I wished to come!'

'But since you've been here it hasn't been at all like it was in Kitzbühel. I thought perhaps it was because, staying in my own home, with Mum and Dad around all the time, you didn't feel so . . . so free. And that was a bit why this evening I tried to – well, tempt you.'

'And I am very easily tempted. Ah, Christine, Christine, you don't know, you don't know!'

She was in his arms at last, but it was too sudden and too violent to be enjoyable. He bruised her lips with the hardness of his mouth, the woollen stole was thrown on one side and he covered her neck and shoulders with kisses. She shuddered and tried to get her arms free so that she could put them round his neck and then, just as suddenly as he had seized hold of her, he put her away from him.

'But it must not be!' he said in a strange, wild voice.

'Why not, why ever not? Gunther, please. One moment you seem to be saying that you love me more than you thought you did and the next you are turning away from me. Why?'

'Listen, I will try to make you understand. You remember how happy we all were in Kitzbühel, you and I and Michael and Mitzi?'

'Of course I remember. It was wonderful.'

'Yes, it was wonderful and I will never be able to go back there again.'

'You mean, because of the Nazis taking over?' Christine asked slowly. 'But they wouldn't make difficulties for you if you went to Austria, would they?'

'The authorities would not, but Mitzi would spit in my face. Christine, *Liebling*, Mitzi's grandmother, her father's mother, was a Jew.'

'But up there, in the mountains, surely nobody cares about that?'

'Up in the mountains, down in the cities, yes, there are people who care. The Ski School no longer belongs to Friedrich, it has been taken away from him. And in spite of all I have thought in the past, I cannot, I *cannot* believe that it was right.'

'You said you thought Hitler was a great man.'

'He is a great man and Germany is a great and wonderful country. We have risen from the ashes, we have rebuilt our nation. I believe it is our destiny to be amongst the leaders of the world. But now I am afraid of the way we are going. Christine, I am afraid.'

He was sitting away from her, leaning forward with his elbows resting on his knees, his head bent as he spoke. Although there was no moon the summer night was light enough for Christine to be able to make out the strong line of his shoulders, the brightness of his hair falling forward as he looked down at his clasped hands. She had given little thought to the international situation except in so far as it might affect her own small plans. She had been impatient to be assured that the *Anschluss* would not stop Gunther coming to visit her that summer. Now she felt ashamed of her thoughtlessness and all the more so because it left her helpless to offer him any comfort in the agony she sensed in him. The little, frothy, careless love she had felt for him, the desire for admiration, the craving for the excitement of his kisses, dropped away. In its place, she began to feel the stirring of an emotion so deep she was afraid.

'You could stay here in England,' she offered. It was the only solution she could think of and as she said it she realized for the first time that she thought of her country as a haven, safe against any evil there might be outside.

'No, I could not do that. I am German. I belong to my own country and, if necessary, I must help to defend it.'

'You think there will be a war?'

'Yes, I do.'

'A war between Britain and Germany? Oh, Gunther, surely not?'

'I pray that it will not be so, but I very greatly fear it. There will be a war and we will win it and what will happen to you, my Christine?'

'You might not win!'

'How can we lose? We are ready and you are not. You are like children! What do you think about? Garden parties and games and what the Queen is wearing in Paris. What is the first thing your father asks about when he comes home each evening? The cricket score!'

'If we were attacked we'd fight.'

'And if we were attacked we, too, would fight. You see, *mein Liebling*, you see? Already, you and I, who love one another, are a little angry because we feel that our countries are threatened.'

'We do love one another, don't we, Gunther?'

'I know that I love you. About you, I am not so sure. I think there is still time for you to draw away.'

Christine shook her head, even though he could not see her, was not even looking at her. 'No,' she said with sudden and great certainty. 'It's too late for me to draw back. I love you so much it hurts me right down to my toes.'

It drew something that was more of a groan than a laugh from him. 'But we must part. Another week and I must leave you.'

'At least we shall have that week,' Christine said. At the back of her mind, unacknowledged and unrecognized, was still a hope that something might happen to rescue them from the unhappiness that threatened to overwhelm them.

She moved closer to him and tried to make him turn to face her.

'I want to comfort you,' she said. 'Darling, darling Gunther, whatever you want I will do. Make love to me, now.'

He put his arms round her, but his lips were stiff and cold against her cheek. 'No, *mein Liebchen*, no. If we are old, experienced lovers then we might make love on this hard seat or I might make you lie down on the cold ground, but when it is for the first time – no.'

They kissed once and then he stood up and pulled her up to join him and they walked slowly back towards the house, their arms round one another.

They were very quiet in the days that followed. They could not bear to be apart and all the time they were together they wanted the comfort of touching one another. Christine would even hitch her chair nearer to Gunther's at the dinner table so that while they were eating their arms could brush against one another and underneath the table her thigh was pressed against him.

'I wish you'd say something to her,' Harry grumbled to Barbara. 'The way they carry on is putting me off my food.'

'I must speak to her, I know,' Barbara agreed. 'Though not about your loss of appetite, my dear.'

'You don't want me to say anything to Gunther, do you? I mean, if anything happened to Chris I'd have his lights and liver, even if I had to go to Berlin to do it.'

'No, say nothing. He knows how you feel without being told. So does Christine, come to that.'

She tried to be tactful, but Christine merely looked at her with blank, unseeing eyes and said: 'You don't understand.'

'I do understand. My darling, you are not the only young woman who has ever been in love. It's very hard for you to believe that it will pass, but it will.'

'You're trying to say that I'll get over it, as if it were the measles! I love Gunther. I want to spend the rest of my life with him. I'd marry him tomorrow if he'd ask me, but he won't.'

'I'm glad he has that much sense! You are far too young to be sure of your own mind.'

'The only thing you've got against him is that he's German.'

'The very short time you've known each other worries me as

much. Two weeks in the winter, three weeks in the summer and a few letters in between! It's not a great deal on which to base a lifelong relationship.'

Christine turned her face away, her mouth set. Desperately Barbara sought for the right words. In another moment she would have lost her. Already she was on the verge of flight.

'If you are given time, which I pray God you are, then it will still be possible for you and Gunther to meet again next year and find out whether you feel the same about each other,' she said gently.

'If we are not fighting one another by that time you mean.'

'It's not something any one of us has any control over. In the meantime . . . my dear, don't do anything that might spoil your life.'

'Oh, don't worry! Gunther agrees with you and he has more self control than you would believe possible!'

She had turned right away from her mother to hide her face, but the words came out with an angry sob.

'I see,' Barbara said. She looked at Christine's averted head with great kindness. 'Yes, I see. My dear, my dear, he's right you know. It's a hard saying, but a very true one, that the appetite grows by what it feeds on. You will find it easier to get over losing Gunther – if you must lose him – if you have not become lovers.'

Christine got up in a wild swirl of movement. 'I don't think you remember what it was like when you were young. I don't think you remember at all.'

Barbara did not repeat this conversation to her husband, but she did touch on it to Connie.

'I'm only forty-three, but Christine obviously thinks I'm long past remembering the agonies of young love. In a way, of course, she's right. Harry was my one and only and we were married before I was twenty-one, after a fairly conventional courtship. I'm really worried about the way she was talking today. Do I give her too much freedom, Con?'

'They all expect to go their own way these days, it seems to me, and more so back home in America than here. Are they out somewhere today?'

'They've gone down to the coast by train, just Christine and

Gunther together. Brighton, I think. They've taken a picnic. It sounds quite harmless, doesn't it? The only thing is, it started badly. Christine came down to breakfast wearing one of these new dirndl dresses. They're all the rage and everyone's wearing them, but of course they are just like the Austrian national dress. Gunther just looked at her as if he'd been frozen and Christine said "I'm sorry" and went and changed. I mean, it just goes to show the difficulties, doesn't it? Poor children.'

In spite of the ominous start to their day out Gunther and Christine did manage to put it behind them and enjoy themselves. It was a relief to be away from people who knew all about them.

'I'm so tired of being watched,' Christine said.

Gunther approved of Brighton, observing its squares and terraces with the interest of an architect. Christine took him to see the Pavilion, warning him beforehand that she considered it quite hideous, and couldn't believe it when he insisted that he liked it.

'It was built by a man who had the courage of his convictions,' he said. 'He wanted fantasy, and why not? It is no more strange, I assure you, than some of the castles poor mad Ludwig built in Bavaria.'

'I wish I could see them.'

'Perhaps, one day.'

They went swimming in the sea, which was colder than it looked, and lay on the beach afterwards to dry.

'Not terribly comfortable on these pebbles,' Christine said. 'Shall we get dressed and take our picnic up on the Downs instead?'

'*Up* on the *downs*? This is something I have not heard before. Please explain.'

'The hills are called Downs – I don't know why. There are the North Downs and the South Downs, and these are the South Downs.'

'The English language is very strange. As soon as I think I

have mastered it something comes along which has no logic at all.'

They took a bus to Rottingdean and climbed the smooth green hills behind the coastline.

'This is beautiful,' Gunther said, pausing to look behind him.

'Peaceful, too. Look at all the people down on the sea shore, like ants.'

They found a quiet hollow, warmed by the sun, well away from the track they had been following.

'I'm ravenous,' Christine said. 'Open up the picnic bag and see what we've got for lunch.'

'Kiss me first.'

He was leaning back against the sloping side of the hollow, his arms behind his head. His shirt was open at the neck and he had rolled his sleeves up above his elbows. Christine went and leaned over him and he pulled her down to kiss her.

'I thought you'd decided to give up making love to me,' she said.

'That is easy to say, but not so easy to do, I find. And I never said I would not kiss you.'

'I've been so unhappy since Saturday night.'

'Yes, I know. Forget it. For today, we will be happy.'

They had their lunch, ham and chicken legs, bread rolls and fruit.

'How much I would like a bottle of good white wine,' Gunther said.

'Have an apple.'

'Thank you – Eve.'

Christine laughed and held the apple tantalizingly just out of his reach. 'Eve was much more successful with Adam than I am with you.'

'Poor Adam, he didn't know what trouble he was bringing on himself.'

It was not an answer that pleased her. She dropped the apple into his outstretched hand and turned her head away. Gunther watched her as he bit into the apple. When he had finished it he threw the core away with an impatient swing of his arm in a great arc.

42

'In twenty years' time there will be an apple tree here and no-one will know why,' Christine said.

'Where will we be then?' Gunther said under his breath.

He lay down on his back again and gazed into the blue sky. Somewhere above them a skylark was singing. The frown between his eyebrows faded and he yawned. 'I'm sleepy.'

'Me, too.'

Christine moved over so that she could lie by his side and he stretched out his arm and pulled her head against his shoulders. They lay for a time quiet and contented, and then Gunther's hand moved against her bare arm and Christine stirred restlessly. She turned to face him and they looked into one another's eyes, so close that he could see the faint soft down along her upper lip. With slow, careful movements he began to undo the buttons of her blouse.

'Someone might come,' Christine protested in a breathless whisper.

'They will be either very shocked or very sympathetic and in either case they will go away quickly.'

He felt round her back for the fastening of her brassiere and undid it. It was Christine who heard the voices and pushed him away. She sat up and began putting her clothes back in order with shaking hands. Gunther rolled away from her and lay on his back with one arm over his eyes, his lips compressed into a thin, bitter line.

Two boys and two girls in shorts and hiking boots climbed into sight on the hillside. Christine was sitting demurely by Gunther's side, the remains of their picnic all round them. One of the girls waved. 'Hot work, toiling up here,' she called.

Christine nodded and managed a small, meaningless smile. As the little group disappeared from sight she pushed her hair back from her forehead.

'It is hot here,' she said. 'I wish we could find some shade.'

'Do you want to go back to the sea shore?'

'No, too many people. Let's walk further inland.'

They wandered on, not touching one another, not speaking. They came to a stile near some rising ground covered by bushes and Gunther climbed over and turned to give his hand to Christine.

'I think the path goes off to the right,' she said doubtfully, seeing that he was moving in the opposite direction.

'It will be quieter round this side of the hill and I think I can find you some shelter.'

She followed him, the bag containing their damp swimsuits and towels over her shoulder. She was beginning to wish she hadn't suggested this walk. Her open sandals weren't really suited to it. She gave an exclamation of pain and hopped on one foot.

'Sorry, stone in my shoe,' she said.

Gunther put the picnic bag down. 'I will go and explore while you take it out,' he said.

There was a tiny track leading into the thick bushes which covered that side of the hill. He walked down it, cautiously because of the thorny bushes which brushed against him on either side. In a minute or two he was back.

He held out his hand. 'Come, this is a very good place,' he said.

Christine thought it looked unnecessarily scratchy, but the sun was right overhead and she thought she might be going to get a headache. The brief interlude in Gunther's arms and its abrupt termination had shaken her. For one moment it had seemed as if she was going to have to face up to the consequences of her insistence that she loved him and wanted him and then it had all come to nothing. As usual, people had come along and spoilt it. She thought rebelliously that she wished they could be alone on a desert island to work it all out on their own. No Hitler, no rumours of war, no mother watching with anxious eyes to see if she had turned into a scarlet woman yet.

He led her along the path, which soon dipped steeply until the bushes rose on either side of them and it seemed almost as if they were walking in a tunnel.

'It's certainly shady, but I'm being scalped,' Christine protested, pausing to disentangle a strand of hair from a thorn.

'We will stop here.'

It was a circle of grass entirely surrounded by gorse and hawthorn bushes. The passage they had forced through the last few yards had closed behind them. To Gunther's experi-

44

enced eye it had borne unmistakable signs of having been used before for the purpose he wanted it for that afternoon, but he had done some quick tidying up before fetching Christine and there was no disreputable debris to distress her as she looked round.

'It's a lovely secret place,' she said, but her voice was a little uncertain.

'There is some shade for you, although I fear it will disappear as the sun goes round. Also, as you have said, it is secret. There will be no *Wandervolk* to trample on us with their boots here.'

He sat down with elaborate nonchalance and patted the grass beside him. He perfectly understood the hesitation with which she joined him. He put an arm round her and smiled the attractive, mischievous smile he had had in Kitzbühel, which had been so much less in evidence while he had been in England.

'Now, what was I doing before we were interrupted?'

The lighthearted way he spoke calmed Christine's nervousness. Two dimples showed in her cheeks as she answered: 'You were being naughty.'

He tilted her back on to the grass and leaned over her, his face alight with laughter.

'I am not *naughty*, I am wicked. I have brought you to this good, private place so that I can show you how wicked I can be.'

'I thought you had,' Christine said. 'Oh dear, I suppose I'm wicked too.'

'Not yet, but soon you will be equally bad with me.' He stroked her face with gentle fingers. 'I can no longer go on as we have been. I must love you. And you wish it, too. You have shown this to me many times. Under your parents' roof it was not possible, but here we will be like two nature children and I will make you very happy.'

'For a little while,' Christine said. 'We'll still have to say goodbye on Saturday. Will you come back to me?'

'I will come back.'

He knew in his heart that at that moment he would have promised her anything. He had made easy promises before in

45

the heat of desire and forgotten them as soon as he was satisfied, but this was different. She was more to him than a lovely girl he lusted after. They belonged together. She was the only person to whom he had been able to confide something of the desperate anxiety he felt about his country and she had been quick to sympathize, in spite of her ignorance. She had spoken of marriage, something he knew would have been impossible even without the threat of war looming ahead. He was not in a position to support a wife, especially such a girl as Christine, accustomed to all the luxuries of life, self-willed, extravagant and unconscious of the fact that she was more than a little spoilt. He saw quite clearly all the reasons why she was not a suitable wife for him, not at this stage of his career, and yet it was impossible not to feel proud that she wanted it.

Because of the very special feeling he had for her he treated her with a tenderness Christine only partially appreciated. They lay together all the long hot afternoon, naked, sunbaked, slippery with perspiration, and she sobbed in ecstasy at the pleasure he bestowed on her with his magnificent body.

The sun began to sink and the shadows to lengthen. Gunther's arms slackened and Christine shivered. He rolled over on to his side and began to feel on the grass for the clothes he had coaxed her to take off. She lay on her back, one knee bent, one arm flung up over her head, her eyes still closed, careless of her nakedness now that he knew her so intimately.

She sensed that he was looking at her and opened her eyes.

'You are a good and generous lover, *mein Liebling*,' Gunther said. He sat back on his heels and began to hand her her clothes. 'Come, you must dress and so must I.'

'Have we got to go back into the world?' she said, her voice no more than a dry, exhausted whisper.

'Yes, we must.'

She blinked at him, with tears on the end of her lashes. 'I am so happy.'

'My dear love.' He put his arms round her and raised her up and kissed her once more on the lips. Since she seemed to be unable to make up her mind to do it herself he began to help her to put on her clothes. After a moment or two Christine roused herself and stood up to step into her skirt and put on her blouse.

'I feel quite dizzy,' she said. 'And I don't think my legs will hold me.'

'Have I been too hard on you, my little one?'

'Oh, no! It was wonderful.' She smiled, a little shyly. 'I didn't know I had it in me to be so shameless.'

She stretched her arms above her head and drew a deep breath. 'Do you know what I'd really like now? Another swim. Or, at least, a dip in the sea. I don't know that I've got the energy to do more than float. I'm all sticky and itchy with bits of grass on my back.'

'That is a very good idea. The water will be warmer than it was this morning after the sun has been on it all day.'

They made their way out of their secret hideaway. Christine was glad that there was no-one about to see them emerge. It would have taken the edge off her happiness if anyone had looked at them with knowing eyes as they came out of the shelter of the bushes.

They wandered down the hill with their arms round one another. The tide was out and they had to go a long way for their brief bathe, but the water was like warm milk with a curdling of foam on the small waves. They ducked and splashed, playing like two children, and then ran back to dry themselves and dress awkwardly on the beach.

They found a café and had a meal. And then at last they had to agree that their day was over and they must go home.

It was late by the time they reached Eveleigh, but the family were still up. Christine did not bother to open the front door, but went round to the back and in by the french windows. They paused in the doorway, blinking in the light from inside the room. Barbara's heart contracted as they stood there, hand in hand, wearing their happiness like a nimbus, deeply contented, careless of all the world. Never in all her life, she thought, had she seen a couple who looked so magnificent together.

Their contentment lasted until Friday, surviving even some pointed remarks from Harry about a festival held in Germany

47

to honour the Nazis who had been executed for the murder of the Austrian President Dollfuss.

'You must realize that in some circles these men are regarded as martyrs,' Gunther said.

He spoke stiffly and Harry mistook his words for a defence of the assassins. He was about to make an angry retort when Barbara caught his eye and shook her head. He pressed his lips together and buried himself behind his newspaper, rustling the pages in frustration, but when on Wednesday he read that Monday's edition of *The Times* had been suppressed in Germany because of adverse comments on the celebration he could not resist mentioning it.

'I do wish you would be more tactful,' Barbara said afterwards. 'You can't hold poor Gunther responsible for all the shortcomings of his Government. You'd be very indignant if a Frenchman took you to task about the doings of a Labour Government, wouldn't you?'

'Hardly the same thing,' Harry pointed out. 'All right, I'll keep a still tongue in my head. I like the boy well enough, but I shan't be sorry to see the back of him.'

The growing tension displayed itself in another way when Michael challenged Gunther to a tennis match. It began lightheartedly enough, but something got into Michael and made him determined to win. They were more evenly matched than was apparent at first. Gunther might be a fine natural athlete, with a strength and an eye for the ball, but Michael had been playing for many years and was better able to judge the angle of his shots and vary his tactics. It was a sufficiently exciting game to attract several onlookers at the Tennis Club. Christine and Lucy sat on a bench side by side, both of them aware in different ways of undercurrents beneath the smiling acknowledgments by the two young men of each other's winning points. There was something vindictive in the way Michael slammed home a return which caught Gunther on the wrong side of the court and hopelessly wrong-footed. He raised his racket in the air and called: '*Gut, gut*' but he learned too quickly for Michael's comfort and in the following game he played the same trick. Michael made a desperate lunge to reach the ball, lost his balance and crashed to the ground. Gunther approached the net and waited for him to get up.

'Are you hurt?' he asked. 'We are equal. Shall we give up the game?'

Michael picked himself up. He had bruised his knee and grazed the palm of his hand. He wiped it against the leg of his white shorts.

'We may as well finish it,' he said and turned away.

He was furious with himself for that lost point and determined to fight to a finish. His normally good-natured face was set in obstinate lines. He was certainly not going to give up like a hurt child because of a few cuts and bruises. It was time Gunther was beaten at something. All that physical superiority was getting a bit trying. Deep in the recesses of his mind was a thought Michael would not have brought out into the open, a primitive urge to thrash the man he suspected was having his sister.

They battled on. Christine was biting the knuckle of her thumb, a habit she had in moments of tension. They reached match point and the game went to deuce. Michael was serving. He guessed that Gunther would expect him to play for his backhand and tried to fool him by placing the ball to the forehand corner, but Gunther returned it successfully. There was a long rally until Gunther smashed the ball with a fine overhead lob. The ball rose fast and at a difficult angle. Michael could do no more than touch it with his racket, but by a fluke the impetus was sufficient to carry it back over the net and Gunther, who had not expected to see a return, failed to get near it. Advantage to Michael. He tried to steady himself, but he was wrought up and he served a fault. He took his second ball and bounced it a couple of times and then, instead of playing for safety, put every ounce of his strength into a sizzling service straight down the centre line. Gunther just managed to get his racket to it, the ball touched the top of the net, hesitated for a second and fell back on his own side of the court.

'Michael's won!' Lucy exclaimed, jumping up.

Gunther came up to the net, smiling in generous pleasure. 'A good game,' he said. 'Congratulations.'

49

Michael held up his hand, grazed and bleeding palm upwards. 'I don't think I'll shake hands, if you don't mind,' he said.

Their eyes met. Michael's face still wore its dogged, obstinate look. Gunther's smile faded. He looked down, touching the toes of his tennis shoes with the edge of his racket. He was almost sure that Michael suspected what had happened between him and Christine and had chosen this way of showing his disapproval. He told himself that it did not matter, but he had a curious sense of loss. A friendship had been withdrawn and it was not until now when it was gone that Gunther knew how much he had come to rely on the pleasant footing he had achieved with Christine's family. Nothing would be said, of that he was sure, but Michael knew and condemned him and no doubt the mother and father would feel even more outraged.

That night Christine finally came out of the cocoon of careless happiness which had surrounded her since their visit to the coast and faced up to the fact that the following day Gunther would be gone. He would, of course, come back. Any other possibility was so unthinkable that she would not even allow it into her mind. He would come back or she would go to him. One day, when they were a little older and he was a successful architect, they would be married.

It was a fairy tale and even as she told it to herself she knew that it was not real. She lay awake, staring into the darkness, trying to hold at bay the wave of misery which was waiting to engulf her. She twisted over and felt for the little clock which stood on her bedside table. It was after two o'clock. She sat up and threw back the bedclothes. Everything was quiet. Christine got out of bed and tiptoed across the floor to her door. With stiff, cautious fingers she very slowly turned the knob and inched the door open.

In the passage outside it was much darker than it had been in her room. Michael's bedroom was opposite hers, her parents were next door, Gunther was at the far end of the passage. She felt along the wall with her hand, moving with infinite caution and very slowly. A board creaked and she paused, holding her breath, but nothing stirred.

She reached Gunther's door and opened it with the same caution she had used on her own. Inside it was lighter. He had pulled back his curtains before going to sleep and the summer night was not entirely dark. She closed the door behind her and moved towards him, speaking his name in a hushed whisper. He was asleep and for one moment she felt outraged that he should find it possible to sleep, but he roused quickly when she touched him. He raised himself on one elbow, not immediately understanding what had woken him.

Christine knelt by the side of his bed, a dim figure in her white cotton nightdress. All her anguish at parting with him was in her desperate whisper: 'You can't go away and leave me tomorrow! You can't!'

She buried her face in his pillow, her body shaking with sobs.

'Sh . . . sh . . . you must be quiet,' Gunther said. He put an arm under her shoulders and raised her up and she crawled into bed beside him, shivering uncontrollably, convulsed by the grief that overwhelmed her.

'*Liebchen*, you must not cry like this. Be quiet, be still.'

He pulled up the bedclothes to stifle the sound of her sobs.

'Don't go, please don't go,' Christine pleaded.

'I must. You know that I must. I will come back, I promise.'

'You won't. They'll keep us apart. There'll be a war and you'll be killed. How can I go on living then?'

Something of her despair began to affect him. He lay stroking her head, holding her tight, soothing her, but his face in the darkness was sombre. He had not intended to unleash this torrent of emotion, still less had he meant to be so deeply affected himself. She was right; it was intolerable that they should be driven apart just at the moment when their love was at its sweetest. Losing her would be a torment to him. If he could have had her beside him then anything might have been tolerable, even the reception he feared was waiting for him in Germany. Together they could have defied the world. But it was not possible for them to be together.

Since there was nothing that could be said between them that would help solve their dilemma he gave her the only comfort that was available to them. He felt for the hem of her

51

nightdress and raised it, smoothing his hand over the soft contours of her body.

'Yes,' Christine said. 'Yes, Gunther. Love me so hard that you won't be able to forget me while you're away from me.'

'We must be quiet,' he cautioned her. 'Very quiet, my little love. And I will not forget you. I can never forget you. I don't want to leave you, you do believe that, don't you?'

She nodded and began to kiss him, writhing her body about in an agony of love, until he said: 'Be still, *Liebling*, be still. You are too wild.'

There was no laughter between them as there had been during their long hot afternoon of loving, only a silent and desperate convulsion of two bodies striving to express a love and despair that could not be put into words, and when it was over he had to send her away, back to her room, creeping alone along the dark and chilly passageway, while he lay awake and longed to have her back again.

Gunther was downstairs early the next morning. All his packing had been done the night before and he was ready to leave. Christine, he guessed, was still asleep. He wondered whether she would wake up in time to say goodbye to him. She would have to, it would look so strange if she did not.

Her father was the only other person in the breakfast room when he went in. They wished one another a good morning and then Harry said, a little awkwardly: 'All ready to go?'

Gunther nodded. Of all the family Harry Brookfield was the one with whom he was least at ease. He felt that he didn't know him as well as the others, since Harry was out all day and usually they'd met only for an hour or two in the evenings. There was a barrier between them, too, because of Harry's strong views about Germany, which he felt inhibited from discussing with Gunther.

Gunther made an effort and said formally: 'Before I go I must thank you sincerely for allowing me to have this time with you. It has been most enjoyable.'

Harry put down the paper he had been pretending to read. 'Glad you enjoyed it,' he said. For the first time he noticed the look of strain on Gunther's face. The boy was not happy, poor young fool, and probably they'd have Christine moping about all over the place as soon as he'd gone.

'About Christine,' Harry said abruptly. 'She's not very old, you know. She seems to have taken it into her head that you're the love of her life. All nonsense at her age, of course. She'll have half a dozen such fancies before she settles down and marries.'

'Perhaps you are right,' Gunther agreed. 'For myself, if circumstances had allowed it I think I would have asked you for permission to call Christine my wife one day.'

'It's out of the question.'

This was more serious than Harry had bargained for and he threw down his paper and began to move restlessly about the room.

'You're a decent youngster and I've got nothing against you, but I'd not allow any daughter of mine to go and live in Germany as things are at present. There, that's being blunt with you, but it's best for me to speak my mind. This business with the Czechs, I don't like it at all.'

'The Sudetenland Germans only want to be allowed to keep their own language and culture,' Gunther said.

'Do they indeed! There's more to it than that, I think. Czechoslovakia is a silly, cobbled-together little country, I know, but it does exist and it ought to be allowed to find its own salvation, without outside interference.'

'Please, I do not know this expression . . . cobbled together.'

'Sewn up out of little pieces.'

'Oh yes, that is very true. The Versailles Treaty was foolish in this respect. The German people still feel German, you understand, no matter what you may call them. If they wish to reunite with the Fatherland . . .'

'They'll get plenty of encouragement from the other side of the border! It can only lead to trouble. There's a speech reported in today's paper by that man Henlein who leads the Sudetenland Germans. At the National Gymnastic Festival, if you please! What's that got to do with politics? But there he is, talking about a united free Germany, and Goebbels backing him up.'

'I can't expect you to understand.'

'I understand all right! I've been through it before. I fought in the last war and I never thought I'd ever live to see another one.'

'We don't want war.'

'No-one does, but we'll get it, all the same.'

He glanced over his shoulder at Gunther, standing very stiff and tall at the other end of the table.

'I've got no quarrel with you, Gunther. All the same, Christine will have to forget you. It's a hard thing to ask, but I'd rather you didn't write to her again once you've gone back to Germany.'

'I'm sorry, I cannot promise that,' Gunther said. 'It would be wrong for me to cut myself off from her with no explanation.'

He just stopped himself in time from adding 'after what there has been between us'.

'Please,' he said, and now he spoke in a low voice and the words came with difficulty. 'Let me have that.'

Harry felt like groaning out loud. He'd got it badly, just as badly as young Christine.

'I wish I'd never let her go to Kitzbühel,' he said.

Gunther managed a very slight smile. 'Yes,' he agreed. 'It would have been better if we had not met. I may write?'

'I can't stop you,' Harry admitted. 'Damn it, I don't want to stop you. But go home and find yourself a nice German girl, that's my advice to you.'

Gunther's smile slipped into a painful grimace. 'You sound just like my sister,' he said.

Chapter Three

All through August the Czechoslovakian crisis dragged on. In Britain people took their holidays and tried not to think about what was happening on the Continent. There was considerable doubt about where exactly Czechoslovakia was and the arguments about the return of Sudetenland to Germany were confusing to the ordinary man and woman. Families like the Brookfields, with a personal interest in the outcome, were the exception. Most people thought vaguely that the Czechs and Germans ought to be left to fight it out on their own without dragging in other people who only wanted to be left in peace.

It was not until September when the Government issued thirty-eight million gas masks and ordered the digging of trenches in the London parks that uneasiness began to turn to alarm. No-one wanted war, that was the one thing everybody could agree about. There was a unanimous feeling that 'that Hitler' ought to be taught a lesson, but not war, that was going too far, especially over a place with a name few people could pronounce and fewer still could spell.

The Prime Minister went to see Hitler and came back with nothing settled. He went a second time to Munich and on the afternoon of 30th September he returned waving a piece of paper and declaring that he had obtained 'peace with honour . . . peace in our time.'

The crowd went wild with relief, a feeling echoed by the rest of the country as soon as the news was broadcast. Only the more farsighted recognized that the respite was no more than temporary.

'It's going to be all right, isn't it?' Christine asked her father.

The only word which had got through to her was 'peace', but there was something about the expression on his face which did not match the hope that had sprung up in her own heart.

'If you don't care what happens to the Czechs,' he said. 'My own feeling is that we've behaved disgracefully, but I know I'm in the minority.'

'Anything rather than war,' Barbara said.

'Anything? I'm not sure I agree. There comes a time when you have to make a stand. I don't happen to like the price we've paid for this peace.'

'But the Germans in the Sudetenland do want to be German again,' Christine said.

'Do they? All of them? Or only the Nazis? And what about the rest of the country, dismembered, defenceless?' He shook his head. 'I wish I was as sure as you are that we've done the right thing.'

There was an uneasy silence. Harry wished he had been less outspoken as he saw the bright hope that had lit up Christine's face begin to fade. The past two months had been hard on her and he raged inwardly at the change that had come over his glowing, carefree girl. She was pale and quiet, with dark circles under her eyes. There was a look of dumb suffering about her which cut him to the heart. He would have done anything to ease her hurt and yet when she said: 'I thought perhaps, if things were all right between us and Germany, I could ask Gunther to come back for another visit at Christmas. Or I could go over and see him', his patience snapped and he answered her with angry sarcasm.

'You're so besotted about that boy you can think of nothing else. Do you imagine a country has been thrown to the dogs so that Christine Brookfield can kiss her boyfriend under the mistletoe? No, you will not go to Germany and I will certainly not have him under my roof again.'

Christine sprang to her feet and her chair crashed to the floor behind her. 'You don't want me to be happy! You're completely prejudiced against the Germans. I love Gunther and I will see him again, I will!'

She rushed out of the room, slamming the door behind her, and they heard her running up the stairs.

'Not very tactful, darling,' Barbara said. 'It was hard to

slam her down just as she'd had the first ray of hope for weeks. I'd better go to her.'

She got up, but as she passed his chair Harry caught hold of her hand. She paused and looked down at him, a long look of love and understanding, and before she went out of the room she bent and kissed him on the forehead. She went slowly up the stairs, trying to think of something to say to her daughter, something comforting, but sensible. She had not found any words by the time she reached Christine's room, but in any case they were not wanted. Christine had locked her door.

A week later she had a letter from Gunther which dashed any hope of another visit from him that year.

'I am sorry to have to tell you that my career has received another setback,' he wrote. 'I have been conscripted to work in a factory. They say it is to be for six months. I hope it will not be longer. At least I am earning a little money, but there will be no holiday for me at Christmas. The best I can hope for is that I shall be free from this commitment next summer.'

The stiff sentences were an attempt to conceal the misery that filled him. His return to Germany had not been happy. He missed Christine with a savage feeling of loss which would not leave him. The girl who had seemed like a child in her lack of experience had revealed herself to be a woman capable of intense and glorious passion. She was acutely responsive, almost as if she could read his mind, just as he had often felt that he could read hers. She was warm and loving and full of laughter. And she was beautiful. The memory of her long golden limbs, her round pink-tipped breasts, the delicacy of her skin and the softness of her hair was a torture to him.

He had made a profound mistake in going to England that summer. Impossible now to put her out of his mind, to think of her as just another girl who had given him pleasure. He had fallen in love with her more deeply than he had intended and once she had realized how her own superficial desire for admiration had hurt him Christine, too, had begun to love him with an intensity that appalled him even while he exulted in it.

Nothing had been as he had expected. The ease and freedom of the Brookfield household had surprised him. The casual way everyone wandered in and out, the way they talked to one another, their arguments and their friendliness, all these were strange to him.

There were still aspects of the Brookfields' life which puzzled him. They had a large house, but they had no servants. Mrs Brookfield seemed to do most of the work with no help but a woman who came in to do some cleaning. The Hofmeyers' apartment in Berlin was spacious, but nothing like as big as the Brookfields' house, and yet they had always had a maid who lived in and did the housework and most of the cooking. Gunther had never helped to wash dishes in his life until he went to England. It was not a man's work. He would quite happily have sat at the table while Christine and her mother waited on him and he had been really astonished when Michael and Jimmy got up and cleared away the plates.

The Brookfields were not, to his way of thinking, cultured people. There were books in the house, but as far as he could see they were rarely read. Above all, there was no music. To Gunther, who had been brought up to regard concert-going as one of the necessities of life, this was a real deprivation. His father had been an Army officer who had died young as a result of wounds received in the 1914–18 war. They were not poor, because his mother had had money of her own, but for as long as he could remember she had added to their income by giving music lessons. She was an accomplished pianist whose ambitions to perform publicly had been frustrated by an old-fashioned father who had considered it an undignified career for the daughter of a family with connections with the minor aristocracy. Her explanation of this had made Gunther look into his family background, only to find that his grand-father's pretensions had been ridiculously inflated. Neither of her children had inherited her talent, but they had been brought up to listen to music with critical enjoyment and in this respect the Brookfields were philistines.

He was deeply attached to his mother, but his relations with her were formal. He would never have walked in and demanded: 'What's for tea then, old lady?' as young Jimmy had done, but then neither would he have accompanied the question by an affectionate bear hug round the shoulders. He did not feel the same protectiveness towards his sister that he sensed in Michael. Frieda was his elder by four years and had always had a dominating streak in her. She thought she had the right to tell him what to do, not the other way round. He was conscious, as he had never been before, of what he had missed by losing his father at an early age. He had been brought up by women – his mother, Frieda and Lotte, the maid. He had looked upon Christine as spoilt, but the truth was that he was equally pampered, though in a different way. The Berlin apartment never resounded to cries of: 'Mum, I can't find my socks.' Gunther's socks were always washed, darned and in the right place and there were three women to see that it was so.

The interruption to his architectural training was a bitter blow. The director of his firm had been regretful, but he had had no choice but to comply when he had been ordered to release the most recent of his recruits for work of 'national importance'. Gunther had little doubt who was to blame for that order. He suspected that while the idea of sending him to England with a camera had been Ulrich's own bid to gain credit with the Party, it had also been a test of Gunther's obedience, and he had failed the test. Gunther had spoken glibly of his regret over the loss of the camera and had offered to pay for it, an offer which Ulrich had been quick to accept, but he doubted whether he had been believed. Ulrich had decided he should be punished. A word in the right ear and it was done. At the stroke of a pen trainee architect Hofmeyer had become a machine operator in a factory making motor components, it was said for a nominal six months, but Gunther in his more despairing moments feared that his prospects had been spoilt for life. He disliked the work in the factory, which was noisy and repetitious. The only bright spot was that he earned a wage which enabled him to pay off his debt to Ulrich quickly.

59

The news of the compromise over Czechoslovakia was as much of a relief to him as it was to Christine. Even though he was almost as uneasy about the way events were moving as Harry Brookfield he still felt a thrill of pride that another step towards the reunification of Germany had been achieved without bloodshed. It was wonderful what a show of strength could do. One might have qualms about the Nazi movement, but there was no doubt that under Hitler's guidance Germany had succeeded in regaining a place in world politics which made it a force to be respected. The British acceptance of the break up of Czechoslovakia accorded well with the impression he had gained during his three-week visit to their country. An easy-going people, ready to make any concession to preserve the comfortable life they enjoyed. They were pleasant, likeable, even in some respects enviable, but he would not have changed his nationality in spite of his present hardships. There was undoubtedly something superior in the German character.

Christine, of course, was different. She had something of the Valkyrie in her. She had dared to scorn the conventional morality of her upbringing and it was Gunther who had counselled prudence and had kept the secret of their love-making. Christine would have eloped with him to Germany if he had encouraged her. Her recklessness had alarmed him, but it had also destroyed the last of his defences against her. He had told himself that once he had had her his longing for her would weaken, but her total, headlong surrender had overthrown all his preconceptions. She was his perfect counterpart. They matched one another not only in their physical splendour, but in a certain turn of mind, a way of looking at the world, a sympathetic understanding which was as sweet as it was unexpected. He wanted her furiously as the weeks went by and, looking grimly into the future, he could see little hope of ever finding another woman who would be her equal.

His satisfaction with the outcome of the Czechoslovakian crisis lasted until the beginning of November. A trainload of German-Polish Jews was sent from Germany to the Polish border. Poland refused to take them in, Germany refused to let them return. International negotiations started and while they were dragging on the deportees sat in the train and starved. A young Jew, living illegally in Paris without a permit, received a letter from his father, one of the victims, describing their sufferings. The seventeen-year-old boy took a revolver and went to the German Embassy and shot the Third Counsellor.

It was murder, and treated as murder, but it was also the excuse the Nazi Party had been waiting for. On the night of 10th November, all over Germany and Austria, organized groups of young Nazis smashed their way into Jewish shops, homes and synagogues, pillaging and burning everything they could lay their hands on.

Gunther had been working a night shift. He returned home early in the morning through a district which had been ravaged, his feet crunching on broken glass, unable to believe what he saw. In a doorway an elderly man was huddled. He had a grey overcoat pulled round him, his head was bent over his drawn up knees, on his back was the yellow star all Jews were required to wear.

A couple of boys in Hitler Youth uniform came running down the street, laughing and tossing something between them. As they drew nearer Gunther caught the flash of colour and saw that it was a beautiful Meissen vase.

When they were level with the doorway one of them called out: 'Here's another of them!'

He caught hold of the old man and dragged him out into the roadway. The old man made no resistance, but squatted in a kneeling position on the ground, his arms wrapped round his body, his head bent.

'Oh, leave him. We've done enough for one night. I'm tired. Let's get home to bed. Here, catch!'

His companion caught the vase, hesitated for a moment, then brought it down with all the force of both arms on the old man's head. His eyes closed, he slumped forward, surrounded by shards of bright porcelain, blood trickling slowly down his forehead.

'You swine! I wanted that for my mother!' the other youth exclaimed.

They ran off down the road, laughing and miming playful blows at one another. Gunther went up to the old Jew and

61

bent over him. He felt completely helpless and yet he could not walk away and leave the man unconscious in the road.

More people were beginning to stir, coming out of their houses to stare at the damage. A car stopped with a screech of brakes. Authoritative footsteps rang on the metalled surface. Gunther looked up and saw a pair of jackboots on a level with his eyes. He stood up slowly and confronted an officer of the SS. The other man looked him over with cold eyes and an impassive face.

'Are you a Jew?' he asked.

'No.'

'Then go away and leave him alone.'

'But . . .'

The SS officer put his hand on the revolver that hung in a holster at his waist. He pushed the man on the ground with the toe of his boot. The old man rolled over and opened his eyes. The blood was beginning to congeal on his forehead. He looked straight up at Gunther, a look of fathomless sadness, like some dumb and suffering animal. Gunther turned on his heel and walked away, sick with disgust at his own impotence.

It did not help to find Frieda giving Ulrich breakfast in their apartment when he got in. Her face was flushed with excitement, her eyes glittering. Ulrich looked up and spoke with his mouth full of cold ham as Gunther went in.

'Done a hard night's work? So have I! We've shown them tonight, the filthy swine.'

'I don't particularly enjoy my work,' Gunther said. 'But at least I did something constructive on my workbench tonight. I *made* something. You and your lot have been indulging in an orgy of wanton destruction.'

'We're fighting against forces which are out to destroy our State. It's as well for you, Gunther Hofmeyer, that you've got a friend in me, or your attitude might call for investigation.'

Gunther went out of the room without replying. He was shaking with anger. To think that it had come to this; he had been afraid to defend a helpless old man and unable to throw an unmannerly lout out of his own home. To ease his feelings he sat down, unwashed and unfed, and poured out all his frustration in a letter to Christine. He took the precaution of writing in English, but he might have spared himself the trouble. Three days later Ulrich called on him again.

'I told you I was your friend,' he said. 'Now perhaps you'll believe me.' He pulled a letter out of his pocket. The envelope was torn and grubby. 'I've been asked to pass on a message to you. When you write to your English girlfriend in future, write in German.'

Gunther picked up the letter. His letter to Christine. Not only his dangerous criticism of the events of the *Kristallnacht*, as it had come to be called from the amount of broken glass that lay around afterwards, but his expressions of love, his admission of his desperate need of her. Who had read it? Ulrich at least was too ignorant to be able to translate it, but presumably some colleague of his had understood enough to send him that warning. He tore up the letter into tiny pieces and the next time he wrote to England it was in formal, stilted phrases which drove Christine wild with disappointment.

Christine completed her secretarial course and found a job working for a merchant bank in the City. She travelled up to town each day with her father and to her surprise she liked her work.

'Christine seems to have settled down,' her father remarked.

'She's too quiet,' her mother said. 'I worry about her. Don't imagine she's got over the Gunther affair just because she doesn't talk about it. She's bottling it all up inside her. I've tried to make her talk to me, but we seem to have lost touch.'

'She still hears from him, doesn't she?'

'Not so frequently. Perhaps he's losing interest and that's what's upsetting her.'

'It must fade away in time, surely?'

'I suppose so, but Christine has always had an obstinate streak. Even as a little girl, once she'd set her heart on something she had to have it. What really worries me is the way she's saving.'

'You don't think she's thinking of going over to Germany? If that's what's in her mind she can drop the idea straight away. She's still under age, I shall forbid her to go.'

63

'Bless you, darling, you've left it a bit late to start playing the heavy father. You might forbid it, but do you really think that would stop her?'

'Probably not,' Harry admitted gloomily.

The unsatisfactory relationship between Christine and her parents dragged on into the spring. She said nothing about her plans and Barbara was too afraid of having her fears confirmed to force her into revealing them. It was a considerable relief when Christine came home from work one day looking more animated than she had been for months and full of a scheme which Barbara was thankful to approve.

'Four of us from the office are thinking of going over to Paris for a week,' she said.

'What a lovely idea, darling! Do I know the other girls?'

'You've heard me speak of them. Clare and Pat and Diana. Diana is the Chairman's secretary. She speaks marvellous French and I think even a short visit would give me a chance to improve mine a bit.'

'Who's footing the bill for this jaunt?' Harry asked when he was told about it. He spoke jocularly, only too pleased to see his daughter looking so bright and cheerful.

'I am,' Christine said quickly. 'I've been saving up.'

'I might be persuaded to make a small contribution,' Harry offered. 'Enough to buy a Paris hat or something.'

He was hurt when Christine hesitated. It was not so long since the child had depended on him for every stitch she wore. Surely he could give her a little present without offending against her new independence?

'Say "Thank you, Daddy", and take it,' Barbara advised quickly. 'He's never offered to buy *me* a Paris hat.'

Her words dispelled the look of strain on Christine's face. 'Thank you, Daddy,' she said demurely. 'I'll try to spend it on something you'll like.'

The visit to Paris did not take place until June. The four girls arrived in the late afternoon and rushed out immediately to stare at the Arc de Triomphe, the Louvre, the Eiffel Tower.

'Can we look round the shops in the morning?' Christine asked. 'I have to buy a hat. It's a present from my father.'

It took the four of them most of the morning to find

something which satisfied Christine, but as soon as she had chosen a dashing little straw boater decorated with cornflowers she said: 'Well, that's that. Now I can leave.'

'Where are you off to?' Diana asked idly. 'It's nearly time for lunch. I thought it would be fun to go over to the Left Bank and find a little bistro and have an omelette or something and then splash out on a really splendid dinner tonight.'

'I'll stay for lunch,' Christine agreed. 'Then I must start packing.'

'Packing? But where are you going? We haven't even started seeing Paris yet.'

'I didn't come to the Continent to see Paris. I'm going to Berlin.'

They argued and pleaded with her, but it was like talking to a brick wall. Nothing would move her. They gave up their plans for the afternoon and went and saw her off on the overnight train.

It cast a blight over their visit to Paris. They were three instead of four and although they agreed not to bother their heads about her they were all secretly anxious about this defiant dash into a country which was now hostile to the British.

By the time Christine arrived in Berlin she, too, had become aware of the undercurrents of bad feeling which greeted her every time she had to produce her passport. No-one was actively rude to her, no-one tried to obstruct her journey, but she felt that the questions that were asked about the reason for her visit were unnecessarily searching and she was uncomfortable about some disparaging remarks she overheard from people who assumed that she did not understand the language.

The streets seemed to be full of soldiers in field grey, airmen in blue, black-uniformed SS and jack-booted Gestapo. It was a curious experience to see the Hitler salute actually being used. In common with most British people she had looked upon the 'Heil Hitler' as something of a joke, but now she saw grown men exchanging the greeting in total earnest and there was nothing funny about it.

She had no plan in her mind except that she was determined to see Gunther. He didn't know she was coming. Somehow she must find out the reason for the change she had noticed in his letters. She told herself that if he had stopped loving her then she would prefer to hear him say so to her face. Anything would be better than the slow erosion of the confident love she had felt for him when they had parted. She was, as her parents recognized, both obstinate and determined. She knew that neither her father nor her mother looked favourably upon her relationship with Gunther and so she had made up her own mind what she would do. The worst thing that could happen would be that he would turn her away, the best thing would be that he would be as overjoyed to see her again as she was at the thought of being with him.

What she had not anticipated was that Gunther would not be at home at all. She went to the Hofmeyers' apartment, nervous now that the moment had come, but trying to appear at her ease. The door was opened by Frieda who had no idea who this tall, fair-haired girl, carrying a suitcase and wearing a frivolous hat, could be. Even Christine's carefully enunciated enquiry for Gunther did not enlighten her. It was not until Christine said, stammering a little under Frieda's critical inspection: 'I am Christine Brookfield . . . from England' that Frieda realized that this was the girl Gunther had been so foolish about the previous summer.

'Gunther is working,' she said, speaking automatically as her mind turned over this unexpected development. 'He will not be home until midnight.'

Frieda correctly interpreted Christine's expression of dismay. The English girl had expected to find her brother at home so that she could tumble into his arms once more. She waited in malicious satisfaction for Christine to speak again, but Christine was entirely at a loss. If Gunther had been expected back within an hour or so she might have asked if she could wait for him, but midnight!

'I suppose . . . I will have to wait until tomorrow to see him,' she said.

'I'll tell him you called,' Frieda said.

Christine began to turn away, unable to think what to do next. Now, when it was too late, she bitterly regretted not having made better arrangements for her visit to Berlin.

An inner door opened and Frau Hofmeyer came out into the entrance hall.

'Who is it, Frieda?' she asked.

Christine paused and looked back over her shoulder. Frieda would have shut the door, but her mother put her hand on it and looked enquiringly at the girl outside.

'It's Gunther's friend from England,' Frieda said reluctantly.

'But she must come in!' Frau Hofmeyer exclaimed. 'What are you thinking of, Frieda, to let her go away with no refreshment when her family has been so kind to Gunther?'

She held the door open wider and smiled at Christine. Her manner was nervous, but she was determined to do the right thing, and Christine found herself being ushered into the living room. She looked round quickly. The furniture was heavy and old-fashioned, but beautifully polished, and the shining wood-block floor looked positively dangerous. How strange the flowery chintzes and floating net curtains of her own home must have looked to Gunther after all this crimson plush.

She sat down on the edge of a chair and accepted a cup of strange-tasting coffee and some delicious cream cake.

'I came to Berlin on . . .' she sought for the German word for 'impulse' and could not find it, 'without making arrangements', she said. 'Can you suggest a hotel, somewhere small and not too expensive, where I could stay for two or three nights?'

Frieda started to reply, but Frau Hofmeyer interrupted. 'You must stay here. Yes, Frieda, it can be arranged. I will share your room for a few nights and Fräulein Brookfield will have mine. It is the least I can do for the daughter of a family which has received my son in their home for three weeks.'

Christine stammered her gratitude. It was what she had hoped for, but she had not anticipated having to extract the invitation from Gunther's mother without his help. She was not entirely comfortable about accepting it, especially since she detected in Frieda something of the same animosity she had already sensed in the minor officials who had interrogated her. Still, Frau Hofmeyer seemed friendly enough, although it was disconcerting to see the way she kept glancing at her daughter as if seeking her approval and looking worried when she did not get it.

The reorganization of the bedroom was carried out with Frau Hofmeyer bustling round, looking pleased and animated as she instructed Lotte about the sheets which were to be put on the bed for Christine and the embroidered pillow slips which were to be used. Christine offered, a little awkwardly, to go out for a meal, since they had not been expecting her, but Frau Hofmeyer wouldn't hear of it.

'So young a girl alone in a restaurant and at night! Your mother would never forgive me. You must share our supper and forgive us for its shortcomings.'

She also overruled Christine's desire to stay up and wait to see Gunther. 'You are exhausted. Yes, I can see it quite clearly. We will leave a note for Gunther to say that you are here and tomorrow you can see him all day.'

Later, when she was alone with her mother, Frieda said: 'You're a fool to encourage her. You should have sent her away.'

'That is no way to speak to me,' Frau Hofmeyer said. Normally she was overawed by Frieda. Her daughter's forceful character and dogmatic views were too much for her to cope with and she was frightened by her strong political opinions. On this occasion her excitement at receiving this visitor from England had overcome her naturally gentle and submissive nature and she was not going to have her pleasure dimmed.

'She will be here for a very short time. I think it is a small return to make for the hospitality that was shown to Gunther. We will say no more about it.'

It was well after midnight by the time Gunther let himself into the flat. Transport was difficult at that time of night and he sometimes toyed with the idea of buying a bicycle. But to do that would be to admit that he was not going to get free from the factory and he could not bring himself to believe that.

There was a note on the table. He picked it up and read it, expecting it to be some anxious message from his mother about heating up some soup before he went to bed. He read it twice before he could really persuade himself that Christine was there, under his own roof, in his mother's room.

68

He walked slowly out of the room, the note still in his hand. He saw the light come on in his mother's bedroom and opened the door and went in.

Christine was sitting up in bed, her eyes enormous in a face white with strain. He stood in the doorway, unable to move. Christine's mouth trembled and she made a small movement with her hands as if she would have held out her arms to him but was afraid of being rebuffed. He moved forward, hardly knowing what he was doing, and sat down on the edge of the bed facing her. She was wearing a white cotton nightdress with an embroidered yoke, just like the one she had worn the last time they had slept together. She was beautiful, even more beautiful than he had remembered. Still unable to think clearly, he put his arms round her, not kissing her but holding her close against him.

Christine clung to him, tears in her eyes, but laughter on her lips. For a moment when she had switched on the light and looked up with dazzled eyes and seen him standing there he had seemed a stranger. She drew away and looked up into his face. She had thought him changed when she had seen him last summer, but the difference between the laughing boy she had known in Kitzbühel and the man she now saw was even more marked. He looked older and more tired and he smelled of dust and sweat, but he was still Gunther.

'I knew everything would be all right if I could only see you,' she said.

She felt for a handkerchief under her pillow and blew her nose. 'Do you still love me?'

'I do. Oh yes, I do,' he said. He pulled her to him and laid his cheek against her soft hair. 'You shouldn't have come. When I've got over the shock I will be angry with you.'

She laughed, too happy at being in his arms again to take him seriously. She looked over his shoulder and saw Frieda standing in the open doorway, her long dressing-gown pulled round her, her face rigid with disapproval. Christine put up a hand to straighten her dishevelled hair and Gunther stood up.

'I must go and let you rest,' he said.

With his back to the door he gave her a tiny wink. He wore a mischievous look which made him seem more like the boy

69

she had first known. Christine's face coloured up and she smiled, the dimples in her cheeks very much in evidence. Frieda said nothing, but the bitter line of her mouth hardened.

As Gunther went out he put a hand on his sister's shoulder and steered her down the passageway. 'There's no need to look like that,' he said. 'Did you expect me to go straight off to bed without checking to see that this extraordinary news was true?'

'Why has she come?'

'To see me.' His hand on her shoulder grew more gentle. 'There is no sinister motive behind it. Christine is as open as the day. She believes herself to be in love with me. She wanted to see me, so she came. It's as simple as that.'

As it happened, the shift that Gunther was working that week was ideal for Christine's visit. He was home until the late afternoon, which meant that he was free to take her around during the day. He took her to the sights of Berlin, not sorry to have the chance to show off his city with its wide modern streets and fine buildings.

They went to the Tiergarten and walked round the gardens which had been made on what had once been a swamp, watching the birds in the rushes and reeds, the alder trees reflected in the water, and the formal flower beds. They strolled down the Kurfürstendamm with all its smart shops and saw the Gedächtniskirche with its steep tower, and the Schloss and the Dom and the Brandenburger Tor, until Christine begged for a break and then they sat down under the striped awning of a wayside café for a cool drink.

As far as Christine was concerned it did not much matter where they went so long as they could be together, and she did not realize the trouble Gunther took to shield her from sights which might distress her and of which he was himself ashamed. Even so, she could not help but see the signs of '*Juden verboten*' even on such simple things as a park bench.

The hours she spent alone with Frau Hofmeyer and Frieda were at times awkward, but she exerted herself to make a good impression and Frau Hofmeyer was charmed by her. Frieda remained aloof and suspicious, but Gunther advised Christine not to let his sister's attitude worry her.

'She is not a happy person,' he said. 'And so I think she grudges happiness to anyone else. I don't like Ulrich Hübner, but I wish he would marry her. Frieda would settle down and make a good little *Hausfrau* if she were only given the chance. It's her misfortune to believe herself in love with a man who makes use of her and gives her nothing in return. As a result, she substitutes her devotion to the Führer for the affection she should be giving to her own husband and family.'

Christine, observing the light of fanaticism in Frieda's eyes whenever she spoke of her Leader, thought that this was true. Hitler must be an extraordinary man to inspire so much devotion. Christine tried to imagine herself giving such uncritical acclaim to a British political leader, or even to the King, and failed completely.

She and Gunther wandered back to the apartment at the end of Friday morning and found Frau Hofmeyer preparing to go out. She clucked her tongue in distress when she heard that they had had no lunch.

'I must go,' she said apologetically. 'Every Friday afternoon I give a piano lesson to a young girl who is relying on me to prepare her for her examination. She is crippled, but with such talent! If I do not arrive she will be heartbroken. And Lotte each Friday goes to confession and then to visit her widowed sister, so there is no-one to prepare your meal.'

She look distracted, but Gunther took her by the shoulders with unusual familiarity and propelled her firmly towards the door.

'There is food in the kitchen. We can prepare something for ourselves.'

'There is some good vegetable soup, and sausage and bread and smoked cheese.'

'A feast! Go now or you will be late.'

When she had gone he turned to Christine with a smile. 'Can you cook?'

'No! Oh, Gunther, how terrible! Now you are going to find out my shortcomings. I can manage a boiled egg.'

'We'll have a cold meal.'

They ate in the kitchen, which would have filled Frau

Hofmeyer with horror, and washed down the strong-tasting sausage and the tomato salad with glasses of red wine.

'I can make coffee,' Christine offered.

Gunther grimaced. 'You must have noticed that we have nothing but *ersatz* coffee,' he said. 'I believe it's made from acorns.'

'I thought it tasted unusual. But why, Gunther?'

'Our population has grown and we can no longer feed ourselves. That's one of the things that has led to our present problems. We have to import food, and coffee is not a necessity. We need more land, more living space.'

'*Lebensraum?*'

'Yes, exactly. But don't look so troubled, *Liebchen*. Forget our lack of coffee and have some more wine instead.'

Christine sat dreaming over her glass of wine, her elbows on the table, tilting her glass to catch the light in the red liquid. Gunther watched her, smiling slightly. She looked up and caught his eye and his smile deepened. She reached out her hand to him across the table and he took it in one of his.

'So – what shall we do this afternoon?' he asked.

Christine shook her head. 'You tell me,' she said.

Gunther opened her hand and looked at the smooth pink palm. 'This is probably the only time we shall have alone together. Shall I tell you what I would like to do or can you guess?'

Christine's hand closed round his once more. 'I can guess. It's what I would like too.'

He stood up. 'Good!'

Christine looked at the cluttered table. 'But we must clear up in the kitchen first.'

She began to stack the dishes together and carry them over to the sink. Gunther came up behind her and nuzzled his face down into the back of her neck. 'Why is it that you are suddenly domesticated when I do not feel in the least like washing plates?'

'Because it would be very embarrassing if your mother or Lotte came home and found everything just like this and we'd been here all the afternoon and done nothing about it.

72

Gunther, stop it! Here, have a tea towel and keep your hands occupied!'

It was a wonder that nothing got broken, but they did succeed in tidying up before they went with their arms round one another towards Christine's bedroom.

'Do you think me completely shameless?' she asked. 'Chasing you halfway across Europe and leaping into bed with you as soon as we are alone?'

'Of course not. It makes me very happy.'

Christine smiled tremulously. 'How silly of me to start having qualms now, when I've got to the point of enticing you into my bedroom.'

'There's no need to entice me. It is the place in all the world where I most wish to be.'

He set himself that afternoon to give her a memory that would carry her through the separation he believed lay in front of them. In the days they had spent together they had avoided any discussion of the future, but at the back of both their minds was the knowledge that this could be their last meeting. That was why Christine had come. He knew that, although she would not say so.

He was curiously touched to find that she was shy of him and had to be coaxed back to the point of intimacy with each other they had reached the previous year.

'It's been so long,' Christine said. 'So long since that night I came creeping along the corridor in the dark. It's been awful since you went. I never dreamed that I would want you back so badly.'

'And there has been no-one else to console you all these sad months?'

'Of course not!' She raised herself up and looked down at him in horror. 'How could there be?'

He guessed from the troubled look that came over her face what her next question would be. 'There hasn't been anyone else for you, has there?'

And Gunther, who had not been able to live through his dreary days without the consolation of a woman occasionally, lied stoutly and swore that he had been true.

He wooed her delicately, finding the sensitive nerve ends

which sent delicious tremors of pleasure running through her, and Christine accepted it as part of the wonder of love and never suspected that she had been so fortunate in finding in her young lover not merely physical harmony but a depth of understanding she might look for in vain in a less sensitive man.

It was not until they lay spent and drowsy, their reluctant hands falling away from one another, that he told her the piece of news he had kept at the back of his mind all the time they had been together. They began to talk, more confidentially now that they had found one another in deep physical satisfaction once more. He spoke of the horror of the *Kristallnacht* and she understood at last the reason for the falling off of his letters. He told her of his hatred of working in the factory.

'Can't you just give in your notice?' Christine asked. 'There must be something else you can do, even if it's not architecture.'

'It is not so simple, but there is a way out and I think I will have to take it.'

'Come back to England with me.'

'No, my darling, that is not the way for me. I can be released from the work I am doing, but only if I transfer to something that is of even more use to the State.'

She started nervously, aware from his reluctance to come to the point that he was going to tell her something that would distress her.

'I am going to volunteer to join the *Luftwaffe*.'

She was silent for so long that he lifted his head to look down at her. She was lying quite still, her head pillowed in the crook of his arm, a look of such deep sorrow on her face that he caught his breath.

'There is going to be a war, isn't there?' she said.

'Yes, *Liebling*, there is going to be a war.'

'And we shall be on opposite sides.' Her voice was a whisper.

He sat up. 'No! Even if our two countries are fighting, you and I, we will still be on the same side.'

'I'll never forget you, never stop loving you. I promise . . .'

Wiser than she was, he stopped her at those words. 'No, we will make no promises. The years go by and it is not always possible to keep the promises one has made. You are free and

I am free. If, one day, you find an Englishman you come to love there must be no guilt in your heart because you have broken a promise to me.'

'And you, will you find a German girl who will be more to you than I have been?'

'Not more, that isn't possible, but it may be that I will find someone else. I am a man who cannot live without a woman,' Gunther said, sadly honest at last. 'We must say goodbye to one another now, this afternoon, while we are alone and can show our sorrow to one another. You will be brave, my little love. You have so much courage. Twice now you have come to me when I have not thought it possible. Now you must face saying goodbye with equal courage and help me to do the same.'

Their parting was terrible to both of them and even Frieda was struck by their silent anguish. It was all nonsense, of course, she told herself, a mixture of sentiment and sex which was really quite revolting to an ordinary sane person, but for once she held her bitter tongue and her manner towards her brother was kinder than he realized at the time.

Christine returned home to find her father more seriously displeased with her than he had ever been before in all her life. She listened to what he had to say without replying and finally he subsided, unable to continue in the face of her stony, dry-eyed composure.

The only words he got out of her were not calculated to mollify him. 'I had to go and I won't say I'm sorry because I'm not.'

He was on the verge of making an angry retort, but Barbara caught his eye and shook her head.

'There's no need to say any more,' she said with a calm she was far from feeling. 'Christine knows that she has been extremely inconsiderate. We were very worried when we heard from Diana what you'd done, darling. That's why Daddy is so upset – as I am. You should have told us your plans.'

'You would have tried to stop me.'

'Where did you stay in Berlin?' Harry asked.

'In Gunther's home. Frau Hofmeyer was very kind. She sent you her compliments and her thanks for your hospitality to Gunther last year.'

She recited her message like a tired, polite child, with the words meaning nothing to her.

Barbara got up and put an arm round her shoulders. 'You look tired out. I think you should go straight to bed.'

She led her away, ran a bath for her, brought her a glass of warm milk and tucked her up as if she were a little girl again and Christine let her do it with a docility which tore at her mother's heart.

In the days that followed Christine seemed to want her mother's company more than anything else. She would seek her out and sit watching her preparing food in the kitchen, not talking but needing her with the persistence of a sick child. She went back to work and found herself cold-shouldered by her friends, still sore because of her desertion in Paris. She offered them no more of an apology than she had given to her parents.

'If she says once more "I had to go", I'll shake her,' Clare said. 'Anyone would think no-one had ever been in love except Christine Brookfield. She fancies herself as a proper little Juliet. I'm fed up with her and I told her so.'

At least one of Barbara's private nightmares came to nothing. She had had visions of her daughter coming home pregnant and when this proved not to be so she was secretly grateful to Gunther. Harry, she knew, when he had learned that Christine had been, as it were, chaperoned by Frau Hofmeyer, cherished a delusion that his daughter retained her virginity. Barbara was sure that this wasn't so, but she didn't say so to him. Her own silence surprised her until she realized that there had been a subtle change in her relationship with her daughter. She no longer looked upon her as a young girl, but as a woman to be treated with the same consideration she would have extended to one of her own contemporaries, and she thought that perhaps it was this silent understanding that made Christine find comfort in her company.

The news grew more and more grave. Michael was down from Oxford, cautiously confident of having gained a reasonable degree, but strangely vague about the next step in his career. He had an interview with one of the big aviation companies from which he returned looking even more abstracted than he had been before. He took advantage of a moment alone with his father that evening to tell him what was on his mind.

'I had a good long talk with the chap who interviewed me today,' he said. 'We both think war is inevitable. I said I was thinking of chucking the idea of joining his firm and he agreed that it would probably be a waste of time because I'll be called up anyway. As far as I can see one might as well volunteer as wait to be called. So I've decided to join the RAF.'

It brought home to all of them the closeness of war. Barbara tried to argue that it would be a terrible mistake to rush into uniform and then find that there was no fighting after all, but Michael was obstinate and she couldn't shake him. She began to turn her mind once more to the possibility of sending Jimmy to America. He was outraged by the idea.

'You can't send me away. I'm not a kid. I could be useful. Dad, tell her you won't let me go.'

His father sympathized, but for once his mother would not be shifted.

Jimmy sailed for the United States during the last week of August, scowling horribly in an effort to hold back the tears which would come in spite of his fifteen years. The house seemed empty without his cheerful, impudent presence.

'Even Michael going into the RAF isn't as hard to accept as this,' Barbara said. 'Oh, God, I do hope I've done the right thing! He'll grow away from us, and he's always been special to me, my last baby.'

A week later Harry, Barbara and Christine listened to Mr Chamberlain's tired voice as he announced the outbreak of war.

When it was over Harry switched off the wireless. Christine got up and went out of the room. Harry and Barbara looked at one another and then Barbara went after her.

Christine was in her bedroom, sitting on the edge of her bed. Barbara sat down beside her and put an arm round her shoulders.

'Gunther has joined the *Luftwaffe*,' Christine said. 'He told me he was going to before I left. Michael is in the RAF. They could kill one another. How am I going to bear it?'

She turned towards her mother and Barbara held her tightly without saying anything. She thought Christine would cry, but she didn't. A long shudder ran through her body and then she freed herself.

'We must help each other,' Barbara said. She stood up, cleared her throat and then continued firmly: 'You have a lover fighting on the wrong side, I've sent one son away from me and the other is going to be in constant risk of his life, and I don't suppose I shall be able to keep your father from charging into danger if he can possibly manage it. In spite of all that, I don't intend to allow the good roast beef I've got downstairs in the oven to spoil and I expect you to sit down and eat it. One step at a time, Christine, that's the way you can bear it.'

Chapter Four

Gunther took to flying like a bird released from a cage. Everything was in his favour: his physical fitness, his swift reactions, even the mathematics he had studied. He put in for training as a fighter pilot and was exultant when he was accepted. It was a role best suited to him both by temperament and inclination. His favourite sports had always been individual ones, such as swimming and ski-ing. He could operate as a team member, but it was the element of individuality in the role of the fighter pilot which appealed to him. He had never wanted to be part of the ground staff, feeling that it was too closely allied to the work he had disliked in the factory. Nor had he wanted to be a bomber pilot. Single combat in the air seemed to him a cleaner way of fighting a war than raining bombs on helpless cities, although his cynical instructors did their best to disabuse their pupils of any such romantic notions.

He relaxed thankfully into the company of his fellow-trainees. They were a good bunch; cheerful, irreverent and keen. They knew that war was just over the horizon and they were spoiling for a fight. His enthusiasm for the coming battle was dimmer than theirs because of his fear of what might happen to Christine, but the more he learned the more convinced he became that the German armed forces were unbeatable. It would surely be a quick war, a swift decisive victory for Germany and, he hoped, a merciful peace. Who could stand against them? Even the Russians, their strangest allies, had seen the necessity of making a pact with Hitler.

He was more fortunate than Christine in having fresh, congenial company and a fascinating new interest to take his mind off their parting. From the start he handled his aircraft with ease and certainty. The only complaint he had was that he could not get enough time in the air.

'A natural,' his instructor said after sending him off on his first solo flight. 'Keep an eye on him. He could turn out to be an ace.'

'He's going to be a good flyer, I grant you that. How will he be when he has to combine it with fighting?' his Station Commander asked.

It was something Gunther sometimes wondered himself. The answer when it came was more simple than he had expected: when he was attacked he fought back.

He was too close to his initial training to take part in the invasion of Poland. The declaration of war by Great Britain and France which followed was greeted by cheers and toasts in the Mess. If he was not as delighted by the news as his colleagues he managed to conceal the sick dismay that filled him and to make a show of joining in their boisterous rejoicing. In a way it was a relief to have it settled at last. All out war now, and they could begin the serious fighting. And winning.

At first events moved as swiftly as he had hoped. War broke out in September and Poland fell within a month. By May 1940 Norway and Denmark were in German hands. On the 10th May Belgium and Holland were invaded by German airborne troops, and at the same time wave after wave of the *Luftwaffe* flew over France attacking airfields and destroying aircraft on the ground. The tanks and troops stormed in after them. It seemed to Gunther that he never slept in the same place two nights running. As the airfields were captured the *Luftwaffe* moved into them, always on the move and always forward.

He spent long hours in the air, no longer doubting his ability to fight but exhilarated by the danger and the exercise of his skill, constantly pitting his wits against opponents who were his equals and sometimes his superiors. He had some lucky escapes, but they were all part of the excitement of the game. When he swopped stories with his fellow pilots they laughed about their near misses and vied with one another to provide the most hair-raising details.

'Did you see that Hurricane? Came right out of the sun at

me. I thought he'd got me. I was watching him too closely to
see Ernst coming up behind and it must have been the same
with him, we were hypnotized by one another. He never knew
what hit him, poor devil.'

'A kill?'

'No doubt about it. Ernst can notch that one up. Do I get
any credit for being the decoy duck?'

'All you get is a warning not to let it happen again. Ernst
says he can't always be playing nursemaid to you.'

They seemed to be always laughing, young and keen and
sure that victory was only a matter of months away. The
fighting was hard, harder than they had thought it would be,
and amongst themselves the pilots admitted that in some
respects the enemy's equipment was superior to theirs. The
Spitfire fighter, for instance, had an edge over the Messerschmitt 109 which Gunther flew, and the RAF pilots were good
– almost as good as the *Luftwaffe*.

The tanks raced through, sweeping across France, pushing
the British Army towards the sea. France was going to fall, no-
one had any doubt about that, and then surely the British
would see the need to come to terms with the victorious
Germans.

In the area around the last beachhead left to them the
British battled desperately to hold on to the ports which were
their only hope of escape. The French fought a gallant
rearguard action, but in the end only Dunkirk was left.

'Have you heard?' Gunther was asked by an excited pilot.
'The Army's holding back. Göring's persuaded the Führer to
let the *Luftwaffe* finish off the British – at least that's the story
I've been told. Great news! We'll smash them into the ground.'

'Great if we are successful,' Gunther said. 'I'm no tactician,
but isn't it going to be rather a long haul for the bombers?'

'Oh, don't be such an old bear! We'll annihilate them!'

Gunther's observation had been no more than a passing
thought, but it proved to be correct. The airfields where the
bombers were stationed were too far from the beaches where
their services were required. Even worse, for three days they
were closed in by fog. Boatload by boatload the British Army

crept away, harassed by Stukas, raked by machine guns, but still surviving.

Gunther, flying over the sandy beaches, saw the long, patient lines of men and wondered at the blind faith that kept them there, waiting for rescue. The RAF was very much in evidence too, as he realized abruptly as he picked out the unmistakable shape of a Spitfire ahead. He began to climb steeply, trying for the advantage of height, but the other aircraft was faster and damnably manoeuvrable. Even the tighter turning circle of the Messerschmitt failed to give him the advantage he needed. He fired at random, knowing he had not found his target, and heard the rattle of bullets in reply. His Messerschmitt shuddered and he fought to control it as the engine coughed. He turned its nose towards home, cursing silently because he was having to make an ignominious escape from a fight that had been all too brief and disconcertingly favourable to the British aircraft.

He tried to keep airborne, but he was losing height. His fuel tank had been hit and he was lucky not to be on fire, a piece of luck which might not last. The Messerschmitt was still flyable, but he was running out of time. He could bale out, but that would mean the destruction of an aircraft which was sorely needed. At the back of his mind he knew that the *Luftwaffe*'s losses had been severe, too severe for comfort; he must save the aeroplane if he could. He was flying over agricultural land and still losing height. He picked out a suitable field and made an unorthodox, bumpy and exceedingly hair-raising landing.

He quickly climbed out of the confined space of the Messerschmitt cockpit, fearing an explosion after the way he had had to put down. His throat was dry and his hands were clumsy inside the silk gloves he was wearing. He shrugged off his bulky life jacket and tossed it back into the cockpit, no point in burdening himself with that on dry land, and he removed the flare cartridges he had clipped to the top of his flying boots so that he could get at them easily in the cramped Me109.

The aircraft sat, lopsided and disconsolate, in the middle of the field. Gunther kicked disparagingly at what looked like the remains of a crop of turnips. He felt disgusted with himself for having been out-manoeuvred, for having to admit defeat. At least the aircraft was salvageable. On the other hand, although he could have flown himself back to base, he had only a vague idea of where he was now that he was on the ground. There seemed to be nothing for it but to start walking.

It occurred to him that a field in France, without the backing of the German army, was not the best place for a solitary *Luftwaffe* pilot. He'd had little contact with the French. The civilians he'd seen were sullen but harmless; the French Air Force had been gallant, even reckless, but ultimately ineffective. It would be ironic indeed if he got himself shot by a local farmer just when it looked as if the war was about to be concluded.

He trudged across the fields, not particularly comfortable in his flying boots, until he could see what looked like a farmhouse and outbuildings ahead. He went forward cautiously, still with the feeling that there was hostility in the air all round him. It brought home to him how sheltered he had been, always surrounded by companions, only fighting in the air, rarely seeing the people whose countries his compatriots had overrun.

There was a truck parked in the courtyard of the farm. Because of the way he had been thinking he was thankful to see the German markings. There seemed to be no-one about, but as he approached he heard voices inside one of the barns. A raucous laugh, a shout and then a woman's scream, a thin, high-pitched wail of terror.

The door of the barn was ajar. Gunther flung it open and stood in the doorway. There were three of them, three soldiers of the *Wehrmacht* in field-grey uniforms, and they had got the woman down on the floor amongst the wisps of golden straw. Two of them had finished with her and were leaning against the wall urging on the efforts of their companion. When the door opened one of them swung round, his hand feeling for the gun he had discarded, but when he saw not a vengeful French farmer but a man in the uniform of the *Luftwaffe*, and an officer at that, he hesitated, his mouth open.

'What the hell do you think you're doing?' Gunther

demanded. He could see at a glance what they were doing, but he knew the question would put them on the defensive.

They looked at one another.

'Just a bit of fun,' one of them said uncertainly.

The one on the floor got up, fumbling awkwardly with his clothes. The woman began to crawl away, whimpering like a hurt animal, towards the back of the barn.

'Get outside and wait for me there,' Gunther ordered.

They obeyed him, but he heard one of them mutter with a touch of bravado: 'Probably wants a go himself.'

Gunther swung round, his face white with anger. 'For you there'll be an added charge of insolence. Now, get out!'

He knelt down by the side of the woman. She was a big, fair girl in her late twenties. They had been rough with her. One cheek was red and swollen, her eye was half closed, her lip was split, a thin trickle of blood ran down her bare legs. She backed away from him along the floor, her eyes blank with shock, incapable of recognizing that this was not another attacker, and all the time that terrible noise of mindless terror came out of her mouth.

His French was nothing like as fluent as his English. Desperately he sought for words to reassure her.

'*Je ne vous ferai pas de mal*,' he said uncertainly, but he doubted whether she was capable of understanding his thick accent.

He touched her bruised and swollen cheek with gentle fingers and his hand brushed against her hair.

'*Je le regrette*,' he said. It sounded hopelessly inadequate, but there seemed to be little more he could do. She needed medical care and perhaps he could arrange that. He got up and left her.

Outside the three soldiers were waiting for him. Dull, stupid louts, he thought scornfully. If they had had their wits about them they would have driven off and left him. As it was, he was going to be forced to take the matter further.

He got in beside the driver and ordered him to take him to their Commanding Officer.

'We meant no harm,' one of them ventured.

Gunther did not answer him. No harm! He thought of the

girl's torn and bleeding body, her damaged mind. Were they animals?

'We've beaten them, after all,' the whining voice persisted. 'The Frenchies did a lot of damage to our unit. Only fair we should have something in return.'

'Be silent!'

The soldier subsided sullenly in response to the curt order.

Gunther was delivered to the temporary headquarters of their unit and explained himself to the smart young major in charge.

'Hard luck about your plane,' the major said. He was all sympathy and very ready with his hospitality . . . 'we've come across some fine cognac in the local château' . . . until Gunther told the rest of his story.

'Oh, bloody hell! I know the three you're talking about. I'll see they're reprimanded.'

Something about the careless way he spoke stung Gunther. He looked him straight in the eye. 'You will, of course, want to charge them and have them properly punished, *Herr Major*,' he said flatly.

It was a tiresome business and it brought Gunther a brief notoriety he could have done without, but the *Wehrmacht* prided itself on the correctness of its behaviour, and because of his insistence the three soldiers were charged, tried and sentenced. Opinion amongst his own companions was divided. A number dismissed the incident as part of the fortunes of war.

'Why couldn't the silly bitch give it to them without making a fuss?' one scornful young pilot snorted.

It was a matter of wry exasperation to Gunther that it was the more dedicated Nazis who congratulated him in all solemnity on his zeal in protecting the righteousness of their cause.

Long before the trial he went with a party of technicians to the field where he had left his Messerschmitt to see whether he was right in thinking that it could be salvaged. There was nothing left of it but a charred skeleton of twisted metal.

'Looks as if you had a lucky escape, sir,' one of the mechanics remarked. 'It must have burst into flames after you'd landed. A few minutes earlier and you'd have gone up with it.'

Gunther walked round the burnt out shell, his face thoughtful. The aircraft had been in no danger of burning when he had left it, he was quite sure of that. There were farmworkers in the next field. One of them paused by the hedge and looked towards the group of Germans, his face impassive. Gunther bent down and touched the ashes lying beneath the aeroplane. They were still warm. He had no doubt at all that the burning of his aircraft had been an act of vengeance. He didn't altogether blame them. The Messerschmitt might have been a write off in any case. He kept his mouth shut and agreed with the mechanics that he had been fortunate in leaving the aircraft when he had.

It was not until the trial was over and he had a brief glimpse of the girl again that he admitted to himself the true reason for his violent sense of outrage. There was no real resemblance, none at all, he told himself, but just for one fleeting moment when he had knelt by her side and his hand had touched her hair she had reminded him of Christine. Suppose that after all the British did not sue for peace, suppose they had to invade England, what would happen to Christine?

France fell and Gunther and his friends went to Paris for a brief, hectic weekend. Released from the stress of battle, intoxicated by their own success, they stalked the boulevards like the young gods they knew themselves to be, brutally healthy, avid for sensation. In the uniform of a *Luftwaffe* pilot, cap tilted at a rakish angle, even the least prepossessing achieved a dashing air and they had little trouble in finding themselves girls who were willing to overlook their nationality.

'Women like conquerors,' one of Gunther's colleagues said. 'I've got my little girl eating out of my hand.'

For once Gunther stayed aloof. He did not like them, he found, those girls who, for money or expediency, were prepared to give themselves to the men who had humiliated their countrymen. He had more respect for the ones who passed by with eyes averted and paid no attention to the whistles and suggestive remarks.

When they returned to their unit he alone amongst his

colleagues could not boast of having scored a hit with a single French girl and once again there were puzzled looks directed at him, as there had been over the matter of the rape. He was a good chap, Leutnant Hofmeyer, and a fine flyer, but something of a lone wolf.

They grew more and more edgy as the days went by, expecting at any minute that the invasion of England would begin. Almost without exception they had been confident that Britain would realize that further resistance was useless. Even Gunther could see no sense in the islanders' obstinate determination to continue the fight. The news they were given was censored, but they heard about Churchill's speech of defiance: 'We shall fight on the beaches . . . we shall fight in the fields and in the streets . . . we shall never surrender . . .' They saw now that this war was not going to be over as quickly as they had thought. It was going to drag on and all because the *verdammte* English refused to admit that they were beaten.

There came back into Gunther's mind a memory he had almost forgotten, of a boy of his own age who had decided that he would win a tennis match and who would not give up in spite of cuts and bruises which must have made holding a racket excruciatingly painful. In the Mess, while the others laughed uncomfortably at the 'warmonger's' speech, Gunther raised his glass in a silent toast and drank to an enemy who was, if nothing else, worthy of respect.

They were ordered to step up the attack against Britain in the air and day after day they flew out, fighters and bombers, in search of their targets. The bright September days were ideal for aerial combat, but they began to grow deathly tired. Where did the British get them, those seemingly endless supplies of men and planes? Was it possible that the figures they were given for aircraft destroyed were not as reliable as they supposed? Why was it they were constantly being told of brilliant successes which must surely be happening to other *Gruppen* because Gunther's lot knew only too well that they were not winning their part of the fight against the RAF? Britain called it 'the Battle of Britain', the Germans never admitted that it was a battle at all. It was merely a series of skirmishes over a few airfields which were better defended than they had believed.

'They know when we're coming and they know where we'll be when we get there,' a weary pilot remarked to Gunther. 'The way they track us is fantastic. Why haven't we got anything as good as that?'

It was not until after Dunkirk that Christine admitted that she was going to have to do something more decisive than just continuing with her peacetime job. It was a year since she had seen Gunther. The thought of him was still like an old wound that hurt when it was touched, but she was no longer the withdrawn, silent ghost she had been. The careless girl who had fallen headlong into love on the ski slopes had gone for ever, but the competent young woman who had replaced her was very much to her father's liking.

He had become an Air Raid Warden and so had Barbara. Christine studied First Aid, but she began to feel that this was not enough. She had been stirred by the story of Dunkirk, as had every Briton, and she was affected the new spirit of determination in the air. They were alone and, in spite of the obvious dangers, accepting the challenge. When it came down to rock-bottom there was no-one capable of showing Jerry what was what except the British; that was the general feeling. It never seemed to occur to anyone that they might be defeated and they would have been incredulous if they had known of the opinion on the other side of the Channel that they were already beaten. It was only just beginning – that was what most of them thought.

It came as no great surprise to her mother when Christine said one day: 'There's a lot of talk about making call-up compulsory for women. I'd rather go of my own accord like Michael did. I'm going to try to get into the WAAFs. I feel closer to them because of Michael and . . .' she stopped abruptly.

'And Gunther,' Barbara said gently. 'You still think about him, don't you?'

'Not as much as I did, but, yes, I still wonder when a

German plane goes over if he might be flying it. Silly, because I don't even known for certain that the *Luftwaffe* accepted him, nor what branch he might have gone into. But somehow I've always seen him like Michael, keen to be a fighter pilot. Don't look so worried, Mum, I'm over the worst of it now. Sometimes a week or more goes by without my even remembering him and then something will happen to bring it back. It still hurts, but having to make such a complete break has helped me get him out of my system. If there'd been any hope . . .'

She sighed and her mother said quickly: 'The only real cure is for you to find someone else.'

'Perhaps, one day. What I need now is new work, new company.'

'I'm sure you're right. Getting away from home will be right for you now. It's time I threw you out of the nest, though my other young fledgling still hasn't forgiven me.' She picked up her letter again with a sigh.

'Is that from Jimmy?'

'Yes. I do wish he wouldn't be so scathing about baseball. After all, it is a national sport. It can't really be the same as rounders, as he claims. He's taken up rifle shooting! Apparently he has the idea that if the Germans invade he'll come over and defend us. My dear old lanky lad! Does he imagine he's going to swim the Atlantic?'

Christine's first few weeks in the WAAF coincided with the stepping up of the German offensive against the RAF. She found herself having to cope not only with the strangeness of sharing a hut with unknown girls and taking in a mass of new regulations and restrictions on her freedom, but also with the hazards of being in what had suddenly become the front line.

She had joined, a little reluctantly, as a clerk. It seemed only sensible to make use of her secretarial training, but she made no secret of the fact that she would prefer to do something different from her peacetime job. When she was asked if she would like to train as a 'Clerk Special Duties' she accepted because it seemed a possible way out of a routine job. She was sent to Yatesbury and so well kept was the secret that she did not discover until the first lecture that she had volunteered to be trained in 'radio direction-finding techniques for the detection of aircraft at long ranges'.

'Me a radar operator! Who would have thought it!' she said when they all returned exhausted to their huts. 'Am I completely dim or was everyone else as much in the dark as I was?'

'I hadn't a notion,' one of the girls agreed. 'I'll never take it all in, I know I won't.'

'It's a very interesting thing to get into, and right up front in operations, too,' Christine said thoughtfully. 'I'm not going to give up easily.'

In the next three weeks they all grumbled and complained that their brains were giving way, but no-one dropped out. The need for secrecy was impressed on them over and over again as they were told about the chain of stations round the coasts which were detecting aircraft at long ranges and passing on the information to Fighter Command. Christine learnt about the basic principle of radio direction finding: that an electrical impulse of radio wave sent out into space and coming into contact with a hard object would then rebound; that the speed of radio waves was known, so that a measurement of the time taken for the wave to travel to an aircraft and back would reveal how far away that aircraft was. She learnt about tracking and plotting – pushing counters about on a large-scale map of the British Isles to show how the aircraft were moving – about wavelengths and frequencies, cathode tubes and magnetic fields.

Her head was still reeling when she finished her course. She was posted to the Kent coast and immediately caught up in the great wave of August air raids. There was no time to feel like a new girl, her services were too urgently required. She had to take her place straight away beside seasoned veterans and to try to equal their concentration and coolness.

It became second nature to don the headset, focus her eyes on the screen and begin reading plots and heights of incoming enemy aircraft while continuously passing the information on over the telephone to Stanmore, ignoring the fact that the hostile aircraft were heading straight for their own station.

The only response to enemy aircraft overhead for the girls in the Ops Room was to put on their tin hats and carry on plotting.

She did think one day that they had been put out of action. Her chair rocked with the force of the blast as a bomb exploded outside the hut. From the operator at Stanmore she could hear the anxious question over her head telephone: 'Do you still read me? Are you still there?'

'Half a minute,' Christine croaked. 'I'm nearly blind and I've got a throatful of dust.'

She wiped her streaming eyes. A second explosion tore the door of the hut from its hinges and one of the girls slid from her chair to the floor. The line of light on Christine's screen flared up and went dead, but the telephones were still working. From Stanmore, Fighter Command were still clamouring for information, but for the moment there was nothing Christine could tell them.

She picked her way over the overthrown desks and chairs. Ellen, the girl on the floor, stirred and opened her eyes.

'Stunned by the blast, I think,' Pilot Officer Cooper said.

'I thought that door was supposed to be bombproof,' Christine said.

She edged through it and out into the open. There was a crater in the compound only a few yards away and a pile of rubble and smashed wood where the cookhouse had been.

Two medical orderlies with a stretcher raced towards her.

'Anyone hurt?'

'One girl knocked out and a few cuts and bruises,' Christine said.

'You've been lucky. The cooks have caught the worst of it.'

A quarter of an hour later, powered by an emergency Diesel, they were operating again. They were shaken, but they tried to calm themselves with forced banter.

'I wonder if Jerry knows he hasn't hit anything essential?' Section Officer Smith remarked.

'What's unessential about food?' Christine asked. 'When they hit my stomach they hit me where it really hurts.'

They were resolutely cheerful, determined to ignore the fact that one cook was dead and another had had to have her leg amputated. If it had been an isolated incident it would have appalled them. Because it was repeated day after day they were forced to acquire a hard outer shell which protected them from the horror with which they were surrounded.

Christine's work brought her a new sense of comradeship with Michael. They had never been quite at ease with one another since Gunther's visit, and Michael's condemnation of his sister's dash to Berlin had been brutally outspoken. Now, of all the family, he was the only one who appreciated what Christine was doing and when they both had leave which happened to coincide he treated her with a respect which impressed her parents all the more because they were kept in the dark about her duties.

They were both shaken by the degree of Michael's exhaustion. Here, if they had only known it, was the answer to the Germans' question about the apparently limitless resources of the RAF: the pilots were driven to the point where only willpower kept them on their feet.

He was stationed at Biggin Hill, in the forefront of the attack on South East England. Day after day he and his fellow pilots lounged round their dispersal huts ready to take off at a moment's notice.

'My wife offered me scrambled eggs for tea when I was on leave and I was halfway down the garden before she got as far as "eggs",' one of them joked, but it was never entirely a joke. They were keyed up to such a pitch of alertness that it was difficult to let go. Their off-duty time was boisterous and Christine came to learn that the apparent high spirits and crazy escapades were as much due to their need to forget the friends who had not survived that day's sorties as the search for relaxation for nerves which might otherwise betray them next time they were in the air.

Michael flew all through the Battle of Britain. He shared the exhilaration of knowing that they were holding firm, but he shared too the loss of men whose comradeship he had valued. As long as he was on duty he could keep going. When he was on leave he let go.

He arrived home on a Friday afternoon, driving his own little car, for which he had been nursing the petrol for weeks.

His mother bit back an exclamation of dismay when she saw his drawn face and sunken eyes.

'Lovely to see you, darling,' she said. 'Christine will be home tonight, too. Isn't that nice? Your father shouldn't be long. He said he'd try to get away early tonight. I've actually managed to make a decent cake so go and sit down and I'll make some tea and cut you a slice, then we can have a chat before everyone else arrives.'

By the time she came back from the kitchen carrying the tea tray Michael was asleep, slumped in his chair. Barbara bent over him, anxiously scanning his worn young face. More than anything else it brought home to her the burden that was being borne by boys like Michael.

She did not touch him, but when Harry came home she said: 'Do you think we ought to wake him? He'll get a better rest in bed.'

Harry nodded. He put his hand on Michael's shoulder and was horrified by the jerk with which he awoke.

'You dropped off in the chair and Mum thinks you'd be more comfortable in bed,' he said. 'Come along, old chap, I'll give you a hand.'

Michael went off up the stairs, blinking his eyes and stumbling slightly. He made no objection when Harry stayed until he was actually in bed. The only thing he said before he closed his eyes and sank back into sleep was: 'It's so quiet here.'

'We've had a fair number of alerts,' Harry said. 'But we're only on the fringes. I know how lucky we've been.'

It was doubtful whether Michael heard him. He was already asleep.

He slept until midday the next day and came down in time for lunch, ravenously hungry and prepared to eat the entire rations for the family for the week. Barbara swallowed her hurt when he spent the afternoon on the telephone talking to his friends and announced that he would be out for the evening.

'He goes back tomorrow. We've hardly seen anything of him,' she said to her husband.

'He doesn't want to be fussed over. Leave him alone,' Harry advised.

He was less sympathetic when his son made a noisy return at one o'clock in the morning, but they both made an heroic effort and refrained from comment. It was Christine who remarked caustically: 'Next time I come home on leave I'm going to make sure you aren't here, you noisy brute. I can do with a rest just as much as you can.'

He grinned at her unrepentantly. 'The evening got a bit hairy,' he admitted. 'Sorry I disturbed your beauty sleep.'

'Was Angela with you?' Christine asked. 'I haven't seen her for ages.'

'She was, but the dear girl has betrayed me – she's joining the ATS. I told her she'd regret it when she met the rude soldiery.'

He glanced at his sister, lying half-supine in a deckchair in the same way as he was himself.

'Why didn't you come along? You've spent your leave sitting around at home.'

'It's what I wanted. I get enough social life on the Station.'

'I'm glad to hear it. You can't go on moping for something you can't have – life's too short.'

Christine closed her eyes. After a moment she said: 'I went to a dance with a Pilot Officer last week. He was dead the next day.'

Michael stirred uneasily in his chair. 'Have you said anything about it here at home?'

'No.'

'Better not. They think they know, but they don't really. Dad tries to get me to talk, but I think he realizes now that I'd rather not. You must have had some rotten moments in the last few weeks.'

'It's been a bit noisy.'

He grunted and nothing more was said, but most unusually when they parted he leant forward and kissed her on the cheek.

'Look after yourself,' he said.

'You too.'

She waved goodbye to him as he zoomed away in his car.

Barbara and Harry were standing just behind her. When she turned she saw that her mother's eyes were wet.

'He'll be all right,' she said.

It was the best she could offer in the way of reassurance and she knew only too well how empty her words might be. The young Pilot Officer she had known for only a brief week or two had been just like her brother and he had been there one day, dancing, laughing, demanding kisses, and the next day he had disappeared into the Channel and his body had not yet been recovered. They did not speak about death amongst themselves. Old so-and-so had 'bought it', they said, purposely vague.

Michael felt rested and keen again after his brief leave, eager to be in the air. The next two weeks were packed with successful action, and then he ran into trouble.

They scrambled when the alert sounded, racing across the worn grass towards their aircraft. He was whistling softly to himself as he prepared to take off, a habit he had picked up to keep himself calm in the nervous moments before he was airborne. He eased a finger round the inside of the silk scarf he wore round his neck in place of a collar. In common with most of the fighter pilots he prized comfort above smartness and the scarf prevented the chafing of the neck they otherwise suffered from as they constantly turned their heads from side to side, searching the sky for the enemy. It had come to be something of the trademark of Fighter Command; that, and the top tunic button left undone and the deliberately battered peaked cap.

As soon as the Hurricane was in the air his nervousness dropped away. He still felt keyed up, but this was the familiar excitement of the chase and he enjoyed it; it was the anticipation that churned up his stomach.

He heard the voice of the Controller from the Ops Room.

'Bandits coming in from the south. Maintain Vector one-zero-zero, making Angels twenty-five.'

There was a laconic acknowledgment from Squadron Leader Telford and then they kept R/T silence until his voice came over the air again: 'Michael, stop that bloody whistling.'

'Sorry,' Michael said with a guilty grin. He had not even known he was doing it.

They were getting further instructions. 'Bandits at Angels fifteen. Start turning now on to two-seven-zero.'

The squadron wheeled on to a course that would bring them face to face with the incoming aircraft from the best position, coming out of the sun.

'What's their strength?'

'Looks like fifty plus,' the Controller replied. 'Target now ten o'clock, range ten.'

Michael wriggled into his parachute harness. One white wisp of cloud drifted by; apart from that the sky was a blazing blue, and empty, damn it, empty.

'Target eleven o'clock, range five.'

The disembodied voice sounded as if it knew what it was saying, but he could see nothing, and then he heard Larry Telford's shout: 'Yoicks! Tally ho!'

The R/T was alive with warnings and instructions. Michael was flying in number two position in Red Section. He could see the enemy aircraft now: Heinkels and Dorniers with an escort of Messerschmitts. He heard the crisp command: 'Red Leader to Red One and Two. Five Me109s above main formation. Take them.'

Michael climbed fast, striving to get above the 109s before they could get the advantage. He got one lined up and pressed his thumb on the trigger, pouring ammunition into the fuselage as he zoomed past. As he banked and turned he heard the confused chatter all round him:

'Break right, Green Two, break right.'

'Behind you, Yellow One.'

'I've got him, Red Leader. Leave him to me.

Michael tried to get his target back in line for another burst, but the Me broke away steeply, successfully evading him. He followed it, intent on a kill, until a voice spoke sharply in his ear:

'Bandit on your right, Red Two.'

He twisted his head and saw it, an Me coming straight for him. He dived beneath it, but it hit him with a burst on the right wing. No serious damage, a lucky escape, and Red

Leader had got him. There was a plume of black smoke and it plummeted down towards the sea.

Michael was into the Dorniers now, past the defensive escort which had been trying to keep him at bay. It was a piece of cake. The rear gunner was pumping out incendiary bullets, but he must be cross-eyed because none of them was reaching target. Michael pressed his own thumb down hard, without apparent result. He eased the throttle back a fraction and gave them another burst. A crimson flame shot out of the fuselage, there was a stream of smoke, and then an explosion that seemed to make the air as turbulent as a rough sea in a gale.

He was sucked into the slipstream as the remains of the Dornier screamed past him and as he fought his way out of it vengeance fell on him from above. He heard the shouted warning as he was trying to recover control of the Hurricane but his reaction was just too late. He banked to evade the Messerschmitt but it was on his tail, guns blazing. He felt a stab of pain and there was a curious sound, like tearing fabric. There was a searing pain all down his right side. He could smell smoke. He was on fire. The Hurricane was spiralling downwards. He would have to bale out.

The fire was getting worse and he couldn't get out. The flames were licking at him, there was acrid smoke in his eyes and nostrils, blinding him, choking him. His hands fumbled with the cockpit, there was a rush of cold, clear air and he was free, but the flames were still all round him. The legs of his trousers were on fire. As he drifted downwards he tried to beat out the flames with his hands. Before he hit the ground he had lost consciousness.

Chapter Five

The first thing Michael was conscious of was pain, then of darkness. He tried to move, but something was holding him down. He tried to open his eyes, but something was bound round them. His mouth was dry. He made an attempt to lick his lips and a voice said: 'You're with us again, are you? Thirsty?'

Something cool and moist touched his mouth and he managed to swallow. The pain was getting worse. It was all down one side and his head felt as if it was on fire.

Fire! A convulsive shudder ran through him and he struggled to sit up. Somebody held him down. There was a murmur of voices and then a pinprick in his arm and oblivion descended on him once more.

The next time he came to the surface he knew that he was in hospital, that he must be badly injured and that his eyes were bandaged. He managed to croak out the first, most immediate question that came into his mind.

'What's happened to my eyes?'

'Nothing serious,' a soothing voice assured him. 'It's only temporary. Don't worry about it.'

He thought they were lying, but he was too weak to argue. He lay still and let them do what they would with him. There were dressings to be changed and the agony was excruciating. Someone was making an awful fuss about it, whimpering and crying like a baby, and somewhere at the back of his disordered mind he thought that it might be him.

He did not speak about his eyes again until he sensed that there was someone by his bed who was in charge of all the others. He was a little stronger. They had managed to get some food into him even though there seemed to be something

98

wrong with his mouth. He nerved himself to ask the question again and this time he put it more strongly.

'Am I blind?'

'I think not. Fortunately, you were wearing your goggles. The sight of one eye will certainly be impaired, though I can't say to what extent until we are able to examine it while you're conscious. The left eye I believe to be merely inflamed. Once that has subsided you should retain the same degree of sight in it as you had before.'

The cool, dispassionate voice was oddly reassuring. It gave him the courage to ask: 'I suppose I look pretty ghastly?'

'No worse than a lot of others I've seen and a lot better than some. You still have all your main features – two ears, two eyes, a nose and a mouth. Some of you careless young devils I have to rebuild from scratch. You may have to have a skin graft. But at the moment I'm mainly concerned with the severe burns to your right thigh.'

The examination that followed tried him to the utmost, but he gritted his teeth – apparently he still had those, too – and tried to bear it without a repetition of the sorry exhibition he believed he had made of himself previously.

'Not bad,' the cool voice remarked. 'Astonishing, the ability of human tissue to renew itself. Yes, thank you, sister, you can put a fresh dressing on. About the face . . .' A hand felt Michael's pulse. 'Yes, we'll leave that until tomorrow. By that time the eyes should be ready for testing.'

They warned him the next day that he would still be in darkness when they took the bandages off his eyes. He still wasn't sure that he believed that he would see even though the man with the quiet voice had said so with such authority. It was unpleasant, waiting to discover whether it was true or not, but when a dim light was gradually allowed into the room he did begin to perceive the difference between dark, solid objects and the empty space between them.

'There'll be a little difficulty in focusing at first. Don't let it worry you,' the ophthalmologist said.

This was a new man, not the one who was treated as if he were God. He was wearing a white coat and he had dark hair and a moustache.

'I can see you!' Michael exclaimed.

'So I should hope! I'm big enough and ugly enough! Now I want you to rest your chin on here while I take a look right into your eyes. Can you do that without hurting yourself?'

'The dressing on my face gets in the way.'

'Just a minute, I'll see if I can adjust the instrument.'

He started by examining the bad eye. 'Can you see the light?' he asked.

'I can, but it's all spread out and blurred.'

The ophthalmologist grunted, but made no other comment. He seemed better pleased when he turned his attention to Michael's left eye.

'Nothing much wrong there,' he said.

Michael waited until he was writing up his notes and then asked: 'What's the verdict?'

'The vision in the right eye is certainly impaired – permanently, I'm afraid – but as Mr Charteris thought, there's nothing wrong with the left eye which a little treatment and rest won't cure.'

'What about flying?'

'I can't hold out much hope that you'll ever return to flying duty.'

Michael's face was too heavily obscured by the dressing on his burns for his expression to be seen, but something about the quality of his silence made the ophthalmologist add: 'I don't have to tell you how important all-round vision is to a pilot.'

'No.'

It was all Michael could bring himself to say. He felt empty for the remainder of the day. He told himself that he was being incredibly stupid. He had spent many terrible hours believing that he had lost his sight. This had proved not to be the case and yet here he was in black despair because he wasn't going to be able to fly again.

'You're very gloomy,' his nurse said as she carefully cleaned his mouth after he had painfully consumed some minced chicken.

'Not going to be able to go back to flying,' Michael mumbled.

'You're a glutton for punishment, aren't you? I dare say they'll find you some useful job on the ground, or you might be invalided out.'

'No! I don't want to be a clerk with pebble glasses and a walking stick and they're not pushing me into Civvy Street if I can help it.'

'Some people don't know when they're well off. I think you've been too much on your own for the last few days. I'll get some of the other chaps to look in and cheer you up.'

She paused in the doorway and looked back. 'You'll find some of them look rather peculiar. Don't be tactful about it, they know exactly what they look like and it may do you good to see the way they take it.'

A few minutes later a head was poked round the door.

'Hello, old chap! Nancy said you were ready for visitors. I understand they're thinking of pushing you out into the main ward with the rest of us hard cases tomorrow so I thought I'd better come along and give you a sight of one of the freaks so that it doesn't come as too much of a shock to you.'

For a moment Michael couldn't speak. The face that was presented to him was barely recognizable as human. It was patterned by patches of light-coloured skin, the nose was no more than two tubes covered by a strange flap of flesh, there was a piece of skin hanging loose from one cheek.

'Don't take any notice of my dingle-dangles,' the apparition said. 'I'm growing myself a new nose and this thing on the side is going to be a replacement ear. It won't function as an ear, of course, but it'll be useful to rest my hat on.'

He lowered himself carefully into the chair by Michael's bed. 'Artificial leg,' he explained. 'Works quite well, but I still have difficulty in bending it when I sit down.'

He appeared oblivious to the effect his appearance had had on Michael, running on in a cheerful, inconsequential fashion. At the end of ten minutes he dragged himself to his feet.

'I've been told not to stay too long. One or two of the other chaps may look in to say hello as they go past. They're a good bunch and we're looking forward to having you join us. It makes a change to see a new face. Though I suppose,' he added thoughtfully, 'You could say we were all new faces. That was meant as a joke.'

When Michael joined his fellow patients in the main ward two days later he was ready to take his place amongst them as a subordinate member of a band of men wrecked by war and refusing to allow their grotesque masks and distorted limbs to reduce them to anything less than humanity.

Michael was in hospital for several months. The treatment was slow, but he did begin to see signs of improvement. He was given a transplant to replace the flesh which had been destroyed on his left thigh and he, too, grew a 'dingle-dangle' to repair his damaged cheek. His lips developed a twist which was straightened out and once that was done he began to feel more normal again. His sight settled down and although he needed glasses for reading he could see well enough without them for ordinary living.

The hospital was too far from home for Barbara and Harry to visit him often, although Barbara had spent the best part of a week in a hotel nearby when he was first wounded and was scarcely conscious of her visits. He was not sorry to be left alone in the early days when he did not really want anyone to see him. It was not until he was close to being released that he began to welcome visitors.

In February Christine took advantage of a weekend leave to pay him a visit and stayed in the small hotel which her mother had used earlier. She had to wait for a bus to take her to the hospital and Michael already had a visitor when she arrived.

She walked down the ward, looking for her brother, resolutely disguising the shock she felt at the sight of the mutilated men who looked her over with undisguised approval. She had lost none of the athletic ease of movement which had once so attracted Gunther and even the severe lines of her uniform could not hide her beautiful figure and long legs. She had a good colour in her face, partly from walking in the cold wind outside and partly because of her consciousness of the admiration with which she was being watched, and her hair shone in the winter sunshine which came streaming through the window.

The man who had been sitting with her brother got slowly

to his feet as he realized that she was stopping by Michael's bed. He was slimly built and brown as a gypsy, with a flush of colour along his high cheekbones and eyes as dark as sloes, watchful and intent. His hair was cut close to his head, showing the fine shape of his skull. He wore his uniform with the deliberate carelessness which was the hallmark of Fighter Command, but nothing could detract from the fine-boned elegance of a body that looked as if it would move with the swiftness of a deer. Christine noted automatically that he had the Distinguished Flying Cross and realized that this must be Squadron Leader Telford, of whom Michael had spoken in the past.

'A good sort of chap,' he had said. 'Crazy as a coot,' which Christine had recognized as high praise.

She saw him realize that he had been staring at her for too long and was amused by his embarrassment. A shy man, not entirely at ease with women, she thought, but his look of boyish diffidence was misleading: he was older than he seemed and there were lines at the corners of his eyes and mouth which betrayed the tension under which he lived. He reminded Christine of a wary animal, only half tamed, who would shy away in alarm if he were approached too abruptly. It would be interesting, and perhaps rewarding, to coax him into friendship.

'This is Larry Telford,' Michael was saying. 'Squadron Leader Telford, I should say, but you can see that for yourself. This is my sister Christine . . . Chris, you've been promoted!'

'Commissioned is the correct term, as you would know if you weren't a mere temporary airman,' she told him. 'Assistant Section Officer, no less.'

'Congratulations,' Larry Telford said. He was still standing and he added: 'I didn't know Michael was expecting a visit from one of his family. Perhaps I should go away and come again another time.'

'Don't do that!' Michael exclaimed. 'Not when you were just about to tell me how the Squadron finds it can't do without me.'

'The darts team misses you,' Larry retorted. 'Apart from that we've been managing reasonably well. We haven't actually won the war, I admit, but our record hasn't been too bad.'

'I'm probably the one who's in the way,' Christine said. 'Do fetch another chair and sit down. I can see Michael is much more interested in hearing what you have to say than in talking to me.'

She sat and listened to the two men as they talked about the airfield where Michael had been stationed, joining in occasionally, but content to be there and to see her brother looking so cheerful.

His apparent good spirits only wavered once and that was when he said abruptly: 'You know that I've been grounded?'

Michael tried to conceal his disappointment when the Squadron Leader said immediately: 'Yes, I'm sorry about that.' He had, he realized now, been hoping for some disclaimer, some slight hope that after all he would be able to return to flying.

Christine saw the shadow cross his face and turned the subject.

'Have you heard from Jimmy lately?' she asked.

'Yes, he and Lucy write to me regularly. Jimmy still thinks his rightful place is in England, nothing will shake him from that, but he seems to be having a great time in America.'

He didn't find it necessary to say so, but the letters from his brother and from Lucy had been one of his lifelines. Lucy, in particular, had a way of writing of little incidents with a light, amusing touch which had sometimes made him laugh out loud even though the world she was describing seemed as remote as the moon from war-torn Britain. Jimmy, too, had developed a laconic sense of humour which showed that he was growing up fast. Michael was inclined to agree with him: he ought to be at home.

Larry Telford got up to go at the end of half an hour and nothing would persuade him to stay longer.

'So that's your Squadron Leader Telford,' Christine said, watching Larry walk away down the ward. 'Not quite what I expected.'

He had something she had rarely encountered in a man

before – grace. He walked like a dancer, or perhaps like a wild, shy deer of which he had reminded her.

'He's got more to him than you might think at first,' Michael said. 'He's a weird bird in some ways, though. He's nuts about nature and that sort of thing.'

He grinned, a lopsided travesty of his old cheerful smile. 'We were very suspicious when he was seen disappearing into the woods every night. You can guess what the boys made of that! And do you know what he was doing? Watching for badgers!'

Christine laughed at his bewilderment.

'Mind you, he's a spot-on pilot,' Michael went on quickly. 'One of those chaps who seem to do it all by instinct. He rides his Spitfire as if it were a horse and he's got an uncanny knack of making himself invisible. The Jerries don't seem to know he's there half the time.'

When Christine left at the end of visiting time she found that Larry Telford was still in the hospital, waiting for her. It was typical of him, she guessed, to have said nothing of his intention.

'I've got a car,' he explained. 'I thought perhaps you might be glad of a lift.'

'Oh yes, please,' Christine said gratefully. She smiled at him, conscious of a lift of her spirits because this attractive, self-contained man was sufficiently interested to put himself out for her.

'Michael's looking a great deal better than I'd feared,' Larry remarked as they drove away.

'Yes, but it's a bitter blow to him that he won't be allowed to fly again. Have you any idea what'll happen to him?'

'Administration or perhaps Training, I imagine.'

'Training might be a good idea. He's got an engineering degree and he's rather a good speaker, so giving lectures would be no hardship to him. Would it be possible to follow that up and come up with some concrete ideas before he begins to get too despondent?'

'Yes, ma'am, I'll look into it.'

'Oh, dear, did I sound bossy? I sometimes think if this war goes on long enough I shall turn into a real old battleaxe.'

He half turned his head to look at her. 'I don't imagine there's any danger of that. You're in radar, aren't you?'

'I've just gone on to plotting.'

'You girls do a grand job.'

They pulled up outside the hotel and he said, with the diffidence she found endearing: 'Have you any plans for this evening? Are you going back to the hospital again?'

'No, there's no more visiting until tomorrow. My only plan is to have as good a meal as the hotel can give me and then to sit by the fire until it's time for bed.'

'Would it be a terrible bore if I came and joined you?'

'Not a bore at all. I'd be glad to have company.'

They spent a quiet evening together. It was pleasant, undemanding, relaxing. They had enough in common in their service life to make it easy for them to talk and by a few carefully casual questions Christine established that Larry was twenty-nine, unmarried and a Regular Air Force officer. She was sufficiently intrigued to make an effort to put him at his ease, slightly amused by her own determination to do so.

He was reticent, but she discovered in him as they talked a vein of romantic patriotism which accounted, she thought, for his fine fighting record. To Larry, England meant the unspoiled countryside: the sweeping Wiltshire Downs of his home, the hidden lanes and hedgerows full of wild flowers, birds swooping in the newly-turned earth behind the plough, the grey spire of the village church, laughter in the local pub from men who worked close to the land, deserted beaches under winter skies. To him the thought of alien feet marching along English roads was a desecration. He did not say so openly. It was Christine who saw behind his laconic phrases and sensed the driving force that could turn this peace-loving man into a ruthless killer in defence of his country.

She had hardly ever met a good-looking, unattached man who made so little play for her, and yet there was no doubt that he admired her. She sensed in him a great reserve of determination, perhaps obstinacy: Larry Telford would be prepared to wait for his badger to leave its sett, his bird to come to hand, his girl to turn to him.

It was not until she remarked apologetically that she was

tired and would like an early night that she discovered he had to drive through the night in order to be on duty in Kent the next morning. She was horrified and worried, and not only because she thought it a rash thing to do. There was something unexpectedly extravagant about his having sacrificed his night's sleep in order to spend an evening in her company. It was not the way she had read his character at all.

She mentioned in an offhand way that they had had a meal together when she saw Michael the next day.

'I think you've made a conquest,' he said. 'Strange. Our Squadron Leader doesn't go much for the girls.'

'You mean he doesn't chase after everything in skirts like the rest of you,' Christine retorted.

'I shan't do much chasing as I am at present,' Michael said. 'Chris, do I look very hideous? It's difficult to judge, surrounded by much worse cases.'

'I'd hardly know there's been anything wrong with you,' she said quickly. 'The new skin on your face isn't quite the same colour as the old, which gives you a patchy appearance. Apart from that, truly, I don't feel in the least put off when I look at you.'

'Oh, good.'

He fell silent and she asked: 'Any special reason for asking?'

He looked up with a cynical expression on his face. 'Angela. She's stationed only thirty miles away so I dropped her a line and suggested she came in to see me. Dash it all, it's never been very serious, but we've gone around together for as long as I can remember. I thought she wouldn't mind making a bit of an effort for old time's sake. It was a disaster. She stayed for half an hour and spent the whole time not looking at me. Then I got a letter saying that "in the circumstances" perhaps it would be better if we didn't meet again. What circumstances? The only thing I can think of is that I've turned into something of a hideous old crock.'

'I never really liked her. Quite apart from that, I can't see that you had any special call on her – I never noticed you being particularly faithful if you could find something better or, at any rate, new. Pull yourself together, brother dear. As soon as you've got back your health and strength you'll be the same Casanova of Eveleigh you've always been.'

He laughed and agreed, but it rankled, that rejection by a girl he had carelessly regarded as his standby in his home town. Once he was home again he missed the thought of having someone he could call upon for company if he happened to feel like it, although since she was stationed so far away she would not have been available anyway, which made his sense of injury all the more illogical.

Michael had been out of hospital for two weeks before he was asked to report, not to his former Station, but to the Air Ministry.

'I wonder what on earth they can want with me in London?' he said with a puzzled frown. 'Not some ghastly desk job at HQ, I hope.'

He took a great deal of trouble to turn himself out smartly on the day of his interview, having his hair cut and pressing his uniform. He refused to carry the stick he had been using to help him get about. That was a mistake. His leg was already aching before he arrived at the Air Ministry. In spite of all the efforts of the hospital there had been some shrinkage of his muscles and his right leg was very slightly shorter than his left. He had been given special shoes with the sole of the right foot built up by a quarter of an inch, but he had still not adjusted to walking long distances without having something to lean on.

He was surprised when he found himself being interviewed by a Squadron Leader and a Wing Commander. The Wing Commander did not do much of the talking, but every now and again Michael would look towards him and find himself being watched with a degree of attention which seemed out of all proportion to the mundane questions being put to a perfectly ordinary Pilot Officer.

When Wing Commander Sinclair did ask a question it seemed to Michael to have very little relevance to his war experience.

'You belonged to the OUDS when you were up at Oxford, didn't you?' he asked abruptly.

'Yes,' Michael agreed.

'You've no particular qualms about standing up and talking in front of an audience?'

'As long as I know what I'm talking about.'

'Have you ever been to the United States?'

'No.'

'Any connections over there?'

'Some old family friends. As a matter of fact, my young brother is living with them at the moment.'

The two officers exchanged a quick glance and then Wing Commander Sinclair said: 'Would you like a chance to see him?'

It took Michael's breath away. 'Me – go to America?'

'A public relations exercise. We need someone to go over there, do a few talks, make some appearances at suitable functions, drum up support for the war effort.'

'I'll go if I have to,' Michael said slowly. 'But I don't much fancy the idea. Would you, in my position?'

'Frankly, no. I sympathize with your feelings. On the other hand, from our rather repulsive point of view, you are ideal. Dashing young pilot, visibly wounded but not repugnant to the eye, an easy talker, not quite fit enough for active duty but well enough to get around, and without any other job at the moment.'

'The only part of that I like is that you say I'm not "quite" fit for active duty. Does that mean I'll get back to something more directly involved with the fighting when I return?'

'I can't make any promises, but you have my sympathy. I'll do what I can to get you a more congenial posting after this jaunt.'

It was not until he was halfway across the Atlantic that the comical side of his mission began to be apparent to Michael. It was, after all, fairly ridiculous. He had been measured for the best-fitting uniform he had ever possessed, but only after earnest discussions had taken place about the merits of allowing him to appear in a more battle-stained rig; he had been briefed with a thoroughness which put some of his flying missions to shame; he had had speeches prepared for him; he was to be received at the British Embassy; he had been assured of hospitality on a scale to make his eyes pop, but had been implored not to allow it to go to his head; he had also been told to remember that the United States was still officially neutral and some Americans were extremely sensitive about their country's status. He felt like a cross between a cockshy and a force-fed goose.

It was a thrill to be flying into Washington, daunting to discover that Press photographers had been organized to take pictures of him, and surprisingly affecting to see young Jimmy again. They grinned at one another, both reluctant to be seen to be moved by their meeting. Jimmy had grown. He was taller than Michael now. He had filled out, too. The 'lanky lad' had developed into a broad-shouldered young man, but the sandy hair was still the same, and the freckles, and the wide, engaging smile. His look of horror at being asked to pose for a picture with his brother was a sight to see.

Michael had Jimmy's company for only two days and then they parted, Jimmy to return to school and Michael to start on a trek which took him from the white dazzle of Washington to six other States before he ended his tour with a visit to Connie and Bob's home in Minneapolis. Everywhere he went he was overwhelmed by kindness and hospitality, but it was tiring, more tiring than he had expected, to be constantly surrounded by strangers, to have to be ready to answer questions all day and every day. Their curiosity about conditions in Britain was insatiable. They seemed to have difficulty in believing that life was going on much the same as usual in spite of shortages and air raids. When he had to admit that the enormous steaks which were placed in front of him were too large for him there were sympathetic murmurs, but he could see that there was a lack of comprehension behind their sympathy.

When he finally arrived at the Jardines' house on the outskirts of Minneapolis he was more than ready for a rest amongst familiar faces.

'What has made the greatest impression on you?' Bob asked curiously as he drove Michael from the airport.

'The lights – I still flinch every time I go out at night and see all those neon signs flashing away in the darkness; the girls – like ripe peaches.' He paused with a look of reminiscent pleasure on his face, then he went on: 'The food, of course; the abundance of everything.'

He fell silent and Bob said: 'Those are the obvious things, I suppose. What about the American view of the war?'

'I think what has struck me more than anything else is the complacency,' Michael said slowly. 'That "of course it couldn't happen here" attitude. It horrifies me. True, you are a long way from Europe, but there are other parts of the world where the United States is highly vulnerable. I hope that doesn't sound rude. I've been bottling it up until I could say it to someone who couldn't misunderstand me.'

'There are plenty of us who'd agree with you. That's why I'm glad to see a young guy like you, who knows what he's talking about, giving us a few hard facts. It's going to be real difficult to get it accepted, but the truth is we'll have to come in ourselves before the war is finally won.'

Connie met them on the front porch, both arms held out. Michael hugged her and then looked over her shoulder at the girl who was hovering in the background.

'Lucy? You've been growing up while my back's been turned.'

He put his hands on her shoulders and looked down into her face. It was something of a relief to find that she had not shot up in the way Jimmy had. She was still rather too thin, but her face had begun to lose its childish contours. Her dark eyes were as expressive as ever and there was something very attractive about her firm, pointed chin, the sweet line of her mouth, her high cheekbones.

'If you aren't careful you're going to turn into a beauty,' Michael said. 'Do I get a kiss?'

Lucy nodded and reached up and kissed him on the shiny new skin on the right side of his face. She turned away quickly to hide the tears that came into her eyes. He had changed and yet he was still Michael; still the same impudent grin and teasing manner, but there was something new about him, quite apart from his limp and altered appearance. There was a look at the back of his eyes that tore at her heart. A look of suffering borne with grim determination, the look of a man who had seen death very close and would never quite forget it.

She discovered another dimension to him when she heard him speak before a large audience the following evening. It was something of a revelation to all of them. He was fluent, easy, amusing and yet authoritative. He gave a dramatic description of a typical air raid, described the rationing system, spoke of the fine effort being made in the factories in Britain and made a graceful reference to American generosity. He only touched on his own experiences very lightly, but since they could see with their own eyes that he had been wounded his understated account of the Battle of Britain was all the more telling.

'That boy should go into politics,' Bob remarked afterwards as Michael sat down to a storm of applause.

Lucy and Jimmy were both on their feet, clapping enthusiastically, their young faces alight with pride, until Jimmy recollected himself and adopted a more offhand attitude.

'He always did have the gift of the gab,' he said tolerantly. 'Interesting, though, wasn't it?'

'It was *marvellous*,' Lucy said.

Her pleasure in the evening was dimmed a few minutes later when she discovered that Michael was not going home with them. He had been invited to a party. She saw him going off with a girl she knew: Jo-Anne Parker, giggling, empty-headed and pretty as a picture. One had thought that Michael had better taste.

She went to bed soon after they got home and tried to go to sleep, but somehow she could not stop herself from listening for Michael's return. It was just after midnight when Lucy heard a car pull up outside. She heard, too, Jo-Anne's unmistakable giggle. With all her heart Lucy longed to be twenty-one, with yellow curls and a prominent bust. Michael had said she was turning into a beauty, but of course he hadn't meant it. To him she remained the same skinny kid she had always been. It was completely unfair, that to her he should still be the most marvellous person in the world. How did you get over it, this terrible, aching love for someone who was worse than indifferent, who was merely kind and brotherly?

What was the cure for this feeling as if all your insides were melting just because he turned his head and laughed or put out a careless arm and hugged a girl who was nothing to him but a childhood friend?

The long, long silence that followed after she had heard the car pull up was very hard to bear. The tears welled up and would not be stopped. Lucy put her face down into the pillow, her whole body wracked by sobs. It never occurred to her that her distress might be overheard, but after a minute or two there was a cautious tap on her door and then it was opened by Jimmy. He stood first on one bare foot and then on the other, his sandy hair standing on end, his dressing gown pulled carelessly round him, his eyes blinking in the light which had been left on on the stairs.

'I say, Luce, is anything wrong?' he asked uncertainly. 'I thought I heard you crying.'

'I'm OK,' Lucy said in a muffled whisper, but she sounded odd to him.

'Shall I fetch Aunt Connie?'

'No!'

He moved towards the bed, not knowing what to do. Tentatively he patted the shoulder which was all he could find to touch. None of the experiments he had so far made with girls had prepared him for comforting anyone in such dire distress. Something had to be done. They had become very good friends, he and Lucy, particularly since they had united in sending cheering-up letters to Michael. He didn't like to see her, his good companion, so unhappy.

'You can tell me,' he said awkwardly. He perched himself on the edge of her bed. 'Come on, Luce. I might be able to help.'

'No-one can help,' Lucy said tragically. 'M-Michael's outside with horrible Jo-Anne Parker.'

'Lucky devil!'

'They've been there *ages*,' Lucy said, ignoring this unhelpful observation. 'How can he? She's not even nice!'

'No, she's not particularly,' Jimmy admitted. 'Smashing goodlooker though. I see what it is,' he added thoughtfully.

'You always were nuts about old Mike. Trouble is, you're a bit young for him.'

'I'm nearly eighteen!'

'I'm nearly seventeen and they won't let me go home and fight for my own country.'

Lucy sat up and he felt in his pocket, found a crumpled handkerchief and handed it to her. 'Here, mop up.'

Somewhere in the darkness a car started up and roared away. The front door opened. They could hear Michael's footsteps on the stairs. Lucy's door was standing wide open. Michael, his mind pleasantly befuddled by an agreeably pneumatic young woman smelling of gardenias and with a nice line in kisses, paused and glanced in. At the sight of his young brother sitting on the edge of Lucy's bed with his arm round her he stopped.

''Allo, 'allo!' he said. ''ow long 'as this been goin' on?'

He spoke facetiously, but there was a touch of sharpness behind his question. It was not quite the thing for young Jimmy to be caught in a girl's bedroom at that time of the night, not when it was Lucy, whose parents had treated him as if he were their own son.

'Nothing's going on,' Jimmy said. 'Lucy was upset about something and I came in to see if I could help, that's all.'

'I'm all right now,' Lucy said, appalled at the thought that Michael might discover that she had been crying over him.

'She's still a bit mopey, you'd better see what you can do,' Jimmy said.

He went quickly out of the room and back to his own bedroom, but as he untied his dressing-gown and let it drop on to the chair by his bed he was frowning. It was weird, in fact it was downright astonishing, but he had just begun to have some inkling of what it was that was giving Lucy so much pain. She was still only old Luce, a year older than him and nothing more than a friend, but for some reason it had hurt, to get up and leave her to his brother to comfort.

Michael plumped himself down on the spot Jimmy had vacated. 'What's the matter, scrap?' he enquired.

'Don't call me that! It's what you used to call me when I was just a kid and now I'm grown up I don't like it.'

He laughed and put his arm round her, just as Jimmy had, but with far more assurance.

'You'll always be "scrap" to me,' he said. 'I'll try to remember you don't like it. Are you feeling better?'

'I guess so.'

'Not going to tell me what was wrong?'

'I'd rather not.'

She moved a little closer to him, unable to resist the temptation of resting her head against his shoulder.

'Did you have a good evening?' she asked.

'Yes, I think it all went very well. Thank goodness that was my last, my very last, speech! I can't tell you what a relief it is to have it all over.'

'What about the party?'

'Very pleasant, but I was tired and my leg ached so I couldn't jitterbug. I think Jo-Anne got a bit bored with me.'

Lucy began to feel far more cheerful. 'I thought she'd fallen for you in a big way.'

Michael laughed again. 'I was a novelty, that's all.'

His fingers moved absentmindedly over Lucy's bare arm. He was, as he had said, tired, but he had not yet completely relaxed from the nervous tension he felt after appearing on a platform. He was slightly lightheaded from Jo-Anne's father's bourbon, and decidedly amorous. Jo-Anne's kisses had been heady, but the small car had been too unaccommodating for anything more satisfying, nor had she really been willing. A bit of a tease, a girl as light and insubstantial as a meringue and as cloying. He was suddenly very conscious of Lucy, curled up in the circle of his arm, small and warm and feminine.

It gave him enough of a jolt to make him say with an abruptness that was almost rude: 'I must go. A minute or two ago I was on the point of criticizing Jimmy for cuddling up to you and here I am doing the same thing. You're turning into a dangerous woman, young Lucy. Two men in your room in one night, and brothers at that! You should be ashamed of yourself.'

Lucy was growing sleepy. 'It's nice having you near me,' she murmured drowsily.

'It's nice for me too.'

He sounded amused in the way that made her love him.

'It really is time for me to go.'

He was still holding her, in spite of what he said. She turned towards him and lifted her face and he bent his head and kissed her. Then he took his arm away and left her.

It struck him, as he was drifting off to sleep, that it was a strange thing that it should be that one chaste kiss from Lucy that lingered in his mind, not the more practised caresses from Jo-Anne. She was uncommonly good to have in one's arms, young Lucy, even though she was a skinny rabbit compared to Jo-Anne. There was something unusually sweet and fresh about her. Jo-Anne's hair had been stiff with some stuff she had put on it to hold it in place, but Lucy's hair was like silk and she had the smoothest skin he had ever touched. He hadn't been exaggerating when he'd told her that she would be a dangerous woman, except that Lucy was too good to be dangerous. There was an element of shining honesty about her. The sort of girl a man might marry if he didn't happen to be a damaged old crock with only one good eye and a leg that ached abominably.

Michael was staying two more days with the Jardines before returning to New York and flying home. It was supposed to be a rest period for him, but he found that there was one more social function for him to attend before he left Minneapolis.

'I'm sorry, Michael,' Connie said. 'But these are old friends of Bob's family. They've invited us all to dinner and it was difficult to find an excuse. It will only be a family party, I promise you.'

'Rather a large family party,' Michael muttered under his breath to Jimmy as they arrived at the Schultz's house that evening.

The house was ablaze with lights, there were several cars drawn up outside and they could hear a cheerful hubbub of voices as they entered the hall.

Mr Schultz came forward, large and beaming. His broad face was flushed with pleasure and he was already perspiring. He looked exactly what he was, a prosperous man with a large, thriving business and a large, thriving family. His hair had once been fair and was now grey, still thick and carefully brushed straight back from his forehead. He had round blue eyes and wore rimless spectacles.

'Come along in, come along in! It's a very great pleasure to have you here and to shake you by the hand. Heard your talk last night. Great, just great! You won't mind my saying it was a mite one-sided? But then, as you'd have guessed from my name, I come of a German family. Now, I don't have to tell you there's two sides to every question. For people like me there's only one course for America. Strict neutrality. So I guess we don't quite see eye to eye.'

Michael smiled, if not with any great cordiality at least without giving offence. It was a bit much, having all this thrown at him almost before he had got through the front door. However, there was no doubt about Mr Schultz's goodwill. He positively radiated it. With an inward sigh Michael foresaw that before the evening was out he was going to have to exert himself yet again and put forward some of the reasoned arguments with which he had been provided in order to convince Mr Schultz that he might be mistaken.

They were ushered into a crowded room and provided with the usual lethal American pre-dinner drinks and then Mr Schultz clapped his hands.

'Now, folks, I've got a small surprise for our friend from England,' he said. 'And I hope he's going to take it in the spirit in which it's meant. I guess that one or two of you know that my wife's nephew is here on a visit. He's not in uniform, but like our friend Michael he's fighting for his country. Only difference is, Kurt is fighting for Germany. Kurt, where are you? Come here.'

A young man stepped forward. He was very slim, very sleek and on his face there was a faint look of amusement which made Michael bristle. If Kurt had shown embarrassment Michael would have been sympathetic, since he himself was wishing that the floor would open up for him, but that supercilious air betrayed that he had been prepared for this confrontation and knew that he had the advantage of Michael.

With a wooden expression on his face Michael waited while Mr Schultz went on: 'Now, this is neutral ground and under

117

my roof enemies have just got to be friends. I want you two young people to shake hands right here in front of us all.'

He put his hand on Michael's shoulder. 'I guess I don't have to tell you, Michael, that the German people have always had the greatest admiration and respect for the British. No-one regrets this war worse than the ordinary man and woman in Germany.'

Michael glanced round at the interested circle of faces. The advice he had been given had been to avoid social meetings with any Germans, but if he walked out it would have a very bad effect. Most of the people were smiling in simple pleasure at this opportunity to spread a little peace and goodwill, but one or two were waiting avidly to see what sort of scene he was going to make. He held out his hand.

'I'm very glad to shake the hand of your charming wife's nephew,' he said. 'While we are enjoying your hospitality I am sure we can forget the differences between us.'

Someone started to clap as the hands of the two young men met. There was a flash as a photograph was taken. Mr Schultz was beaming all over his round face. How kind he was, how well meaning – and how naive.

The German clicked his heels and gave a little bow. 'Kurt Waldenheim,' he said. He had black hair, brushed away from a high bony forehead. The skin was stretched tight over the bones of his face, which gave him a skull-like appearance, but he was doing his best to appear friendly.

'What are you doing in America?' Michael asked, since it seemed to be expected that they should exchange some conversation together.

'Much the same as you, I imagine,' Kurt Waldenheim said. 'Visiting my relatives and spreading the word about the great German war effort.'

'A propaganda exercise, in other words.'

'As yours is.'

It was true and by his silence Michael admitted as much.

'I see you have been wounded,' Kurt remarked. His eyes, dark and opaque, rested thoughtfully on Michael's face. 'I'm sorry. I dislike to see a brave man disfigured.'

His English was impeccable, with only the trace of an

accent. Perhaps it was uncharitable to assume that he had deliberately chosen the word which would be most likely to hurt.

'You should have seen me before they patched me up,' Michael said lightly. 'A hideous sight, I can tell you.'

He smiled and turned away. Surely that was as much as could be expected of him?

'Michael, my dear boy, I'm so upset I hardly know what to say,' Connie said as they drifted towards the other end of the room. 'I wouldn't have had such a thing happen for the world. I could cheerfully shake Herman Schultz until his silly little eyes drop out.'

'It's not important,' Michael said. 'He means well, but I doubt if he realizes that he's being used. Kurt strikes me as being a real snake. He's right, of course, about us both being here for the same reason, but I don't relish being put in the same class as him.'

'I agree. Would you like to go?'

'Certainly not! I'm not going to leave the field free for Kurt! Let's have another drink and pretend we're enjoying ourselves.' He looked thoughtfully towards the corner of the room where Kurt was surrounded by a group of people. 'I'd like to know a bit more about him.'

'I can tell you about him,' Lucy said. 'I know the Schultzs' daughter and she's told me all about her cousin Kurt. He may not be in uniform at the moment, but he's an officer in the SS.'

'A dyed-in-the-wool Nazi,' Michael said. 'I'm going to spend the rest of the evening keeping out of his way.'

He stuck to this resolve, unobtrusively melting out of the way every time Kurt moved towards him, but Jimmy was less wary. Partly out of curiosity at being confronted by one of the enemy, partly out of a certain natural pugnaciousness which made him feel that Michael's tactics were rather too tame, he lingered near Kurt and listened to him talking, until some of the remarks he overheard made his blood boil.

Kurt spoke with an apparently modest pride of Germany's remarkable victories in Europe. He was regretful about Great Britain's determination to continue the fight.

'We believed that the British would want peace once France

had conceded defeat,' he said truthfully. 'Unfortunately, under that well-known warmonger, Churchill, they seem to be blind to their best interests.'

'You have to admit they've done pretty well in the air battles over Britain,' someone remarked with a touch of sharpness.

'But at what cost!' He looked towards Michael who was studiously ignoring him on the other side of the room. 'I wonder how many of his friends are similarly disabled?'

'I guess they've made a few sacrifices, but at least they've staved off the danger of invasion.'

Kurt shrugged. 'So far Germany has held back from that step because of our very earnest desire to persuade the British to see reason. If it becomes necessary then we'll have no hesitation in invading and Britain, like France, will be over-run.'

It was too much. Jimmy could keep quiet no longer.

'I g-guess you don't quite understand about England,' he said. 'All right, you might invade – although I think you've left it a bit late. It's just possible that you might overrun the country, but that doesn't mean that we would ever be defeated. You must have heard what Churchill said about fighting on the beaches and all that. Well, it was true. Everyone would fight – all the men, and the women. All the children, too. We'd never give in. The country itself would turn against you. The stones on the beaches would trip you up, the cliffs would crumble when you trod on them, the rivers would rise up and drown you. You could even kill us all and we would still not be defeated because we just wouldn't ever admit we were beaten. And the fight would go on while there was still one person left in the world with a drop of English blood in him. You think we ought to ask for peace, but what you don't seem to have grasped is that we're going to *win*.'

He felt in his pocket and pulled out a crumpled notebook. 'Here, write down your name and address in Germany. After the war is over and you've been beaten I'll get in touch with you and give you any help I can. Believe me, you're going to need it.'

It raised a few smiles, but on the whole they were sympathetic. There was something about the way he poured it all out with absolute conviction that made people fall silent. Kurt's easy assurance slipped visibly. For one moment he looked malevolent. Then he recovered himself, took the notebook from Jimmy and began to write.

'Certainly I will give you my address,' he said. 'And for exactly the opposite reason. I think you will be more in need of help than I will when the war comes to an end.'

He handed back the notebook and added: 'I didn't realize I was to meet two Englishmen this evening. What are you doing over here?'

'I was evacuated to the States before the war began,' Jimmy admitted reluctantly.

'Ah! Your parents sent you here to be safe! That speaks for itself, doesn't it?'

He smiled and moved away. All the colour that had risen to Jimmy's face during his outburst drained away. He turned so white that Michael went up to him and put a hand on his shoulder.

'Come on, Jim, we'll have to go now, there's nothing else for it,' he said. 'It was a magnificent speech, youngster.'

'You heard what he said,' Jimmy said. 'Mike, I ought to be at home. Can't you do something to get me away?'

Michael shook his head. 'I'm sorry, old chap, but you're going to have to be patient a bit longer. If it goes on until you're old enough to be called up you might manage to get yourself shipped back.'

Jimmy's expression was mutinous. He'd get home somehow, with or without his brother's help.

Chapter Six

On 22nd June 1941 Germany invaded Russia. Gunther had been posted to the Eastern border some weeks earlier. It was not a popular posting. Anyone who could bring any influence to bear had themselves removed from the list and remained in France, or Italy, or Greece, or North Africa: the extent of Germany's commitment to war grew more extensive all the time. The only good thing Gunther could see about his new field of operations was that it relieved him from making sorties over England, where he still clung to the feeling that he had friends. Apart from that, there was nothing to be said in favour of duty on the Russian border, even in midsummer.

With the opening of the campaign against Russia he was once again in the thick of fighting. His score of enemy aircraft destroyed mounted. It began to look as if he might achieve his Knight's Cross, the coveted award which marked the shooting down of twenty enemy aircraft.

The only thing he could see that was likely to hold him back was lack of an aeroplane to take him into the air. The supplies situation was making them all uneasy. Undercarriages of bombers and fighters were constantly being damaged by landing on the hard-baked, deeply-rutted fields they were forced to use. It was a melancholy sight to see rows of aircraft waiting for repair and to know that there were no spare parts available. For all the vaunted efficiency of the Nazi war machine it did not seem to be very good at actually getting the goods to the place where they were needed.

It was supposed to be a quick, sharp campaign 'over by Christmas'. Had there ever been a war that was not going to be 'over by Christmas', Gunther wondered cynically, but he kept that thought to himself. His attitude was already suspect in some quarters and if he had not been such a highly respected pilot he might have had to answer for his lack of enthusiasm in joining in the fulsome praise of Hitler and Göring that was expected of a good *Luftwaffe* officer.

Thanks to the intervention of Feldmarschall Milch the *Luftwaffe* were issued with winter clothing – woollen underwear, warm stockings, big fur boots and sheepskin jackets. The *Wehrmacht* was less fortunate. They did not start indenting for heavy duty winter clothing until the autumn was well advanced, and when it was not forthcoming the *Luftwaffe*, grumbling bitterly, was forced to relinquish some of its stores of clothing to equip the soldiers.

Gunther owed his first leave for many months to what he considered a minor scrap. The weather was foul; no snow yet, but cold and constantly raining. When they were alerted to fend off a Russian air attack Gunther and his companions ran across the sodden grass, clumsy in their heavy boots and thick jackets, but laughing and shouting to one another, eager for some action in place of the interminable sitting around watching the wide, empty landscape and waiting for an advance which seemed to be a long time in coming.

The Russians were obstinate fighters and a bombing mission on its way was difficult to turn back, but Gunther's *Gruppe* had had several slack days and they were spoiling for a fight. They swept into the air, seasoned, professional killers on the hunt for the enemy.

They made contact with the Russians and tore into them, darting and weaving amongst the heavy bombers and the fighters which tried to defend them. Gunther picked out a MiG-3 and was annoyed when it eluded him. He climbed again, trying to get his sights on another quarry. The air was full of machine gun bullets. He thought his Messerschmitt had collected a graze or two, but the damage must be minor because it didn't seem to be affecting its performance.

The attackers were headed towards his own airfield. Gunther, uneasily aware of the rows of aircraft lined up on the ground waiting for servicing, knew that it would be a real disaster for his *Gruppe* if the Russians got through. There was a Russian MiG above him to the right, but Ernst Reinhardt was keeping it fully occupied. He could see another MiG ahead, out of his range unless he closed with it rapidly. The Russian pilot banked and turned to go to the rescue of his companion. It had to be a split second decision – to go for the fighter ahead or to take advantage of the gap in the defences and try for a Tupolev bomber. Gunther breathed a silent prayer that Ernst would be able to cope with two attackers and sideslipped towards the heavy bombers droning along below him.

He came in on his target at an acute angle, making it almost impossible for the gunners to get a burst against him. He knew he had secured a hit, but apparently not on any vital part, since the Tu-2 was still maintaining its course. Other bombers were also in trouble and at least one of them jettisoned its bombs short of the target and turned away. Gunther's dive had carried him beyond the Tu-2 he was after. He turned and climbed, so steeply that for a brief second he was afraid that he'd asked too much of his Messerschmitt and the engine was going to stall. But it was this nerve to push his aircraft to its utmost, just within the limits of tolerance, which had made Gunther such an outstanding pilot. His judgment had not been at fault, he was still in control; he swallowed the sour taste of fear, turned and dived. The bomber hadn't a hope of escaping him. His thumb was steady on the button, the red hot lead pumped out of the gun; the Tu-2 corkscrewed downwards, billowing out smoke, and exploded as it reached the ground in a field frighteningly near to where the German aeroplanes were lying helpless.

Gunther thought his leave was due to the fact that his kill had been so close to home and the right officer had been watching. That and the wound he received from a piece of shrapnel which had torn through his cockpit and caught him on the cheek. It left him with a scar like one of the sabre marks so cherished in the old days by the duelling officers of the Emperor's Army. He was told it would fade as it healed, but it gained him ten days' sick leave.

Gunther was fortunate in managing to hitch a lift on a flight to Berlin – this saved him a whole day which would otherwise have been wasted on travel. He kept himself in the background when he saw that the other travellers were high-ranking officers, but one of them at least knew him by sight and called him forward.

'Hofmeyer, isn't it? One of our excellent young fighter pilots, Herr General. A real fire eater. We're hoping for a Knight's Cross for him in the next few months.'

General Obermann nodded amiably. Gunther caught a whiff of brandy on his breath and guessed that they had all lunched well enough to feel expansive.

'Come and sit by me,' General Obermann said. 'We'll dispense with formality for this short journey. It isn't often a General gets the chance to hear the views of the man on the ground – or should I say, in your case, in the air. How do you feel the campaign against Russia is going?'

Apart from a savage wish that he had, after all, travelled by train, Gunther's mind was blank, but the General was waiting for an answer so at last he said reluctantly, but truthfully:

'Perhaps we were too elated by our successes at the start. In June and July it was felt that we would win a resounding victory in a very short time. Now we seem to have come to a halt, even to have had to make some retreats. It's already October and the winter will be on us shortly.'

'It might be easier to manoeuvre on hard-packed snow than on these damned boggy, sandy tracks they call roads in this god-forsaken country.'

'Possibly,' Gunther agreed.

'You don't sound very convinced.'

'I'm confident of ultimate victory, of course,' Gunther said. 'But if you want me to talk frankly, Herr General, then I must tell you we've already had worries about the shortage of essential supplies. Is that situation likely to improve when the winter closes in?'

'Feldmarschall Milch has reported on the situation regarding your precious aeroplanes. He's a man who gets things done. There will be improvements.'

'Yes, sir.'

'Well, any more helpful observations? How would you have settled the war against Russia, Leutnant Hofmeyer?'

'A large question, Herr General! I think perhaps I would

have pushed straight on to Moscow in August instead of going into Southern Russia.'

'That was the Führer's own decision.'

Hurriedly, Gunther attempted to retrieve his mistake.

'I'm sure the Führer has a better view of the overall picture than a junior pilot can get, even from the vantage point of five thousand feet.'

The General grunted. He leaned towards Gunther and said in a confidential undertone: 'I'm not saying, with the benefit of hindsight, you understand, that you are wrong.'

Decidedly he must have lunched well, to have allowed himself to indulge in such an implied criticism of the Führer's strategy. Gunther thought it wiser not to reply to such an indiscretion. He was relieved when General Obermann slumped down in his seat, closed his eyes and went to sleep.

There were cars drawn up for the General and his companions on arrival at the airport. Gunther saluted and turned away, but General Obermann said: 'Wait a minute, Leutnant, where do you live?'

'Just on the fringe of Wilmersdorf, Herr General.'

'In that case my driver can take you on after he has dropped me in Charlottenburg.'

He did not wait to be thanked, but went back to say goodbye to the other gold-braided officers who had accompanied him, while Gunther handed over his one battered suitcase to the poker-faced driver.

General Obermann lived in an apartment in an expensive part of the city. Gunther, feeling he must be punctiliously correct in gratitude for the General's geniality, got out and stood on the pavement as he heaved himself out of the car.

'Enjoyed meeting you,' General Obermann said. 'Have a good leave. Not married, are you?'

'No, sir.'

'Well, have a good time. I hope we don't have too many air raids while you're at home.'

Gunther got back into the car and waited until the driver returned from delivering the General's luggage. He had a feeling he was being watched. He looked up and saw a face at one of the windows. One of the General's family, presumably.

He found his mother alone when he reached their apartment. Frieda had been sent into the country with a party of children for a short rest from the air raids.

'Why not leave them there?' Gunther asked.

'I'm sure I don't know. Except . . . there have been rumours that the camps they were sent to weren't quite satisfactory. I don't understand why they can't make proper arrangements for the children because the air raids still continue, but then most of what is happening is beyond me. It's such a struggle to exist. How I am to feed you while you're at home I'm sure I don't know. Frieda manages the rations for me. She's so strong and never waivers.'

Frau Hofmeyer glanced fearfully over her shoulder although there was no-one else in the apartment but Lotte.

'Well, of course I know it will all come right in the end. I have every confidence in the Führer. If only the British would let us have some rest. I shall feel better with you here.'

She touched his face briefly and began to cry. 'Your poor cheek. But at least you are still alive. So many of my friends have lost a husband or a son. War is cruel.'

Gunther put his arm round her and smoothed her hair.

'Don't cry, *Mutti*, or I'll think you aren't pleased to see me. It's nothing but a scratch on my face. As for food, I'm quite accustomed to living on cabbage soup and black bread. If you can give me something different from that I'll be satisfied.'

To cheer her up he told her about his flight home and she opened her eyes wide and straightened herself up proudly at the thought of him mixing with such high-ranking officers.

'They will have forgotten all about me by now,' he assured her. 'Even General Obermann.'

That he was wrong about this he discovered the next day when he received an invitation, delivered by the expressionless driver, to a reception at the General's apartment.

He did not really want to go; it was not a form of entertainment that appealed to him, but he had to agree with his mother when she pointed out how unwise it would be to refuse.

She put Lotte to work on his uniform, brushing and pressing, and both women exclaimed in proud admiration when he was ready to leave. Gunther laughed and kissed them both, which drew delighted squeals from elderly Lotte, but he still thought it an eccentricity on the part of General Obermann to have invited a chance-met junior *Luftwaffe* officer to his home.

The apartment was a revelation of sophisticated elegance, all cream walls, black leather furniture, smoked glass and chrome tables. General Obermann's hostess was his daughter, Elsa.

Within minutes of meeting Elsa Obermann Gunther understood who had been responsible for inviting him to this overcrowded party. He also knew that the rest of his leave was going to be very enjoyable indeed.

She was small, her head barely reaching his shoulder, but exquisitely proportioned. Everything about her was perfect, from the top of her burnished head to her fine-spun ankles and narrow feet. She was dark and she wore her short brown hair quite straight and cut in a heavy fringe across her forehead. Her face was round, with broad cheekbones which, together with her velvety eyes, tilting upwards at the outer corners, gave her a Slav look. Her skin had an unusual texture, creamy, thick and opaque, like the waxy flowers of orange blossom. She had high, pointed breasts, very noticeable under her thin silk dress, and a waist which looked as if it really could be spanned by a man's two hands. Her own hands, tipped with polished nails, fluttered restlessly as she talked. Her voice was husky, slightly breathless, with a childish intonation to it, but it needed no more than a glance or two from those dark, assessing eyes to tell Gunther that this was no child.

She wore a scent that troubled his senses, musky and penetrating. She moved in it as if in a cloud, a mist of sexual allure. Every man in the room was conscious of her and she knew all about the effect she was creating.

She tilted back her head to look up into Gunther's face and smiled. There was something about the quality of that smile that drew an immediate answering gleam from him. It was mischievous, conspiratorial, as if she were offering to share with him, and him alone, some pleasurable secret.

'You travelled back from the horrible Eastern front with

Vati,' she said. 'How long do you have before you must go back again?'

'Only eight days,' he said regretfully.

She pouted, as if in disappointment, which was ridiculous considering that they had only just met, but highly flattering.

'I saw you from the window when *Vati* arrived home,' she said with devastating frankness. 'I asked who you were and then I sent Otto – his driver, you know – with an invitation for this tiresome party. If you look round you'll see why. You and I are the only people here under fifty – except for Kurt, and he's so *dedicated* it really makes him the most terrible bore.'

Gunther glanced round the room and saw that what she said was almost certainly true. Apart from a young man in the black uniform of the SS they were the youngest people present.

'Kurt has just been to *America!* Can you imagine anything more interesting? If only one could get him to talk about something besides politics. He thinks I'm frivolous.'

She looked up into Gunther's face, all mock solemnity. 'He *almost* asked me to marry him, such a good connection for him, you know, and Kurt is terribly ambitious, but at the last moment he decided I was too light-minded for a serious man.'

'Did he tell you so?' Gunther enquired, fascinated by this revelation, only half believing that it could be true. It did not really matter what they said to one another, far more interesting communication was going on beneath the surface.

'Not in so many words,' she admitted. 'But I knew what he was thinking, poor Kurt, so *obvious*. Are you a serious man, Leutnant Hofmeyer?'

'My name is Gunther – Fräulein Obermann.'

'Gunther. You must call me Elsa. And about your seriousness?'

'I'm prepared to be anything you like provided I can be sure of seeing you again.'

She laughed and laid her hand on his arm, a fleeting touch which had an effect out of all proportion to its importance. 'I must go and do my duty by all these boring old men and women. Come and see me tomorrow afternoon. About four o'clock.'

The apartment was empty when he called the following

afternoon. Elsa herself let him in. He had brought her flowers and she exclaimed with as much delight as if it was the first bouquet that had ever been presented to her.

'*Don't* say that they are to thank me for that terribly dull party yesterday,' she begged. 'You can't possibly have enjoyed it.'

'It would be impossible for any man not to enjoy himself at a party if you were there.'

'Such a pretty speech! I must put these lovely flowers in water.'

She flitted around, finding a crystal vase, darting away to fill it with water, arranging the flowers, trying out the effect first on one table and then on another, but finally she sat down beside him on one of the black leather couches and curled herself up, one arm resting on the back of the couch, half turned towards him, her feet underneath her. She was wearing a blouse of dark red satin and a grey pleated skirt, her waist cinched in by a wide black belt. She looked, if possible, even more devastating than she had the day before. She leaned towards him and touched his cheek.

'Your poor face. What happened?'

'A very slight wound. The merest scratch.'

She did not take her hand away. Gunther turned his head until his lips touched the soft palm. She laughed and moved away from him.

'Tell me about yourself,' she commanded.

She listened intently as he told her what little there was to tell. He thought it as well to be scrupulously honest. No point in letting her imagine that he was anything but a hard-up wartime officer with poor prospects and no connections. She hardly seemed bothered by that part of his story.

'Oh, don't go on about what you are going to do after the war,' she interrupted him. 'I live for *today*.'

'Perhaps you are right.'

'Of course I am. That's why when I see something I want I go *absolutely* straight for it.'

She smiled at him, her wicked, mischievous, inviting smile. With a throat that was so dry he had difficulty in speaking Gunther asked: 'Have you seen something you want?'

'Yes, please.'

Before he could speak again she went on: 'I do seem to be making all the running, don't I? Your turn. If someone were to grant your most *fervent* wish right at this moment, what would it be?'

'To pick you up and carry you off to the nearest bed and make love to you.'

'Oh, good! *Absolutely* the right answer, darling, except perhaps the carrying off bit. I do think you should conserve your strength.' She stood up. '*Vati* absolutely never comes home before six o'clock, but perhaps I'd better put the chain on the door, just in case.'

She paused in the doorway and looked back over her shoulder. 'I really ought to warn you that I am utterly, *utterly* depraved.'

By the time she pushed him out of the apartment at the last possible moment, a few minutes before six o'clock, he was enslaved. Nothing in all his considerable experience had prepared him for Elsa Obermann. Even the last traces of regret for the golden girl he had known in England faded from his mind. The combination of her small, exquisite body, her devastating frankness, the things she said in her fluting, childlike voice and her sexual skill was overwhelming.

For the remainder of his leave he came and went at her command like some well drilled automaton. He neglected his mother, but she only teased him about being in love and looked pleased. Frieda came home and he hardly noticed. Every waking moment that she would spare him was spent with Elsa.

'Absolutely *hate* to see you go,' she mourned on the day before his departure. 'We have been good together, haven't we, darling?'

'Perfect.'

They were, as usual, in her bedroom, closely entwined amongst the peach-coloured satin sheets. Somewhere deep in the recesses of Gunther's mind he was vaguely shocked by Elsa's profligacy: those satin sheets, her French perfumes, her beautiful clothes, the caviare she gave him, sitting back naked on her heels on the bed and nibbling at it on a biscuit. There was a war on. People like his mother had difficulty in finding enough to eat. Where did it come from, all this luxury?

Nevertheless, when she said: 'I'm supposed to go to a dull old dinner this evening. Shall I have a naughty headache and stay here with you instead?' he said: 'Yes.'

She leaned over him. 'Are you sure you aren't too tired?'

He tilted her back on the pillow and kissed her. 'I dare say you'll find some way of reviving me.'

'You'll have to stay in here and keep very quiet while I tell *Vati* about my dreadful headache.'

There was a strange, unpleasant excitement about lying there in her bed listening to the General moving about the flat getting ready to go out again. He heard Elsa's voice, giving her fluent, false explanation, and then she came back and joined him.

'I've told him I've simply got to go back to bed,' she breathed into Gunther's ear. 'He's promised not to come in and disturb me before he goes.'

She began to tease him with her hands, nipping him painfully, stroking and squeezing, but he could do nothing until after the heavy front door had closed behind the General, then he fell on her with a voraciousness that reduced her to sobbing, wordless compliance.

It was late before he got home that night. He let himself in, surprised to see that there was a light on in the living room. He went in and found that Frieda was still up although his mother had gone to bed. The table was laid for three, the food was untouched.

Frieda spoke. 'You said you would be in this evening,' she said, and something in her flat, expressionless voice conveyed a depth of disappointment that jolted him. It was true, he had said he would be at home for this last evening, and they had prepared a farewell meal for him. Slowly he took in the details of that meagre, carefully-hoarded feast. They had not touched it when he had failed to appear. Some of it, presumably, would be salvageable, but what would it mean to them, without him?

'I'm sorry,' he said.

'Mother went to bed.'

'I'd better go and see her.'

His mother's bedroom was in darkness, but she was still awake and answered immediately when he tapped on the door. She did not put on the light, but he could tell from the huskiness of her voice that she had been crying.

'I was delayed,' he said lamely.

'Were you with that girl?'

'Yes.'

'Are you going to marry her?'

The idea had never occurred to him. 'No.'

'All that good food wasted,' Frau Hofmeyer said. 'I wish you could have let us know you would be eating out tonight.'

'As a matter of fact, I haven't had any proper dinner,' Gunther said, surprised to realize that this was the truth. 'Is it too late to heat up some of the food? I really am quite hungry.'

'I suppose we could . . . it will give you indigestion at this time of night,' Frau Hofmeyer said doubtfully.

'Not a bit of it! Come along, *Mutti*, rouse yourself. Come and give your bad boy something to eat, even if he doesn't deserve it.'

It was a curious meal, and the gaiety he infused into it was forced at first, but gradually they warmed to the occasion; Frau Hofmeyer, dressed again but with her hair still in long grey plaits; Frieda, unexpectedly willing to be won over; even Lotte, roused from sleep and blinking like an owl in the light.

It was Frieda and Gunther who did the clearing up when their mother and Lotte had been sent off to bed. They worked in silence, both tired, both conscious of words held back which would have spoilt the warmth in which the evening had ended.

Frieda wiped the last of the dishes and put a hand to her aching head. She gave her brother a strange look.

'I disapprove of practically everything you do,' she said. 'Your morals are deplorable. But you have a good heart.'

He wondered for a moment if she was being spiteful when she asked abruptly: 'Do you ever think about your English girl?' but there was nothing in her voice but curiosity.

'I've tried not to,' Gunther said. 'I don't suppose I'll ever see her again.'

133

'At least this new girl is German. You haven't told us much about her except that she's a General's daughter.'

'There's not much to tell. She's helped me to pass a very enjoyable leave – though looking back I admit I've been a bit selfish, allowing her to monopolize me. I doubt whether she's much of a letter writer. Who knows when I shall be home again? I'm afraid Elsa may find some other diversion.'

He saw that Frieda was looking scornful, but with the new tolerance she was so unexpectedly displaying she refrained from making any comment.

They parted and he was borne away on the long train journey back to the front, a tiresome, cold and miserable journey, surrounded by other members of the armed forces who made no secret of the fact that they hated the idea of continuing the fight in the Russian winter.

As the weeks went by Gunther felt that he was beginning to understand the inherent melancholy of the Russian people. Across the vast, empty landscape the German forces moved like pygmies, and miles began to seem like yards when there was nothing in front of them but more empty space inhabited by nothing but the wind which howled round them like a living thing, whipping up snow and sending it driving into their faces, penetrating even the comfortable clothing with which the *Luftwaffe* had provided itself while the less fortunate soldiers complained that the blood was frozen in their veins.

By the beginning of December they had penetrated to the very suburbs of Moscow, but the main offensive was still held up in the forests surrounding the city. The Russian counter-offensive began. The Germans, worn out and ill-prepared for the conditions in which they were fighting, started to fall back.

The top command of the Army began to fall into disarray. In the South, Feldmarschall von Rundstedt, foiled in an attempt to hold Rostov, wanted to retreat to a defensive position on the Mins river, but Hitler forbade it. Runstedt asked to be relieved of his command and was taken at his word, but the withdrawal took place just the same. Within two weeks two more top commanders, General von Brauchitsch and Feldmarschall von Bock, both pleaded ill health and retired from the field. A fourth, Feldmarschall von Zeen, resigned because Hitler rejected his appeal for withdrawal on the Northern front near Leningrad. Hitler appointed himself Commander-in-Chief of the Army. As Christmas approached, General Heinz Guderian, the brilliant tank commander who had master-minded the victorious sweep of the German armoured divisions across France in 1940, and who had had a clear idea of the necessity to drive on to Moscow at the commencement of the Russian campaign, made a decision to withdraw troops which was disputed by his new Commander-in-Chief, who promptly got rid of him.

The causes of these changes hardly penetrated to the lower ranks, but it could not be concealed that the Generals were departing and the knowledge did nothing to build up morale. From the other side of the world came news which elated some and worried others amongst the German troops beleaguered by winter.

'The Japanese have attacked the American Fleet at a place called Pearl Harbour,' an excited pilot told Gunther. 'Those little yellow devils will keep the Americans busy, and the British too if they overrun the Far East. Good news, isn't it?'

'I'm not so sure,' Gunther said. 'It gives the pro-war party in the United States the chance they've been looking for. They'll declare war on us next and they are a big country, as big as this damned Russia. And with vast resources. Perhaps it won't worry them as much as you might think to have to fight in more than one arena. I think it would have been better for us if they'd stayed out of it.'

Chapter Seven

On 24th October 1941, the day after his seventeenth birthday, Jimmy disappeared. He left a note behind for Connie and Bob saying he was sorry for any upset this might cause and 'tell Mum not to worry', but there was no clue as to his whereabouts.

'I blame myself for not taking him seriously when I saw him in June,' Michael said.

He had managed to get forty-eight hours' compassionate leave from the training school to which he had been posted on his return from the United States, on the grounds that he was the last of his immediate family to have seen Jimmy. But there was little he could do or say to help his distracted mother.

' "Tell Mum not to worry",' Barbara commented bitterly. 'As if that makes it all right! Michael, haven't you any idea where he's gone?'

'It's only a guess, but I suspect he's gone over the Canadian border and joined up,' Michael said.

'Then we must try to get him out again. He's a very bad boy and I'll tell him so when I see him.'

'He's seventeen years old and built like a young ox,' Michael said drily. 'Your little boy has grown up while he's been away. And he's probably having the time of his life.'

Enquiries were put in hand, but no trace could be found of James Robert Brookfield.

'Gave a false name, the young devil,' his father said. He tried to keep it hidden, but he was tickled by his younger son's initiative.

'Stop grinning like a Cheshire cat,' Barbara said crossly. 'You may think he's been clever, but I don't. Harry, isn't it enough for you to have one son ruined for life and a daughter who comes home looking like something that's been put through a wringer, without giving another son?'

'I haven't given him, he's chosen to go of his own accord,' Harry pointed out. 'I admire him for it, I admit. The boy's got spunk.'

It was six weeks before they received a letter from Jimmy and then it contained the bare minimum of information. He admitted to being in Canada and that he had joined up. He insisted that he was perfectly fit and well, but he didn't give an address nor did he say which of the Forces he had joined.

'Ten to one it's the Air Force,' Harry said.

'You need a holiday,' Christine remarked to her mother when she came home towards the end of the year.

'Look who's talking! You look like a ghost.'

'I'm all right. At least I do get home for a rest occasionally. Civilians never get leave.'

'I suppose there's no hope that you'll be home for Christmas?'

'I'm afraid not. Some time in the New Year is the best I can hope for and as a matter of fact I've rather promised to spend my next leave with someone else, if you don't mind.'

'Of course not, darling, if that's what you want to do. Where are you going?'

'Both Michael and I have mentioned Larry Telford. He was Michael's Squadron Leader. He's asked me to visit his home, in Wiltshire.'

Her mother sat up with a jerk, her attention thoroughly caught. 'My dear! Is this serious?'

'It is on his side,' Christine admitted. 'For me, I don't know. We've been in touch since we met in February, but we haven't had much chance to spend more than a few hours together. Let's just say I'm sufficiently interested to want to see how it works out if we can manage to get a long leave together and spend a whole week under the same roof.'

'How very wise, dear,' was all Barbara said, but Christine could see from her satisfied expression that she had the highest expectations of this new development in her daughter's life.

It had been a strain, all that time apart, both for Christine and Larry. Their brief, snatched meetings were unsatisfactory, particularly since they left Christine still undecided about the future. The week they spent at Larry's home, folded away in a hollow of the Wiltshire Downs, isolated by a fall of snow, did more to settle her mind than all the previous months of letters and telephone calls and evenings spent in cinemas. His parents were comfortable, welcoming people, rather older than her own mother and father, but very much the same type: uncomplicated, happy in their own marriage, wanting the best possible life for their son.

The house was delightful, or would have been in peacetime, when it could have been properly kept. It was stone-built, not large, but old and full of unexpected twists and corners.

'Full of draughts, too,' Mrs Telford said. 'We do our best to keep it warm, but I'm afraid we've given up the dining room for the duration of the war. We eat in the kitchen or on a card table in front of the fire in the drawing room when we are on our own, and in this freezing weather I think we shall have to go on doing that.'

She was a little round-faced woman with a shy smile and a bustling manner. She had a way of putting her head on one side which reminded Christine of a robin and it was from her that Larry got his dark eyes and smooth brown skin. She wore strong, sensible country shoes with woollen ankle socks, thick stockings, an ancient tweed skirt and a shapeless cardigan. When she went outside she pulled something on her head that looked remarkably like a knitted tea cosy and she fed the hens in an old fur coat that moulted round her as she walked.

Larry's father was tall and thin, with grey hair and a bristling moustache, and the sweet, vague smile of the slightly deaf. Christine had never met anyone more punctiliously polite, he invariably got to his feet when she entered a room, always opened the door for her, pulled out her chair at the table. He was an ex-Army Officer who had retired to this quiet country house and now found that in wartime it was too big for his needs.

'It's a family house,' Mrs Telford confided. 'It would be a lovely place to bring up children. We had evacuees at the beginning of the war and it really came alive. I was sorry when their parents took them away. So unwise with all the bombing we've had since. Now that we no longer entertain as we did in peacetime it's something of an encumbrance to us. But George clings to it because he hopes that Larry will want to take it over one day. If he were to marry and have two or three children . . .'

She broke off and smiled sympathetically at Christine's rising colour. 'Well, my dear, I gather that nothing is settled, but you must let me tell you how much we both like you.'

She patted Christine's hand with her own plump little hand, hardened now by mixing up chicken feed and scrubbing stone floors.

For all her remarks about no longer entertaining, she did arrange one dinner party while her son was at home and Christine, who had been warned that this might happen, realized that she was on show for the benefit of Larry's friends and neighbours and dressed up in a long dress of clinging blue crepe which dated back to pre-war days.

She was surprised by the number of people who were prepared to turn out on a cold January night, but Mrs Telford had no refusals and they sat down sixteen to dinner, with an enormous goose as the main course. Christine gathered from the talk amongst the women that there had been donations to eke out the rations, but the wine came from Colonel Telford's own cellar and was warm as sunshine to the palate, deep red and smooth as silk.

'Not much of it left,' he said apologetically. 'Might as well use it up. Let me refill your glass, Christine.'

They made an effort to avoid talking about the war, but inevitably it cropped up. Christine learned that one couple had a son who was a prisoner-of-war and another woman said, almost under her breath: 'At least he's alive.' She caught Christine's eye and made a pitiful attempt to smile.

'She had two sons in the Navy, both lost at sea,' Larry said afterwards. 'I was at school with the elder of the two. He was a grand chap. Left a wife and two small children.'

The inevitable clearing up in the icy cold scullery was something of an anti-climax when the party was over. Christine was given an enormous apron and directed to wipe the beautiful crystal glasses Mrs Telford had brought out for the occasion. She was in mortal fear that her numb fingers would let one drop on the stone-flagged floor. It was a relief when the job was finished.

Larry caught her hand in his as they all left the kitchen. 'You'd better come and get warm before you go up to bed,' he said.

'Good idea,' Colonel Telford said, but his wife caught his arm and gave it a little tug and he took the hint and left Larry and Christine to go back alone to the remains of the log fire that still smouldered on the hearth in the drawing room.

Larry was still holding Christine's hand. He sat down in the big wing chair by the side of the hearth and pulled her towards him. She curled up on his lap in the circle of his arm with her cheek against him.

'It was a lovely party,' she said.

'Everyone took to you,' Larry said. 'I'm not surprised. You looked lovely, darling. You took my breath away when you came into the room, but then you do that every time I see you.'

Christine twisted round a little more and clung to him as he moved his head to kiss her. He had not up to this time been a particularly demanding lover. Perhaps if he had always been as urgent as he was tonight they would have arrived at a solution to their relationship before this. Certainly his love-making was not unwelcome to her. His mouth was firm and warm on hers and she liked the feel of his lean body as she pressed against it.

She let her fingers play with the soft, short hair at the nape of his neck. His arms closed round her so hard that it was painful, but she did not want to move away. His voice was thick as he said: 'Chris, you are going to marry me, aren't you? Darling, I love you so much. I've adored you ever since I looked up and saw you coming towards me in that hospital ward.'

'I think so,' she said softly. She kissed him again very gently and quickly. 'Give me until the end of the week.'

'I wish I could give you some of my own certainty. I have no doubts at all. You're everything I've ever dreamed of and it isn't given to every man to meet his dream.'

'I'm real,' she protested. 'An ordinary, flesh and blood woman, not a dream girl.'

'Indeed you are. That's what makes it difficult to wait for you to make up your mind. I haven't pressed you, Christine.'

'No. Perhaps you've been too patient.'

'Right! From now on I'll be very impatient. I've got to do something to make you see that we're meant for one another.'

She found the certainty she was seeking quite suddenly the next day. They had gone out walking together, climbing a hill in the crisp, cold air, laughing and struggling through the soft snow, Christine wearing borrowed Wellington boots which were slightly too large for her. When they reached the top they stood leaning against one another, out of breath but glowing with warmth. Larry hugged her tight and they kissed, their cold lips warming under the pressure of mouth on mouth.

When they parted Christine tucked her hair back under the red knitted cap she wore. A memory hovered somewhere on the fringe of her mind, something to do with a red knitted hat and snow and a man, another man. But Larry caught her hand in his and it went again.

They looked down into the valley to where the house stood, sombre and grey except for one lighted window, a plume of smoke rising unwaveringly into the still air.

'Could you learn to be a country girl?' Larry asked. 'It's what I want – to finish my time in the RAF and then to follow Dad's example and live off the land. Perhaps here. He's hinted that he wouldn't mind handing the house over to me. We'd never be rich, but it would be a good, satisfying life.'

Christine had a sudden vision of the future, so vivid that it seemed quite real. Herself and Larry, living in the house in the valley, a peaceful, hardworking existence with dogs that had to be taken for walks, ground that had to be dug, animals that needed tending. And a couple of children. A serious, brown-haired boy like Larry, a blonde little girl like herself.

She turned towards him, her face alight with the conviction that had come to her.

'I want to marry you,' she said. 'Larry, I do, I do! I love

you, of course I love you. Darling, how could I ever have doubted it?'

The wedding was to be in April. Both Christine and Larry agreed that they wanted to be married in the church at Eveleigh, but when she suggested that they should both wear uniform she saw that Larry looked disappointed.

'You don't really want me floating up the aisle in white satin and a veil, do you?' she asked in amusement. 'Not very practical in wartime, darling.'

'I sort of see you in a dress when I think about it,' Larry admitted. 'I don't care about the details, but not uniform – please.'

If you want me in a dress you shall have me in a dress,' Christine said firmly.

They had met in a café in a town halfway between their two camps to discuss arrangements for the wedding and they had only a couple of hours together. It was a wet day and there was nothing to do but sit over cups of lukewarm tea, looking at one another and longing to be alone. What they needed was a bed, Christine told herself with an honest acknowledgment of her own nature, but Larry had never suggested anticipating their marriage and something held her back from making the first overtures. He was a funny lad, her Larry, sensitive and reticent, with a head full of dreams. She stretched out her hand to him over the café table and he gripped it hard and smiled at her. It was when he looked at her like that, with his dark eyes alight with love, the lines of his fine-boned face tense with desire, that she longed to take him in her arms and give him the comfort of her body.

It was not the setting she would have chosen to say something to him which had been in her mind ever since their engagement. But time was running short and they might not meet again before the wedding.

'Strictly speaking, I'm not entitled to the white satin,' she said deliberately, plunging in before she could let the opportunity slip once again. 'I'm not . . . you won't be the first man who has made love to me, Larry.'

142

She was fiddling with the tea spoon in her saucer, not wanting to look at him while she said it. But when he remained silent she looked up and saw that he was completely at a loss to know what to say.

'I don't suppose I'm your first girl either?' she said, trying to help him.

'No, that's true,' Larry admitted. 'Look, there's no point in either of us going into the confessional. What's past is past. Let's put it behind us and forget about it.'

Again Christine stretched out a hand to him. The warm tide of love in her threatened to spill over into tears.

'Bless you, darling,' she said. 'I knew you'd understand, but I couldn't feel quite easy until I'd told you.'

'I envy him,' Larry admitted, clasping her hand tightly. He paused uncertainly. 'Him? Them?'

'Him,' Christine said firmly.

'Well, I envy him because you loved him, but I'm sorry for him, too, because he lost you. Unless . . . was he killed?'

'I don't know. He could easily be dead. I have no way of telling. Darling, we said no details, let's stick to that. I love you. With all my heart.'

'That's all I need to know.'

'Come on,' Christine said, standing up. 'It's nearly time for your bus and even a Squadron Leader is allowed ten minutes' huddle in the bus shelter with the girl he's going to marry.'

Christine wore ice-blue taffeta on her wedding day, adapted from a pre-war evening gown belonging to her mother, the wide neckline filled in with white cotton lace from a pair of curtains the blackout had made impractical. It was a fine spring day with sunshine flooding through the windows of the church as she arrived on her father's arm. She looked radiantly happy and very beautiful. Her veil had been lent by Mrs Telford, and she carried a posy of blue and white flowers.

The question of the honeymoon had presented difficulties. Larry had wanted Scotland, but the time they could take was too short to make that practicable. He had thought their final choice of a small village in Sussex decidedly tame, but once the excitement of the wedding was over he had to admit he was glad that they didn't have a long journey in front of them.

143

The hotel had been highly recommended and it proved to be everything they had been told; small, pretty and welcoming. The proprietor spotted them as a honeymoon couple straight away, even without the trail of homemade confetti which emerged from their suitcases. His knowing smile brought an extra colour into Christine's face and made Larry clear his throat uneasily.

It amused Christine to realize as they unpacked that it was Larry who was embarrassed by their new proximity. She kissed him quickly on the cheek as she passed him with an armful of underclothes.

'Go downstairs and sit in the lounge,' she suggested. 'I'll unpack for you – the first of my wifely duties.'

They had dinner in the small dining room, no longer caring that everyone had guessed that they were a honeymoon couple, absorbed in one another and scarcely conscious of the food that was put in front of them.

They went outside after dinner and strolled down the village street. At the point where the pavement ended it was pitch dark. Christine stumbled and Larry's arm went round her, holding her strongly. She turned towards him, feeling with her hand for his chin and then putting her arm round his neck. They clung together in the cool spring darkness, kissing eagerly. Christine slid her hands down Larry's back. He had changed out of his uniform after the wedding ceremony into civilian clothes. She felt the rough tweed of his jacket under her fingers and then the smoother fabric of his trousers. She dug her hands into the back of his thighs and felt the shock of excitement that went through him. Suddenly she felt wild with impatience. What were they doing out here in the street when they could be back in their own room and together at last.

'Let's go back to the hotel,' she said.

They began to walk back with their arms round one another. They pushed their way through the heavy blackout curtain that shielded the front door and blinked in the sudden dazzle of light inside.

'Do you want a drink?' Larry said.

'No, I'd rather go straight up.'

'Shall I . . .' He looked at her uncertainly and she realized that he simply did not know what she wanted. 'Shall I wait down here?'

'No, come up with me.'

He caught her eye and smiled ruefully, a tacit admission that he was out of his depth, and the familiar wave of love engulfed her, the warmth she always felt when he looked like that, young and uncertain.

The hotel was an old inn, parts of it dating back to the sixteenth century. Their room had whitewashed walls criss-crossed by dark timbers. The ceiling was low and in one corner it sloped down to the floor. The floor was of polished wood, scattered with rugs which slipped under their feet. While they had been at dinner the white cotton quilt had been removed from the bed and the corners of the sheets turned down. It looked much more like a bed than it had earlier in the evening. Christine's pink satin nightdress had been laid out on one pillow, Larry's blue and white striped pyjamas on the other.

'It looks very domesticated,' Christine said.

She was surprised to find that she was nervous. Her throat felt dry and it was unexpectedly difficult to look at Larry. She took a quick, surreptitious glance. He was still Larry, rather serious looking, but nothing unfamiliar. He took off his jacket and put it over the back of a chair, then he undid his tie, folded it in half, and put it over the jacket. He sat down on the side of the bed and bent down to undo his shoes. Christine looked at his back and his bent head affectionately, a little bubble of amusement rising inside her.

'Do you always undress in the same order?' she asked.

He looked up, surprised by the question. 'I suppose I do,' he admitted. 'Why?'

'I just had a thought that in ten years' time I shall look at you sitting on the side of the bed undoing your shoes, just the same as you are tonight.'

'Do I seem so set in my ways? I suppose one gets into these habits unconsciously.'

He stood up and turned to face her. Without his shoes, jacket and tie he looked oddly young and vulnerable. Christine went over to him and began to unfasten the buttons of his shirt.

145

'There's a very long zipper on the back of this dress,' she said. 'Would you like to undo it for me?'

As the dress slipped away from her shoulders Larry bent forward and buried his face against her half-revealed breasts. She could hear his breath rasping in his chest. She drew away from him and said apologetically: 'Darling, I must go down the corridor to the bathroom. I'll be back in a minute, I promise.'

She thought ruefully as she slipped along the corridor with her dressing gown pulled tightly round her that none of the great seduction scenes in films and novels ever mentioned the necessity of going to the lavatory or brushing one's teeth. She ought to have had the sense to attend to these mundane details before being so inviting.

The room was empty when she returned to it. Larry must have gone in search of a second bathroom. She finished undressing and pulled the pink satin nightdress over her head. It settled round her, sleek and voluptuous, and she got into bed. Larry's pyjamas had gone from the other pillow and his clothes were scattered round the room. She smiled. He wasn't so orderly as she thought.

She was sitting propped up against the pillows when Larry came back. He undid his dressing gown with his eyes fixed on her face and let it fall to the floor unheeded.

'You look beautiful,' he said. 'So beautiful.'

Christine held out her arms and he got in beside her. She felt that he was actually shaking with the force of his passion for her and she was filled not only with desire but with a curious compassion for him, her darling Larry who had waited for her so patiently.

But for all her understanding of his need she had expected that he would still be able to hold himself in check until she too was fully aroused. Instead, he kissed her once, digging his tongue deep inside her mouth, fumbled blindly for her breasts and then entered her with a force that made her cry out more in pain than pleasure.

She told herself, when he had separated from her, that her previous experience had been relatively slight. That because there had been no-one since Gunther the recollection of the

146

way it had been with him had become too highly-coloured in her mind. She had built up a memory of a fairyland of delight which bore little relation to reality. This was reality, this rough, desperate union with a man who had kept himself apart from her for too long. Larry was a kind and loving man, and he adored her. It was early days and the frustration he had suffered must have been hard to bear. They would soon get to know one another better. And then he wouldn't leave her with this physical soreness and a little, nagging feeling of disappointment.

Larry lay very still, one arm still stretched across her, his head on the pillow by her shoulder. She sensed him making an effort to control his breathing and then he said flatly: 'I'm sorry. I didn't mean it to be like that.'

She slid lower down on the pillow so that their heads were level.

'It doesn't matter,' she said.

'It does. I behaved like a selfish brute and I wanted it to be wonderful for you – oh, damn!'

'Darling, we're *married*,' Christine protested. 'We've got years ahead of us to . . . to work things out, make it good for both of us.'

She stopped, uncertain whether she was saying the right thing.

Larry put his arms round her again and held her tightly. 'I will make you happy,' he promised.

'You've already done that,' Christine said. 'Giving you what you want is my happiness.'

'Bless you.' He managed to sound more like his usual self as he said with an attempt at flippancy: 'Good job it wasn't the first time. Might have put you off for life.'

Christine had a sudden presentiment that he was going to ask her to make some comparison between him and Gunther. It was a relief, even though she knew it was a mistake to bring it up at all, when he said: 'Chris, I know we said we'd never talk about it, but that other chap, he couldn't be anyone I know, could he?'

'No, that's absolutely impossible.' In her anxiety to reassure

147

him Christine said too much. 'It was a long time ago, before the war. I was very young. I got to know a German boy . . .'

'A *German*?'

'Yes. We were . . . we believed ourselves to be very much in love. We knew we had to part. I was very unhappy and so . . . it happened.'

'A German. That's something I would never have thought possible.'

She did not answer and Larry went on in a low voice: 'I hate them so much. They are destroyers. Chris, how could you?'

'His nationality didn't seem important at the time,' Christine said stiffly. 'Not to me at any rate. I told you I was very young.'

'You must have been if it was before the war. I suppose the truth is he was a plausible type who took advantage of you. You must have been just a kid.'

Sadly, Christine remembered how she had crept down the dark passage in the night to Gunther's bed; how she had defied her family and pursued him halfway across Europe; his honesty and the way he had tried to protect her from the passion that consumed them. Even to save her marriage she owed him more than to acquiesce in that lie.

'No,' she said. 'I knew what I was doing and I was determined to have him. I can't make any excuses.'

He was still dissatisfied, she could tell that. She slipped her arms round him and kissed him.

'Darling, it's all over. It was *years* ago. It's you I love. It's you I married.'

'Yes, of course, that's true.'

He allowed himself to be won over and, a little tentatively, to begin making love to her again. And Christine encouraged him and put more into her response than she really felt because any deception was better than leaving him feeling unhappy and inadequate.

The week passed all too quickly. They went walking on the sweeping hills of the South Downs, they visited the coast and found it a melancholy sight with the shore obscured by barbed wire. Cautiously, they felt their way towards a more settled relationship, even though Larry still seemed to need constant reassurance and Christine worried secretly in case it was her own lack of experience which made it necessary for him to ask her so often whether she really did love him.

There was one side of Larry which always delighted her, and that was his feeling for the countryside. Most of their meetings had been in towns and the only time she had seen him at home in Wiltshire the snow had been thick on the ground. She was enchanted to find that he could answer all her questions and make a walk in the fields an entrance into realms of wonder and beauty.

He laughed at her and teased her for being a suburbanite who thought of spring in terms of sugar pink almond blossom and the hard yellow of laburnum overhanging the pavements. Spring in the country was wilder and more tender. Larry knew where there would be primroses; he parted the wet grass with careful fingers to show her the sweet wild violets; he could tell her that the delicate mauve flowers lining the bank were called ladies' smocks and when she wrinkled her nose as they walked through a wood he told her she was treading on a patch of wild garlic which would soon burst into dazzling white flowers.

He knew how old the lambs were and which crops were showing in the fields and what the farmers were doing with the machines which were a mystery to Christine. He could point out a bird's nest in a hedge and give her the names of the birds, but Christine was his equal when it came to identifying the aeroplanes which flew overhead: Spitfire, Mosquito, Hurricane.

'We never get away from them, do we?' she said. 'Britain is just one vast airfield.'

The uncertain April sun went behind a cloud, there was a sudden flurry of raindrops and Larry caught her hand in his and they ran down the hill together, back to the shelter of their hotel.

It was days like these which made Christine look forward eagerly to the future. There was so much they could do together, so much Larry could share with her. She coaxed him into talking about his home and he was enthusiastic about the changes he would make if his father handed over the house and land to him.

149

'It's not big enough to be a working farm, that's the only thing that worries me,' he said. 'It might be quite hard to scratch a living. On the other hand, our next-door neighbour is getting on and I've an idea that he wouldn't mind selling out. Joined together – as they once were in the past – the two properties would be a workable size. Of course, it would take money, but I've got a reasonable amount saved. I might be able to do it.'

'*We* might be able to do it,' Christine said with determined emphasis.

He turned towards her with a smile that lit up his face. 'Yes. That will be the best thing, Chris. Working together for something we really want. Building a proper life for ourselves.'

'And our family.'

He bent down and kissed her. 'After the war, my darling, after the war.'

It was not until their fourth night together that she discovered that Larry had nightmares. She was awakened by a harsh cry. He was thrashing around, muttering incoherently, fighting to get free of the bedclothes which had twisted round him. It took her some minutes to wake him and he was drenched with perspiration.

'Darling, you were dreaming,' she said.

'Yes . . . oh, damn! I hoped it wouldn't happen while I was with you. Sorry.'

'What causes it? What do you dream about?'

'It's always more or less the same,' he admitted. He spoke reluctantly, but Christine persisted and at last he explained. 'It's a sort of claustrophobia, I suppose. I'm flying, get into a fight, my aircraft is out of control or on fire and I can't get out. I'm jammed in my seat, or the cockpit won't open. I start to struggle and then I wake up. While it lasts it's horrible.'

She stroked the damp hair away from his forehead. 'How many missions have you flown?' she asked.

'Too many. But it hasn't been possible to do anything else. And please don't suggest I apply to be grounded. That's one thing I'll never do. This is just a stupid weakness I'll have to overcome.'

'Have you seen the MO?'

'No, and I'm not going to.'

'If you knew that one of your squadron – a young pilot like Michael for instance – had this problem, what would you make him do?'

'Exactly the opposite to what I'm doing myself.'

'I don't want to sound as if I'm blackmailing you, but you might remember that you have me to consider now. I don't want to be a widow.'

'It's not just selfishness,' he said with the diffidence which so endeared him to her. 'Each one of us really is needed. Having this quiet rest this week has done wonders for me. And being with you. It's been a strain, waiting for you to make up your mind, then waiting for the wedding.'

'I wish we hadn't got to separate at the end of the week,' Christine said.

She was deeply troubled, blaming herself for not having realized how near he was to the end of his tether. She saw now that he was never entirely relaxed, but she had grown so used to his nervous energy that she had thought it a natural part of him. Perhaps that was why his lovemaking was so precipitate and unsatisfying. If she could only help him to relax and take life more easily then everything might improve.

She tackled him the following night in the hope of talking him out of taking precautions. 'Darling, can't I persuade you to change your mind about starting a family? If I were expecting a baby I could get out of the WAAF and make a home for you.'

In all her thoughts about her marriage Christine had seen herself in a domestic setting with a house and family. How long was she going to have to wait to achieve that? How long would the war continue? Now more than ever she felt that Larry needed that kind of stable background to offset the strain of the life he was forced to lead. She tried to make him see how she felt, but he was adamant: no family while the war was on.

'Our children must have a really good start,' he said. 'A proper home, a father and a mother, peace and some kind of certainty to life.'

She knew that he would realize from her silence that she

151

disagreed with him. He moved closer and spoke with his mouth against her hair.

'Chris, I'm still fighting a war. I could be killed. I can't run the risk of leaving you a widow with a child to bring up on your own.'

For the first time since he had known her, her courage faltered. 'Don't talk like that,' she said in a fierce, desperate whisper.

She clung to him and he could feel her face wet against his bare shoulder. 'Nothing is going to happen to you. It can't! I love you too much.'

'My precious girl. Of course nothing is going to happen to me. I'll live to be ninety and we'll have a dozen children, but after the war, my darling, after the war. Oh, God, can you wonder I hate the Germans?'

Chapter Eight

In the Spring of 1942 Hitler launched an offensive in Russia which had two main aims: in the short term to capture the Caucasian oil fields, without which he believed that Germany would not be able to continue the war, and in the long term to take Moscow. The German armies swept South and East and once again there seemed to be nothing which could stop them. They took Sebastopol on 2nd July and the oil town of Maikop fell to them on 9th August. Stalingrad was the next objective.

In contrast to the bitter winter, the heat was sweltering. Morale was not as high as it had been during similar victorious periods in the earlier months of the war. These battles were too hard won, the distances were too great; every step, every roll of the wheels, seemed to take the German soldiers further from their homeland. What were they to do with all this vast country when it was won? Everyone was short-tempered and there was uneasy talk of atrocities committed against the Russians. There were difficulties over supplies, particularly fuel.

'We'll be grounded tomorrow if we don't get something to put in the fuel tanks,' Gunther's *Kommandant* grumbled. 'Hard luck on you, Hofmeyer, when you are so near to getting your twenty.'

Gunther shrugged. 'I dare say there'll be plenty of opportunities,' he said.

'God, yes! This bloody war looks as if it'll go on for ever.'

Their fuel supplies reached them in time to prevent the catastrophe of having the whole *Gruppe* grounded and Gunther was able to claim his twentieth and twenty-first kill. There were celebrations in the Mess, congratulations from his Commander. He knew that he had been recommended for the

Knight's Cross, but it came as a surprise to learn that he had been granted two weeks' leave and was to go to Berlin to receive the award from the hands of Reichsmarschall Göring.

It was nearly a year since he had last been home. It would be good to see them again – and Elsa, if she still remembered him. He smiled to himself as he thought of Elsa and there was affection in the smile. As he had expected, she had proved to be a poor correspondent. Three scrappy notes in ten months. No doubt she had been amusing herself with someone else. Strangely, he didn't particularly mind. It was impossible to imagine Elsa living alone.

It was the autumn before he was actually in Berlin. Stalingrad was under siege, but it had not fallen. Another winter threatened them. More than ever he felt uneasy about the way the Russian offensive was going.

It should have been a pleasure to arrive on a still, cool day when the sun shone in a blue sky and yellow leaves drifted down from the trees that had survived on the 'Ku-Damm', but the serenity of the day only emphasized the rawness of the bomb damage all round him. He had not dreamed the extent to which whole areas had been flattened, leaving jagged gaps instead of remembered landmarks, and heaps of rubble where there had once been homes and shops. Metal girders, twisted into grotesque shapes, were silhouetted against the crisp, clear sky.

The destruction and desolation of the scene was like a physical blow. How guarded his mother's letters had been, with scarcely a hint of the war in the air which had brought the civilian population of Berlin into the front line.

He wondered whether Elsa would still be living in the same apartment or whether she had left for the greater safety of the country; whether, a chilling thought, the block of flats had been damaged in the bombing.

He had had reassuring letters from his mother and Frieda and knew that at the time they had written they were still safe and his own home intact, but what if Elsa's silence, which he had shrugged off indulgently, arose not from neglect but because something had happened to her? He was startled by the depth of his concern for her, that naughty, amoral purveyor of delicious sex.

He did not attempt to contact Elsa for the first forty-eight hours of his leave, determined not to allow her to monopolize him in the way she had when they had first met. Then he gave in and telephoned her. With a feeling of anticipation mixed with anxiety he waited for an answer. He glanced at his watch. At eleven o'clock in the morning the little wretch could surely not be in bed, either alone or with anyone else. When he heard her voice his relief was so strong that for a moment he could not speak.

He had half expected that he would have to remind her who he was, but Elsa said immediately: 'Gunther! Darling Gunther! Are you at home? Oh, lovely, lovely, lovely! *Must* see you! When?'

'Are you free this afternoon?'

'Oh, darling, I'm not! What a bore! Tomorrow?'

'At four o'clock?'

He heard her gurgle of amusement. 'Just like old times. Yes, four o'clock.'

He was reluctant to let her go. 'You're still at the same apartment? I was afraid you might have been bombed.'

'No, we are still intact, apart from some broken glass. Of course, one does have to go to the cellar at night. I have the most comfortable little bolthole, but it is a bore having to share with other people. One has to confine one's more interesting activities to the afternoon.'

'You always did,' he reminded her.

'I know, but now it's "instead of" and not "as well as". I mean, one is positively *deprived*.'

'Poor neglected girl. Am I to have the chance of making it up to you tomorrow?'

'Of course! Looking forward to it *so* much, darling. Must go now. Do you love me?'

'More than you deserve, you wicked woman.'

He told her the next day the reason for his visit to Berlin.

'Darling, not really! An actual medal put round your neck by fat old Göring in person. How ghastly for you.'

Gunther's bare shoulders shook with laughter. 'You are the

155

only person who has shown me any sympathy,' he said. 'Everyone else thinks it's wonderful.'

'They probably don't know him as well as I do. Such a play actor.'

He pulled her towards him and kissed her soundly. 'You mustn't talk about our great leaders like that.'

They went about with one another more than they had on his previous leave. Gunther was a hero of the Reich, with his photograph in all the papers, fêted and entertained, with more invitations than he knew what to do with. Elsa was his companion at a party the day after his decoration by Reichsmarschall Göring and the sight of him, backed into a corner, glass in hand, striving to be courteous while a strident-voiced woman told him her version of what was happening on the Eastern front, reduced Elsa to helpless laughter.

'You don't really care for this kind of party, do you?' she enquired.

'It strikes me as immoral. Men are dying to keep this crowd in brandy and cigars. Why do you put up with it, Elsa?'

'These people can be useful,' she said. 'One tolerates them for the sake of what they can do for you.'

'Privileges? Black market?'

'Hush, dear. The black market doesn't exist.' Her vivid little face mocked him for his innocence. She tucked a hand under his arm. 'Difficult for us to disappear when you are so big and beautiful and poor dear Klara's main attraction of the evening. Half the people here – especially the *female* half, darling – came to see you. Perhaps if I just *hinted* at an engagement with the Führer?'

He was appalled by her audacity, but a confidential word in their hostess's ear, a smile, a shrug, and they were free to leave the smoke-filled room full of complacent stay-at-homes.

The concert they attended together was far more successful. Elsa's interest in music was as serious as Gunther's own. She listened appreciatively and her comments afterwards were discerning. They strolled back to her father's flat together afterwards, arm in arm and reluctant to part. The air raid warning sounded just before they reached the building.

'Damn,' Gunther said, pausing uncertainly. 'I ought to try

to get home. Mother will be frantic at the thought of me being caught in an air raid. It doesn't seem to occur to her that I face even greater dangers every day at the front.'

'You would be foolish to try to walk through the streets during a raid. You'll have to come and see my little hidey-hole, sweetheart. And please hurry.'

The cellar was quite large, but not large enough for privacy. The occupants of the apartments, the concierge, the servants, all huddled together as best they could, some on the floor, some on bunk beds, one or two in battered armchairs.

'This is our corner,' Elsa guided Gunther over the recumbent bodies towards an inflated beach bed and a pile of cushions.

They propped themselves against the wall. After a moment Gunther put his arm round Elsa's shoulders. No-one paid any attention to them. They all seemed sunk in apathy. There was no sign of the General. They could hear guns overhead and the shriek and thud of bombs. He felt Elsa's shoulders shake and looked down. To his astonishment tears were running unchecked down her face. He bent his head towards her.

'What is it?' he asked in a low voice. 'Are you frightened?'

She shook her head. 'It's so horrible,' she said in a furious whisper. She turned her head and laid her cheek against his chest. 'So *horrible*! Look at us! Herded together like animals. Sitting here, doing nothing, waiting for death to come and find us. I hate it, Gunther, I can't tell you how much I hate it.'

He was astonished by the depth of feeling in her voice, even though she spoke in a whisper. Little, wicked, laughing Elsa, who seemed to think of nothing but the gratification of her senses.

She went on: 'Every night more people die; helpless, innocent people. What have they done to deserve it? Whose fault is it that they are being punished for nothing more than the fact that they happen to live in Berlin?'

'The British . . .' he said helplessly.

'No, not the British. They obey the orders they are given, just as our own soldiers do. The fault is with people like my father, who saw what was happening and did nothing to stop it.'

He was appalled, as much by her bitterness as by her words.

The racket outside increased. Somewhere in the dimly lit cellar an old woman was crying with a mewing noise like an injured cat. Her husband patted her hand helplessly; tears running unheeded down his own cheeks.

Gunther put his face right down against Elsa's. 'I agree with you,' he said. 'But it's too late to turn back now. We must go on to the end.'

Her voice came to him as the merest thread of sound. 'We shall be defeated.'

It was the first time he had ever heard anyone say such a thing and it gave him a sick jolt in the pit of his stomach. It wasn't true, it couldn't be true. There were setbacks in any war, but their achievements had been remarkable. Even the Russians were on the run.

'You mustn't say such things,' he said.

'No, I know I mustn't,' Elsa agreed and there was a tinge of irony in her voice. 'We must keep on pretending, and I'm very good at that.'

The long night wore away. Elsa slept at last, her head pillowed against his shoulder. Gunther was cramped and cold. He couldn't sleep. The building above rattled and shook. Someone was snoring. The old woman who had been crying was asleep, her head fallen forward on her chest.

It was dawn before they were able to leave the cellar. They came up into the grey morning, yawning and blinking, and stretching their stiff limbs. Down the street a house had burned to the ground; nothing remained but a brick chimney stack pointing a blackened finger at the sky. A group of firemen, sullen with defeat, sagging with weariness, water still dribbling from their ineffectual hoses, crunched over the damp ashes.

Directly across the road a block of flats had been sliced in half. All the inner rooms were exposed, like a child's doll's house with the front standing open. Shreds of curtains blew gently in the air. The people who had already come up from the shelters stood in apathetic groups, staring at the ruins of their homes, or moved aimlessly over the rubble, searching for anything that might have survived.

'Is there nothing we can do for them?' Gunther asked.

'They'll be looked after,' Elsa said. She sounded exhausted.

'I don't like to leave you,' Gunther said uncertainly. 'But I must go to my mother and sister. Will you be all right?'

Elsa nodded. Her creamy skin looked yellow in the morning light, stretched tight over her wide cheekbones, with deep shadows under her eyes.

'Come and see me tomorrow,' she said. 'Not today.'

'At four o'clock,' Gunther said and she managed to raise a small smile for him.

When he called on her the following day she appeared just the same as usual: frivolous, sensual, dressed in silk and surrounded by perfume, an enchanting little animal with no thought in her head but to give and receive pleasure. And yet, on his last day, most unusually she came right down to the street with him to say goodbye and as he turned away he saw that her eyes were full of tears.

On 23rd October 1942 General Montgomery launched an attack on El Alamein in North Africa, but to Barbara the date meant only one thing: it was Jimmy's eighteenth birthday and a year since they had heard of his disappearance. She so rarely spoke of him that the memory of the date had faded from Harry's mind. He thought she was particularly silent over the breakfast table, but she had become noticeably quieter during the last year and he did not connect it with any particular unhappiness until the middle of the morning when he had a telephone call from Christine.

'Dad, I've only got a few minutes,' she said. 'I thought I'd ring home this evening, but I just wanted to ask if Mum was particularly upset.'

'What about?' he asked. 'Nothing's happened, has it? You're all right?'

'It's Jimmy's birthday,' Christine said. She spoke impatiently, exasperated by his forgetfulness. She had to admit that her father's reaction was suitably contrite.

'Bless you, Chris, for reminding me. You're quite right, of course. She'll be feeling low.'

He tried to make up for it when he got home that evening.

'Nothing in the post?' he asked, carefully casual.

'No,' Barbara said. 'Were you expecting something?'

'I thought we might have heard from Jimmy.'

She turned to him, blind with tears, and he put his arms round her and held her tight.

'I thought you'd forgotten.'

'I had. Christine rang up and reminded me. She's getting in touch this evening. I'm sorry, darling. It's not that I don't think about him and worry about him. The date just slipped my mind.'

Barbara drew away and wiped her eyes. 'Sometimes I think I'll skin him alive if he ever does come home,' she said. 'Do you think he's all right?'

'I'm sure of it. He always had nine lives. Come and sit down, love, and I'll see if I can find you a drink.'

'Elderberry wine is all we've got,' Barbara said. 'Very nice in its way, but not terribly consoling.'

The autumn days gave way to winter. Another Guy Fawkes Day without fireworks, except those provided by the Germans, another Christmas looming ahead and it looked as if Barbara and Harry would spend it alone. The North African campaign was going unexpectedly well; the British had become unaccustomed to victories, but this time Rommel was retreating. There had been Allied landings in French North Africa and American uniforms were beginning to be quite a common sight in Britain.

Barbara decided to make an effort for Christmas even if it was not going to be particularly gay, and cycled into Epsom to have a fresh permanent wave. She wondered, as she rode home in the wind and the rain, how much of her new wave would survive. Probably it would be hopelessly frizzy and she would look a fright, she thought gloomily.

There was no other thought but this in her mind as she put her bicycle away in the garage where the car for which they could get no petrol stood waiting for better days. She hurried into the house with her thoughts fixed on a hot drink and the preparations for an evening meal for Harry and nearly fell over a large kit-bag lying on the floor in the hall. Her face brightened. One of the children had come home unexpectedly, probably Michael. She thought at first that this guess had been correct when she opened the living room door and saw a pair of legs in Air Force blue stretched out from the depths of an armchair. Then she realized that there was something not quite right. The legs were too long, the colour of the uniform was subtly different.

A very large young man with sandy hair, an enormous grin and slightly anxious eyes unfolded himself from the chair. Barbara stood where she was, her damp raincoat half unbuttoned, her headscarf dangling from her fingers, unable to speak, unable to move.

'Hello, Mum,' he said. 'I say, the old cookie jar isn't what it used to be and I'm starving.'

'Jimmy.' It came out as a breathless croak. 'Jimmy.'

'Yes, it's me. The prodigal son. Are you going to bawl me out?'

'You wretched boy. Darling, how are you? Oh, Jimmy, Jimmy!'

She stumbled towards him, almost falling over in her anxiety to touch him. He caught her up in a magnificent sweep of his long arms and hugged her.

'No need to get all weepy,' he said gruffly.

'You've grown,' she sobbed.

'Well, that's no reason to cry, is it? Come on, Mum, snap out of it.'

'Why didn't you let us know you were coming?' she asked.

'I didn't know myself until this morning. My outfit arrived in England a week ago. I've been trying ever since to get a bit of leave.'

'How long have you got?'

'Only forty-eight hours, and lucky to have that. I confessed to the CO and he said I'd better come home and try to make my peace. You aren't going to be stroppy about it, are you?'

'It's over and done with now. Sit down, darling – you're so *big* – and tell me everything that's been happening to you.'

'That's a tall order. Putting it in a nutshell, I got tired of sitting around doing nothing, especially after seeing Mike and the way they'd damaged him. As soon as I could pull it off I went over the border and joined the Canadian Air Force. I've spent the last year training.' He held out his arm proudly. 'See that? Flight Sergeant. Of course, they were under the impression that I was nineteen, but I don't think they're going to take it away from me now.'

'We made enquiries but we couldn't trace you.'

'No, I thought of that. I used a birth certificate belonging to one of my classmates. He's older than me, you see. Would you believe that I've been going under the name of Hiram Wynters for the last year? I told them I was called Jim, but even then it took some getting used to.'

Barbara glanced at the clock. 'No point in trying to get hold of your father,' she said. 'He'll be home in less than an hour. I'll make up the bed in your old room straight away and put a hot water bottle in it.'

'Come off it, Mum! No need to coddle me. I'm tough.'

'The bed must be aired,' she said firmly. 'Then I must try to think what I'm going to give you to eat.'

'There's a tin of ham for you in my kit bag and a bottle of whiskey for Dad. American, I'm afraid, but I hope it will soften his heart towards me.'

Barbara was in the kitchen when Harry let himself in at the front door. The kit bag had been taken upstairs, so he had nothing to prepare him. Jimmy stood up, more nervous of this meeting than he had been of the one with his mother.

'Hello, it's me,' he said.

Harry stopped stockstill in the doorway, much as his wife had done.

'I can see it is,' he said. 'And twice as much of you as there was when you went away. What have they been feeding you on?'

'It's the corn-fed beef that does it,' Jimmy said.

He was still eyeing his father warily. Obviously the old man wasn't going to fall on his neck like his mother had done, but he didn't look particularly hostile. He held out his hand.

'I'm sorry about all the worry and upset, Dad,' he said.

'So you should be,' Harry said.

He put his hand out and winced at the force with which it

was wrung, but when he saw how his son relaxed at this acceptance of his apology he looked thoughtful.

'How do you think your mother is looking?' he asked deliberately.

Jimmy hesitated. 'It's more than three years since I last saw her,' he hedged.

'And you think she's looking older. She didn't start looking like that until a year ago.'

Jimmy flushed uncomfortably. 'I've said I'm sorry,' he said.

'And you think that makes it all right. Oh, she's forgiven you – probably forgotten all about it because she's so pleased to have you back – but I'm not going to be so easily put off. I've been saving this up for a long time and before we all sink back in a glow of delight because you've condescended to come home I'd just like to tell you what I think of you. You've been thoughtless, selfish, inconsiderate and ungrateful. You've driven your mother almost to the point of a nervous breakdown.'

'I did write,' Jimmy said desperately. 'I told you I was all right.'

'Half a dozen notes in thirteen months. Very reassuring.'

Barbara came back once again, looking rather more relaxed. 'I think everything's under control.'

She glanced quickly from one to the other of them. 'Oh, dear, have you two been having words?'

'I guess I had it coming,' Jimmy said.

'Darling, you sound so American – or should I say Canadian? We have been very anxious about you, of course, but it's such a blessing to have you here, safe and sound.'

She put her hand on her husband's arm and looked up into his face: 'Harry?'

'If he wasn't twice my size I'd take him outside and thrash the living daylights out of him,' Harry said. 'All right, I've said my say. It's over now.' He looked at his son. 'Just keep it in mind for the future, that's all.'

The tension in the atmosphere began to subside. 'Where are you stationed?' Harry asked.

'Middleton St George. Not far away by Canadian standards,' Jimmy said. 'It's funny how small everything looks over here now. Even this house. And the queer little fields. Shabby, too, but I guess that's the effect of the war. I came through London though and it didn't seem as badly damaged as I'd expected.'

'A lot of the fronts of the buildings are still standing,' Harry said. 'Behind the façades there are acres of damage, especially in the City and round the Docks.'

They settled down, peaceful and relaxed, a family circle once more.

'If only Michael and Christine could be here,' Barbara mourned. 'I must write to them tonight before I go to bed. I'm sure Michael will do his best to arrange to see you as soon as he possibly can. It's more difficult for Christine, of course, having to save all her spare time to be with Larry.'

'Who's Larry?' Jimmy asked.

'Of course, you don't know! Christine is married.'

'Never! Good grief! Who to?'

'Larry Telford – he was Michael's Squadron Leader. We all like him immensely, but it is difficult for him and Christine, continually being torn apart.'

More than anything else the fact that his sister had got married and he had known nothing about it brought home to Jimmy the gap that his year's absence had caused in the family history. Old Chris getting married to a man he had never met and knew nothing about really gave him a jolt.

None of the family managed to get home for Christmas, nor was Christine able to join Larry as she had hoped. Their meetings since their honeymoon had been scrappy and unsatisfactory. They were on edge with one another when they did meet. She had to make a conscious effort beforehand to remind herself that Larry was under an even greater strain than she was herself. During the year he had been trained for night fighting and she knew that he was escorting bombing missions over the Channel on their way to Germany.

She did manage to get them together for a weekend in April which almost coincided with their wedding anniversary. They went back to the same small hotel. Sentimental or not, Christine had the feeling that her marriage needed the cement of these little reminders of what they had already shared.

It was a relief to find Larry looking more relaxed than he

had the last time, when they had had an acutely frustrating meeting in a tea shop. She had had an overnight pass and he had not been able to stay with her.

They were moving about their bedroom, unpacking and chatting desultorily. Christine had discovered in the brief meetings they had snatched during the past year that it took them both a little while to adjust to being together again. It was wise not to rush things. If she allowed Larry to find his own pace everything went well. She had only once made the mistake of suggesting that they should go straight to bed on arrival at a hotel and it had been a disaster. The inner tension from which he was never quite free had communicated itself to her. Instead of helping him to relax she had felt herself grow more and more taut until their union had ended in a failure which had distressed both of them. Too new to one another to laugh about it, too unsure of the other one's reactions to talk about it freely, they had glossed over their mutual pain and never referred to it again, but Christine knew only too well that the nagging memory was there, making Larry edgy with her whenever they first met.

It took her by surprise on this occasion when he caught her by the arm as she passed him and said: 'Chris, stop pottering about. I want you so badly. Let's not waste any more time.'

She went to him gladly. At the back of her mind was the thought that this time Larry might give her the baby she longed for, but for all his urgency he was not forgetful. She sighed to herself but said nothing.

They went downstairs to dinner later on, outwardly decorous, but with the atmosphere of their afternoon of love still hanging about them. Larry raised his glass to Christine in a silent toast and she moved her foot towards him so that it rested against his. He closed one eye in a slow wink and she smiled back at him, not caring that their absorption in one another was earning them amused glances from the other guests.

'Are you going to eat your dinner?' Larry asked.

Christine looked down at her plate. 'I'd forgotten about it,' she admitted.

'Eat up. Must keep up your strength. What you are going to need this weekend, my girl, is stamina!'

It was far and away the best time they had had together. The hours passed in a delirium of love and laughter. To herself Christine admitted that it was the honeymoon she had hoped for in the beginning. A year late, but that was the fault of the times they lived in. As good as it was with Gunther, she thought to herself lazily in an unwary moment, and then pulled herself up in horror. The one thing she had sworn never to do was to make comparisons. Even to let Gunther's name come into her mind seemed to her a disloyalty. What she had felt for him was a mere youthful infatuation, mostly physical, she thought, wiping out the memory of the companionship there had been between them. Larry was her husband, the man she loved now that she was a woman.

She stirred restlessly in his arms.

'What are you thinking?' Larry whispered.

'About how much I love you,' Christine said.

The only thing that marred their leave was that Larry would have to return on Sunday afternoon while Christine could, if she wished, stay on until the following morning. She would have left when he did, but Larry insisted that she should take all the leave that was due to her. They dragged themselves out of bed on Sunday morning just in time to get breakfast and then, because Larry would always rather be outside than in, they set out for a walk.

'Not that I'm feeling particularly energetic,' Larry remarked thoughtfully.

He looked carefree and relaxed, strolling along with his dark hair ruffled in the breeze and his face lifted towards the sun. The sidelong, conspiratorial look he gave Christine brought the colour up into her cheeks and made her choke with laughter.

The weather was kinder to them than it had been the year before; and billowing white clouds sailed along the horizon without massing together and showering them with rain, the air was warm and sweet. They climbed the hill out of the village and looked down into the valley, over the rooftops of irregular red tiles to the grey church spire.

'I miss the bells,' Larry said. 'It was something I particularly liked, the sound of them coming across the fields on a Sunday morning.'

'Like "Summertime on Bredon",' Christine said.

'In a way,' Larry agreed. 'Except, of course, that I had no love to lie with me and watch the clouds go by until you came along.'

'No?'

She was teasing him, looking back over her shoulder from just above him on the hill and laughing. Larry caught up with her and pulled her closer with an arm round her waist. She leaned against him, delighting in the feel of his hard muscles.

'No,' he said firmly. 'I was a solitary boy. Not lonely exactly, because I was always perfectly happy roaming about on my own.'

'It's my belief you are three parts gypsy,' Christine said, looking up into his brown, smiling face. 'Did you ever go poaching?'

'I did,' he admitted. 'I had a friend, a real old rascal, who used to take me out in the woods at night and more than once we made off with a pheasant. I couldn't take them home because I was supposed to be in bed and asleep, so old Rob had them. He lived in a wooden shack, not much more than a shed, the poorest of the poor, but the old devil never went hungry. He could walk through a wood without disturbing a leaf, take a bird or a rabbit, even tickle a trout, find a handful of mushrooms, pinch a few vegetables out of the fields and cook a meal over a wood fire that was fit for a king.'

'Is he still alive?'

'No, he died years ago. I was very upset, but I know my parents were relieved. I admit that he was dirty, smelly and dishonest, but he gave me an understanding of wildlife and I'll always be grateful for that.'

Christine said: 'Go on, tell me some more. Do you realize we've been married a whole year and there's so much I don't know about you? Did you go on haunting the wild, wet woods after old Bob died?'

'It had become a habit,' Larry admitted. 'I could still live off the land if I had to. Next time we have some leave why don't we go camping? I've still got a tent at home. We could go somewhere quiet and I could show you how fascinating it is, the simple life.'

'Cold water to wash in and spiders in the bed,' Christine said suspiciously.

'Bed? What do you mean bed? I might pull up some bracken for you. If I felt like spoiling you, city girl.'

She aimed a blow at him which he dodged, laughing, and they scrambled up the last few yards of bare chalk and stopped to get their breath back. Christine felt aglow with happiness, lit up like a lamp. Everything conspired to fill her with contentment: the golden day, the new ease between them, the release and joy of their successful lovemaking, the way Larry had suddenly opened out and talked about his boyhood.

'We're so lucky,' she said impulsively.

'Be careful,' Larry said quickly. 'Don't boast about good fortune.'

'You pagan!' Christine exclaimed. 'You think the gods are waiting to pounce on poor mortals who admit to being happy! I ought to have made to come to church this morning instead of coming to worship Mother Nature.'

She dropped down on the short, springy grass and patted the ground by her side. Larry sprawled beside her.

'I've done my quota of church parades lately,' he said. 'I don't think I'd have gone, though I hate to refuse you anything. I got so riled by the Padre's sermon last week I nearly got up and walked out.'

'What did he say to upset you so much?' Christine asked.

'He was going on about forgiving our enemies and the way we ought to "treat them with compassion" after the war. Early days for that sort of talk. Best to wait until after we've beaten them. I want to see them on their knees and crawling. And no charity handouts until they've paid for the damage they've done.'

'The Padre was bound to say what he did,' Christine said. 'You can't hold that against the poor man. And besides, he was right. If we behave like the Nazis we'll end up being like them.'

Larry's mouth tightened into a thin, obstinate line. 'If we

168

put them back on their feet they'd only start all over again. They did it before,' he said. 'Is that what you want?'

'God forbid! But, Larry not all the Germans are Nazis. Some are decent and not so different from us. We have to give them a helping hand, otherwise it will just mean the strongest – and the most ruthless – coming to the top again.'

She meant it to be no more than a reasonable argument. But Larry rolled over on his side and spoke in an angry mutter with his face turned away from her.

'As far as I'm concerned there's no such thing as a good German,' he said. 'Of course, I haven't had your special opportunities for judging, have I? He must have been a real charmer, that boy you were in love with before the war, or is it that you just can't admit to yourself that you once made love to a Nazi thug?'

The abrupt change of mood, the depth of his resentment, came as such a shock that all Christine could find to say, flatly, was: 'He was not a Nazi thug.'

Larry did not reply, but his nervous fingers tore savagely at the blades of grass beneath his hands.

Christine made an effort to retrieve the situation, trying to speak reasonably. 'I was talking in the abstract,' she said. 'Not thinking about any particular person. Larry, how could you? Because I disagree with you, you turn my words against me in a way which is totally unfair. I'm entitled to an opinion of my own, aren't I?'

She got no answer. There was a closed, remote look on Larry's face and she realized that nothing was going to make him admit that he had been in the wrong. He stood up, looked at his watch, and all he said was: 'We'll be late for lunch if we don't go down.'

He held out his hand, but Christine ignored it and got to her feet without his help. He turned away and began to walk down the hill ahead of her, leaving Christine to follow in a state of mutinous resentment: he had been so unjust to bring the subject up like that.

They walked back to the hotel in almost unbroken silence and hardly spoke again until they went into the bar for a drink before lunch. There was no sherry, no whisky, no gin. Christine settled for a shandy. When Larry followed her example she broke the uncomfortable silence by asking quickly: 'When are you flying again?'

'Tonight.'

He carried their glasses over to a table near the window. Christine sat down without looking at him.

'You took me up too sharply,' Larry said abruptly, as if there had been no interruption to their conversation outside. 'No doubt the way you think is admirable, but I don't happen to agree with it. I'm entitled to my opinion, too.'

'Yes, of course,' Christine said, totally noncommittal. 'It's a thing on which we'll have to agree to differ.'

They had slid away from the real issue and they were both aware of it, but Larry's semi-apology and Christine's forbearance enabled them to paper over the crack and got them through their last lunch together.

It was better when they went upstairs to collect his things before he left. 'I do love him,' Christine thought helplessly. There was something about the line of his spine as he bent over his suitcase, something vulnerable about the bones at the back of his neck, that made her melt inside. She touched him, a little tentatively, and he turned towards her with something of the same desperation she felt herself.

'We're a couple of fools,' Christine said. 'Arguing and spoiling our lovely weekend.'

'It has been good, hasn't it?' He sounded as if he needed reassurance and she gave it to him, with all her heart in her words.

'It's been wonderful. The best we've ever had. Darling, the war can't last for ever. When we're together all the time we won't have these silly misunderstandings.'

They clung together, kissing urgently, lips and hands reluctant to part now that it was too late to do anything about it.

'I've got to go,' Larry said at last. 'My lovely girl. I hate to leave you. You're right; once we can settle down like an old married couple we won't be so foolish.'

'You know my answer to that. I've been trying all this weekend to trap you into making me pregnant.'

'I thought perhaps you had. I don't know, Chris. You seem so sure about it. To me it seems the wrong time to bring a child into the world.'

It was the nearest he had ever come to sounding in the least uncertain and she felt suddenly hopeful of winning him over.

They walked down the road to the bus stop and as they stood leaning against one another Larry said: 'Some time this summer we ought to be due for a longer leave together. We'll talk it out then, this feeling you have about starting a baby.'

The bus came round the corner and they kissed goodbye. Larry, normally so reticent in public, seemed unable to let her go. It was only when the bus driver tooted his horn that they broke apart. They did not speak again, not even to say goodbye. Larry climbed into the bus and found a seat. She stood on the pavement and looked at him, shut away from her behind a window stuck over with paper to prevent splintering from blast. He raised his hand and she held hers out towards him, then the bus started and he was carried away.

Chapter Nine

It was generally felt by the Allies that 1943 was going to be the decisive year of the war. On all fronts it had begun to look as if the tide was turning against the Germans. Stalingrad was surrounded and General Paulus's 6th Army was being destroyed; Rommel's Afrika Corps was being pushed across North Africa towards Tunisia; the United States were fighting back strongly against the Japanese. The ordinary German people had only a limited understanding of these events, but to anyone in a position to take a wider view the situation was grim.

General Obermann and his daughter did not often have a meal alone together, but since it did not conflict with any more interesting plans, Elsa was all compliance when he told her curtly one morning that he wanted her undivided attention that evening. She pointed out that it was the servant's day off and suggested that they should go out to a restaurant to eat, but her father shook his head impatiently.

'I know we'll be alone. After all the money I spent on your education surely you can manage to arrange a meal for us here. Something cold will do.'

'You speak as if food were to be had for the asking,' Elsa remarked. 'I have to tell you, darling, that it isn't, not even for Generals and their daughters. However, I can, if I'm forced into it, make a tolerable omelette. I do wish you'd tell me what this is all about. I'll be dying of curiosity all day.'

She got no response to this remark, but General Obermann, lost in thoughts which seemed to give him little satisfaction, would have been surprised by the shrewdness in her dark brown eyes as she looked at him.

All the same, Elsa was not prepared that evening when her

father said abruptly as he finished off the remains of a rather better meal than her careless words had implied: 'Have you ever thought of marrying any of those hordes of men who gather round you?'

She looked at him in such blank astonishment that he went on: 'I can see you haven't. Then think about it now.'

'But why?'

'Because I think it would be a good idea if you had a different name, if you separated yourself from me.'

'Are you in trouble?'

'Not yet. I may be at some time in the future. You must know nothing about it. Now, tell me: do you favour any of your young men above the others? It must be someone safe.'

'Like Kurt Waldenheim?'

The General grimaced distastefully. 'Too close to the centre. I don't want him as a son-in-law. Don't tell me you really prefer him?'

'He has a certain macabre fascination. No, I don't like him enough to marry him.'

'Someone outside our normal circle,' he pressed her.

'There's Gunther,' Elsa said slowly.

'You'll have to remind me who he is.'

'The *Luftwaffe* pilot. We saw quite a lot of one another last year and again more recently when he was decorated with the Knight's Cross.'

'What's his background?'

'Oh, completely bourgeois. Widowed mother, sister who's a teacher, father was in the Army – an officer, but quite lowly. Before the war Gunther intended to become an architect, but never completed his training. Quite penniless, poor darling.' She paused and added thoughtfully: 'The most *delicious* lover.'

'I don't need to know the sordid details of your love life. It's time you got married. I've had more than one hint that the way you live is a scandal.'

'The dear Führer is such a puritan,' Elsa said, quite unmoved by this. 'Except, of course, with Eva Braun.'

In spite of the fact that he knew they were alone in the apartment the General snapped: 'Be quiet. Never forget that

173

there are such things as hidden microphones. One breath of criticism of the Führer could ruin everything.'

Elsa opened her eyes wide. 'I wasn't criticizing him,' she protested. 'On the contrary, the one thing I know in his favour is that he has a human weakness for a pretty face. She's a banal little thing, of course, but she seems to suit him.'

'Elsa, will you please show a little more discretion – and I wish you'd take me seriously.'

'Very well. You are involved in some plot . . .'

'Don't call it that!'

'Why not? Don't try to fool me with your talk of hidden microphones. You wouldn't have talked to me here unless you were sure that it was safe.'

'For the moment this apartment is secure. As to the details of what is going on, the less you know about it the better. Could you stomach marriage to this Gunther of yours? He sounds ideal. I could let it be known that I'm not pleased at your marrying someone so far beneath you. We could quarrel and you could keep away from me.'

'But how would I live?' Elsa asked plaintively.

'I'd see you were all right for money. If everything turns out well we can be reconciled. As for the future – there's always divorce if you want to get rid of him.'

There was a long pause while she licked the last of her brandied cherries from her spoon.

'I don't know whether I would want to get rid of him. He's frightfully presentable. One might make something of him.'

'Are you in love with him?'

'I almost might be. There is just one *tiny* difficulty, darling. He's in Russia.'

'I can fix that. It may take a week or two, but if I get him to Berlin can you persuade him to the altar?'

'When so much is at stake? I'm sure I can. I'd better start writing to him, to let him know how much I miss him. As a matter of fact, it's true. There's no-one around at the moment quite like Gunther.' She sighed. 'How much longer is this ghastly war going on?'

He did not answer. Elsa asked another question and this time she was deadly serious: 'Can we still win?'

'We can still negotiate an honourable peace,' her father said slowly. 'But only if that megalomaniac who calls himself our Commander-in-Chief is out of the way.'

'Now who's being indiscreet?'

He looked at her with sombre eyes. 'I've told you it would be better if you knew nothing. Already I've said more than I intended, but you're no-one's fool, Elsa. You know what has to be done. Keep your mouth shut – and keep away from me.'

Frau Hofmeyer was astonished a few days later to receive a visit from the girl who had taken up so much of Gunther's time on his last two leaves. She stood in the hallway, ravishingly pretty and remarkably smart for the fourth year of a war that had reduced most women to threadbare shabbiness. She managed to look very young and slightly nervous as she explained who she was.

'I hope you will forgive me for calling on you like this,' she said. 'Suddenly it seemed so wrong for us not to be acquainted.'

With her head in a whirl Frau Hofmeyer invited her in. She was not given to probing deeply into her son's affairs – he was a man and must run his life himself – but nothing about the way he had spoken of Elsa had prepared her for this visit. She had something of the family pride which had once inspired her father to refuse to allow her to be a concert pianist and she did not consider anyone too good for Gunther, especially since he had been decorated by Feldmarschall Göring himself. Nevertheless, she had regarded his friendship with the daughter of a General on the Führer's personal staff as something quite separate from his ordinary family life. Yet here was Elsa – within the first ten minutes she had exclaimed against formality and begged to be called 'Elsa' – sitting in the drawing room drinking coffee and behaving as if it was all perfectly normal.

Elsa heroically finished her cup of *ersatz* coffee and looked round her surreptitiously. Frau Hofmeyer was rather a dear in a dim kind of way; slightly vague, perhaps that was due to her artistic temperament. The apartment was fusty, especially now that it was darkened by having a blown-out window boarded up, but it was comfortable. Provided it survived the bombing it would be a reasonably acceptable place in which to live. There was an old servant woman who seemed quite competent. That was important. Elsa was prepared to forgo the luxuries to which she had been accustomed in better times, but she had no intention of doing all her own cooking and cleaning.

Frau Hofmeyer was lonely, that was obvious. She would probably welcome an addition to her family, especially a pretty, deferential daughter-in-law. One would have to live without sex, which would be frightful, but even that could be accepted if it were necessary to one's survival.

Few people held out against Elsa when she chose to charm them, certainly not anyone as eager to be pleased as Frau Hofmeyer. The visit was a high point of excitement in a life which had become increasingly drab and lonely in recent months.

'My daughter is teaching in a camp for girls in Czechoslovakia,' she said. 'I'm glad, of course, that she's away from the bombing, but it means that I'm very much on my own. Lotte has been with me for so long that I look upon her as a member of the family, but I can't talk with her as, for instance, I can with you. You may know that in the past I taught music – to some very fine musicians, I may say. Some of them have had quite distinguished careers. However, there is little call for piano lessons now. I miss the contact with other musicians.'

She missed the income, too. If it hadn't been for the allowances she received from Frieda and Gunther, she would have been hard put to it to live, but she did not find it necessary to touch on that when talking to Elsa Obermann.

'I have two tickets for a Philharmonic concert,' Elsa said. 'Would you give me the pleasure of your company?'

She spoke on impulse, driven by genuine compassion for this proud, quiet woman so obviously living on the borderline of poverty. She was rewarded by the light that came into Frau Hofmeyer's face, but to her surprise the older woman hesitated.

'It's an afternoon concert, we'd be home before any air raids started,' she urged, but that was not the reason why Frau Hofmeyer was looking doubtful.

'This war has made things so difficult,' she said. Her hand smoothed over her worn grey skirt. 'I really don't know that I have anything to wear that wouldn't disgrace you.'

176

'My dear Frau Hofmeyer! We are all shabby together. It's a badge of pride,' Elsa said blithely ignoring the fact that any shortcomings in her wardrobe were hidden under a splendid ocelot coat.

Frau Hofmeyer's shoulders straightened. 'If you are quite sure you wouldn't be ashamed to be seen with me . . .'

'Of course not. In any case, one doesn't go to a concert to be seen, but to listen to the music.'

She had no idea of the anxious brushing and steaming and pressing that went into making Frau Hofmeyer's old brown coat and skirt fit to be worn, but she did recognize the state of ecstatic pleasure induced in Gunther's mother by the concert. A strange woman, not at all like Gunther, except that possibly it was from her that he derived the sensitivity which made him such an entrancing lover.

Elsa was well pleased by the start of her campaign to change her standing with Gunther. She persisted in her visits and little attentions. By the time Gunther, to his puzzlement and relief, found that he was being posted away from the horror of the Eastern Front, his mother had begun to look upon Elsa almost in the light of his fiancée.

By special invitation she was there in his home when he arrived. Gunther looked at her with dull bewilderment, but his fatigue prevented him from taking in the full implications of her presence.

'You look so tired!' his mother exclaimed. She was appalled by his appearance, grey-faced and sunken-eyed. Her hands clutched together nervously and she looked to Elsa for guidance.

'Poor Gunther, you must rest,' Elsa said decisively. She stood on tiptoe and kissed him on the cheek.

'Some hot soup,' Frau Hofmeyer suggested. 'Elsa was able to get me a chicken and Lotte has made soup with the carcase.'

He accepted the soup and drank it hungrily. It was tastier than anything he had eaten for months.

Elsa sat at the table and watched him, her chin propped on her hands. When his mother went out of the room Gunther said: 'I didn't expect to see you here. I'm pleased, of course, but I don't understand.'

'I was anxious about you. I got in touch with your mother and we became friends. I spend quite a lot of time with her.'

He shook his head. 'I'm sorry,' he said. 'I suppose it makes sense, but I'm too tired to understand.'

'You must go to bed.'

'Yes,' he agreed. The ghost of his old mischievous smile flickered across his face. 'Alone.'

Elsa stood up. 'Definitely alone,' she said. 'Dear Gunther, I'm so pleased to have you back.'

As she went past him she touched his cheek with the back of her hand. 'I love you,' she said. She sounded surprised.

She left it to his mother to reveal the status she had assumed in his home and Frau Hofmeyer was very ready to do so. Her talk was all of Elsa. Elsa had taken her to a concert; Elsa knew a man who would provide occasional pieces of meat; Elsa had given her a jacket – of wool, real wool, and only slightly worn.

'Elsa,' said Gunther thoughtfully when he was at last alone with her, 'seems to have been remarkably busy.'

She was still living in her father's apartment, though its elegance was only a shadow of what it had been when he had first seen it. No matter how often the surfaces were wiped, the glass-topped tables and black leather furniture showed a film of dust produced by the constant vibration of the building in the bombing raids. The pink satin sheets were wearing thin and the building was no longer centrally heated but relied on individual stoves which required constant attention and a supply of fuel not always available.

Once he had recovered to some extent from his stupor of fatigue Gunther had been avid for her, as she was for him.

'My lovely Gunther,' she murmured. 'Dear, kind, strong Gunther.'

Her small, lithe body was thinner than it had been. He put his hands on her pelvis and was disturbed by the way her hip bones jutted out under the skin.

'Do you get enough to eat?' he asked.

'No, darling. Even your little Elsa is going hungry. Must we talk about it now? It isn't food I'm hungry for at this moment.'

'Anyone would think you'd been living a life of chastity,' Gunther remarked.

178

'I have! There are no men. Besides . . .' she hesitated and then she said: 'It was you I wanted.'

Again he was astonished, but the admission filled him with a special tenderness. He remembered that she had cried the last time he had left her. Her attentions to his mother, so unexpected and so welcome, could only have arisen from a wish to be in touch with someone close to him. It was something he would have to think about when his head was clearer, not clouded by mounting passion.

She clung to him, wrapping her arms and legs round him and whispering endearments in his ear and he put away from him the recollection of blind white days and nights with men crawling through the snow in a trail of blood and slime and corpses with blackened faces and bodies gnawed by ravenous animals. Elsa was warm and sensual and the ghost of her old perfume still clung to her. She twisted and turned in his arms, smoothing his body with her soft, clever hands and all the time she kept up that murmur of love words in a husky undertone until every pulse in his body was united, every thought in his head was obliterated and he was nothing but one aching point of desire. She lifted herself towards him, and he was so lost to everything but his own driving need that he did not even hear her moan of pleasure as he took her.

When they were quiet again Elsa remarked in an exhausted whisper: 'But, darling, you've become a sledgehammer since I last saw you!'

Gunther gathered her closer and kissed her on the forehead. 'I didn't hurt you, did I?'

'Yes – it was *lovely!*'

He gave a smothered laugh and kissed her again.

'Have you been having a very bad time, my treasure?' Elsa asked.

'Very bad,' he said. 'We should never have gone into Russia. It will be the death of us.'

The war was back with them again and their brief interlude of forgetfulness was over.

'Your mother has been so good to me,' Elsa said with an abruptness that took him by surprise. 'I'm going to have to leave here. Father is hardly ever at home. I can't go on living

179

in this vast empty place alone. Your mother, too, is lonely. We get on well together. I've been thinking – if you have no objection – of suggesting she has me as a lodger in your apartment.'

'I can't imagine that would work,' Gunther said. 'Your company would be welcome to Mother, I am sure; she seems to have taken a great liking to you; but you, Elsa, can you really see yourself fitting into our middle class home successfully? It's not at all the way you have been used to living.'

'The way I lived even a year ago has disappeared,' Elsa said. 'I was totally self-indulgent – oh, yes, I knew it even at the time, and I didn't care.'

'It was one of the things I liked about you. You were totally unashamed of enjoying your life.'

'Things are different now. There are few luxuries and I've become surprisingly moral now that there's nothing to tempt me but decrepit old men and spotty boys.'

'Oh, come now, Elsa. There's an occasional soldier on leave, surely?'

'Only you, my brave *Luftwaffe* hero. I don't want anyone else.'

He was becoming more and more astonished by her apparent sincerity. She had said that she loved him, she had hinted that she had been faithful to him – and even that she was prepared to go on being faithful to him.

'I couldn't take you to bed like this if you were living in my mother's apartment,' he remarked.

'No, I suppose not, unless . . .'

She let her voice trail away and Gunther completed the sentence for her, only half in earnest: 'Unless we were married.'

She remained silent and he asked, still not taking her seriously: 'Would you marry me, Elsa? I must admit the thought is new to me.'

'Yes, I would marry you,' she said. 'I would be glad to marry you. Is it what you would like, Gunther?'

'I have so little to offer you. An absent husband whose survival is uncertain. Not much money and no prospects for the future.'

'I remember telling you when we first met that I lived for

today. That's still true. Let's leave tomorrow to take care of itself and enjoy what we can get now.'

He did not make any response to that and she went on: 'Are you hesitating because I have been so wicked in the past? That is over. I am older and sadder and perhaps a little wiser. I'm prepared to be a good wife.'

She was relieved to see that he was beginning to smile. 'Will you learn to cook and sew and be a proper little *Hausfrau*?' he teased her.

'I can already do those things. I was given a very good convent education and I sew beautifully.'

'A convent education!' Gunther began to shake with laughter. 'I would never have suspected it!'

Elsa joined in his laughter. 'Perhaps the good nuns would not be *entirely* pleased with me,' she admitted. 'But think how happy it would make them if they knew I was going to reform!'

'Don't reform just yet,' he begged. 'Not right at this moment. I'm just about to start working myself up to celebrate our engagement.'

'You will marry me? You will? Oh, Gunther, you don't know how happy that makes me!'

'Yes, I'll marry you, you baggage. Heaven help me when peace comes, but at the moment I can't resist you. Darling Elsa, my wicked sweet witch. Do you love me? Is it possible?'

'Yes, I do, I do! Only you, Gunther, I *promise* you.'

They were married within the week. General Obermann did not attend the ceremony and Elsa let it be known that he was not pleased by her marriage. It troubled Frau Hofmeyer more than anyone else, just as she was the only one who wept at the briefness of the civil wedding: neither Gunther nor Elsa was prepared to go through a religious ceremony.

He took her into the country for a few days, so that they would not have to spend their wedding night in an air raid shelter.

'I'm relieved to find that being married doesn't have any inhibiting effect on you,' he remarked after their first few hectic hours together.

'On the contrary, I have a feeling of release,' Elsa said in her fluting, childish voice. 'Such a strange experience, to be doing it when it's legal.'

She took enormous trouble to please him, surprising herself by the genuineness of her feeling for him. He was magnificent; splendid to look at, courteous and considerate, a delightful lover and a hero into the bargain. Whatever the outcome of this atrocious war she had achieved a worthy husband. By anyone's standards Gunther was a good catch, except as regards money, and that, no doubt, was something that could be taken care of in easier times, if they ever came.

The great thing was to survive. Elsa's blood ran cold in her veins whenever she thought about the implications behind her father's command that she should separate herself from him. If there were a successful coup against Hitler then General Obermann would be riding on the crest of the wave, his daughter would be one of the most prominent women in Germany. If the planned revolt failed, the revenge of the Nazi Party would be too dreadful to think about. Elsa shivered and clung closer to her new husband. Gunther would protect her. One could only hope that the plot was a long way ahead, long enough for Elsa Obermann to disappear into the obscurity of being Elsa Hofmeyer.

Gunther's new posting coincided with the stepping up of the Allied bombing offensive against the great German cities. On the night of 1st March the Squadrons of the Royal Canadian Air Force which formed No 6 Group of Bomber Command flew their first mission over Berlin. It was an exceptionally clear night. Flight Sergeant Jimmy Brookfield, flying from Middleton St George as a rear gunner in a Lancaster, was astonished by the fine visibility. Below him he could see the fires already raging from the bombs which had been dropped by earlier crews. All round him the flak from the anti-aircraft defences made patterns of light and star-bursts in the sky.

There were Messerschmitts and Focker-Wolffes about. He tried to keep his eyes skinned for them, but there was so much noise and danger and excitement, that he missed the Me109 that cut across his tail, guns blazing. He opened fire, but he knew he was too late, too slow in his reactions. He cursed himself afterwards because it was the only real chance he had during the raid to secure a hit. He was guiltily aware that it was only luck and perhaps an off-day for the German, too, which had saved him and all the crew from a sudden, ugly death.

The bombs were away, they circled and turned towards home; the flak and the explosions receded into the distance. Nothing now but the drone of the engines. And the possibility of interception before they reached the coast. It hadn't been quite as he'd expected, the long flight towards the target, the fear he'd experienced at their hot reception, his reaction to the movement of the aircraft as they met an air pocket or the pilot took evasive action. It had never bothered him before, but that night he had been all too conscious of his lonely, vulnerable position and every time his stomach lurched he had been convinced that they had been hit. He felt deadly tired, a little sick. It had been a great adventure, but now he was secretly glad that it was over. And it was all to do again in a few nights' time – and again, and again, and again.

On the night of 5th March 1943 the RAF's night bombing campaign started in earnest. Essen was attacked by a large force. One after the other the squadrons of bombers: Mosquitoes, Halifaxes, Stirlings, Wellingtons and Lancasters, approached the target and off-loaded their bombs. Reconnaissance photographs afterwards showed that a 160-acre area of Essen had been completely levelled. Over a larger area of 450 acres, more than three-quarters of the buildings had been severely damaged. In particular, the Krupps factories had been badly hit.

Three nights later it was the turn of Nuremburg. On 12th March Essen was again attacked, but this time Gunther, flying as a night fighter for the first time, was able to claim that he had damaged a Wellington, although he could not add it to his list of 'kills'.

The British public was told about this new heavy bombing programme, and inevitably, Christine in her work in the Operations Room was all too well informed about the dangers and successes of the men she knew and feared for.

She knew all about the life expectation – or lack of it – of a rear gunner and she listened to the bombers passing overhead or watched the movement of the counters on the operations table and often spared a thought for her young brother. She no longer worried to quite the same extent about Larry. He was a very experienced pilot. She didn't like him being a night fighter, especially forming part of the escort for the great fleets which set out night after night for Germany, but the fighter aircraft did not have the range to take them all the way, and the knowledge that he was forced to turn back before they reached the Ruhr made her optimistic about his safety.

They had hopes of a week together in August and she had reminded him that he had promised to discuss her yearning to have a baby. It was strange to her, this deep-rooted desire to bear a child. She had never thought of herself as a particularly maternal type and she had to agree that in many ways Larry was right in saying that this was not the time to bring a new life into the world; and yet she found herself turning her head away from the sight of babies in perambulators, filled with a fierce primitive urge to feel his child growing inside her, to hold her own baby in her arms.

Because she wanted him to understand how deeply she felt she had written to him recently trying to put into words something she did not really quite understand herself. She hadn't had his reply, but she longed for it to be sympathetic.

She was particularly interested in the raid which was being carried out on Hamburg on the night of 24th July because it was to be the first time Bomber Command had made use of a device called 'Window' – strips of tinfoil cut to the wavelength of the German radar. Christine had had this process, which jammed the radar signal, explained to her and she was anxious to know how well it worked.

She was aware, as she watched the Ops table, of someone coming into the Ops Room, of a conference going on between two of the RAF officers behind her, but she paid no attention to it until she felt a touch on the shoulder. She removed her headphones and turned round in surprise. One of her colleagues was behind her.

'I'm relieving you,' she said.

'But I'm not due off for another hour.'

'Flight Officer Mayhew wants to see you. Better get cracking. You know her ladyship doesn't like to be kept waiting.'

'I can't think of any great crime I've committed lately.' Christine joked. 'Any idea what it's about?'

'None at all.' The girl's attention seemed to be fixed on the table and she sounded absentminded, but as Christine walked away she looked after her with a compassion that would have told Christine everything if she had seen it.

Christine smoothed her hair as best she could with the palms of her hands and put on her cap. It seemed dark outside, but as her eyes became accustomed to the gloom she realized that the summer night was still quite light. The air was cool and fresh. She breathed it in gratefully after the stuffy atmosphere of the Ops Room. The Flight Officer's office was in a Nissen hut about three hundred yards away, but she took her time walking over to it, enjoying being out in the open.

She did not begin to feel apprehensive until Flight Officer Mayhew told her to sit down. This wasn't standard procedure, not unless there was something seriously wrong. Even then, her first thought was of Jimmy. Was he on that raid tonight? She hadn't thought the Canadians were involved, but she didn't know all the details of the operation and she could have been wrong. Dear God, surely nothing had happened to Jimmy.

'I'm sorry, I have bad news for you,' the Flight Officer said. She looked down at her hands, clasped in front of her on the desk. 'Your husband . . .'

Larry! Christine heard herself say in a disbelieving whisper: 'Oh, no, not Larry!'

'Yes, I'm afraid so.'

'Dead?'

'No, but very badly injured. He was in a fight over the French coast, I understand. His aircraft was badly damaged. He flew back to base, but crashed on landing.'

A faint hope stirred in Christine. He was still alive.

'I must go to him,' she said.

'Yes, arrangements are in hand. He's in hospital in Ipswich.'
Flight Officer Mayhew looked with compassion at the white,

still face of the girl in front of her. 'This has been a great shock to you. Do you feel well enough to go and do your packing straight away?'

'Yes, of course.'

'Very well.' She hesitated and then, reluctantly, she continued. 'My dear, don't build too much on the fact that he has survived the crash. He's very badly hurt.'

For the first time something like understanding showed in Christine's eyes. 'He may die before I get to him?'

'It is possible.'

She shook her head. 'No, he'll hang on, no matter what it costs him. He won't die without seeing me first.'

During the hours she spent travelling Christine was completely unconscious of the passage of time. All her thoughts were on Larry. She pictured him in his narrow hospital bed and with every ounce of her willpower she silently begged him to hold on, to go on living.

The doctors and nurses who were caring for him did not hold out any real hope that he would survive. But there was still a flicker of life in him when Christine arrived. She sat by his side and spoke to him in a low voice, urging him as she had done all the way there in her mind to fight for his life. Twelve hours later he was still alive. His pulse began to beat more strongly; his eyes flickered once or twice; when Christine put her hand on his she thought that he moved his fingers as if he were trying to grasp it.

It was three days before the doctors admitted that he was out of immediate danger; it was another twenty-four hours before they told Christine that he would never walk again.

It had not occurred to her that his immobility was due to anything more than extreme weakness. Now it was explained that his spine was irretrievably damaged, the nerves severed, the vertebrae smashed. She remembered with horror the way she had begged him to go on living. It might have been better to let him die.

She said the words out loud and the two doctors looked uncomfortable.

'Life can be enjoyed, even by paraplegics,' one of them said at last.

'Life! Do you call it that, for a man like Larry!'

She tried to calm herself and made an effort to apologize. 'I'm sorry. Will he be completely paralysed?'

'It's difficult to tell until he's strong enough to stand some tests,' the younger doctor said. 'He can move his arms and his head. It may be that he'll be able to sit up unaided. Below the waist we think he'll be paralysed.'

He glanced at his companion and the older man carried on. It was a brutal thing to have to say, but it was better to get it over.

'You will have to face the fact that marital relations will be impossible,' he said.

Christine turned away. She hadn't even thought of that and she resented being told in such a way. Her impassioned plea to Larry to give her a child jolted back into her mind and her eyes filled with tears.

'Who will tell Larry?' she asked in a dull voice.

'We'll do that, but not yet – not until he is stronger.'

'Keep it from him as long as you can,' Christine said. 'He'll take it badly.'

She was already on indefinite leave. She wrote to her Commanding Officer and explained the position. She tried to think about the future, but it was all too new and too difficult. Presumably she would be released from the WAAF. Once Larry was able to leave hospital he would need her to look after him. Where would they live? How would they manage? Try as she might she couldn't imagine what it would be like.

She wrote to her mother, a short, stark report, not asking for any sympathy. Larry's parents had already arrived and were staying in the same hotel as herself. She wished desperately that they were not there. It would be impossible to face them and not tell them.

She broke it to them in much the same brief words as the doctors had used to her. Larry would live, but he would not be able to walk. Mrs Telford understood immediately. Her mouth trembled and she put a shaking hand to her face. Colonel Telford looked from one to the other, blankly uncomprehending, and Christine saw that he wasn't wearing his hearing aid. Either he hadn't heard or else he was unable to believe what he thought he'd heard. She could not bring herself to repeat the words. She put her hand on Mrs Telford's arm and turned her towards her husband. And then, unable to speak, Christine went out of the room.

Christine's letter reached her mother on a morning when Barbara was fortunate in hearing from all three of her young. The postman didn't come until after Harry had left for the office. She looked at the clock. She was keeping hens and the little horrors still had to be fed, and she must get to the butcher early if there was to be the slightest hope of getting some of the offal he had hinted might be available that day. She couldn't really spare even a quarter of an hour, but all the same she poured herself an extra cup of tea and settled down to the luxury of her letters.

Jimmy's first. She couldn't help it, he was the one she worried about most, perhaps because he was the youngest, perhaps because of the long time he had been missing from her life, perhaps because he was the one in the most immediate danger. His letter was much the same as usual, cheerful, but not particularly informative. Everything, according to Jimmy was 'bang on'. Barbara grimaced to herself as she put it away. Tiresome boy, he never gave her the news she really wanted to hear, but it was something that he was still safe and in good spirits.

Michael's next and at least he had something interesting to tell her. Michael had had a surprise, a very pleasant surprise, and something of his sense of shock came through.

He was still at the training school, regretful about his own inability to fly as a pilot, but more resigned to it than he had been. The hard experience the RAF had won in the early years of the war made their training methods of particular interest to all the Allies, especially the Americans, and Michael had already delivered lectures to US pilots. They were keen, anxious to learn, sometimes embarrassingly deferential to a veteran pilot, sometimes a little brash and sure that they knew it all already. He'd liked them and it had proved a useful point of contact to be able to say that he had visited some of their home towns, however briefly.

He knew vaguely that there was a high-ranking American officer visiting the training school one day in July, but he hadn't been called upon to take any part in the programme. He'd had a free period in the morning and had gone down to the village shop, mainly for the pleasure of the walk. He still had a limp, but he never used a stick now, and although his leg sometimes ached, he was usually able to ignore it. As for his face, he was reconciled to the fact that it would never look any better. The surgeons had done their best and he was by no means repulsive to look at. More than that couldn't be expected.

As he walked up the drive in the warm July sunshine he could see the big, gleaming American car waiting outside the front door of the mansion which had been taken over as a training school. A nice job, that car, he thought. If the driver was anywhere about, he'd be interested in asking a few questions.

The driver was there all right, standing on the far side of the car, as neat and trim a figure as he had seen in a long time. Of course he ought to have guessed that it would be a girl. She was standing with her back to him. She had taken off her jacket and rolled up the sleeves of her shirt. Her cap was off, too. She was holding it up in front of her, moving it backwards and forwards like a fan, trying to create a breeze in the sultry air. She was small and slim, with dark, waving hair cut very short. He didn't have to see her face to know that she would be very attractive.

She heard his footsteps, with their characteristic slightly uneven rhythm, and turned her head. It was Lucy.

'Lucy?' Michael said. 'For heaven's sake! Lucy!'

The colour came up into her face and she smiled widely.

'I guess I ought to salute, but it seems sort of unnatural,' she said.

'But . . . Lucy! I'm stunned,' Michael said.

'It's not quite such a coincidence as it seems,' she said. 'I knew you were here. When I heard Colonel Linklater was

189

coming down I volunteered to be his driver in the hope of seeing you. How are you, Michael? You're looking great.'

'So are you. I'm all right,' Michael said. He still looked dazed. 'I didn't even know you'd joined up.'

'You haven't written to me lately, you stinker, so I kept the news to myself – and I was lucky, got myself posted to England almost straight away. How are all the family? I was planning to give your mother a call, maybe go and see her when I can get away. I'm stationed in London.'

'She'll be thrilled,' Michael said. 'We're all OK.'

'How about Jimmy?'

'Finding out that war is harder than he'd expected, unless I'm much mistaken.'

'I guess you can say that about all of us from the other side of the Atlantic. No matter what you expect, it comes as a shock to see the bomb damage and everything.'

'You're mad to have come,' he said, with his eyes fixed on her face.

'Well, thank you! That's a fine welcome! Do you feel like that about all the American forces?'

'Far from it,' he admitted. 'The fighting men are more than welcome. But a girl like you . . .'

'You think I may be more of a liability than an asset?'

'Not that,' he protested.

'Huh! I can see it's what you do think. If I can drive my Colonel around it frees a man who would otherwise be doing it. Right?'

'Yes, but . . .'

'Aren't I good enough to join in your war?'

'Too good. OK, I'm being ridiculous. Just take care of yourself, that's all.'

'I'll do that,' she promised.

'Have you had lunch? Have you got to stay out here in this hot sun? How about a cool drink inside?'

'Is that allowed, you being an officer and a gentleman and me being one of the lower ranks?'

She chuckled at his look of dismay. 'I guess it isn't. Don't look so worried, Michael, I've only been out here a few minutes. I went inside, asked for you, found you were out –

which I admit made me wish I'd been more open about paying you a visit – was treated *very* hospitably by a real nice Sergeant . . .'

'I'll bet you were,' Michael said glumly.

'And now I'm waiting for my Colonel and taking him on to lunch somewhere. They'll feed me too, I guess. I may say I've found your boys to be very kind and welcoming wherever I've been so far.'

'I'm not surprised. When did you start getting so pretty?'

'Since you last saw me, obviously, or you'd have noticed it before. Of course, you were taken up with Jo-Anne Parker at that time, weren't you?'

'Jo-Anne who?'

'You don't remember, after the rush you were giving her? Oh, Michael!'

'I have a feeling you're teasing me,' Michael said. 'I don't remember any Jo-Anne thing. Look, before this Colonel of yours reappears we must make arrangements to meet.'

'I'll give you my address,' Lucy said. 'Give me a call when you're in town and perhaps we'll be able to arrange something.'

'Perhaps!'

'I do keep kind of busy. You know how it is, our boys are a long way from home and they're keen to be with a girl from the States.'

'Yes, but we're such old friends.' He hesitated and then he said: 'You wouldn't mind being seen out with a man with only half a face?'

'That's a real nasty thing to say,' Lucy told him. 'And what's more, it's blackmail. You think you can shame me into going out with you. I've known you too long to fall for that, Michael Brookfield! Ring me when you're free and if I'm available you shall have first call on my time – that's a promise.'

'Thank you. Thank you very much,' Michael said. 'That's most generous of you. If I don't have anything better to do next time I'm off duty I might just call you.'

They were both laughing, but in spite of the smile on his face Michael felt nettled. Little Lucy, laying down the law about whether she would see him or not. She'd changed, and not only in appearance. He'd always thought her a pleasant looking youngster, but now she really could be called beautiful. Perhaps it was that short, boyish haircut which seemed to make her high-cheekboned face particularly appealing, perhaps it was the extra assurance she had gained, perhaps it was the fact that she had outgrown the angular boniness he remembered and now had a remarkably good figure. Whatever it was, he'd had a jolt. He wanted to see her again to make sure that he was right, that there was really something quite out of the ordinary about Lucy, the way she was now.

He kept his remarks to his mother deliberately offhand. 'Young Lucy has turned out to be quite pretty,' he said in his letter. 'A competent driver, too, as far as I could judge. We only had time for a few words, but I hope to see her again soon.'

Barbara folded up the letter and put it back in its envelope. She was nearly as surprised as Michael. Why hadn't Connie written to tell? Come to think about it, it was some time since she'd heard from Connie. Perhaps a letter had been lost at sea. She pushed the gloomy thought out of her mind and opened Christine's letter. It was very short, no more than a straightforward statement of the facts: Larry had crashed on landing after he had been shot up in a fight; he was very seriously wounded, but it looked as if he would live; the doctors had warned her that it was not likely that he would ever walk again.

'My poor little girl,' Barbara whispered, all alone in her sunny kitchen with the breakfast dishes still waiting to be washed up. 'My poor little girl, how ever is she going to be able to bear it?'

Chapter Ten

Michael's plans to see Lucy again were frustrated. On the
only occasion when he was able to get to London she was
away on a long driving job. To his indignation it was Jimmy
who had the good luck to be at home when Lucy found an
opportunity of dropping in to see his mother.

'I mustn't stay long,' she said apologetically. 'I'm on my
way back to base and I've made a small detour to see you. I'll
be shot at dawn if I'm caught. Aunt Barbara, Michael wrote
and told me the terrible news about Christine's husband.
There's no improvement, I suppose?'

'None at all,' Barbara said. 'He's better than he was, getting
quite strong, but of course that means he'll soon be able to
understand what's happened to him. Christine spends every
minute she can at the hospital. I haven't seen her.'

A small, warm hand clasped hers. 'You're feeling shut out,'
Lucy said. 'But Christine will turn to you if she needs you –
you must know that.'

There was a resounding crash from the front door and
Barbara smiled tremulously.

'Contrary to what you may think, that's not a herd of
elephants, it's just Jimmy coming in,' she said.

'Jimmy? He's home? Oh, that's great!'

The sitting room door flew open and Jimmy came in. He
stood in the doorway, grinning all over his face.

'Well, well, if it isn't me ole Luce, all done up like a soldier,
and looking a fair treat,' he said.

'Jimmy, it's just wonderful to see you. Not that I've forgiven
you for the way you ran off.'

'You were the one person I might have told,' he admitted.

'But I would have had to swear you to secrecy and I didn't think it was fair to do that.'

He looked wistfully at the table. 'Any tea? I'm starving.'

'You always are,' his mother said. 'I'll make some tea and cut some bread and butter. Lucy has brought me a tin of beautiful butter.'

She went out of the room and Jimmy said with satisfaction: 'Good. Now I can say hello to you properly.'

He put his hands on Lucy's arms and pulled her to her feet. Lucy started to protest, half laughing and half in earnest, but he held on to her and kissed her. His lips were firm and warm and rather more demanding than Lucy had been prepared for. Jimmy had learned a thing or two since they had last been together.

She struggled to free herself and he let her go. He was looking rather pleased with himself and he would have done it again, but Lucy drew away and said: 'No, that's enough, Jimmy. I won't have it. That's not the way things are between you and me.'

'That's not the way things *were*,' he said. 'No reason why they shouldn't change.'

'Yes there is. I like you, I'm fond of you, but I don't want to . . . to get involved.'

He moved away from her and went to look out of the window. His hand jingled some loose change in his pocket.

'Is it still Michael?' he asked.

She did not answer and he turned his head to look at her.

'Yes, I can see it is. He doesn't know how lucky he is. Couldn't you make do with me instead?'

Lucy shook her head. Jimmy shrugged his shoulders. 'Oh well, no harm in trying, was there?'

Again she shook her head. She was looking puzzled and worried.

'Jimmy, when you ran away, it wasn't anything to do with me, was it?' she asked abruptly.

'It was everything to do with you, sweetheart. You knew that really.'

'That's not true. You were mad to get into the war long before . . .'

'Before I started waking up to the way I felt about you? Yes, of course I was, but it was being in the same house as you, being treated like a kid brother when I wasn't feeling like a brother, knowing that it wasn't ever going to be any good, that gave me the extra push I needed to make me run off.'

'You were younger than me,' she said helplessly.

'I still am. Not so noticeable now, is it?'

It was true. He had aged. Once she had thought of him as a boy. Now there was no doubt that he was a man. He looked precisely what he was, a tough and experienced fighting man. And enormously attractive, Lucy had to admit that. If it hadn't been for the persistent, unceasing love she still felt for his brother it would not have been difficult to turn to Jimmy. As it was, it was hopeless.

'I never told anybody,' she said, going off at a tangent. 'That I suspected you fancied you were a bit in love with me, I mean.'

'Not much to tell, was there? I made a couple of botched attempts to make love to you, you were politely off-putting, I went and joined the Canadian Air Force. Hardly the love story of the century.'

'No. I didn't realize that it was so important to you. I thought you were just, well, experimenting. It made me rather cross, in fact, being, as I thought, used like that.'

A slight, rueful smile crossed his face. 'I knew that was the way you saw it. So I upped and went for a soldier – or rather an airman.'

'Any regrets?'

'No! It's been great. The only thing is . . .'

She waited and he said: 'I didn't think at all, at first, about the effect of the bombing. The cities we've raided are devastated. Some of the people killed just have to be civilians. Women and children amongst them, I guess. It bothers me.'

'You're under orders,' she said gently.

'Don't say that! That's what the Germans say.'

He grinned. 'One thing helps, though. Do you remember the Nazi at that party when Michael was over? I tell myself every time that he might be on the receiving end of one of our bombs.'

'I certainly do remember. And the great patriotic speech you made.'

'I was just a kid.'

Lucy was thankful that they had turned the conversation. What Jimmy had said had troubled her. Always, at the back of her mind, she had known that he had begun to cherish a boyish infatuation for her before he had disappeared from her parents' house. She'd laughed it off, even, as she had admitted, been slightly indignant about it. It seemed that his feelings had been stronger than she'd realized and she felt bothered and a little sad.

It made her less forthcoming than she might otherwise have been when she and Michael at last got together. He was still Michael, the centre of her universe, but she couldn't help remembering that he was Jimmy's brother. He accused her of not listening to him and she confessed that her mind had wandered.

'Thinking of someone else?' he enquired.

'Yes, I was,' she said.

At any other time his barely suppressed indignation would have thrilled her, but her worry was too real for her to pay much attention to his scarcely recognized jealousy. She continued to be abstracted and slightly offhand and Michael went back to his training school disgruntled. Lucy was spoilt, not at all what she used to be. He wasn't sure that he would trouble to see her again.

The realization that what was different about Lucy was that in the past, whether he had ever acknowledged it or not, she had belonged exclusively to him, and that this was what he was missing, came to him only slowly. His decision not to see her again was a joke. He thought about her altogether too much for comfort. He had to see her and he wanted her to be just what she had always been. Only it seemed to be too late. Lucy spent an evening with him thinking about someone else and he had no idea what he was going to do about it.

The news that Lucy was in England was of little importance to Christine. The last time she had seen Lucy all her attention had been fixed on Gunther and Lucy had been only a child. What a long time ago that seemed now. She looked back to the selfish, lovesick girl she had been and could hardly believe that she was the same person.

Christine managed to find lodgings near the hospital. They were cheaper and more convenient than the hotel where she had stayed at first. Larry's parents had gone back to Wiltshire. There was a vague arrangement that they would return after a few weeks and give her a chance to get away, but she didn't really want to go. She went to the hospital every day. She had not yet put in her application to leave the WAAF, but doing so, for her, was no more than a formality.

She dreaded the moment when Larry would have to know the full extent of his injuries, but the long delay before he was strong enough to be told was a torment. He had two operations, neither of which did anything to restore life and feeling to his deadened limbs. He was very ill, too weak to recognize what was happening to him. He knew her when she was there, and would smile feebly and hold her hand. But there was no understanding in his eyes.

It was September. In Europe Mussolini had fallen, the Allies had conquered Sicily, the Russians had taken Kharkov. Four years after the start of the war the Italians surrendered, but the Germans went on fighting in Italy and the Allies landed at Salerno. Christine listened to the news on the wireless every night in her lonely room, but it no longer meant a great deal to her. Her war had narrowed down to a hospital ward and a man who lay on the borderline of death and still did not know that his life, if he won through, might prove to be an intolerable burden to him.

On 12th September, the day the Italian Fleet surrendered at Malta, Larry's surgeon left a message asking Christine to see him before she visited Larry. She waited for him in a small, untidy office with just room for a cluttered desk, two chairs and a filing cabinet. When he came in, frowning and preoccupied, she saw that he had to think for a moment why he wanted to see her.

'Oh, yes, Mrs Telford. I wanted to talk to you before you

saw your husband today. He understands now that we aren't going to be able to help him to walk again.'

Christine turned so white that he was afraid she might faint, but she closed her eyes for a moment and then said: 'I was so afraid after all this delay that you were going to ask me to break it to him.'

'No, it was best done by a medical man.'

'Does he understand . . .'

'Everything.'

'How did he take it?'

'Very quietly.'

'Yes, he could.' She stood up, feeling blindly for the back of the chair to steady herself. 'I'd better go to him.'

'You're a very brave girl,' the surgeon said. 'There's not much I can say except that there are people who specialize in the problems of men like your husband. Later, when he's ready to leave hospital, I can arrange for you to receive advice and counselling.'

'Thank you. For the moment it will be better not to have too many people talking to him about it. Just me. I understand him, you see.'

She was wearing civilian clothes. Her old tweed skirt was slightly too short and she wore a handknitted twinset with it which had had to be darned on the elbows of the cardigan, but which was still a clear, bright blue. It never occurred to her that to Larry, lying with his eyes fixed on the door, waiting for her to come in, she looked as desirable and unattainable as the dream girl he had once called her.

She saw him flinch as she entered the ward and was thankful that she'd been warned that he knew the truth. He didn't say anything as she sat down by the side of his bed. He was propped up a little higher on his pillows than he had been. His face was gaunt and his eyes were sunk in his head, with dark hollows underneath them.

Christine knew that the only thing to do was to speak to him at once about the news he'd been given. She took his hand and said: 'Mr Hudson has told me that you know. Darling, it's not the end of the world. You're still alive and by the time you are ready to leave hospital I'll be free to look after you. We'll still be together.'

His fingers moved over her head, caressing it slowly. 'I knew you'd say that. It's no use, Chris, I can't let you do it. I can't keep you tied to half a man for the rest of your life.'

'I've known about it for weeks, while you were still too ill to be told,' she said steadily. 'I've had time to get used to the idea. I've no intention of letting you throw me over.'

'You've got to be free to make a life for yourself.'

'You are my life.'

'It's not right.'

' "For richer, for poorer; for better, for worse; in sickness and in health." Do you think I didn't mean it?'

'I never thought it would turn out like this. I meant to give you a wonderful life. God knows I should have known better; I saw plenty of other men being killed and maimed. I ought never to have married you.'

Christine's lips quivered, but she kept her voice steady.

'That would have been a pity,' she said. 'No matter what happened I would have wanted the memory of being married to you.'

He turned his head away and she saw that he was as near to tears as she was herself.

'I can't bear it,' he said. 'Chris, I can't bear it.'

'My love. My dear love. We'll bear it together.'

She believed when she left him that she had reassured him. For herself she refused to have any doubts. Buoyed up by the love his helplessness aroused in her she felt herself equal to any task. She began to make a plan for the way they would live, but when she tried to discuss it with Larry she found him unresponsive.

'I think the best thing would be for us to go to your parents,' Christine said. 'You're used to the house and it's big enough for all of us. Best of all, there are rooms on the ground floor which could be adapted to give us a little place of our own. I haven't spoken to your mother and father, but I'm sure they'll agree. There's a downstairs cloakroom, too, and we could take the back drawing room as our bedroom . . .'

'Our bedroom? Are you proposing to sleep in the same room as me?'

'Of course. In the same bed, if it's not too uncomfortable for you.'

She saw the way his mouth tightened into a thin, bitter line and plunged on in blind determination to bring out into the open the most delicate of their problems.

'My dear, I know what you're thinking, but there are still ways in which we can express our love for one another. We still have hands and lips . . .'

'Don't!' He flung up his arms across his eyes. 'Don't talk like that.'

She got up from the side of his bed and stood over him. Deliberately she took hold of the hand with which he was hiding his face from her and held it against her breast.

'Darling,' she said. 'You must trust me and believe that you can make me happy.'

'What about the child you were so keen to have?'

She put his hand down very carefully on the tight hospital blanket. 'That's something I do regret,' she said. 'But I can live with it, even be glad that I'm free to give you all my care and attention.'

If he had shown even the slightest sign that she was winning her fight to assure him of her continuing love it would not have been so exhausting, but he never gave in. The most she felt she had achieved was that he stopped talking about her leaving him. He wasn't complaining, only silent. And she could get him to take no interest in the future.

One day she arrived to find that he had been promoted to a wheel chair. She thought that this mobility might cheer him, but if anything he spoke more bitterly than usual as he said, indicating a tangled mass of cane on his bedside table: 'They're teaching me to make a basket. Can you imagine it? Basketwork! Me!'

'It's better than sitting doing nothing,' Christine said, but she spoke automatically. Suddenly she was tired out, reduced to the last ounce of her strength by the constant battle to keep up his spirits, to make him believe that there was a life ahead for them.

'Three months ago I flew a machine worth thousands of pounds, I had command over men who trusted me with their lives.'

Christine's control snapped. 'Perhaps you might try to use the sort of discipline you needed then to face up to what your life is now,' she said. 'You might make *some* effort to accept it and fight back, Larry.'

He made no reply. She rallied herself to make one last effort.

'If I were in your shoes, paralysed and helpless, would you desert me?' she asked.

His head jerked up. 'No, of course not.'

'You'd expect me to go on living, to let you care for me and help me to make what I could of my life?'

'Yes,' he admitted reluctantly.

'You don't think I'm equal to you in courage, do you? But let me tell you I think women are stronger than men. If I were in your place I wouldn't lie back and think about nothing but how hopeless everything was. I'd take every opportunity I could to make something worthwhile of what life I had. And I wouldn't turn away from the help that the person who loved me best in the world could give me. I'd accept it and glory in it.'

There was a long silence until at last Christine whispered: 'I'm sorry.'

She thought he was just going to go on lying there, ignoring her. She could hardly believe her ears when Larry said: 'No, you were right to say what was in your mind.'

He gave an odd little laugh. 'You've utterly confounded me. I thought I was doing pretty well by not actually complaining and I believed I was right in refusing to accept the sacrifice of your life. You keep telling me it's not a sacrifice, which is ridiculous, but if you're hell-bent on throwing yourself away I suppose I can't stop you. It's not going to be easy, being more positive, but I will try.'

It was such a resounding victory that she could think of no reply, particularly when he went on with a wry attempt at a smile: 'Perhaps I should start by making a decent basket.'

She turned away and picked up the basket to conceal her tears. 'You haven't made a bad start,' she said.

'That's mostly done by the physiotherapist. Poor girl, I didn't show much interest. In fact, I was fairly ungracious. But, honestly, Chris – baskets!'

'Actually, it might not be such a bad idea,' Christine said slowly. 'Listen, Larry, there are so many shortages now – even shopping baskets. When you leave here we'll think of some work to do. Materials are in short supply, but in a country district it must be possible to get hold of wood and . . . and straw, and . . . oh, I don't know, I'm not enough of a country girl. Couldn't we think along the lines of setting up a workshop for country crafts? Small, useful things – like baskets.'

She was thrilled when she saw that she had caught his interest.

'It might be possible,' he admitted. 'Dad's always been good with his hands and he's got a workbench in one of the outhouses. It would have to be lowered so that I could reach the top from my chair.'

'Think about it,' Christine urged. 'You understand these things so much better than me.'

She was conscious that that last sentence had descended into cunning and she saw from his smile that Larry realized it too, but he made no comment.

She got up to go feeling better than she had for a long time. She was even more encouraged when Larry said: 'Kiss me, Chris.'

She bent over him and they exchanged their first real kiss since his injury. As she drew away he said in a low voice: 'Thank you, darling.'

The next time she went to the hospital she thought that Larry was looking tired.

'I've got a stiff neck,' he admitted. 'And cramp in my hand.'

'I suppose you've been trying to do too much after being completely immobile for so long. Just like you – you can't do things by halves, can you?'

They laughed about it, both of them relieved that they could suddenly laugh together again, but when the stiffness and the clumsiness with his hands persisted Larry mentioned it to the physiotherapist.

'What do you recommend – rest or exercise?' he enquired.

He looked critically at his handiwork. 'Shall I go on with this lopsided effort or shall I take a day off?'

'Give me your hand,' she said. 'Now, grip mine as hard as you can.'

'You'll be in trouble if my wife comes in,' he warned her.

He was smiling, but he was watching her closely, and he didn't miss her slight involuntary frown at the feebleness of his clasp.

'Give yourself a rest,' she said. 'Your muscles probably need toning up. I'll think about some exercises for you. I'll have a word with the surgeon about it.'

Larry was as aware of the surgeon's elaborate casualness as he had been of the physiotherapist's worried reaction.

'I hear you've been overdoing the basketwork. I've brought Dr Galloway, our consultant neurologist, along to have a look at you.'

They examined him, asked him questions, tested his reactions. He had grown accustomed to the routine, but this time he watched their serious, noncommittal faces with more anxiety than he had ever known before. When they told him afterwards that he had made a splendid recovery he was not deceived. There was something wrong and they weren't telling him. He asked no questions, but lay back on his bed, tired and dispirited.

The two men smiled at him, wished him good-day. Courteous and distant, they went out of the ward. Outside, they looked at one another.

'I don't like it,' the surgeon said.

'Neither do I,' Dr Galloway admitted. 'We'll do some X-rays tomorrow.'

Larry submitted to the fresh X-rays without comment. Christine knew about them, but he had deliberately given her the impression that they were merely to confirm that all was well with his original injury.

'They may make me a bit tired,' he said. 'Why don't you take a day off tomorrow? Come in and visit me the day after.'

'Darling, are you sure? You know I like to see you every day.' She picked up the neglected basket and shook her head at him. 'Not much progress. You'll have to do better than this when our livelihood depends on it.'

'I'm obeying orders not to overdo it,' he protested.

When the painstaking X-rays had been completed he asked to see the surgeon.

'This afternoon,' the sister promised. 'The poor man does have other patients besides you and he won't be able to tell you anything until he's examined the X-rays and consulted with Dr Galloway.'

She wasn't aware that she had tacitly admitted that there was a new complication, but Larry noted it and added the knowledge to his growing conviction that all was not well.

He tackled the surgeon obliquely that afternoon. 'I want to start making plans,' he said abruptly. 'When will I be able to leave hospital?'

'There may be a little setback to that. I'm going to arrange for you to see a specialist about this numbness in your hands.'

'You don't know what's causing it, in spite of the X-rays?'

'We're not sure.'

'Will I have to have another operation?'

'I doubt if it will get any better of its own accord,' was all the surgeon would commit himself to saying. He was being cautious, too cautious. With an effort Larry concealed the sick horror that had begun to fill his mind.

'I see,' he said mechanically. 'I'd better see this new man then.' He looked down at the hands that lay flaccidly on his lap, on top of his helpless legs. 'Can we keep it from my wife?'

For the first time the surgeon betrayed something of the worry that lay behind his careful clinical manner. 'I'm afraid not. She must be told.'

Larry nodded. 'I'll tell her when she comes in tomorrow,' he said. 'When is the specialist coming?'

'Thursday of next week. I'll have a word with your wife myself before that.'

After the surgeon had left him Larry stretched out his right hand in front of him. He tried to bend his fingers to touch the palm of his hand. They went halfway and stopped and nothing he could do would persuade them to go any further, although when he took his other hand and pressed the fingers down there seemed to be nothing physically wrong to stop them moving.

He asked to be put in his wheelchair and began a restless perambulation of the corridors outside his ward. He was on the fifth floor and it was too late in the day and too chilly to be asked to be taken outside. He wheeled himself down the long corridor to the window where he had several times sat and watched for Christine to come up the drive. It was a long French window, opening right to the floor, with a low metal grill outside, not a balcony, just a barrier to stop anyone inadvertently walking straight out of the window.

'You'll get cold, sitting there, Squadron Leader,' a passing nurse remarked. She came up beside him and closed the window. 'My word, autumn has set in with a vengeance. Hasn't your wife come in to see you today?'

'No, not today,' Larry said. 'She'll be here tomorrow.'

When Christine arrived the next afternoon the weather had veered round and was bright and sunny.

'I've been picking up conkers,' she said. 'Look!'

She held out her hand to reveal a smooth brown horse chestnut.

'The trees in the drive are beautiful. Do you want to go out, darling? I could push you as far as the gate and back.'

He agreed, glad that there would be some occupation during her visit which would keep her from running into the surgeon and hearing the news that Larry wanted to keep from her. Glad, too, that if they were out of the ward she wouldn't see the untouched state of the basket he had had to neglect.

The autumn sunshine was brilliant, with a more mellow glow than it had had in the summer. The sky overhead was deep blue, with a soft haze in the distance, the grass was a dark, lush green, the flat-fingered leaves of the horse chestnut trees were rust and gold. Christine pushed the chair along the gravel drive and then over a grassy track to a small, secluded garden surrounded on three sides by a hedge. There were late roses in the hedge, dropping their crimson petals on the grass.

'Pouf! I'm out of condition,' Christine said. 'I wonder if the grass is damp? Or would it tip up your chair if I sat on the step of your chair?'

'Sit on my lap.'

'Darling, do you think I should?'

'I can't see why not.'

Very gingerly, she lowered herself on to his motionless knees, turning sideways towards him. His arms went round her and they held one another closely.

'Oh, that's lovely!' Christine said. 'Hold me tight, Larry. I'm not hurting you, am I?'

'No, it's wonderful to have my arms round you again.'

They kissed with a passion that had never been possible in the confinement of the hospital ward.

'The sooner I have you at home and in my own care the better,' Christine murmured. 'Darling, you do see, don't you, that everything will be all right between us?'

'I can see that you believe it,' Larry said.

She was wearing her tweed skirt and the blue jumper, with a jacket over the top. He put his hands under the bottom of the jumper and touched the taut smooth flesh of her waist. Christine gasped and clung to him convulsively for a moment.

'Goodness, what cold hands,' she said. 'Darling, I don't want to break this up, but I really think I ought to take you back inside.'

He nodded and she got up and gave herself a little shake, smoothing down her skirt and jumper. She saw that he was watching her and wrinkled her nose in a small, conspiratorial smile. It was disappointing that he didn't respond, but she felt that they had made such strides forward that afternoon that his abrupt change of mood was of minor importance.

She took him back inside, but not to the ward. 'I'll watch you go from the window,' Larry said and she left him there, on the fifth floor, by the open window.

He sat and waited for her to come into sight below. When she did, she turned to look up at him and wave. He lifted his hand in response and watched her as she walked away, tall and vigorous and healthy, with her swinging stride and the sunlight glinting on her hair.

'My lovely girl,' he said.

Only the right-hand side of the window was open. The left-hand side was secured by a bolt at floor level. He bent down, fumbling with his awkward fingers, and pulled it up, setting both parts of the window wide open. He sat for a moment, looking at the wrought iron parapet. Then he took away the blanket that covered his legs so that it should not impede him. He looked round quickly. Everything depended now on no-one coming into the corridor. With his hands on the wheels he backed his chair away, then set it in motion forward, as hard and as fast as he could.

He took his hands away and lifted them in the air, the wheelchair crashed through the open window, hit the low parapet and he was pitched forward. For one second he thought he had misjudged it and in that moment he tried to save himself. His hands scrabbled at the smooth, black-painted ironwork, but their grasp was not sufficiently strong to hold him. He was hanging over the edge of the barrier, caught at knee level between it and the chair. Then the wheels of the chair spun round on the slippery surface. It tilted and he was free and falling.

Christine, walking fast, had reached the lodge gates. She looked back over her shoulder, but the hospital was almost hidden by the trees in the drive. The low rays of the autumn sunset turned the windows of the upper floors to sheets of molten gold. She turned away and walked on.

Chapter Eleven

There was an inquest. Christine gave evidence. In a dull, monotonous voice she told of her last visit to Larry. She spoke of their plans for the future. She said he had been cheerful. She described how he had asked her to leave him by the open window so that he could watch her go and how she had turned back and waved to him. In response to a question she said that she was quite sure that only one half of the long window had been open.

The finding was merciful. Although it could not be known for certain, it seemed as if Squadron Leader Telford had opened the second half of the window and leaned out to watch his wife walking down the drive, had overbalanced and fallen. He had tried to save himself: the black paint below his finger nails was evidence of that. It was an accidental death.

Christine might have believed it if it hadn't been for the evidence dragged out of a reluctant Mr Hudson. He didn't volunteer the information, but in response to a question he was forced to disclose that there had been a further deterioration in his patient's condition which called for a fresh opinion.

It was a piece of evidence that might have been taken either of two ways. The Coroner directed one piercing look at the surgeon and then said flatly: 'This loss of gripping ability in his hands would have made it more difficult for him to grasp the iron railing?'

'Unfortunately, yes.'

Nothing in the faces of the two men betrayed that a difficult moment had been passed. There was an exclamation of alarm from the body of the courtroom, a chair scraped along the floor and Christine slumped forward in a dead faint. In the confusion that followed, with everyone trying to get to her to help, the Coroner signed to the surgeon to step down. By the time he reached Christine's side she was already recovering consciousness. He bent over her and she looked straight up into his eyes. Neither of them spoke, but in that one long look he saw that both of them knew the truth. Christine's eyes closed again and two slow tears ran down her cheeks.

She never spoke of her knowledge to anyone. She spent a fortnight at home, not ill, but obviously unfit to return to duty, followed by a desperately unhappy week with Larry's parents.

They were shattered by their son's death. Both of them suddenly looked old. Colonel Telford in particular had withdrawn into a world in which he appeared to hear and feel nothing. Remote and silent, he seemed to be constantly listening to an inner voice which had more reality for him than the world outside. Mrs Telford, her small, round face lined with sadness, was more worried about him than about herself.

'I feel as if I'd lost him as well as Larry,' she said.

Christine schooled herself to listen for a week to Mrs Telford's memories of Larry, to looking at photographs of him as a baby, as a schoolboy, as a young officer. Talking about him was the only consolation his mother had left and she seemed to believe that it would help Christine too. But some of the things she said grated on Christine's raw nerves until she could have screamed out loud.

'I hope you won't mind my saying it, dear, but I do regret that you never had a child. If I had a grandchild, something of his to remember him by, I wouldn't feel as if it had been such a terrible waste.'

'You had him for longer than I did,' Christine said through stiff lips. 'At least you can look back to when he was a child himself.'

'Yes dear, that's true. I wish I could say it helped, but it doesn't. If only you had had a baby.'

'It was Larry's decision not to bring a child into the world until after the war.'

'Was it?'

To Christine it sounded almost as if Mrs Telford did not believe her.

Even harder to bear was Mrs Telford's attempt to persuade herself that Larry's death had been for the best.

'It *was* a merciful release,' she said, trying to convince herself. 'What would his life have been, poor boy? Helpless, tied to a wheelchair. Truly, sometimes I feel ashamed of wishing him back.'

'I would have looked after him,' Christine said.

'Yes, you've been wonderful all along. But it would have been hard on Larry, seeing you wasting your life.'

'That was what he thought,' Christine said. 'He didn't believe I could bear it, but I would have done.'

It was a relief to be able to go back to her work in the WAAF. She had asked to be posted to a different station, away from the place where she had served all through their scrappy courtship and the painful separations of their married life. At the end of her leave she was sent to the Isle of Wight. She had had enough of reminders of Larry. Deliberately, she cut herself off from her family and friends.

It was Michael who heard the first real news of her. He had gone to London to meet Lucy. He'd been hoping for an evening alone with her, but he was resigned by now to the fact that Lucy was a popular girl, not only because of her charm and good looks, which seemed to attract every one of the American boys who swarmed round her, but also for the sweet, warm sympathy that made it possible for her to sit and listen to anyone's troubles.

'We're invited to a party,' she told him that evening.

'Must we go?'

' 'Fraid so. It's an engagement party and the poor kids have been through so much, trying to get together, I feel I must go along and wish them well.'

She saw that he was looking unenthusiastic and added: 'They're all dying to meet you – the Battle of Britain hero.'

A look of acute pain crossed Michael's face. 'I can see I'm in for a wow of an evening,' he said, but he went because at least he would be with Lucy and with any luck he would be able to coax her into leaving early.

It was, he had to admit, a good party. The American drink flowed freely, there was music and dancing and a lot of laughter. Michael wondered whether Lucy realized that there was a limit to the amount of dancing he could do with his damaged leg. It was beginning to ache abominably, but nothing would make him admit that he was not able to keep going with the best of them. He retired momentarily to a corner, absentmindedly accepted another drink though vaguely conscious that he'd had enough already, and watched while Lucy performed energetically with a GI who appeared to be made out of india-rubber. Out of uniform, wearing something silky in cherry red with a pleated skirt that revealed her legs as he swung her round, she was worth watching.

'Great party,' another GI at Michael's side said. He was flushed and dishevelled, his jacket off, his shirt open at the neck.

'Your English girls sure know how to cut loose when they get going.'

Obviously he meant it as a compliment. Michael smiled stiffly and said nothing.

'Last party I was at was over on the Isle of Wight – say, that's a real pretty place. At least I guess it would be in peacetime. I met a girl there – say, did that little chick show me a good time!'

Michael began to see some justice in the complaints he'd heard about the GI's running off with all the girls. Like that one with Lucy, for instance.

'I wish I could get the luck to be posted near that baby,' the GI said yearningly. 'One of those cool blondes who really sizzle when you get them wound up. What a doll that Christine was. A widow, and a merry one all right. You know what I mean?'

'In the WAAF?' Michael asked. His hand was clenched white around his glass.

'That's right,' the GI said in surprise. 'Chris Telford. You don't mean to say you know her, too? I didn't think she was that famous. Or should I say notorious?'

He laughed, too drunk to see that he was giving offence. Michael put down his glass. He was almost sick with anger, seething with a need to knock this oaf across the middle of the crowded room. He said:

'Come outside with me for a minute.'

The party was being held in a second floor flat. On the landing it was dark and quiet. The American followed Michael unsuspectingly, stumbling as the colder air reached him.

'The girl you met on the Isle of Wight was my sister,' Michael said. 'Take back what you said or I'll knock you into the middle of next week.'

'Well, gee, I'm sorry,' the GI said, totally taken aback. 'All I said was she showed me a good time.'

'You implied . . . Chris isn't like that. She's a decent kid. She took a hard knock when her husband died. Maybe she's been trying too hard to forget, but that doesn't mean she's easy game.'

The GI had recovered from his surprise and was turning belligerent. 'You could have fooled me. I thought she was anyone's girl,' he drawled.

Michael hit him. For one second he felt nothing but wholehearted satisfaction as the American's head jerked, he fell back against the wall and then slid down it to sit in a dazed huddle on the floor. And then Michael realized that he'd caused exactly the kind of scene he'd meant to avoid.

The door of the flat opened and a stream of light lit up the two men. Lucy stood in the doorway.

'Michael, what on earth's going on?' she demanded.

'He said things about Christine and I knocked him down.'

Lucy caught hold of the American boy's arm as he scrambled, swaying, to his feet.

'Let me get at him! I'll tear him apart,' he said.

'Oh, no you won't! Jerry, I won't have it. This is a party and I'm not going to let you spoil it.'

'He started it!'

'No, I didn't,' Michael retorted. 'It was your dirty mouth.'

'I think you've both had too much to drink,' Lucy snapped as the American lunged at Michael. 'Jerry, go back inside. Michael, I'm taking you away.'

'He hit me when I wasn't even looking,' Jerry growled.

'I did,' Michael admitted. 'Oh, hell! I'm sorry.'

He held out his hand, not very hopefully, but after a

moment's hesitation and a nudge from Lucy the GI just touched it and then went back to the party.

'I'm thoroughly ashamed of you,' Lucy said to Michael. 'Get your coat and we'll go and have a cup of coffee somewhere.'

In spite of her annoyance, when she got him away and they were sitting opposite one another in a dimly lit café she couldn't help feeling amusement at the mixture of sheepishness and pride in his expression.

'You're trying not to feel pleased with yourself,' she said. 'I know you, Michael Brookfield.'

'He was bigger than me.'

'What was it all about? Christine, you said?'

He was hesitant at first, but eventually it all came out, everything the GI had said and implied, Michael's own uneasiness about his sister.

'It's not a bit like Christine,' he concluded.

'Yes, it is,' Lucy said. 'It's exactly like Christine. You know how she always throws herself headlong into everything. Surely you remember the way she was with Gunther? I certainly do. And her total devotion to Larry when he was injured. She's wholehearted about everything she does. If she's decided to go to the devil then, being Christine, she'll sure go the whole hog.'

'So what's a blundering brother to do? A lecture from me isn't going to turn her into a plaster saint.'

'No, but the day will come when she'll suddenly hate herself and then she'll be even more unhappy. I guess the first thing is to stop her cutting herself off from us all. Got any leave to come, Michael?'

'I've got forty-eight hours due before the next course starts, but if you're suggesting I should go and see her . . . I don't know, Lucy. I just wouldn't know what to say to her.'

'I'd come with you.'

She chuckled at the look of stunned disbelief on his face.

'If you'd like to have me along, that is,' she said.

'You'd spend your leave with me on the Isle of Wight?'

'Strictly on a mission of mercy. Separate rooms and no hanky-panky, Michael Brookfield.'

'That's shattered my hopes,' he said. He stretched out his hand and squeezed hers tightly. 'Thanks, Lucy. It'll make all the difference. Though I still don't know what you plan to do for Christine.'

'I don't either, but at least we can show we care, that she's not alone, even though she's trying her darndest to be just that.'

It was not a particularly pleasant trip in the middle of winter, nor did Christine seem pleased to see them when they arrived.

'I can't think what possessed you to visit this dead-and-alive hole,' she said.

'I've always wanted to see the Isle of Wight,' Lucy said.

'If you wanted to spend a weekend together there must be more convenient spots.'

She made it sound offensive, but Lucy remained placid.

'We wanted to see you, too.'

'To find out how I'm taking my widowhood? I'm managing very nicely, thank you.'

She smiled with a glittering gaiety that deceived neither Michael nor Lucy. She had changed, there was no doubt about that. She was thinner and she looked remarkably beautiful. Before, she had had the attraction of youth and good health, lovely colouring and clear skin. Now, the hollows in her cheeks revealed her fine facial bone structure, her eyes looked larger and she had developed the angular body and stalking grace of a hunting cat.

She had taken up smoking and her long-fingered hands tapped out one cigarette only to light another immediately. There was something artificial about her: her voice was too high and she had a way of looking every man in the face with a bold and challenging stare which certainly attracted attention.

It was only Lucy's presence that kept Michael from telling his sister, in no uncertain terms what he thought of her, but he had the sense to realize, once he had got over his first irritation, that his criticisms would have been fatal.

Lucy persisted in treating everything as perfectly normal. She chatted easily about seeing their parents, about the latest news she'd had of Jimmy, about the show she'd seen in London recently – not with him, Michael noted jealously. Slowly, Christine began to relax. She laughed less frequently and even asked about Lucy's own parents.

Later, Michael said to Lucy: 'We've come on a wild goose chase, haven't we? There's nothing wrong with Christine, except that she's still getting over the shock of Larry's death.'

'There's more to it than that,' Lucy said. 'She's terribly unhappy. I'll try to get her to talk to me, but I'm not sure she will.'

'That American friend of yours, do you think he was exaggerating?'

'No, I guess she slept with him all right.' Lucy's nose wrinkled thoughtfully. 'I only wish I could believe she enjoyed it. Jerry's a nice enough boy in his way and I guess he might be real good in bed in a wham-bang kind of way, so perhaps Christine got something out of it. But if she did it didn't last and she's back to feeling rotten again, and maybe guilty too, which would make it worse.'

'My hair is rising on my scalp in horror,' Michael said. 'Where did you find out about such things, young Lucy?'

Lucy laughed, that warm, amused chuckle that made him feel weak at the knees.

'Now there's a question you must never ask,' she said. 'It's none of your business, Mike.'

It might be none of his business, but it kept him awake for hours. She was only a couple of doors away from him and if he had known the answers to the questions that raced round his mind he might have nerved himself to go and tap on her door. Had she? Did she? Come to that, most important of all, would she – with him? Little Lucy. Sweet Lucy. Damn her, he could cheerfully wring her neck.

Lucy was just as aware of Michael's nearness as he was of hers and she smiled to herself as she got ready for bed. Dear Michael, after all these years he was beginning to take her seriously at last. She was not at all sure what she would have done if she had heard his hand on her door. She half expected it and was quite unable to make up her mind whether she was glad or sorry when he stuck to their bargain and didn't come near her.

She, too, lay awake, but she was more occupied with thoughts of Christine. Lucy had seen something which Michael had apparently missed, the look Christine had given them when they had left her, a long, desolate look which said to Lucy as clearly as if the words had been spoken out loud: 'Help me.'

She managed to get Christine on her own the next day. Christine wandered into their hotel and announced that she had a couple of hours free.

'Michael's visiting some Squadron Leader he knows on your station,' Lucy said. 'Stay and have some tea with me.'

'Tea? Oh, yes, all right. I suppose it's a bit early for a drink.'

'If you can get a drink at four o'clock in the afternoon you must know things about the British licensing hours that I don't,' Lucy remarked.

The tea came and there was something about the early darkness, the cold, wet day outside, the comfort of the warm aromatic drink that encouraged confidences.

'Are you and Michael lovers?' Christine asked with an abruptness she would never have used in the past.

'Not yet. I'm planning on marrying him.'

She'd surprised Christine who looked genuinely amused as she asked: 'Does he know?'

'He's a mite slow on the uptake. I've always been in love with him, ever since I can remember. The time is coming when he's either got to love me back or else I'm going to have to wrench myself free and find someone else.'

'It was always Michael for you,' Christine said. 'I remember it from way back. Could you make do with someone else?'

'It wouldn't be the same, but if I was sure it was quite hopeless I'd try to make myself forget him – as you did with Gunther.'

She wasn't prepared for the way Christine flinched and said: 'Don't talk about him.'

'Honey, I'm sorry. I didn't think, after all this time, it would hurt you to talk about him.'

'You don't know . . .'

As Christine turned her head away, Lucy saw that she was biting her lips to fight back tears. It bewildered her, but with an instinctive understanding of Christine's need to talk, she said: 'Tell me, Chris, tell me what's bothering you so much.'

'I have dreams,' Christine said; her voice was low and she seemed to have difficulty in finding the words. 'Terrible dreams, Lucy – you wouldn't understand, if I told you . . .'

'Erotic dreams,' Lucy said.

'How on earth did you know? Yes. And it's Gunther, always Gunther. I want it to be Larry. It wouldn't seem so bad if it were him. But he won't come back to me, I can't make him come back. It's always Gunther, and he's enormous and terrible, like a great blond giant. Why does he haunt me like this? Why? I did love Larry best, I *did*!'

She was crying wildly and Lucy went and sat beside her on the windowseat and put an arm round her.

'Poor Chris. Don't stop crying, honey. I guess it's just as well to let it all come out. I don't know why you should dream about Gunther except that perhaps it hurts less than dreaming about Larry. Because Gunther's further away in the past. It may seem wicked, but maybe you're protecting yourself by thinking of him instead of Larry.'

'I don't think so. I don't know.'

'Did Larry know about Gunther?'

'Yes, and he found it hard to accept.'

'And you felt guilty? There's that, too. A sort of punishment you're inflicting on yourself because something you did hurt someone you loved, who died.'

Christine slowly raised her head. She stopped crying and nodded.

'Here I am talking like an amateur psychiatrist,' Lucy said apologetically. 'Why don't you take professional advice?'

'A head shrinker? That's very American.'

'I am American. What's wrong about asking for help? You can't go on the way you are. Poor Christine. I guess sex is sort of a tricky thing to handle. Maybe I'd better not start.'

'Haven't you? How have you managed to stave off all those hotblooded American boys?'

217

'By thinking about Michael. Have some more tea, Christine.'

She poured away the cold tea and gave her a fresh cup. Then she said: 'There's something else, isn't there? It's not just the bad dreams.'

Christine was silent for a long time, but at last she said in a low voice: 'Larry killed himself.'

Lucy felt a cold chill down her back, but she said firmly: 'You can't be sure of that, Chris.'

'I *know*. He believed he was going to become even more helpless and he kept it from me. Why? Because he'd made up his mind what he was going to do. I ought to have guessed there was something wrong. That last day, he was so sweet and loving. He was saying goodbye and I just walked away and left him. It meant I'd failed in everything I'd tried to tell him and show him. He didn't believe I loved him enough.'

'Then the failure was his, not yours.'

Christine turned haunted, tearstained eyes on her. 'Why couldn't I convince him?'

Lucy didn't know what to say. She felt out of her depth. Her heart aching and her eyes full of tears, she searched for words. 'It would be very hard to accept that kind of sacrifice unless you were sure you were worth it. If Larry had been the kind of person who took it for granted that you'd give up everything for him would you have felt quite the same about him?'

She thought she might have struck the right note when Christine agreed: 'Perhaps not.'

'I wish I'd met him,' Lucy said. 'Michael admired him enormously, I know. He enjoyed serving under him.'

'I had a lot of letters after he died all saying much the same thing. He was rather a man's man, I think. Women were something of a mystery to him.'

'Which is maybe why he didn't understand your feelings about his helplessness,' Lucy pointed out gently. 'If he did take his own life it may have been wrong, but it showed a lot of courage. It seems sort of wrong for such an act of bravery to be wasted because you won't accept it. Are you happy about the way you're living?'

'That's why you and Michael are here, isn't it? To try and reform me.'

'Michael met someone who spoke about you as a good-time girl. Mike blew his top. As for me, I'd say good luck to you if I thought you were happy, but you're not, are you?'

Christine shook her head. 'It's difficult to break out of the groove once you've got into it. Too much to drink every night, sex when it's available, silly jokes and dirty talk – and always at the back of your mind the feeling that it isn't worth it.'

'I don't think you really needed a visit from Michael and me. You were already beginning to snap out of it.'

'It's been a help, talking to you. I haven't made any women friends here. Naturally enough, I suppose. I've been on the prowl after their boyfriends.' She glanced at Lucy. 'You aren't shocked?'

Lucy shook her head and Christine suddenly laughed. 'You ought to be,' she said. 'You're a gem, Lucy, but we haven't found any answers, have we? My life seems to ricochet from one crisis to another and I just end up more and more battered.'

They parted affectionately. As Christine had said, nothing had been settled, and yet she felt better. The kaleidoscope had been given a thorough shake and she saw the world through different colours.

Lucy and Michael were alone that evening. She told him about Christine's conviction that Larry had committed suicide, but not about the bad dreams: that was something private.

'I always suspected it,' Michael admitted. 'He had more courage than I would have had.'

'Did you say so to Christine?'

'Of course not.'

'Why not? If you'd brought it out in the open and talked about it perhaps the poor girl wouldn't have been so haunted. She blames herself. Can you imagine that? After all she did for him?'

'Poor kid. Did you get her to admit that she's making a fool of herself now?'

'We didn't put it quite like that. She'll be all right. This bad time will pass.'

'You're quite a girl, Lucy. I don't know why I didn't see it years ago.'

'You're as blind as a bat,' Lucy said placidly.

'Not quite that. But if we're talking about my actual sight, I do have a bit of a disability. I don't wear my specs if I can help it, but I need them.'

He played with the food on his plate and didn't look at her. 'I can understand how Larry felt about keeping a girl tied to him. I'm not as badly handicapped as he was, but I'm no oil painting even after the surgeons have done their best for me, and the scars you haven't seen are even worse.'

'Are you going to show them to me?' Lucy asked with interest.

Michael looked up with a faint, rueful grin on his face. 'I'd like to. I'm in love with you. Hopelessly, head over heels. In spite of which, I don't think I have the slightest right to ask you to marry me.'

Nothing about Lucy's calmly attentive face betrayed the fact that her heart was beating so fast that she was afraid it would choke her.

'Is that a sneaky way of getting me to go to bed with you without having to marry me?' she asked.

'No, it's not! I'm being high-minded and self-sacrificing.'

'And a downright idiot. OK, so I'll sleep with you tonight and see if I can bear the sight of your horrible disfigured body.'

The look of shock on his face made her laugh, but Michael recovered himself and said: 'It's the rest of your life I want, not one night in a hotel bedroom.'

'For a man who doesn't intend getting married that comes mighty near a proposal. I think I'll take you up on it. I'll marry you.'

'No! Yes . . . Lucy, you *can't*.'

'I can, you know. Michael, I've been in love with you since the summer of 1938. If you really love me then I'm certainly not going to let you go. We'll get married.'

'When?'

'That's better. You look quite eager.'

'Eager! I'm beside myself. I never meant this to happen.'

'Liar!'

Lucy smiled at him with brilliant happiness, her dark eyes glowing with the love she could at last let him see.

Michael pushed back his chair. 'Let's get out of here,' he said urgently. 'I never bargained on getting engaged in full view of a room full of people.'

Since most of the residents were in the dining room they had the hallway at the foot of the stairs to themselves for a few minutes. Michael pushed back the soft hair from Lucy's forehead with hands that were not quite steady.

'Darling Lucy. You wonderful girl,' he said.

They had kissed before, but this was different. They clung to one another in a delirium of love, delighting in their newness to one another.

When they drew apart Lucy looked up at him with shy, bemused eyes, knowing that she had betrayed the passion that consumed her, and Michael was smiling all over his face because he recognized a desire that equalled his own.

'Why has it taken me all these years to realize I love you?' he asked. 'It didn't occur to me, not until you suddenly turned up looking like a million dollars and I saw the way every other man looked at you. I've been out of my mind, wanting you, struggling with my conscience because I wasn't sure I had any right to try to make you love me . . .'

Lucy put her hand on his lips. 'To me you're the most wonderful man in the world and I love you with all my heart. I always have and I always will.'

Michael turned his lips against the soft pink palm of her hand. 'Bless you, my darling. Lucy, would you . . . would you really like a preview of my hideous scars?'

She smiled at him, radiant with love. 'Yes, my darling,' she said. 'Yes.'

Chapter Twelve

General Obermann's hint of a plot against Hitler took longer to explode into action than Elsa had anticipated. She waited, holed up like a tiny mouse, she thought plaintively, all through the devastating winter of 1943 and into the spring of 1944. She had expected to be bored, had even wondered guiltily whether she would be able to bear the monotony of her days with Gunther's mother without breaking into some wild and foolish escapade, but the reality proved so grim, the struggle to survive so all-demanding that she had little time or energy for the diversions she had once believed vital to her existence. No word came from her father, she was cut off from the sources which had once fed her with gossip and rumours, she was as dependent as the ordinary men and women of Berlin on the official news, which was given out with a spurious optimism that struck a chill to Elsa's heart.

The dreary months were enlivened only once by a brief visit from Gunther in March during which they frightened Frau Hofmeyer by refusing to sleep in an air raid shelter, preferring to risk sudden death for the sake of the privacy of their tumultuous bed.

'Darling, sometimes I'm not sure whether it's a bomb exploding or me,' Elsa remarked.

'You're as wonderful as ever. Have you missed me?' Gunther demanded.

'Mm. Missed you, missed you, missed you. Horrible war, is it going on for ever?'

'It'll go on until the British and Americans try to open the Western Front. If we can manage to beat them back and hold off the Russians as well then we might get them to talk about peace terms.'

'Are you optimistic?'

'There's still a chance of victory, Elsa. Our men are magnificent fighters, and we have wonderful technical resources. Even I was surprised . . .'

His voice trailed away and Elsa raised herself on her elbow to look down at him and ask: 'You're pleased about something, aren't you? Tell me.'

It was hardly a secret, with the new twin-jet Messerschmitts already going into production, and so he told her that he'd been selected for training to fly the new aircraft.

'The speed! It's unbelievable. I'm thrilled about it, I admit. I don't think the other side have anything to touch us. If only we'd had them sooner!'

It was July before the Messerschmitt 262s were in operation with the *Luftwaffe* and by that time it was, as Gunther had always feared, too late.

In April, a month after Gunther had gone back to his unit, the Germans launched a strong counter-offensive against the Russians, releasing eighteen divisions of the 1st Panzer Army, which had been trapped east of the Dniester, but even successes like this could not stem the inexorable tide of the Russian advance for long. By 17th April the Russian army had reached Sevastopel and there they took 37,000 prisoners, men who could ill be spared from the depleted forces of the German Army. In spite of this there were extensive tank battles in May which beat back the Russians and were hailed as a great German victory.

At the beginning of June the Führer was staying at his mountain retreat in Obersalzburg. An invasion by the Western Allies was expected that summer. It must come soon or the invaders would lose the advantage of the good weather. The High Command had argued about the possible landing place, spending long hours studying the state of the tides, trying to estimate the probable date. It must be imminent, on that everyone agreed. But when would it be?

The morning of 6th June dawned rough and windy and the belief was that no invasion would take place when weather conditions in the English Channel were so unfavourable, but early in the day news came through which no-one on Hitler's staff wanted to give him.

'The Führer has given orders that he is not to be disturbed,' a nervous *aide* said.

The message was passed from hand to hand.

'What does Rommel say?' an SS officer asked.

'The Feldmarschall is away from Normandy, visiting his wife: it's her birthday.'

By the time Hitler was in possession of the facts the Allied beach-head on the Normandy coast was established. North-west of Paris the Panzer Corps, which might have been thrown in to stiffen the German defences if Feldmarschall Rommel had been able to get the Führer's permission in time, stood by and waited for orders which did not come.

'It's his damned insistence on being Commander-in-Chief and keeping control of everything that drives me to despair,' General Obermann said to the Chief of Staff of the Reserve Army, Colonel Claus Graf von Stauffenberg, who shared his view of the Führer as a war leader. 'Why in God's name can't he see the futility of holding a defensive position in the far West? Why not retreat to a line which could be held strongly while our forces are rallied for a counter-offensive?'

' "Retreat" is a word Adolph Hitler refuses to acknowledge,' Colonel von Stauffenberg said. 'He insists we maintain our positions no matter the cost until the new V-weapon – the flying bomb – is ready. According to him it's going to bring the British population to its knees and demoralize the armed forces.'

The flying bombs were despatched, not against military targets but against the civilian population, and they did not have the expected effect. The Allied forces were winning ground in Normandy. Hitler sacked Feldmarschall von Runstedt and replaced him by a Commander from the Eastern Front, Feldmarschall von Kluges, whose initial optimism, which was pleasing to the Führer, soon gave way to a more sober assessment of the situation which did not suit his ideas at all.

On 20th July Colonel von Stauffenberg attended a military conference at the Führer's headquarters in Rastenburg, East

Prussia. Unobtrusively, he placed a briefcase beneath the map table where Hitler liked to stand to confer with his advisers. When Colonel von Stauffenberg left the room the briefcase remained behind. A few minutes after his departure the time bomb inside the case exploded. Hitler survived.

The news of the failed coup came to Elsa over the radio as she listened with Frau Hofmeyer. The older woman exclaimed in horror at an attempt being made on the Führer's life, since she, like the majority of her fellow-countrymen, still clung to the belief that without him they were doomed. Elsa choked back her bitter fury and retreated to her own room. Once she was alone, she paced up and down, consumed with rage.

'Incompetent, stupid, bungling idiots,' she muttered.

The thought of her father was like a knife in her heart. How deeply was he implicated? How far was he suspected? It was only with that thought that fear for herself began to break through her anger. He had told her to separate herself from him and she had done so. Would it be sufficient to have had no contact with him for a year? Surely no-one could suspect her of having any part in the plot?

She lived in suspense for days. There were reports of a purge of dissident *Wehrmacht* officers, but no mention was made of General Obermann. Elsa began to wonder whether her father had been successful in covering his tracks.

She had taken it on herself to do most of the shopping since she had begun to live with Frau Hofmeyer. It was an exacting business, touring the shops to find sufficient food from their depleted stocks, and Elsa seemed to be more successful than Frau Hofmeyer, although it was Lotte who made occasional sorties into the country and returned with precious vegetables, sometimes even an egg or two, or a piece of meat. If Frau Hofmeyer guessed that these visits and Elsa's small triumphs were financed out of Elsa's pocket she said nothing. Elsa had no scruples about getting what she could where she could. In theory Frau Hofmeyer was against the *Schwarzmarkt*, but that didn't stop her from exclaiming in pleasure at the sight of a good fresh cabbage and a piece of salt pork when Elsa brought them in.

'You have a visitor, my dear,' she said, laying out the food on the kitchen table. 'I asked him to wait in the sitting room since I knew you wouldn't be long. An officer in the SS.' She glanced at Elsa and it was obvious that the visit had made her nervous. 'He said he knew you before your marriage. Perhaps he has news of your father, or even a message from him. It does distress me, you know, that you have never been reconciled to him. It isn't right. Please, Elsa, promise me that you won't be too proud to make up the quarrel if you're given the chance.'

Elsa nodded. Her throat was so dry for the moment she could not speak. She took her time about going to meet her visitor, removing her jacket, running a comb through her hair. Her eyes looked enormous and very frightened as she looked into the mirror, her cheeks were white. She pinched them hard with her fingers to give herself some colour and then, with her head held high, she went through into the sitting room.

For a moment she did not recognize the tall, thin man in his black uniform who was standing looking out of the window at the piles of rubble in the street below, then he turned round and she exclaimed: 'Why, it's Kurt! Frau Hofmeyer didn't give me your name. How pleasant to see you again, Kurt.'

Kurt Waldenheim's face did not reflect the pleasure she was trying so hard to convey.

'I have bad news for you,' he said. 'Your father is dead.'

Elsa closed her eyes, put a hand to her head and collapsed into the nearest chair. Kurt made no move to help her.

'Was he killed in action?' Elsa asked in a whisper.

'No. He died by his own hand. He swallowed a poison capsule.'

The fear that Elsa had been carrying inside her grew more intense. She felt it like a monstrous growth, threatening to choke the life out of her. She managed to speak a few words of mechanical protest.

'Oh, no! I can't believe it! Why should he do such a thing?'

'Come now, Elsa. You must have heard that the Gestapo has been stamping out the cells of disloyalty which have been uncovered following the attempt on the Führer's life. Your father, knowing his guilt, didn't wait to be arrested.'

'My father was never disloyal, never!'

'Then why not stay alive? He was certainly implicated. We regret not having had the chance to treat him in the same way as the other traitors. They've been hanged with piano wire.'

'No death is too dreadful for a traitor,' Elsa said automatically.

'The Führer agrees with you. He had a film made of the deaths and takes great satisfaction in watching it.'

A spasm of nausea contorted Elsa's face. To conceal it she put her head down in her hands.

'No matter what he may have done I can't help grieving for my father,' she said.

'Your feeling does credit to your heart, if not your head.'

His cold black eyes rested for a moment on that glossy brown head, bent over her hands, and he ran his tongue over his lips.

'The second part of the investigation has begun. The families and close intimates of the guilty men are being arrested.'

Elsa shuddered and Kurt went on in a silky whisper: 'It could be your turn next.'

She forced herself to look him in the face.

'I've done nothing. I quarrelled with my father when I married and I've seen nothing of him for more than a year.'

'Nevertheless, I think you will be taken into custody. If you have nothing to hide you won't be afraid of being questioned.'

In spite of the sickness that threatened to overwhelm her Elsa managed a small, ironic smile. 'Being questioned by the Gestapo isn't pleasant for the guilty or the innocent. I can't believe it will be necessary in my case. No-one could possibly believe I had a hand in the plot against Hitler. You know how little interest I always took in politics.'

'I know you have a mischievous tongue and in the past you were certainly not discreet. I can remember hearing you refer to Reichsmarschall Göring as a fat old fool.'

'Hardly evidence of deep conspiracy, darling.'

He didn't answer. Was there a chance she could win him over to her side?'

'Why did you come here today, Kurt? To warn me?'

'Perhaps.'

'We were good friends once.'

227

She was manoeuvring, seeking an advantage, and she thought she might have gained one when he replied. 'More than that. I was once foolish enough to believe myself in love with you.'

The fact that he had spoken of his earlier feelings gave Elsa hope. She pushed the thought of her father's death resolutely to the back of her mind and said: 'Poor Kurt! Did I flirt with you? What a naughty girl I was. But you were so handsome in that black uniform of yours.'

He went to her and put his hand round her throat, forcing her head back so that he could stare down into her face.

'You played with me, but you're not going to do that now. As the close relative of a guilty man you're likely to be arrested at any moment. If the Gestapo believe you to have had any knowledge of the plot nothing I can do will save you. However, I'm prepared to let it be known in the right quarters that I believe you to be innocent.'

'That's good of you,' she whispered, but she was terrified by the black, glittering hate in his eyes.

'There's a price to be paid.'

His hand moved down over her throat to her breast and she winced as his fingers closed over the soft flesh. 'Give me what I want, what I've always wanted from you, Elsa Obermann, and I'll save you from the hands of the Gestapo.'

She wasted no time in pretending to misunderstand him, and even succeeded in hiding the repulsion that filled her at the thought of submitting to him. She had begun to expect a proposition like this from the moment he had touched her throat.

She asked: 'If I do what you want how do I know that you won't denounce me afterwards?'

He laughed and his fingers kneaded into her breast. 'You can't. On the other hand, if you refuse you can be quite sure that your next caller will be from the Gestapo.'

'Are you still in love with me?' she asked.

His hand dropped away. 'I've long since got over that foolishness. I want to humiliate you, to pay you out for playing with me. I'm going to treat you like the whore you've always been and when it's over I'll pay you with your life – for what it's worth.'

She still did not answer him and he went on softly: 'The Führer is haunted by this wave of disloyalty. Whole families are being arrested – brothers, sisters, wives, children. Your fine *Luftwaffe* hero won't look so good when he's been stripped of his medals and his neck is stretched by piano wire, and that mousy little woman who let me in, a few months' solitary confinement will probably finish her.

Strangely, it was the threat to Frau Hofmeyer which jerked Elsa out of the trance of fear into which she had fallen. The quiet, nervous woman had been good to her. They had become fond of one another. It was bitterly unjust that anyone so harmless should be caught in Kurt's web.

He was still standing close to her, so close that she had to tilt her head to look up into his face. Her great brown eyes were sad, her mouth drooped in a wistful line, but behind her apparent subjection her mind raced. He had said he wasn't in love with her and certainly he had no knowledge of love as Gunther understood it, but Elsa was too well versed in reading the signs to be deceived. Beneath his cool manner Kurt was in the grip of violent sexual excitement.

'It can't be here,' she said abruptly. 'If you can find a suitable meeting place, I'll come to you.'

She had thought that he might insist on receiving his blood price there and then, but Kurt had laid his plans before he came to her.

'Be at the bottom of the stairs at nine o'clock,' he said. 'I've taken a hotel room for three nights. You will go there with me tonight and stay until I say you are free to leave.'

'You were so sure I would agree?' Elsa asked.

'Oh, yes, I was sure!' He laughed and once again she sensed that he was more vulnerable than he believed.

He pulled her to her feet.

'Kiss me,' he commanded.

She raised herself on tiptoe and put her arms round his neck and he bent his head and kissed her savagely, his lascivious tongue pushing into her open mouth. He was laughing again when he released her, but she had felt his trembling in her arms and she was inwardly both exultant and contemptuous.

He left immediately and Elsa, dry-eyed and composed, went into the kitchen to tell her mother-in-law that her father was dead, that there were family affairs to be arranged and Kurt Waldenheim was going to take her away for a short time so that she could deal with them. She doubted whether the manner of General Obermann's death would be revealed to the public and so she did not enlarge on it to Frau Hofmeyer. Instead, she pretended a distress she had had no time to feel and escaped to her own room.

She locked the door behind her and then very slowly she took off all her clothes and stood in front of the mirror. She was thinner than she had once been, but she was still as supple as a willow wand, her small, high breasts were firm, her skin was the colour of smooth cream. Like a young athlete she raised her arms above her head and flexed her muscles, and as she did so she smiled, not pleasantly but with dangerous amusement.

'I have my weapons, too,' she said aloud.

She dropped her arms and shivered, not from cold but from the memory of Kurt's caresses. Then with cool deliberation she began to plan his enslavement.

Elsa kept her part of the bargain meticulously. She was ready and waiting when Kurt called for her, she went with him to the hotel room he had taken and did not flinch from his lovemaking. On the contrary, she set herself to please him as if she had in truth been the courtesan he had called her, but when it was over she said in her fluting voice: 'Say thank you nicely to Elsa.'

Kurt raised his head. 'Why should I thank you, you creature?'

'Because if you don't I shall go away and not come back again.'

He gave a short, hard laugh. 'You forget what will happen to you if you don't do what I want.'

'What use will I be to you in prison?' Her fingers moved over his buttocks and she pinched him painfully. 'Say thank you.'

He laughed again, but this time with excitement. 'Thank you,' he said with his lips against the soft curve of her shoulder.

'That's a good boy.' She turned her head so that her mouth just touched his ear. 'Do you love me, darling?' she whispered.

'No!'

Elsa took the lobe of his ear between her teeth and bit it. 'I think you do. Say it, darling.'

'No.'

He clutched her to him and she could feel that every muscle in his body was tense. She began to move against him, gentle, undulating movements that made him gasp and shiver.

'No more loving until you say it,' she said in the same quiet, reasonable voice.

'I can't, I won't!'

'You always wanted me,' she prompted him.

'Yes, always. Why did you turn away from me? You took other men, you bitch. Why not me?'

'I didn't know how much you loved me. You do, don't you?'

'I . . .'

'Well?'

'Yes. I love you. Elsa, I love you, I love you.'

There were tears running down his cheeks. He was gasping and choking with emotion, but his body had gone slack and useless.

She let him recover from the emotional storm that wracked him and then she gave him his reward, using all the tricks she knew to arouse him again.

At the end of the third day he knelt in front of her and kissed her feet. Elsa looked over his stooping head and saw their two naked bodies reflected pallidly in the dusty mirror. She smiled in scorn and disgust and knew that her reading of him had been correct. What Kurt had wanted was not conquest, but subjugation.

There was no more talk of the Gestapo and it was Elsa who dictated the course of their affair. She kept up the pretence of attending to family matters, which allowed her to meet him when she felt it was expedient. As she had expected, there was little publicity over her father's death. It was Kurt who told her that Feldmarschall von Kluge had taken the same way out after being sacked by Hitler for his failure to hold back the American breakthrough at Avranches.

She despised Kurt and used him, both to give her sexual release and to gather the news and favours she had missed during her exile from the upper echelons of power. She told Frau Hofmeyer that her 'friend' was able to give her a little extra butter or some similar luxury from time to time and implied that he did it because of his admiration for her late father, a piece of irony Elsa enjoyed.

Gunther's letters were brief and spasmodic. From what he said it seemed that he was heavily occupied fighting over France. Unless he was wounded there could be little chance of his coming on leave, for which Elsa could only be thankful.

In the East, Frieda was growing more and more anxious about the position of her school camp. There was no doubt that the Russians were uncomfortably close. The girls picked up rumours – God knows where from – of atrocities which kept them in a constant state of hysterical excitement. The little ones barely knew what rape meant, but there were girls of fourteen and fifteen amongst her pupils who knew well what was going to happen to them if all the stories they heard were true.

'I can't understand why we're not ordered home,' Fräulein Munster, Frieda's superior, said. But when Frieda urged her to act on her own initiative she said fretfully: 'You know I'm not allowed to release them without special permission.'

To Frieda's more practical turn of mind her waverings seemed foolish. The only thing she said which made sense was that possibly the Führer had some plan in mind for turning back the Russians which would make it unnecessary for the girls to go back to Berlin.

It was not that Frieda thought that Adolph Hitler knew anything about an obscure girls' camp in Czechoslovakia, but she still retained her faith in him. The news of the attempt to kill him had been a shock. She would not have believed that there could be people in personal contact with the Führer who wished him ill. It explained the setbacks the *Wehrmacht* had received. There had been corruption at the top, but now that it was known and the culprits had been removed the Army would recover its former vigour and Germany would be victorious again.

It was a comfortable line of thought, but it did not fit the facts. Germany was not victorious. The Allies were advancing in the west, the Russians were advancing in the east, the Italians were useless, Rommel had been pushed out of Africa, even the Japanese were not the support they had once seemed to be. The thought of defeat crept into Frieda's mind and would not be dislodged. It did seem by mid-September that the Allied advance had been slowed down. They had penetrated into Belgium, taken Brussels and Antwerp, but they had not been able to press on to the Rhine. The *Wehrmacht*, knowing that the Allies would accept nothing but 'unconditional surrender' fought on doggedly.

In December Hitler ordered the launching of his counter-offensive in the Ardennes. With the memory of the way the tanks had swept through France at the beginning of the war and pushed the British Army into the sea, there were grounds for hoping that this might be another turning point, but the attack failed. Hitler, distrustful of his own Generals, stuck blindly to his policy of 'no withdrawal'; the Generals could find no way of convincing him that it was a mistake to be forced into slow retreat, losing men every step of the way.

Frieda and her camp of increasingly unhappy girls stayed on in Czechoslovakia. Fräulein Munster wavered this way and that, one day persuaded that in spite of her failure to make contact with the Hitler Youth headquarters she should take the girls back to their homes, the next digging in her heels and refusing to budge. It was not until the father of one of their pupils, a badly wounded *Wehrmacht* officer on leave from the Eastern front, came to the camp to take his daughter away that Fräulein Munster was convinced of the necessity to make a move.

'Go while you can,' he said. 'Authorization? People have better things to do than worry about reproving you for showing common sense. Get the girls away. I'm taking Ilse today. I don't give a damn about permission. I've seen the Russians in action. I want my girl under my eye where I can shoot her, if necessary.'

'Shoot *her!*' Frieda cried.

He looked at her with the weary tolerance of a hardened soldier. 'Oh, yes. I'll kill her and my wife before I let them fall into the hands of those barbarians. Then I'll fight until there's only one bullet left and use it on myself.'

'Have you no hope?' she asked in a low voice.

'None.'

It was that one uncompromising word that decided Frieda, even though she told herself that she did not believe it. She called a meeting and made a speech which many of her pupils thought inspired. She spoke of their duty to the Fatherland, the necessity for every German to make a contribution towards repulsing the enemies of their country. She told them that they would return to Berlin and help in its defence, even the smallest of them, and the children, homesick and longing for the comfort of being with their mothers and fathers – those of them who still had fathers at home – were wildly excited at the prospect of going back.

They walked into town the next day followed by a rumbling cart holding their luggage. Frieda had allowed two hours for the walk and it took all of that, stumbling along the slippery road. She need not have felt anxious; the train was more than an hour late arriving. They climbed on board and found seats. The girls were excited and difficult to control. The other two teachers were almost useless. Fräulein Munster retreated to a first-class compartment saying that train journeys always gave her migraine and that was the last Frieda saw of her.

She got her charges settled at last and sank down thankfully into the seat they had been keeping for her. The train was making good speed; she began to feel more hopeful. At least they were on their way home. Once they were inside Germany Frieda felt that a great load of responsibility would be lifted off her shoulders.

The feeling of relief lasted for less than an hour. The train slowed and then stopped. They waited, but nothing happened. The girls began to grow restless, looking out of the windows to try and see what was happening. A man coming along the corridor said that he'd heard that there was damage to the line ahead.

Once the girls had started moving around it was difficult to get them back into their seats again. In desperation, Frieda started them singing some of the patriotic songs they had learned in camp. To her it sounded cheerful and reassuring; she was dismayed by the sour looks they received from some of the other passengers.

The train started up again, jerkily and very slowly. They crawled past a locomotive lying on its side, shattered and burnt out, and the girls fell silent. Frieda glanced at her watch. They were already three hours late.

She had thought that conditions would be better inside Germany, but they were worse. A petty official tried to make trouble out of their lack of authorization. But Frieda had expected this.

'By all means get out at the next station and telephone for permission from the Hitler Youth,' she said. 'I hope you'll be more successful than I've been. My pupils and I will sit on the train and wait for you.'

'The telephone lines are down,' he admitted.

'And have been for some days,' Frieda snapped. 'It astonishes me that things are not better organized. In the circumstances I can't see why you are obstructing us in this way and I shall make a point of reporting it when I reach Berlin. Do you want these girls – the mothers of the future race – to fall into the hands of the Bolsheviks?'

'They might do that yet, even in Berlin,' he muttered.

'How dare you say such a thing?' Frieda demanded. 'No invader will cross our frontier. You are a defeatist! The Gestapo should know about people like you.'

He ran his tongue over his lips. 'I'm as good a German as the next one, but you ought to have a letter of authority and well you know it, *Fräulein.*'

He went away and Frieda sat down and closed her eyes, exhausted.

The train moved even more slowly, sometimes no more than half a kilometre at a time. No fresh water was taken on. Frieda went down the corridor to the toilet and retreated again as the stench reached her. She held a handkerchief over her mouth and forced herself to go back in, her stomach heaving.

The train stopped again and all the lights went out. A whisper began to go round: 'Air raid, air raid.' There were anti-aircraft guns somewhere nearby, closer than any guns Frieda had ever heard before. The train shook with the vibrations. They could hear aeroplanes overhead and the shriek of shells and bombs. In the darkness the girls were whimpering and crying. Frieda moved amongst them as best she could in the thick, noisy darkness, trying to reassure them as they crouched on the floor amongst the grime and debris. She squatted with her arms tight round two of the youngest girls as a bomb screamed down and exploded, shattering the glass in the windows. Someone screamed and Frieda crawled over the huddled bodies to a hysterical girl. There was a long splinter of glass embedded in her cheek. By the spasmodic flashes of the guns and the flickering light of a building burning on the embankment Frieda felt for the sliver of glass. It moved under her fingers; she gritted her teeth and pulled. It came away, she thought cleanly, but the girl continued screaming. Her own hands were covered with blood and she couldn't be sure whether it was from the girl's face or from her own cut fingers. She gave the girl her handkerchief to press against the cut, held her close until she quietened and then left her; there was nothing more she could do.

The noise of the aircraft died away, the guns stopped firing. 'We'll soon be on our way,' Frieda said. But it was hours before the lines ahead of them were clear and the train could grope its way forward. The grubby, hungry, tear-stained children were too exhausted to care, when at last they reached Berlin.

Gesundbrunnen Station was like Bedlam. Nothing had prepared any of the travellers for the sight of their stricken city. They knew there had been air raids, even that they had been 'heavy' and not even the most rigorous censorship could have stopped the girls from hearing when their own homes had been hit, but now Frieda discovered that the majority of her pupils' parents were homeless. They were living in cellars, with neighbours who had been more fortunate, or in shelters built against the walls of their former homes.

Transport was the greatest difficulty, as Frieda found, tramping round holding the cold hands of pupils who had to be taken individually to the care of any relatives she could find until, at last, she was free to turn towards her own home.

Frieda had almost forgotten about the girl Gunther had married. She was so exhausted that she only had an impression on that first night of a small figure, smelling faintly of some exotic perfume, with a sweet, concerned voice, who flitted about the apartment and seemed unreal compared with the solid comfort of being with her mother and old Lotte once again.

Frieda's return presented difficulties for Elsa. Once she had recovered from her fatigue she was far more shrewd than Frau Hofmeyer and wholly disapproving of Elsa's dealings in the black market. She knew to a gramme how much food they were entitled to receive and would have stuck rigidly to the rules.

What Elsa really feared was that Frieda would denounce her connection with Kurt. On the whole she had Kurt just where she wanted him and provided she met him regularly, bullied him and made love to him, he would do anything for her. But she knew him to be unstable. He might suddenly veer round and turn against her and certainly a scene with her sister-in-law would have a most adverse effect on him.

As it happened, one of the few things Frieda approved of in her sister-in-law was her friendship with an SS officer who conformed in every way to her idea of a genuine Nazi. She wondered why he was not fighting at the Front, until it was explained to her that he was attached to the Führer's personal staff. After that her regard for him bordered on worship. When he told her that she'd done wrong in bringing her pupils home without waiting for orders she nearly wept.

Elsa approved of her action, in spite of the difficulties caused by the arrival of an extra person to feed whose ration card was not in order.

'I'm sure you were *absolutely* right,' she said. 'These silly little bureaucrats who sit in offices have no *idea*. Of course, it might have been better to take the girls further west because I suppose the Russians are likely to get here before anyone else and then we shall all be raped to death. Such a horrible prospect. I've been debating whether it would be better to put on a welcoming smile and declare open house or whether to defend my honour to the last drop. Such a difficult decision.'

'The Russians will never take Berlin,' Frieda said. 'We won't let them pass. The Führer is here with us.'

The rest of Elsa's remarks she ignored. Of course no German woman would give in willingly to the invaders. Elsa was frivolous and stupid. It was typical of Gunther to have taken such an unsuitable wife.

'Have you heard from Gunther recently?' she asked, following the trend of her own thoughts.

'A tiny note. He's well. He does seem to bear a charmed life.'

'Thank God.'

'Thank God indeed.'

She spoke with genuine fervour. Her feeling for Gunther was the nearest she had ever come to a real love and looking into the future she thought that a life with him would provide the best she could hope for once the war was over. It wouldn't be easy, but Gunther would always be strong and she thought there might be a possibility of their building a new life together. Provided, of course, that one survived.

She didn't want Gunther to find out about her affair with Kurt, yet even that could be confessed to him, if it became necessary, and Elsa thought that he would understand. He would be hurt and angry and perhaps a little disgusted, but he would not entirely condemn her and she didn't believe he would throw her out because of something that had been forced on her. The fact that subduing Kurt had become an interesting campaign in a sexual war which fed her sense of power and titillated her appetite need not be revealed to him. To Gunther she would be the unwilling victim of a depraved monster who had threatened not only Elsa herself but also her husband and her mother-in-law. Seen in that light, going to bed with Kurt became a high-minded sacrifice.

In the meantime, since Elsa cherished no such dreams as Frieda of a great German revival, one could only pray that the Americans would arrive before the Russians, although it began to seem unlikely. Absolutely impossible, Elsa thought regretfully, to start learning Russian at this point. She looked through the old schoolbooks in Gunther's bedroom and began to brush up her English.

By March no-one retained any illusions about the invincibility of the German people. The Americans had crossed the Rhine on 21st March and Montgomery's great assault took the troops serving under him across it two days later. Hitler ordered that the battle should be conducted without regard to the needs of the German people. All industrial plants, all electricity works, water works, gas works, all food and clothing stores were to be destroyed. A desert was to be created. For once his orders were disobeyed. His own end might be near, but there were still people who believed that the German nation could survive even the crushing defeat that was about to be inflicted on it. The Army and the industrial chiefs delayed putting his orders into effect until it was too late.

The devastating raids on the great German cities continued. On 31st March Halifaxes of No 6 Group of Bomber Command, the Royal Canadian Air Force Group, flew to Hamburg. Sergeant Jimmy Brookfield sat in the confined space of his rear gunner's compartment and whistled softly to himself. He was in particularly good spirits because he had had a letter from Lucy that morning. He had, he told himself, long since got over the boyish fancy he had had for Lucy; there were plenty of other girls in the world and a lot of them were inclined to be remarkably kind to a six-foot boy with sandy hair and an engaging grin who wore the uniform of the Canadian Air Force. Besides, she was his brother's wife now and the news she had written to tell him was that he was going to be an uncle, which put her into a different category altogether. All the same, he would always have a soft spot for old Luce. He must drop her a line when he got back. Come to that, he ought to write and congratulate his brother.

They were late over the target and, as a result, there was no fighter escort, which was nasty. As they drew near to Hamburg he stopped whistling and fingered his gun with experienced hands. Not much longer now before the war would be over – unless he was sent to the Far East. The idea was not particularly attractive. Better to think about what he was going to do when peace came. It was going to be difficult to break to his parents, but he was strongly attracted to the idea of making a life for himself in Canada. He had chatted to one or two of the boys about it and they'd all been encouraging.

The Messerschmitt 262s swooped out of the sky, jets screaming, incredibly fast. Jimmy knew all about them. Their speed advantage over the piston-engined fighters had already been demonstrated. Against the heavier bombers, without fighter back-up, the advantage was overwhelming. His gun, firing in staccato bursts, was hardly silent for a second, but no sooner had he got his sights on one of them than it was gone, hurtling above them out of sight, falling back again out of the sky.

The Me262s carried air-to-air rockets on under-wing rails. If one of them struck home the aircraft had had it. Jimmy could hear intermittent chatter going on, the high-pitched talk of men on the edge of excitement and fear. The bombs were away; he had the familiar sensation of being swept upwards in an airpocket as the load lightened; they were turning for home. But the Me262s were still with them. He saw one of the Halifaxes go, twisting and turning, blazing as it fell. There had been others, too, he knew, and he wasn't at all sure that he had managed to get even a near miss on the damnably elusive jets.

There was something not quite right about their own Halifax, it was slower than it ought to have been. He heard the pilot's voice say something reassuring about minor damage and then another Messerschmitt swooped into view. With a whoop of joy Jimmy opened fire. He got it; he was sure he'd scored a hit; but at the same moment he heard an explosion, a cold blast of air whistled round his legs, he felt a searing pain and, looking down, he saw a jagged piece of metal had been torn from the fuselage and blood was seeping from the leg of his trousers.

He gritted his teeth as the pain hit home and then he saw the Messerschmitt come back. With automatic reflexes, Jimmy lined up his sights, pressed on the button and poured out bullets. The enemy aircraft looked as if it was going into an

240

epileptic fit. It twisted wildly round in the air, a great plume of black smoke burst from it and it plummeted for the ground.

The Halifax made it back to base, but the rear gunner was unconscious all the way home. Before they could lift him out they had to cut him free from the torn metal which was embedded in his thigh. He was rushed to hospital and operated on straight away. For half a day after the operation his life hung in the balance. He recovered consciousness once. A girl was bending over him, a dark-haired, brown-eyed girl with cool hands.

'Lucy,' he said, and believed that he had spoken out loud, although all the nurse saw was that his lips moved before he lapsed into a coma again.

When he came round the second time there were lights burning in the ward and a nurse was sitting by his side, but to Jimmy everything was black and he was alone.

'Mum,' he said uncertainly. 'Mum, where are you?'

And in that moment, like a child afraid of the dark and calling for his mother, Jimmy died.

Chapter Thirteen

Berlin was a city of old people, women, foreign workers and refugees. All the fit men of fighting age were at the Front. Boys of fifteen were being recruited to help defend their homes. The streets were a mass of tumbled rubble. Nearly half the houses had been damaged and one out of every three was uninhabitable. Fifty-two thousand people had been killed in air raids and double that number had been seriously injured. It was almost impossible to find a coffin in which to bury the dead and bodies were shovelled hurriedly into the first available hole and never given decent burial. The stench of their decay seeped through the crevices and joined the stink from broken sewers.

Very few people believed now in the possibility of saving Berlin. Kurt Waldenheim was one of the believers, but even so he offered Elsa the chance of leaving the city and moving to the south, travelling in one of the official cars marked by the silver swastika of the Nazi Party. She considered it, but to Elsa the idea of survival tied to Kurt seemed more risky than remaining where she was.

'I'll take my chance,' she said, and stayed put.

Kurt was like a man possessed. He was thinner than ever, nothing but skin and bone, full of restless energy. His eyes gleamed with fanatical fervour. Elsa began to wonder whether he was drugged, but the fever that ran in Kurt's veins was blind faith in the Nazi cause.

'Nothing can defeat us,' he said. 'No matter what happens, we will rise again. Our great Leader will rally us to him.'

She was growing bored with him and the time was coming when he would no longer have any power over her, but she did not dare to laugh. If she had scoffed at him at that moment he might have killed her. She wished she could hear from Gunther. There had been no news from him for two weeks and she feared that he had been taken prisoner. He would know about the ordeal they were enduring and he would be worried out of his mind about them.

They lived now almost entirely below ground. When Frieda came home wearing the armband of the *Volkssturm*, the Home Guard, Elsa knew that she had abandoned any hope that Berlin would not become part of the front line and accepted that the only thing left was to defend the city for as long as possible.

There was still some doubt as to whether the Anglo-American Forces or the Russians would reach Berlin first. The Berliners were openly anxious that it should be the Western Allies who took the city. In mid-March it had looked like a decided possibility, and then General Eisenhower, having assessed the situation and weighed up the lives it would cost, sent a cable direct to Marshal Stalin outlining his plans and putting forward the proposal that he should make his main effort along the Erfurt-Leipzig-Dresden axis in the area to which the main German Government departments were being moved.

As regards Berlin, Eisenhower told his Allies: '. . . that place has become, as far as I am concerned, nothing but a geographical location, and I have never been interested in those.'

Not even a direct plea from Winston Churchill could shake him. 'I do not consider,' wrote Churchill, 'that Berlin has lost its military and certainly not its political significance. While Berlin holds out, great masses of Germans will feel it their duty to go down fighting.'

Churchill's persistent battering at the subject was to no avail. On 12th April 1945 the ailing President of the United States, Franklin Roosevelt, died at his desk in Warm Spring. On 14th April General Eisenhower declared that Berlin was no longer a military objective. The US troops, some of them only forty-five miles away, turned back west and left the city to the Russians. Two days later the battle for Berlin began.

Most Berliners knew by eight o'clock on the morning of 16th April that there had been heavy Russian attacks on the Oder front. They listened to the news on the radio and knew that the moment they had been waiting for in dread had arrived. Strangely, just as he had been when the Normandy landings took place, Hitler was asleep, this time in the Führerbunker below the Chancellery and did not know about the opening of the campaign until after many ordinary inhabitants of the city.

In 'fortress Berlin' trenches were dug, barricades were erected – pitifully inadequate defences against a fully equipped army. The Russian forces were held at bay by some of the stiffest resistance they encountered in the entire war, but the faces which turned towards the west looked in vain for the Allied advance they had hoped for.

The 20th April was Hitler's birthday. Amongst the people who watched him inspecting an SS detachment and a group of boys from the Hitler Youth in the ruined gardens of the *Reichskanzlei* was Kurt Waldenheim. He hadn't seen the Führer for some weeks and his appearance shocked him. He walked with a stoop and his hands trembled. He seemed to drag one foot as he moved. And yet, when he lifted his head, Kurt felt the old thrill. Some power still emanated from the man who had led his people to the brink of destruction, something that convinced Kurt that there was yet a chance that their Leader's tremendous willpower might win them victory.

In the four days between the beginning of the battle and the Führer's birthday the life of the city deteriorated. The attempts which had been made to carry on normally were grinding to a halt. Trams no longer ran, the underground railway had closed except for the transport of workers classed as essential. Rubbish was piling up in stinking heaps in the streets. Even if Gunther had written, his letters would no longer have been delivered. The sound of artillery fire was incessant and low-flying MiGs swept over the town, machine-gunning everything that moved.

And yet it was necessary to try to survive. It was Elsa's turn to stand in line at the bakery for bread. The queue of people was almost silent, shuffling forward slowly. It appeared that the only worry in their minds was whether the supplies would run out before their own turn came. They pressed themselves against the walls and felt the bricks and mortar shake with the thunder of the guns.

When Elsa reached the head of the queue she seized her allocation of bread, thrust the money into the outstretched hand and ran down the road in a momentary lull in the bombardment. It didn't last long. A shell whined overhead. She pressed herself into a doorway, all that remained standing of a block of flats she remembered as being five storeys high. She heard a high-pitched scream, men shouting and the sound of running footsteps.

A boy in uniform was running down the street, pursued by three older men in SS uniform. Elsa squeezed herself further back into the shadow of the ruined doorway. The men caught up with the boy. One of them pinioned his arms behind his back and forced him to his knees. Another had a length of cord twisted round his arm. He shook it free, tied it into a noose and threw it round the boy's neck. The youngster fought like a madman, screaming wildly, the men pulled him to his feet, shouting: 'Coward, stinking little coward.' They wrote something with a bit of charred wood on a piece of board from the nearby rubbish, thrust it into the boy's hand and forced him to hold it. Then they tossed the end of the cord over the nearest lamp post, pulled it tight and hanged him.

They stood and watched him, jerking and moving as if he were trying to find a foothold in the air, and then, when they were sure he was dead, they turned away.

Elsa crept past the dangling body. The piece of board fell from the boy's slack fingers. On it was written one word: 'Traitor'.

When she got back to the Hofmeyer's apartment the other three women: Frau Hofmeyer, Frieda and old Lotte, were all in the sitting room. Elsa was ashen-faced and shaken as she told them what had happened. Lotte shook her head and muttered something that might have been a curse, but Frieda said: 'They were within their rights if he ran away. He failed to do his duty.'

'He was a *child!*' Elsa whispered. 'I swear he was no more than fifteen.'

Lotte looked at Frieda with rheumy, shortsighted eyes. 'I've known you since you were a baby, Fräulein Frieda. You know as well as I do that it's not right.'

Frieda shook her head, but said no more. Instead, she turned the conversation back to what they'd been discussing when Elsa came in.

'Lotte has a plan for making a hiding place for us in the cellar,' she said. 'I hope it won't be necessary, but . . .'

'I think it will be necessary,' her mother said. There was a quiet finality about her voice. 'Lotte is right. If . . . when the Russians come you girls must be kept out of sight.'

'All three of you,' Lotte insisted. 'It doesn't matter about me. It's so long since I've had a man between my legs the Russkis will get no more satisfaction out of me than they would out of a dry old cow.'

She chuckled at Frau Hofmeyer's frown. 'No use using anything but plain speech now, Frau Hofmeyer. The Russkis are savages. I know what they'll want after they've got through fighting; drink, loot and women. You come down in the cellar with me and I'll show you what I've fixed up for you.'

She led them down the stairs to the cellar. It was, in fact, a storage area and each of the flats had a small lock-up room allotted to it in which, in happier times, most people had kept luggage, bits of furniture they no longer used and bric-à-brac they had forgotten about.

The Hofmeyers' storage room had long since been converted into a sleeping place, but Lotte led them past their own cubicle and produced a different key.

'After Herr Schwarz was killed and Frau Schwarz went to live with her son in the country I got hold of their key,' she said.

She pushed her way past the piles of dusty junk inside the room and lit a candle. The Schwarz's storage place was at the end of the building and extended backwards further than the rest, but this wasn't obvious at first glance, certainly not in that uncertain light.

'Now, what I'm saying is that if we pull that great oak wardrobe across as if it was standing flat against the wall, in line with where the other places end, there'd be just about room for the three of you to hide behind it. After you're inside

246

I'll pile up the rest of this stuff so that it looks as if it's not been disturbed. It's not much of a hiding place, but it's better than nothing.'

The light from the candle flickered in a draught of air, the shadows of the four women wavered grotesquely across the wall. There was a crump overhead as a shell landed and the building shivered.

'I think it's a good idea,' Elsa said. 'Frieda, you'll come, won't you?'

For a moment it looked as if Frieda might refuse, but at last she said: 'If they really do break through, yes. It'll be bitter to have to admit that we've come to this.'

'Swallow your pride, Fräulein Frieda,' Lotte advised. 'I'll see you have food and water and a bucket. It won't be so bad. This isn't my first war. I know what I know. Men are pigs. Nazis, Russkis, Yanks or Tommies. All pigs.'

'There's no need for me to come down here,' Frau Hofmeyer said.

'I think you should,' Elsa said. 'I met a doctor a few days ago who'd been treating the refugee women from the East. From what she told me I doubt whether even Lotte is as safe as she thinks.'

Old Lotte gave a sudden chuckle. 'That'll be a thrill,' she said. 'Now be sensible, Frau Hofmeyer. What's young Gunther going to say if he comes home and finds his mother's been ravished by a Russki, and all for the want of taking proper precautions?'

'If he comes home,' Frau Hofmeyer said in a low voice.

'Him? Born under a lucky star. I always told you that.'

Elsa looked at her curiously. Lotte had never had a great deal to say to her. She had a feeling that the old woman didn't entirely approve of Gunther's marriage and Lotte, she thought, was the only person who suspected her affair with Kurt. She was a shrewd old devil.

Elsa shuddered as she thought of Kurt. It was all too easy to imagine him helping to string up boys who failed to 'do their duty'.

'It's cold down here,' Frieda said, mistaking the reason for her shiver.

'There's a bit of a grating high up in the wall,' Lotte said. 'Good thing. It'll give you some air. Come now, you'll need to shift the blankets in here and anything else you need.'

They slept that night in the confined space behind the old wardrobe. There was just room for the three of them to lie down, Frau Hofmeyer and Frieda lying one way and Elsa between them with her feet towards their heads. Lotte spent the night in the cellar, too, but in the open area they had all shared during the air raids.

All night the building reverberated to the sound of bombs and gunfire. They got little rest. There were other people in the cellar. Whenever there was a lull in the firing overhead Elsa heard the snores of the woman whose noisy sleep had plagued them every night over the last few months.

They knew it was morning when a bar of light came through the grill above their heads. They could hear voices outside and the sound of people moving about, collecting their bedding, grumbling about their bad night's sleep. Frieda stood up and stretched her cramped limbs, but they had agreed that no-one else should be allowed to know about their hiding place and so they stayed silent until Lotte came to let them out.

When she heard the key turn in the lock to the Schwarz's cubicle, Elsa exclaimed: 'She's locked us in! If anything happened to Lotte we wouldn't be able to get out.'

They remonstrated with Lotte, but she was unmoved. 'Nothing's going to happen to me,' she said. 'You stay where you are until I've been up to the street to see what's happening. I'll let you know if it's safe to come out.'

She was back in a few minutes. 'There are Russian tanks outside,' she said.

As she spoke there was a burst of machine-gun fire, then the howl of a grenade launcher. The light from the grating was suddenly dimmed and looking up they could see the outline of a foot against the grill. They stood, unconsciously clutching one another, not moving, not speaking, until the boot of the Russian soldier moved away.

'They're orderly enough at the moment,' Lotte said. 'Because there's still fighting to be done. Once it's over and

248

they're let loose they'll be searching for drink and women. You must stay down here.'

Frau Hofmeyer started to protest, but Lotte was adamant.

'I've told the neighbours you've gone away. One of Frau Elsa's fancy friends got you out of town, I said. No-one knows you're here. If it gets out there are three women here, two of them young and pretty, them Russkis will be back as soon as they've got time on their hands. Take my advice and stay put.'

'She's right,' Elsa said. She felt cold, tired and afraid. Why the hell hadn't she accepted Kurt's offer to get her out of this?

'But it may be for days!' Frau Hofmeyer said.

'Best part of a week, I reckon,' Lotte said. 'Now, use the bucket so that I can take it up as if it was the usual night's slops. I'll get you some food as soon as it looks safe.'

'We need water to wash,' Frieda said.

'That's a luxury you'll have to do without for now. What do you want me to do, carry you down a bath? Food is as much as I can manage and you may have to go without that until there's no-one around to see me.'

As she stomped away, Elsa said: 'She's taken charge, hasn't she? Who would have thought it?'

'She's always been a domineering old woman,' Frieda said. 'And she's enjoying having us at her mercy.'

'We might owe her our lives,' Frau Hofmeyer said quietly.

They stayed where they were all through the day. Overhead they could hear the guns, the tanks, the sounds of marching, shouts and screams and breaking glass, but it wasn't until after dark had fallen that the Russian soldiers broke into the house. They could hear them storming up the staircase, pounding on doors and breaking them down when they got no reply. The people in the open part of the cellar were crying and moaning, but nobody moved to defend their property.

In their dark, confined space, Frau Hofmeyer, Elsa and Frieda heard the cellar door crash open and then chaos. The soldiers were looking for something to drink, anything alcoholic, and they wouldn't believe that the cellar had been used for storage for furniture and not for bottles of wine. They had picked up one or two words of German. 'Schnapps' was one of them; 'Frau' was another.

There were shouts, a shot was fired and then another. A woman screamed. There was the sound of running footsteps, a body was hurled against the outer door of the Schwarz's storeroom, and then some laughter, drunken and raucous. They could hear a woman's voice: 'No, no, no, no' on and on and on. Frieda shuddered and covered her ears with her hands. Elsa sat motionless. There were more men coming down the stairs. It was impossible to guess how many. The woman was still shouting her endless, futile protest: 'No, no, no, no.' There was another shot and then silence.

They were trying to open the Schwarz's door. Elsa heard Lotte's voice and then the key turned in the lock. Frau Hofmeyer's hand crept out and caught hold of hers. They all sat like statues. On the other side of the great old-fashioned wardrobe, so tall that it almost reached the ceiling, they heard Lotte's loud, patient voice: 'Nothing here. No *Schnapps*. No *Frau*. Nothing.'

The door of the wardrobe was locked. There was a splintering crash, and exclamations in the strange, throaty Russian voices. Somebody laughed. Only the back of the wardrobe separated the three women from the soldiers. But they'd found something in the wardrobe and whatever it was, it seemed to satisfy them. There was more laughter, a brief argument and then they went. There was noise in the building overhead, but the cellar was quiet apart from someone crying a weak, exhausted sound somewhere in the darkness.

Lotte told them what had happened.

'Two of the women were raped and one of them was shot. They shot the girl's old father, too. I don't know how many of them had her, but she's badly hurt. She couldn't walk. We carried her upstairs and put her to bed. They found some old clothes in this wardrobe. You should have seen them. Trying them on! Dirty, dusty old things – a purple velvet evening dress that must have gone back to the twenties, dropping to pieces with mothholes. Like children, they were.'

'Children!' Frieda exclaimed.

'Easily diverted. All they wanted was a novelty.'

'Is it safe to come out?'

'No! I'll see about getting you some food – if there's any left.'

They took what they could find, but I've a few things hidden away.'

They spent three more days and three more nights in the cellar. It was invaded every night, but since it was obvious that there was nothing left worth taking, the soldiers rarely stayed for long.

On the fourth night they heard a group of soldiers arguing with old Lotte. It seemed that she understood what they wanted.

'They've taken her upstairs, I think,' Frieda said. 'I hope she'll be all right.'

At the end of the long night they waited, but Lotte did not come down to them. The grey light of dawn gave way to a shaft of sunlight and still she didn't come.

'I think we ought to try and get out,' Elsa said.

Together, she and Frieda managed to shift the oddments which had been stacked against the small gap between the end of the wardrobe and the wall until Elsa, the slenderer of the two, could crawl out. The door of the Schwarz's storeroom was broken and swinging on its hinges. She pulled some more junk away and helped Frieda and Frau Hofmeyer out. Everything seemed quiet. There was not even the sound of gunfire or tanks rumbling down the street.

'Can we risk going upstairs?' Frieda asked.

'I think we must,' Elsa said.

They found, when they began to climb the stairs, that their legs had grown weak after the days in the confined space. The two girls helped Frau Hofmeyer, whose knees gave way after the first flight. There was no sound of life anywhere in the building.

The door of the Hofmeyers' apartment was ajar. Frau Hofmeyer pushed it open. Nothing stirred. They went in and Frau Hofmeyer gave a little moan of distress as she saw the condition of her once comfortable home.

Frieda called out cautiously: 'Lotte, Lotte, where are you?'

'She might have gone out in search of food,' Elsa said doubtfully.

Frau Hofmeyer pushed open the door of the kitchen.

She was lying on the floor, her skirts pushed up round her

waist, her old, veined legs sprawling, her decent, baggy knickers ripped in half. There was congealed food in pots on the stove and on the plates on the table. A bottle with its neck broken off had been upset and the spilt wine was still dripping slowly off the end of the table. Someone had vomited in the sink. The room stank of rancid food and dried blood.

Elsa put both hands over her mouth to hold back the nausea that rose in her throat. She heard Frieda say in a queer, high voice: 'Dear God.'

Frau Hofmeyer knelt down and touched the old woman's face.

'She *is* dead, isn't she?' Elsa asked.

'Yes.' Frau Hofmeyer did not move. 'They've taken her crucifix,' she said. 'She always wore it round her neck. And her wedding ring.' She moved the dead woman's hand and the broken fingers fell back awkwardly into their contorted position.

'But she was nearly *seventy*!'

Frau Hofmeyer stood up. 'We can't leave her here like this. We must make her decent. And this filth must be cleaned up.' Her lips trembled and she paused, but then went on steadily: 'I don't know what we're going to do about getting her buried. One of us will have to go out, no matter what is happening out there.'

'I'll go,' Frieda said.

After a moment's pause, her mother said: 'Yes. Try to find out if there are any . . . any arrangements for burying the dead. And what is happening.' She glanced at Elsa. 'You'll have to help me with Lotte.'

'I've never touched a dead body,' Elsa said, a look of horror on her face.

'I can't do it alone.' She looked again at her daughter. 'Make yourself look dirty and ugly, and as old as you can.'

Frieda nodded and went out of the room. She put on old, flat shoes, a shapeless raincoat, and covered her head with a scarf. She rubbed her hands in the dust which lay thickly on every surface and smeared it over her face. In the mirror her reflection looked back at her, very white, streaked with dirt, with dark circles under the eyes. She put her hands in her

252

pockets and hunched her shoulders, but she still looked like a young woman; unappetizing to any normal man, but could the animals who had killed old Lotte be called men?

Out in the street the air smelt of smoke and putrefaction. A small bird hopped into the gutter by her foot and pecked at the ground. She looked at it disbelievingly. Was it really possible that such innocent things as birds still existed? There were only a few people about, mostly old men and women. No soldiers, as far as she could see. Perhaps the fighting had passed on somewhere else.

She turned the corner and saw a tank coming towards her. She felt herself freeze in horror. She stood still because she was too afraid to move, but it rumbled past her and on down the road.

She had no idea where to go until she saw the church. Only half of it was still standing, but she went in. There was one old man, sitting on a splittered seat, and a priest on the steps of what had been the altar.

She went up to him and faltered out her story.

He nodded. 'Mass graves are being dug in the parks. Give me your address and I'll see that your friend is collected.'

'She was a good Catholic,' Frieda said. 'Will you pray for her?'

The man she had taken for a priest smiled with great sweetness. 'My dear child, I am a Lutheran. This church – you are right, it was once Catholic. I came in because it is the first holy place I have seen today which is not entirely destroyed. It felt like home. Yes, I will pray for your friend, and for you and for all of us. God help us and God forgive us.'

When Frieda got outside she looked round. Since she was out she might as well try to discover whether there was any hope of finding food. She walked quickly, forgetting to disguise her youth. There was a queue outside a shop so she joined it.

'What's it for?' she asked the woman in front of her.

'They say there may be some vegetables,' the woman replied. She looked up apprehensively into the sky. 'If only we can get something before it all starts again.'

The queue shuffled forward. One or two people exchanged bitter stories about what they had suffered in the last few days, but most of them kept silent, stunned into helpless apathy. Only once, when someone said in a harsh voice: 'Bloody Nazis!' was there a general growl of agreement. Frieda looked at them scornfully. They had all been Nazis once, she thought, when things were going well.

She got three potatoes and half a dozen carrots as a reward for the long wait. She put them in her pockets since she hadn't thought to bring a bag. It added to her shapeless apppearance, which perhaps was just as well.

As she turned towards home the lull ended. The ground beneath her feet seemed to quiver, the noise was deafening, the air was full of dust. A Russian plane swept over her. She crouched in the gutter and watched the dirt spurting up as the bullets hit the ground. When it had passed she got up and ran awkwardly, the vegetables in her pockets banging against her legs. In front of her another woman, carrying a child, was trying to run. She looked over her shoulder when she heard Frieda's footsteps, her mouth twisted with fear.

'Oh, God, I thought it was one of them,' she gasped. She leaned against the wall, shaking and crying. 'I can't go on, I can't! Anna's so heavy and I'm so frightened!' Her hand pawed at Frieda's arm. 'They caught me, two nights ago. Three of them. I didn't struggle. There was the baby to think of. They might have killed me. Oh, God, what's my husband going to do when he finds out?'

The child in her arms began to cry. She was a little girl of about two, a heavy burden to carry any distance.

'Give me the child. I'll help you,' Frieda said. 'Come on, we must hurry. Where are you going?'

'My mother-in-law's place. Our own flat has been bombed. It's in Wotanplatz Strasse. Number 57.'

She handed over the little girl to Frieda and picked up the suitcase she had been carrying.

They stumbled on together, not talking, picking their way over the fallen masonry and scattered bricks, until another loud explosion sent them both cowering against the wall once more. This time the bombardment didn't stop. Frieda felt every explosion vibrating through her body. The baby was crying, her mouth wide open, her face contorted, but Frieda couldn't hear the sounds of distress that came from her.

A car, swinging wildly from side to side over the broken ground, came hurtling down the road, driven by a boy in Hitler Youth uniform. The back window had been shattered and through the jagged glass poked a machine gun. It was firing at a Russian armoured car close behind. The girls pressed closer against the building, Frieda trying to shield the baby with her body. The Russian soldiers were spraying the whole street with machine gun bullets. Frieda felt the other girl's body jerk and heard a choking cry and a strange gurgle.

Frieda raised her head as the cars sped out of sight. The baby's mother was lying on her back. Her eyes were wide open and blood was running out of her mouth. She was dead.

The little girl was still crying, and struggling to get out of Frieda's arms to reach her mother. Frieda stood up, holding her tightly, and took the suitcase from beside the dead woman. 57 Wotanplatz Strasse she had said. Frieda left her body and stumbled on, crouching to avoid the deluge of shrapnel falling all round her.

She found Wotanplatz Strasse and stopped. Number 57 was a flattened ruin. So were all the other numbers. The whole street of houses had disappeared. There was nothing left but a vast anonymous sea of rubble.

The child was still struggling to get down.

'Be quiet,' Frieda said and because she spoke sharply the little girl fell silent. She put her thumb in her mouth and looked up doubtfully into the face of the strange woman who held her.

Frieda turned back towards her own home. Three Russian soldiers, their guns over their shoulders turned into the street. She froze in her tracks. They were coming towards her. They were going to stop.

They crowded round her, smiling and chatting. One of them poked a finger at the little girl and the others laughed. Frieda's arms closed round the child protectively. The soldier nodded vigorously and said: 'Gut! Gut!'

He had a big knapsack on his back. He pulled out something wrapped in newspaper and oozing blood. Frieda's head swam.

She had a terrible fear that she was going to faint at their feet. He was holding it out to her, smiling and nodding. It was a piece of meat, at least a kilo of what looked like beef.

Scarcely knowing what she was doing, she took it. Through dry lips she muttered: *'Danke.'* Still laughing, the soldiers went off down the road together.

They lived for the rest of the week on the meat and vegetables Frieda had brought back, cooked over an improvised fire on the floor of the cellar. There was no gas, no electricity, and water only for those brave enough to go out and fetch it from the pump in the road. The artillery bombardment went on day and night, the high-pitched whining of the shells and the murderous rain of shrapnel. There was hand-to-hand fighting in and out of the ruined buildings. The wounded lay in the streets until they died and the dead stayed where they were and rotted.

The little girl, Anna, was a problem. Frieda had examined the suitcase she had brought back and found it contained a few clothes, some tins of food and the family papers. The child's name was Anna Theresa Neumann. Her dead mother had been called Rosa and her father was Wilhelm Neumann, described as a book-keeper. She had been born in January 1943, so she was, as Frieda had thought, a little over two years old. There was a silver-framed photograph amongst the clothes showing a smiling girl holding the arm of a man in a pin-striped suit. It was probably their wedding photograph.

Anna was perpetually frightened. She clung to any grown-up who would hold her, her body shaking, her face hidden. She asked in a small voice, husky with crying, for *'Mutti, Mutti'*, and only stared with bewildered eyes when she had to be told that *'Mutti'* couldn't come.

'Thank God she's no younger,' Frau Hofmeyer said in an exhausted voice when Anna had at last fallen asleep on the first night she spent with them. 'At least she can eat what we have, such as it is. I don't know what we would have done if we'd had to find milk for her.'

'I had to bring her. What else could I do?' Frieda asked.

'Of course, my dear. We'll find her relations when . . . when all this is over.'

Elsa kept her thoughts to herself. To her it seemed unlikely that any order would ever be restored from the chaos outside. She took little part in caring for the child. She had never taken much interest in children and her ignorance made her awkward. Frau Hofmeyer, who had borne two herself, was the person to take charge of little Anna.

On the morning of 2nd May, an old man who had gone out into the street came stumbling back into the cellar.

'Hitler's dead!' he called out. 'It happened yesterday. A man outside just told me. It was on the wireless last night.'

'How did he die?' someone asked.

'Don't know, but the announcer said he fought for us to his last breath.'

There was a derisive laugh. 'All I can say is, good riddance,' a woman remarked. 'Perhaps now we'll have a chance of peace.'

Frieda left them. There was only one place where she could be alone. She crawled back behind the old wardrobe and crouched on the rough blankets which had made her bed for so many sleepless nights. The tears ran down her face in an endless, silent stream. It was not the man who was dead for whom she wept, but for her own lost youth and the dream that was ended, for the time when she had believed she belonged to a race set apart for greatness, for the days of joy and power.

It was Anna who found her, crawling into her sleeping place looking for 'Auntie F'ieda'. Her little hands patted Frieda consolingly when she felt her face wet with tears.

'Better soon,' she said. 'Better soon, Auntie F'ieda.'

Frieda caught her up and held her close in an agony of grief. Who would ever give her a child now? Where were all the men. Where was Ulrich, who had disappeared on the Eastern Front? Where was her brother?

Anna began to struggle and Frieda realized that she was frightening the child and let her go. Her moment of weakness was over. She would not cry again.

257

They went up into the daylight again on 4th May. Everything was quiet, but they emerged into a frightening world. Anarchy and starvation ruled. They took it in turns to roam the streets searching desperately for something, anything to eat. Anna grew weak and pale.

The Hofmeyers were fortunate in having a roof over their heads. The apartment had survived the bombing, the shelling, the attacks of marauding soldiers. It was damaged, there were no windows and the furniture was soiled and hacked about, but it was habitable. Some of the people who had taken refuge in the cellar were still living down there. Bands of homeless, parentless children eked out a scanty living, stealing what food they could and disappearing into holes in the ground to devour their spoils.

There was no news of Gunther. Sometimes Elsa believed that he had been taken prisoner. At other times it seemed more likely that he had been killed. Whatever had happened to him, she could feel nothing but dull apathy. If he came home he would just be one more mouth to feed.

The war in Europe came to an official end on 7th May, but had, in fact, been over several days earlier. The fighting was finished. Very slowly, through May and June, the men of the *Wehrmacht* began to creep home. They could be seen in the streets, walking like zombies, their feet swathed in sacking rags, their uniforms torn, dirty and stripped of insignia, looking for homes they had left when they went off to war, and usually looking in vain.

Notices began to appear, tacked to trees or lamp posts, fluttering in the breeze, asking for news of relatives, offering articles for barter. 'Heinrich, I have gone to my sister in Neustadt. Your mother and father are dead. Gerda'; 'Information, please, on the Gottard family, formerly of No 66'; 'Lost on the night of 24th April, when their mother was wounded, two children, Gottfried and Hansel Möller, aged 8 and 6. Any information to Frau Möller, waiting each day by the third lamp post.'

Frieda put one up in Wotanplatz Strasse, near the house where Anna's grandparents had once lived. 'Anna Theresa, aged 2½, daughter of Rosa and Wilhelm Neumann, is being cared for at 26 Linzer Gasse, off Holsteinische Strasse. Apply to Fräulein Frieda Hofmeyer for further information.'

They endured from day to day until July and then the British and Americans joined the Russians in the administration of Berlin and Wilmersdorf fell into the British Zone of Control.

There were different uniforms in the streets. An attempt was made to bring back some order out of the chaos into which Berlin had descended. In spite of orders against fraternization the British made friends with the children, the Americans rushed everywhere in jeeps and whistled at the girls.

A week later there was a loud knock on the door of the Hofmeyers' flat one evening. Elsa went to it and began the laborious task of untying the string with which they had secured it since it had been broken open. Outside was a very large American Sergeant, leaning against the door jamb and chewing gum.

When Elsa at last got the door open he shifted his gum into his cheek, straightened up, made a sketchy salute and said: 'Hi! Anyone here speak English?'

'I speak . . . a little,' Elsa said.

'Great. I've got a letter here from Lootnant Gunther Hofmeyer for his wife. That you?'

Elsa nodded, unable to speak. She held the door open wider. 'Please to come in. Gunther's mother also is here.'

He followed her in, big and amiable and seemingly untouched by the battles he had recently fought. Frau Hofmeyer was trying to feed Anna with mashed potato, which the child was obstinately refusing to swallow even though it was the only food they had been able to provide for her that day. Frieda was sitting at the table mending a tear in one of her dresses.

'There is news of Gunther,' Elsa said quickly. 'A letter.' She turned to the American and said in English: 'He is well – not wounded?'

'No, he's fine. We took him prisoner, but now he's with the British, doing some interpreting for them.'

Elsa explained this to the other two. Tears began to run

down Frau Hofmeyer's cheeks. Frieda went to her and put an arm round her shoulders.

'I cannot tell you what this means to us,' Elsa said to the American Sergeant. 'It is the first news we have had of Gunther since many months. We had begun to believe that he was dead.'

Her own voice broke and the American looked uncomfortable at all this emotion he had unleashed. To hide his embarrassment he tickled Anna under the chin.

'Cute kid,' he said. 'She yours?'

'No. Anna is a child my husband's sister has found in the street. Her mother has been killed by the Russians.'

'Gee, that's awful! Poor kid! What about the rest of her family?'

Elsa shook her head. 'We do not know. Perhaps one day it will be possible to find them.'

Anna, excited by the interest that was being shown in her, drummed with her heels on the chair, picked up her spoon and brought it down with a smack in the unappetizing concoction on the plate in front of her. The Sergeant's face broke into a smile.

'I've got one at home just like her,' he said. He felt in an inner pocket and brought out a wallet. 'Like to see her picture?'

They passed round the photograph he produced and exclaimed politely. He recognized the word '*schöne*' and said: 'She sure is! The prettiest, cutest little thing you can imagine.'

No-one mentioned the contrast between the round face and sturdy limbs of the American child and wan little Anna, but he seemed to guess what they were thinking and he went on awkwardly: 'I've heard food's a bit tight with you people right now. I brought along one or two things . . . a tin of bully beef, some cans of beans, a slab of chocolate. If I'd known about the little girl I'd have tried for some dried milk. Maybe I can call back in a day or two.'

They looked at the things he piled on the table, opulently packaged, desirable beyond words.

'You are most kind,' Elsa said. 'We are very hungry.'

The simple words made him look uncomfortable again. She

260

decided to push their luck a little further and asked: 'Have you perhaps a cigarette?'

'Sure!' He held out an open packet. 'Just a second, I've got my lighter right here. Anyone else . . . ?'

They all shook their heads. 'We do not smoke ourselves,' Elsa explained. 'The cigarette is for . . .' she searched for the word she needed and could not find it: '. . . for changing for other things,' she said.

'For barter, you mean? Gee, in that case you'd better take the pack.'

His anxious generosity overwhelmed them. They tried to get him to stay, but he seemed to want to get away. In the doorway he paused and looked back at the dilapidated room, the worn-out women, the hungry child and said: 'I just want to say we're all glad the fighting is over. We didn't want it to be like this.'

'You are a kind man,' Elsa said. 'Please, you have not told us your name.'

'Sergeant Charlie Jackson, ma'am. I'm glad to have made your acquaintance. I'll be back.'

Frieda was already opening the tin of meat as Elsa showed him out, but Frau Hofmeyer said: 'We haven't read Gunther's letter!' and she paused, ashamed of her forgetfulness.

It was not a long letter, but it gave them an address to which they could write and confirmed that he was alive and well. He had heard terrible stories of the atrocities committed by the Russians in Berlin and was desperately anxious for news of them all. He sent them all his fondest love.

They were all in tears by the time Elsa had finished reading the letter. Anna looked at them anxiously. 'Auntie F'ieda?' she said. 'Auntie Elsa?' She took a large spoonful of the mashed potato and held it out to Frieda. 'Nice tattie,' she said persuasively. She looked bewildered when they all wiped their eyes and began to laugh.

The knowledge that Gunther was alive and would be coming back to them put a new spirit into the household. The only thing that dimmed it was the news that Frieda would no longer be allowed to teach. She had hoped that she would take part in the attempts that were being made to round up the homeless children and take them into some sort of care, but even this was refused her. She had filled up the questionnaire with which they had been issued – the *Frageboden* – the document which was to come to rule their lives – and had answered truthfully that she had been a member of the Nazi Party. After that, all contact with the minds of young children was barred to her. She was bitterly hurt, and all the more so because she knew she had been a good teacher.

She still took most of the responsibility for looking after Anna, since she had been the one who brought her into the family. She was attached to the little thing, as was Frau Hofmeyer, who saw in her the grandchildren she might now hope to have one day, but Elsa kept aloof.

'It will be different when you have your own,' Frau Hofmeyer said and only Frieda noticed the slight wrinkling of the nose which betrayed that Elsa had no great desire to have any of her own.

Now that things were more settled Frieda was beginning to be critical of her sister-in-law. Elsa had been a resourceful companion while they had all been in danger, but Frieda was distrustful of the swiftness with which she had allied herself with the new authorities and particularly of the capital she was making out of her status as the daughter of a General who had been involved in the plot against Hitler. It was the first Frieda had heard of this and it disturbed her. The man had been a traitor and his daughter had not been over-anxious to advertise her connection with him while the Führer was still alive. Now he was dead, and all their hopes with him, and Elsa was suddenly a minor heroine because her father had taken a poison pill rather than face what was due to him.

One afternoon in August Frieda and Anna were alone in the apartment when there was a knock on the door. Outside, when Frieda opened the door, was a small, thin man in the remnants of a *Wehrmacht* uniform which he was wearing incongruously with a flat cap and brown boots.

'Fräulein Hofmeyer?' he asked. 'My name is Willy Neumann. There is a notice on a tree in Wotanplatz Strasse. It says you have a child with you . . . Anna?'

'You're Anna's father!' Frieda exclaimed. 'Come in, please.'

He followed her inside. 'She's really safe?' he asked.

'See for yourself.'

Anna was on the floor, playing with an old shoe to which she had become devoted. She filled it up with bits and pieces and pushed it round the floor like a little truck. Her appearance had begun to improve as she gained weight and colour. Her flaxen hair curled riotously all over her head and Frieda was beginning to wonder what they were going to do as she started to outgrow her clothes.

Frieda heard Willy Neumann's sharp intake of breath as the child looked up. He dropped down on his knees by her side. Anna looked at him doubtfully, then beyond him to Frieda, her face anxious. Her memory was short, but men to Anna meant noise and fear and it was only the fact that 'Auntie F'ieda' was smiling that kept her from crying. When her father stretched out a hand towards her she flinched and moved away.

'I'm afraid she doesn't know you,' Frieda said apologetically.

He got up from the floor. 'Of course not. I haven't seen her since she was a fortnight old.'

He turned towards Frieda and she knew from the way he braced himself what his next question was going to be.

'My wife?'

'Dead. I'm sorry.'

He nodded. 'I knew it must be so when I saw your notice. Do you know how . . . ?'

'I was with her.' Briefly she described how Anna's mother had met her death.

Willy put up a hand and shielded his eyes for a moment. 'My poor Rosa. At least it was a clean death. Those swine . . . they didn't touch her?'

Frieda remembered the dead woman's words . . . 'three of them . . . two nights ago . . .'

'No,' she said. 'It was very quick. There was a fight and we were caught in the crossfire. Your wife was hit, I was unhurt. I'm sorry.'

'And you took Anna. I'm more grateful to you than I can say.'

263

There seemed to be little more that they could say, but Frieda asked: 'You want to take Anna away now?'

'Yes. I'm going to live with my brother. He's got a small farm just beyond Lübars. When I found our place was in ruins I went to my parents' home, but that had gone too. I was too distracted to look at bits of paper pinned on trees, didn't even realize what they were. I went out to my brother's place in the hope . . . but I think my parents must be dead. My brother has had no news of them for weeks. I came back into Berlin today, walking the streets to try to get some news. That was when I saw your notice.'

'Your wife was on her way to your parents' home when I met her, but the house was already completely destroyed. I put my notice up nearby because it was the only address I had. Thank God you saw it. Look, do sit down for a few minutes. We've been given some coffee. My sister-in-law is out trying to barter half of it for some meat, but we've kept some for our own use. You'll have a cup with me before . . . before you take Anna away?'

He accepted and before she made the coffee she fetched the papers which had been in his wife's suitcase. He sat with them on his lap, turning the photograph over in his hands, and she saw him wiping away tears from his eyes.

The aromatic smell of coffee filled the kitchen.

'Sometimes I think that just smelling it again gives me more pleasure than actually drinking it,' Frieda said.

They sat down at the table and little Anna crawled round their feet, pushing her old shoe in and out between the table legs, reassured that this strange man was not going to harm her.

'I've grown fond of her – we all have,' Frieda said. 'But, of course, her place is with you.'

'My brother has two of his own. He and his wife say that having Anna with them will be no trouble. I'm going to work with him on the farm. It seems the best chance of earning a living as things are at present.'

'You were a book-keeper, weren't you?'

'Yes, but the firm I worked for has been bombed out of existence. What about you? What do you do?'

264

'I was a teacher.' She spread out her work-worn hands for inspection. 'Now I'm one of the "rubble women". I work all day shifting bricks and wheeling barrowloads of rubbish from the bombed sites. I was a Nazi, you see. One of the untouchables. It's the only work they'll give me. How fortunate it is that Anna is too young for me to have contaminated her mind.'

He looked uncomfortable at her bitterness. 'I can see you are a good woman,' he said. 'I was never one of the Party myself and I always had doubts about the way we were going . . .'

'Oh, everyone says that – now!' Frieda interrupted him. 'I sometimes ask myself whether I imagined the thousands who stood in the streets and cheered the Führer!' She stopped. 'I'm sorry. I've paid dearly for my beliefs and even more dearly for admitting that I'm not entirely sure we were wrong. If the French and the British and the Americans had allied themselves with us against the Bolsheviks we might have saved the world from a great evil.'

'We joined up with the Reds ourselves at one time,' he pointed out.

'We were forced into that. It was a mistake, I admit.'

'And the Jews?' he asked in a low voice. 'What about the Jews? How could we expect those other countries to condone what we did to them?'

'Do you believe the disgusting propaganda that's been put out about the concentration camps? It's all lies. I'll never believe it, never. They were places of correction for the enemies of the State. They went hungry? We all did that. We had a right to put our enemies into a place of safety.'

'It's not propaganda,' he said. 'I've seen with my own eyes . . . at Buchenwald. It's all true. The starvation, the gas chambers, the mass graves. Warehouses full of the victims' belongings. Men and women like walking skeletons. Torture and disgusting medical experiments. If I gave you the details it would make you sick. Dear God, what one man can do to another! Animals in the jungle are merciful compared with us.'

He looked at her in bleak pity. 'You must believe that it is true. While there are people left who are still deluded there's no hope for us.'

She put her head down on her arms on the table, shaken to the innermost depths of her being by his revelation. After a moment, Willy got up and stood over her, one arm laid awkwardly across her shoulders. Anna sensing that something was wrong, got up and stood by her side, pulling at her skirt. Automatically, Frieda put out a hand to draw her closer and then she remembered that Anna was no longer hers and took her hand away again.

'You'd better take her away quickly,' she said. She stood up and straightened her shoulders. Her eyes were dry, but her mouth was set in a thin, bitter line. 'She may be a little upset at first, but she'll soon forget. I'll put her things together. There's not much, I'm afraid.'

When the small suitcase was packed Willy said: 'You've been good to Anna. I can see she's attached to you. I'll be coming into town from time to time. We haven't got a lot to spare, but a few vegetables might come in useful. Perhaps later on you might be able to visit the farm.'

'Even though I was a Nazi?'

'We've got to start forgiving one another some time. I still think you're a good woman. Mistaken, perhaps, but good in yourself.'

'Thank you.' She looked at him with desperate, unhappy eyes. A nondescript man, but staunch in his way. One of the little people she had always secretly thought inferior in the days when she believed that she and her friends were going to rule the world. Now, she felt grateful for his charity.

'Perhaps, one day, it will be possible for me to visit you and Anna,' she said.

Chapter Fourteen

For Germany the war was over, but not for Britain. Although 'Victory in Europe' was celebrated with bonfires and fireworks the families with sons and husbands in the Far East spoke sourly of the 'Forgotten Army'.

For the Brookfields, 'VE Day' so short a time after Jimmy's death was a bitter irony.

'Five weeks,' Barbara said. 'Jimmy died to keep the war going for five more weeks.'

Neither she nor Harry joined in the local celebrations. It was a public holiday and they spent it quietly at home, alone together.

Christine was very conscious of her mother's bitterness when she came home on leave a few weeks after VE Day. She saw, too, the neglected look of the house, with dust thick on every surface, the weeds growing in the garden, the lack of interest Barbara took in her own appearance, dragging on the same clothes every day and merely passing a comb through her hair, without so much as a dash of lipstick.

On her second morning at home Christine got out the vacuum cleaner and began giving the rooms the cleaning they had obviously lacked for weeks.

'I haven't felt like doing anything,' her mother said, and even the fact that she made that half apology encouraged Christine to believe that she could be brought back to her old self again.

'I've been spoilt, never having to do much housework,' Christine said. 'I'm quite exhausted. Could we have a cup of tea, Mum?'

They sat in the kitchen to drink the cup of tea Barbara had roused herself to make.

'Have you started thinking what you are going to do when you come out of the WAAF?' she asked.

'I'm not coming out just yet,' Christine said. 'As a matter of fact, I've been offered the chance of a rather interesting posting. The only thing is, it means going to Germany.'

Barbara put down her cup with a clatter that betrayed how her hands were shaking. 'You can't do that! How can you even think of going there?'

'Conditions will be bad,' Christine said, deliberately misunderstanding her. 'All the same, I think I'll go. I've been asked to be part of a special team investigating German radar systems. I don't think I can turn my back on such a chance. It could make all the difference to any future career I take up.'

'You won't need a career,' Barbara said. 'A lovely girl like you. You'll get married again.'

'Possibly, but if I do it's going to be a very long time ahead. I need something now, Mum. Something to keep me busy and interested. What else am I to do? You don't want me sitting around at home under your feet, do you?'

'I suppose not,' Barbara agreed reluctantly.

She took a surreptitious look at her daughter as Christine collected their cups together and went to wash them up. She was, she admitted to herself, a little overwhelmed by the Christine who had grown out of the pretty, self-centred youngster she remembered from before the war. This new Christine, with her fine-drawn elegance and her air of cool competence, had a cutting edge about her which frightened her mother. It seemed likely that she would make a success of any career she chose, but in doing so she might sacrifice what to Barbara still seemed her best chance of happiness, and that was a second marriage. Christine wasn't born to live alone.

Christine just had time before she left for Germany a few weeks later for one quick visit to Michael and Lucy to see her new-born nephew.

'I was quite sure I'd have a boy,' Lucy said. 'Isn't he an absolute duck?'

Christine bent over the small dark head and crumpled face of the baby and did not reply. Lucy raised herself on one elbow and said quietly: 'Your turn will come, Chris.'

Christine straightened up. 'I'm no longer sure that it's what I want,' she said. 'He's a lovely baby, Lucy. Are you really calling him after Jimmy?'

Yes, he's to be James Michael – known as Jamie. You will be his godmother, won't you?'

'I'll be in Germany,' Christine pointed out.

'I'm sure we can arrange something with a stand-in. I must say that this new job of yours sounds really great, although I'm not sure I'd want to go to Germany right now. It must be terrible over there,'

'It'll be no picnic,' Christine admitted.

Her brother said much the same thing when they were talking together later in the evening.

'Will you be going to Berlin?' he asked.

'We won't be based there. The Headquarters of the Air Division is at Detmold, but I gather we shall be mostly at the main HQ of the British Control Commission in Lubbecke. I'm hoping to travel around a bit with the members of the team.'

'If you go to Berlin do you have any idea of looking up Gunther and his family?'

'I have thought about it,' Christine admitted. 'I'm going to wait and see whether it seems like the right thing to do when I'm there.'

Michael went over to a desk and opened the top drawer. When he turned round he was holding a newspaper cutting and a torn page from a notebook.

'There's someone else you might try to contact,' he said. 'This was amongst Jimmy's effects.'

He handed over the newspaper cutting and Christine exclaimed: 'It's a picture of you! Who's the other man?'

'A German called . . .' he consulted the other scrap of paper, 'Kurt Waldenheim. I'd forgotten his name, but I remember the occasion vividly.'

He described to her the meeting in Minneapolis with the young SS officer and the well-meaning Mr Schultz's efforts to promote friendship between them.

'Jimmy made the speech of a lifetime,' he concluded. 'I didn't know whether to laugh or cry. He promised to look this

Kurt up after the war and heap coals of fire on his head. He really meant it, or he wouldn't have hung on to that picture and the chap's address all that time. I'd like to do something about it.'

'A memorial to Jimmy?' Christine asked.

'Does it seem too fanciful? I'd do it myself if I could.'

'I'll try.' She looked at the picture again. Kurt's face stared out, tight-skinned, a supercilious smile on his lips. 'Did you like him?' she asked curiously.

'No, I thought he was an arrogant bastard. Perhaps I shouldn't ask you to involve yourself with him.'

Christine shrugged. 'What harm can he do me now? Even if he's alive, which I doubt.'

Christine was deeply shocked by the conditions she found in Germany. She had read newspaper accounts of the devastation, but now she saw the sordid reality: the lack of sanitation, the shuffling queues of people waiting to draw water from the taps in the streets, the total breakdown of any civil administration to deal with hunger and disease and, in the British sector in particular, the predicament of the hordes of refugees fleeing over the border from Czechoslovakia and Poland, victims of the victory that should have brought them peace.

Above all, because she had known it in peacetime when she had been young and in love, she was affected by what had happened to Berlin. It had been six years since she had last seen it, but she remembered the Schloss, now smashed and pitted by mortars; she looked for the copper dome of the Dom and found nothing left but the bare ribs, stark against the sky; along the Unter den Linden there was nothing but embankments of burned-out buildings; the Kurfürstendamm with its night clubs and luxury shops was just a heap of ruins; the steep-towered Gedächtniskirche was destroyed. The Tiergarten, where she had wandered hand in hand with Gunther amongst the flower gardens and the alder trees reflected in sheets of water, was an obscene waste of churned-up mud littered with wreckage, its pools viscous with oil.

Her first sight of the ruins made her despair of finding any of the Hofmeyer family alive, but she forced herself to go to the little street which had once been a quiet turning off the Holsteinische Strasse, hardly daring to believe that their apartment building could still be standing. It was difficult to find her way back to it with all the half-remembered landmarks gone, but a small boy led her to the right street, and held his hand out afterwards, hopefully demanding a cigarette.

She gave him one, no longer surprised by the way he snatched it from her. She watched him scamper down the street before any larger child could take it from him, and remembered the bitter title of a current revue – *'Alles für 10 Zigaretten'*.

The building was still there, damaged, battered and partly roofless, but apparently inhabited. She climbed the stairs, remembering the first time she had come there from Paris with her suitcase in her hand, frightened yet determined. She realized as she went up the second flight of stairs that she was almost as nervous now. Would Gunther be at home? What was she going to say to him?

She paused, on the point of turning round and going away again, when light, running footsteps came up the stairs behind her. She turned to look and saw a girl of about her own age with brown, swinging hair and large brown eyes and a very bright lipstick.

She looked at Christine enquiringly, running a rapid, experienced eye over her uniform, and then asked in English: 'You look for someone? Can I help you?'

'I am looking for . . . for Frau Hofmeyer,' Christine said.

'I am Frau Hofmeyer.'

'You?'

The girl laughed. 'You wish perhaps the older Frau Hofmeyer? My husband's mother?'

Christine nodded. 'Yes.'

'She is at home. Come.'

She went on past Christine, feeling in her handbag for her key. When Christine did not follow she looked back over her shoulder enquiringly.

'You must be Gunther's wife?' Christine asked.

'Yes, that is so. And you?'

'I am . . . I was Christine Brookfield. I knew Gunther . . . the family . . . before the war.'

'And you have come now to see them? But that is so kind! Please to come in.'

Christine followed her in a daze. Of course Gunther had married. Why not? She had done the same herself. He must still be alive. The girl who was his wife had not spoken as if he were dead, nor did she look like a widow.

Elsa took her straight through into the kitchen, the only room they were able to heat. Christine recognized Frau Hofmeyer at once, but it was difficult to believe that the woman sitting slumped at the table in patched and grubby clothes, her rough hands cupped round a saucerless cup of coffee, could be the trim, haughty Frieda. Gunther was not there, and Christine wasn't sure whether she was glad or sorry.

She didn't want to ask after him. It would look as if she had come in search of him, which wasn't true. She'd been moved by a compassionate impulse towards the whole family and not just the boy she had once loved. On the other hand, it would look strange not to mention his name, but every minute that went by made it more difficult to frame the necessary question.

It was Frau Hofmeyer who gave her the news she wanted to hear.

'Gunther is home with us once more, safe and well, thank God,' she said. 'He is working now for the new British administration here in Wilmersdorf.'

'Collaborating with the British,' Frieda said.

They might have got on more easily if Frieda hadn't been there; as it was, it was difficult to keep the conversation going, in spite of Christine's fluent German. If it hadn't been for Elsa the pauses would have been even more prolonged, but she displayed a lively interest in Christine and her vivacity kept the difficult meeting going until Christine felt that it would be reasonable to leave. She produced the small gifts she had brought, stammering self-consciously under Frieda's contemptuous eye as she laid them on the table. She was grateful for the dignified way Frau Hofmeyer accepted them.

'But you must not go! Surely you wish to see Gunther? He will be home very shortly.'

'No, I must go,' Christine said quickly. 'Please tell him that I am sorry to have missed seeing him. That I am glad . . .'

She broke off. They had all heard the sound of the front door opening and closing. Then the kitchen door opened and Gunther came in.

Christine was standing by the table, ready to leave. She was the first person he saw when he entered the room. She was in uniform, very tall and slim, her cap and gloves clutched in one hand. The soft fair hair which had curled round her face before the war had been subdued into a sleek roll at the back of her head, her face was thinner, but Gunther said, after one long look at her: 'Christine? It isn't possible!'

She nodded, her hands moving nervously along the edge of her cap. Without realizing it, her recollection of him had been coloured by the dreams she had endured after Larry's death. Now she saw that he was nothing like the great, blond predator who had stalked her night after night, lustful and shamefully desired. The memory faded and was gone, to be replaced immediately by fresh impressions.

He had changed more than she had, she thought. Nothing could disguise his height and the breadth of his shoulders, and his hair still lay like a lick of bright paint across his forehead, but she felt that if she'd been shown a photograph of him she wouldn't have recognized him. Could this really be the boy she had known, this grim-faced man with lines on his face, who looked at her and frowned instead of smiling?

She had to sit down again, to tell him about the work she was doing and how she came to be in Berlin. She had to admit that she was in his country to help gather information about the radio systems on which, as she realized now for the first time, his own life had depended not so long ago.

He said little, but he watched her, almost as if, like herself, he could not quite believe what he saw. When she got up to go, he asked abruptly: 'You came alone? Is that permitted?'

'It's frowned on,' she admitted. 'I didn't want to tell anyone where I was going.'

273

'It wasn't wise. You shouldn't go out alone, not in that uniform.'

'I thought the uniform would be a safeguard.'

'There are desperate people roaming the streets. You are wearing a watch aren't you? You were carrying . . .' he glanced at the table, '. . . cigarettes, chocolate. You have money. I think it best if I walk back with you.'

He ignored her stammered refusal of his company as she tried to insist that she was sure it wasn't necessary. Elsa looked at them with malicious amusement until she caught Gunther's eye and saw him frown.

They walked down the road together, unconsciously dropping into the same long-legged stride that had once taken them over the hills of Sussex together. They hardly spoke until Christine, beginning to find the silence embarrassing, blurted out: 'Your wife is very pretty.'

'Yes, Elsa is very much admired.' There was a flatness in his voice which she didn't understand.

'I got married, too,' she said, and that at least made him turn his head to look at her.

'Of course, I should have realized. So what is your name now?'

'Telford. My husband was in the RAF.'

'Was?'

'He died.'

'I'm sorry.'

There seemed to be nothing more they could say about that. Then Gunther said: 'I haven't asked about the rest of your family. Your mother and father?'

'They're both all right. Michael was shot down and badly burnt, but he survived. He's married – he married Lucy, you remember her?'

'The American girl? She was charming.'

'They've just had a baby, a little boy.'

'And there was another brother. I've forgotten his name.'

'Jimmy was killed.'

Again he said mechanically: 'I'm sorry.'

They had reached the more populated streets. Gunther stopped and said: 'You will be safe now. I'll say goodbye.'

She held out her hand and he took it, she thought reluctantly. She had expected that his touch would be familiar to her, but he was a stranger.

They stood looking at one another until Gunther said, almost as if the words were forced out of him: 'Your husband, both your brothers, but it seems you don't hate us. Why?'

'I don't know. Many people at home are very bitter. But here, in Germany, I've seen the suffering. The only ones I can hate, truly hate, are the ones who gave orders in the concentration camps. The others . . . they are so like ourselves.'

'That view is too simple. We are all guilty.' He held up his hand to stop her protest. 'You forgive my people more easily than I do and you are not the only one. I find it condescending, that easy writing off of past crimes.'

She wondered why they had suddenly begun talking so earnestly when they were just about to part, but it was not a conversation for a street corner.

'Shall I see you again?' she asked.

'I would like to say not, but that would be selfish. If there is anything you can do to help my mother I must swallow my pride and be grateful.'

It was an effort to reply without betraying how much he had hurt her. 'I'll keep in touch with Frau Hofmeyer,' she promised.

She turned away, her chin in the air, moving blindly, but she heard him call her name in an urgent voice: 'Christine!'

For a moment she thought she would ignore him and then she turned her head and looked back over her shoulder. He had come up behind her and now he said in a low voice: 'You always had the most generous heart of anyone I ever knew. I am more grateful than I sound.'

He did not wait to see her response, but turned on his heel and left her, moving impatiently, as if he couldn't wait to put a distance between them.

Her work took her away from Berlin the following week, but she was back in time for Christmas and wished that she was not. There was a pitiful attempt to hold the traditional fair, the *Weihnachtsmarkt*, and Christine could have wept at the sight of the queues of parents waiting to give their children a brief moment of pleasure on the *Karusselle*. She paid a visit to the Hofmeyers' apartment, but this time she managed to go during the morning and she found Frau Hofmeyer alone.

She had brought a few small gifts and she put them on the table diffidently, feeling how inadequate they were, but Frau Hofmeyer exclaimed in pleasure.

'I will put them away for a surprise,' she said. 'The lavender water for Frieda, the lipstick for Elsa, the warm scarf for Gunther and the chocolates I will keep for myself, but I will take the ribbon off because I have a use for it.'

'The chocolates are American,' Christine said. 'We don't have fancy wrappings in England any more.'

She watched as Frau Hofmeyer carefully removed the strip of bright ribbon.

'It's just what I needed,' she said. 'I am making a doll, look!'

She held up a rag doll, dressed in scraps she had culled from their scanty wardrobes.

'It's for a little girl Frieda rescued,' she said. 'Poor little Anna, she has few toys.'

She told Christine how Anna had come to them. She did not dramatize it, but Christine understood the stark tragedy that lay behind her simple story.

Frau Hofmeyer looked up and saw her eyes full of tears. 'You have a more tender heart than many of your people,' she said gently. 'They say it was our own fault.'

'Yes, I know. Perhaps if I hadn't known you and Gunther before the war I might feel the same. I lost my husband and my brother, I could feel bitter about that but somehow I don't. Just tired and very sad. And now, seeing the way you have to live . . .' Her voice trailed into silence.

'We are more fortunate than most. Elsa has American friends who are very kind to her. My poor Frieda, who works so hard, doesn't like to take their charity, but I have no such qualms.'

They talked for a few more minutes, mostly about Frau Hofmeyer's recollections of Christmas and the New Year in the past.

'Ah, the goose stuffed with apples!' she said nostalgically.

276

'And the big fish – the *Silversterkarpfen*. It was so good. Shall I ever see those days return?'

'I hope so,' Christine said. She got up to go, mindful of the fact that there was a car and a driver waiting for her down below and that she was really supposed to be on her way to the American sector.

She had up to that time made no attempt to trace Kurt Waldenheim. She understood, now that she was in Germany, that it was not simply a matter of going to an address and asking if he was still living there and, if not, where he had gone. Too often the address was nothing but a heap of rubble and people had lost track of even their nearest relatives. But since he had been an SS officer there was a strong possibility that he might be in prison on a charge of war crimes and so, a little reluctantly, she began to make enquiries through official channels.

'Kurt Waldenheim? Never heard of him,' a cheerful lieutenant at the British HQ said. 'I'll have a look in the records, but unless we've nailed him as a War Criminal he'll be out roaming the streets somewhere, free as air and not a damned thing we can do about it.'

He came back with a file in his hand, looking thoughtful.

'We haven't got him, but we wish we had,' he said. 'I think, if you don't mind the Major would like a word with you.'

Christine regretted even more that she'd followed up Michael's suggestion of tracing this ex-Nazi. She was very much on the defensive when she was called in to be interviewed by Major Dawson.

'Sit down, Section Officer,' he said. 'Now, what's your interest in Hauptmann Waldenheim?'

She explained and showed him the newspaper cutting. He grimaced and then said decisively: 'Drop it. He's a dangerous man. We'd like to get our hands on him. He was responsible for a lot of people going to their death, particularly after the attempt on Hitler's life. We've questioned the ones who were still alive and in prison when we arrived and again and again the name that crops up is 'Kurt Waldenheim'. If he's still alive he's gone into hiding and very successfully. He'll turn on anyone who flushes him out.'

He saw that she was looking unconvinced and added: 'If any clue should come your way I would, of course, expect you to report it. And the next thing that would happen would be that you'd find yourself flying back to England. I wouldn't risk keeping you in the country if he knew you were responsible for turning him in.'

This time Christine did not trouble to hide her incredulity. 'What could he do?' she asked. 'The Nazis' organization is broken.'

'Oh, is it? Let me tell you, my naïve child, that there's a sewer beneath the surface. Some of the biggest criminals have got clean away. How? Because there are people willing to help them. Because there are people who believe that they'll come to power again. There are even fanatics who think that Hitler himself isn't dead. You see the poor suffering devils in the streets and feel sorry for them. Scratch the surface and you'll find hatred, a desire for revenge and a brute determination to come out on top again.'

He sighed and pushed a hand through his thinning hair. 'Look, I didn't call you in here to give you a lecture on German psychology. They're a curious people, stamping around in jackboots one day, wallowing in humiliation the next. I've liked the individuals I've met and yet, collectively, they're totally lacking in moral sense. All I want to say to you is – leave Kurt Waldenheim alone!'

She would have obeyed if she hadn't heard, a few days later, a second reference to the assassination attempt on Hitler. She had called a third time on the Hofmeyers, this time with a tentative suggestion about a way in which Frau Hofmeyer might earn a little money. One of the girls in the clerical team she controlled had been regretting that there was nothing she could buy to send home as a present for her little sister.

'I know someone who makes rag dolls,' Christine said.

'I wish I'd known that!' the girl exclaimed. 'Would she make one for me for Linda's birthday, do you think?'

'She might. I could ask her. The trouble is, it's difficult for her to get hold of materials.'

'We could scrape round and see what we could get together,' another girl suggested.

Just after the New Year, Christine went along with a bag full of cast-off stockings for stuffing, an old satin slip, a torn Service shirt, some unravelled knitting wool and odds and ends of sewing thread and put her idea to Frau Hofmeyer. She was nervous about making the suggestion, but to her relief the older woman seized on it eagerly.

'Anything I can do to help the family,' she said. 'I have a great deal of time on my hands. Once, as you know, I taught music – those days are over. The work will be a pleasure to me, and to be paid for it, that will be wonderful.'

'It would be more useful if you could be paid in goods instead of money,' Elsa remarked.

She picked up the old satin slip and fingered it regretfully. It was too worn to be used for anything but cutting up for dolls' clothes.

'I can't encourage the girls to give away their food,' Christine said firmly. 'It must be money, I'm afraid.'

They were still discussing the doll which was to be made as a model and the orders that might follow when Frieda came in. She looked exhausted and very dirty.

'It's snowing,' she said. She nodded in a surly way to Christine and then went over to the sink and began running water to wash her hands. She stared in lethargic despair at the thin trickle that came out of the tap. 'The water pressure's down again.'

'So many of the mains are fractured,' Frau Hofmeyer explained to Christine. She sounded as if she were apologizing. 'Sometimes we have water, sometimes we don't. And, of course, we boil every drop we drink.'

'The sewage seeps into it,' Frieda explained. She leaned against the sink and her mother exclaimed: 'How tired you look, Frieda!'

'I'm worn out.' She looked with malevolent spite at Elsa, lounging by the side of the closed stove in the warmest spot in the room. 'I'm not fortunate enough to have American friends who give me an easy job serving drinks to officers.'

'You know why I got my job,' Elsa said with an air of indifference. She glanced at Christine and said deliberately:

'They respect me because my father martyred himself in the attempt to rid our country of Adolf Hitler.'

Christine had no wish to involve herself in what threatened to turn into a family quarrel, but she had to ask: 'Really? Who was your father?'

'General Gottfried Obermann. He took poison rather than fall into the hands of the Gestapo when his part in the plot was discovered.'

'How terrible!' As Elsa had anticipated, Christine looked at her with a new interest. 'You were lucky not to have been arrested yourself, weren't you?' she asked.

Frieda gave a strange, ironic little laugh, which Elsa ignored. 'I had quarrelled with my father over my marriage to Gunther,' she said. 'We had not been in touch for a year and so I was left alone.'

Christine looked slightly disappointed. 'Then you didn't actually know about the plot?' she asked.

Elsa produced the version of her story which had been so successful with the Americans. 'I did know,' she said. 'My quarrel with *Vati* was mostly pretence, so that I wouldn't seem to be implicated. I was very, very fortunate that the Gestapo believed my story.'

'You were indeed! I've heard that in some cases whole families, even distant relatives, were tortured, thrown into prison, killed.' She looked at Elsa curiously. 'It's strange that you should mention the Generals' Plot. I was given details about it because of a man I was trying to trace. His name was Kurt Waldenheim. I don't suppose you ever knew him?'

A silence descended on the room, so profound that a drip from the tap Frieda had been trying to use made Christine jump nervously.

Elsa spoke, very slowly, as if she were choosing her words with great care. 'I did know him. Inevitably. My father was close to the centre and so was he. He disappeared at the time of Hitler's death.'

It was Frieda who asked: 'Why are you trying to trace him?'

Once again Christine told her story. It sounded fantastic and she could see that none of them quite understood her motive for trying to discover the whereabouts of a fanatical Nazi.'

Frieda shook her head in disbelief. 'You're a curious people,' she said.

Elsa moistened her lips. 'Have you had any success in your search?' she asked.

'None at all. And now I've been told to give it up. Apparently he's regarded as a dangerous man. I was told he was responsible for the arrest of many innocent people. You were lucky to escape.'

'Yes, wasn't she?' Frieda murmured. 'Do tell us, Elsa, how *did* you manage to persuade Kurt not to arrest you? You saw him often enough at the time.'

'He interrogated me, I persuaded him that I knew nothing, and he let me go,' Elsa said. She looked hard at Christine. 'You are wise not to go on looking for him. I think he is dead, but if he is alive then he is certainly dangerous.'

Christine left as soon as she could after that. The undercurrent of antagonism between Frieda and Elsa made her uneasy and she very much wished that she hadn't brought up the subject of Kurt Waldenheim. The reaction had been very strange. Elsa had been frightened and Frieda had seemed to be jeering at her.

She was so preoccupied that she nearly collided with Gunther at the foot of the stairs.

He looked at her with a frown. As Frieda had said, it was snowing outside and he had a scattering of white flakes over the shoulders of the *Luftwaffe* overcoat he still wore, shorn of its insignia, and there were droplets of melted snow in his hair.

'Are you on your own again? I've told you it's not safe.'

'I stayed longer than I meant to. It's not dark yet, is it?'

'That's not the point. I'd better walk down the road with you.'

She looked out at the gathering gloom. The sky was a sullen yellow, the vast empty heaps of tumbled bricks stretched away into the distance. Something scuttled across the road. It was a rat. Christine shivered. Instead of protesting, she let him turn round and walk back down the road with her.

They walked along without speaking. Christine pulled her

cap down and turned up her coat collar. The wind drove the snow into her face and made it smart.

When they reached the corner where they had parted before she turned to say goodbye, but Gunther said abruptly: 'It's the New Year. For God's sake let's stick to some of the civilized customs. Will you let me buy you a drink? Or are you afraid of being pulled in by the Military Police for fraternizing with a German?'

'That nonsense about fraternization has been dropped and I'd be glad of something to warm me,' Christine said. 'There's a bar down the road where we're allowed to go. I don't suppose anyone will notice or care what nationality you are.'

It was too early for the bar to be crowded. No-one paid any attention to them. Christine sat down at a small table with a white marble top, a relic of an earlier, more gracious age. Gunther didn't ask her what she would like to drink. He went straight to the counter and when he came to join her he was carrying two steaming glasses. The smell of hot spiced wine filled the air.

As Christine took her glass from him she was carried back across the years. Snow, and Gunther – and *Glühwein*. She looked up at Gunther and saw that he was smiling.

'Yes, I was remembering, too,' he said. 'Kitzbühel.'

'Such a long time ago. How young we were – and how innocent!'

'*You* were innocent,' he corrected her. He paused for a moment and then he said: 'No, you are right, we were both innocent.'

'It was a good time,' Christine said. She lifted her glass. 'What shall we drink to, Gunther?'

'A happier New Year than either of us has known for the past six years?'

She nodded and they drank and then sat in silence until they both looked up and started to speak together.

Christine said: 'You first.'

'I was going to tell you how much it had surprised me to see you in uniform. Our women didn't join the armed forces to anything like the same extent as yours did. I never once thought of you as having joined up.'

'You did think about me sometimes?'

As soon as the question was out she wished she hadn't asked it: it sounded as if she was trying to get something more from him than the cool friendship he had shown towards her.

She thought from the brevity with which Gunther answered, 'Yes, I did,' that he thought the same. She hurried on to speak of her service in the WAAF.

'We had compulsory call-up from 1942, but I went in before that. I was in radar.' She hesitated and then said apologetically, 'I'm not really supposed to talk about it, even though the war is over.'

'It was a very efficient system,' he said. 'You met your husband through being in the RAF?'

'I met him when he visited Michael in hospital.' Haltingly at first, she began to tell him about Larry. The *Glühwein* grew cool in the glasses in front of them. Gunther listened intently, gathering as much from the changing expression on her face as from her words. She spoke in a mixture of English and German and when she paused for a word he helped her out.

'You loved him very much,' he said.

'Yes, I did. I still grieve over his death.'

'A terrible accident, after he had been through so much.'

She looked at him with a slight, sad smile and shook her head.

'I see. He was indeed a brave man.'

'I think it would have been braver to go on living.'

'You expected too much of him,' he said gently. 'In his place, I think I would have done the same thing – if I could have found the courage.'

To try to chase away the sadness from her eyes he said: 'Drink your wine, Christine. Now, what were you going to ask me?'

'Only what you were doing now.' She sipped her wine obediently. 'I wonder where they got these spices?'

'On the black market, probably stolen from the Americans. I'm trying to help in setting up some sort of administration for this poor torn city. Don't ask why me – the only reason I can think of is that I speak English.

283

She considered him carefully. 'You look like a person used to authority.' She sounded surprised, which made him smile.

'I hate to think of you being a prisoner,' Christine added abruptly. 'Did they treat you well?'

'Oh, yes. We were all very civilized about it. I gave up without a struggle when I saw defeat was inevitable. I suppose it might have been more noble to have fought to the death, but I didn't see much point in fighting for a cause in which I'd lost faith.'

He looked down at his wine and said carefully: 'Some of my people, including Frieda, despise me for working now with the British. For my part, I think *someone* has got to make a start in helping to build a new Germany. I'm not, and never will be, a politician, but I'm quite good at organizing things, I find. But I don't want to end up as a civil servant. I'll bow out as soon as I can. When they find administrators who are not old men or discredited Nazis.'

'Do you still want to be an architect?'

'You haven't forgotten that? Yes, it's still what I'd really like to do. If only I'd qualified before the war.'

'Michael has the same problem, but he's discovered that he likes teaching and he may go into that.'

'Does he know you've made contact with me?'

'Yes.' She laughed at the recollection of Michael's last letter. 'He doesn't want to admit it, but he'd dying to know about your war record. Can I write home and tell him you were a *Luftwaffe* ace?'

He looked at her strangely. 'Will he hold it against me if I say yes?'

'I don't think so. The boys in the RAF seemed to hate the Germans *en masse*, but had quite a respect for the *Luftwaffe* pilots they fought, especially in the sort of single combat you and Michael were engaged in.'

'I got the Knight's Cross.'

'That's quite an award, isn't it?' she asked slowly.

'It means that I shot down more than twenty aircraft. I was most truly your enemy, Christine.'

'But not now – not *now*, Gunther.'

284

He shrugged and did not answer. At last he said: 'It is a bitter thing, to be defeated.'

'Even though you didn't believe in what you were fighting for?'

'It's not logical, but yes. I wanted to get rid of the Nazis and I wanted Germany to win – and the two things were not compatible.'

'Some people thought both could be achieved. Your wife told me about her father being in the plot against Hitler.'

'Dear Elsa! Now she's a true politician; she always knows which side will come out on top.'

He spoke with an irony that made her wonder about his relations with the attractive Elsa, but he asked her a question about conditions in England and the talk drifted away to other things.

Christine felt warm and comfortable, with a pleasant glow inside from the hot wine. Gunther sat opposite her, turned sideways to the table, with one long leg crossed over the other and one elbow resting on the table. They talked easily in the strange, polyglot language they had unconsciously adopted. It was not until he glanced at his wrist and then quickly looked away again that Christine realized that he had been accustomed to wearing a watch that he no longer possessed. It gave her a jolt, that small, unthinking gesture. As did the shadow on his face as he was brought back to the realization of all he had lost.

She was careful not to look at her own watch, as she said: 'I must go.' She pulled her bag on to her shoulder and smiled at him. 'Thank you, Gunther. For the drink and for sparing the time to talk to me. I've enjoyed it.'

It was when they stood up that it happened. Christine caught her foot against the chair leg and stumbled; Gunther put out his arm quickly and caught her, supporting her just under the elbow. She caught her breath and he asked in a concerned voice: 'You didn't hurt yourself?'

She shook her head, unable to control her voice sufficiently to speak. For the first time since they had met she thought to herself incredulously: 'This is *Gunther*.' Gunther, who had held her naked in his arms all through a long hot summer's afternoon; Gunther who had comforted her when she had fled to him in the dark of the night; Gunther, for whose sake she had defied her parents and journeyed half-way across Europe. Her dear enemy, who had been in her thoughts all through the first dark year of the war.

She avoided looking at him, afraid that he would read her eyes and know what had happened to her. She must get over it, and quickly. It was not reasonable, this sudden stab of remembered passion for a man who no longer thought of her in that way, who was married to someone else.

They went out into the dark night. The wind had dropped and the snow was falling steadily. In the light from the café the flakes whirled round them. They paused and Christine said: 'I'm leaving Berlin in the morning. I don't know whether I'll be coming back again.'

'We must say goodbye then.'

'Yes, goodbye,' she said mechanically.

She was filled with blank astonishment that it should hurt so much that this might be their last meeting. Her lips moved stiffly as she pretended to smile and then she turned away and hurried down the road away from him. She did not look round and didn't know that Gunther watched until she was out of sight, standing quite motionless, the snow gathering on his head and shoulders.

When she got back to her cold little room Christine hung up her coat and took off her wet shoes, moving automatically with no idea of what she was doing. She began to walk up and down the room, clasping her upper arms with her hands, trying to get warm and to hold in the pain. How could it have happened, between one breath and the next, to be stricken to the bone by desire for a man she only half remembered? But he was not a stranger. He was Gunther, and she longed for his strength and his tenderness, for the power of his body and the gentleness of his hands. It was as if some seed which had been lying dormant beneath the surface all these years had suddenly been fed and watered and had sprung into life.

She told herself it was too sudden a growth to be taken seriously, that this feeling would die of neglect as long as she never saw him again and put her mind resolutely towards forgetting him. It wasn't as if he had given the slightest sign that he'd been affected in the same way. He had been friendly, nothing more. As friendly as any considerate man might be towards an old mistress, she thought bitterly. He was married. He had spoken of his wife only that evening as 'dear Elsa'. He loved her, he would never love Christine, never again. She must make up her mind that it was hopeless. If she was strong, in time she would get over it, just as she had the first time she had loved him.

Gunther walked home quickly, his hands in his pockets and his shoulders hunched against the cold. As soon as he entered the kitchen he knew there had been a quarrel. His mother was looking distressed. There were patches of colour high on her cheekbones and her hands moved uncertainly amongst the scraps of material which littered the table. Elsa was smoking a cigarette, and that alone might have explained the smouldering atmosphere, since Frieda would see it as a wanton waste of an asset which could be converted into food or fuel. Frieda was angrily banging plates together in the sink in a way that made Frau Hofmeyer wince.

It was Frieda who said with a snap as Gunther came in: 'You're late.'

'I was delayed. It's snowing hard,' he said. He was not sure why he avoided mentioning his meeting with Christine. He hadn't made a conscious decision to conceal it. He just didn't want to talk about it.

'Your English girlfriend has been here,' Elsa remarked.

It was the moment when he ought to have replied: 'Yes, I know', but he did not.

Instead, he picked up a strip of faded pink satin and fingered it absentmindedly. His mother said, with an obvious attempt to turn the conversation towards something pleasant: 'She's suggested I should make some dolls and sell them. And she brought these bits of material to help me. Such a kind thought, and I shall enjoy the work.'

The movement of Gunther's fingers over the scrap of satin stopped. This, whatever it had been – an undergarment, a nightdress – had belonged to Christine. It had known the touch of her warm, sweet flesh, had slithered softly over her breasts and hips. Christine, with her new seriousness, her shadowed eyes, her air of cool authority. Christine, with her generous spirit, who had sought out his family and tried to help them, who seemed to bear no ill-will towards them because of the tragedy that had touched her life. Christine, whom he had once loved.

He put the piece of material down and said in an expressionless voice: 'Have we anything to eat?'

'Vegetable soup, a piece of sausage, some bread,' Frieda answered. 'Elsa will get it for you. She does little else around here.'

Elsa stubbed out her cigarette, half smoked. Gunther could see Frieda grit her teeth in an effort to hold back a bitter comment. Elsa was smiling, knowing how provoking she was being. She stretched her arms above her head, flexing her body like a cat.

'I get tired,' she said.

There was something about her smile, about her sensuous enjoyment of the movement that made Gunther narrow his eyes. Elsa was altogether too pleased with herself these days.

They went to bed early to save fuel and the meagre supply of oil for the lamp that was their only light.

'Horrible winter!' Elsa grumbled. 'I do so long to be warm.'

She snuggled up against Gunther and he put his arms round her, but they neither of them wanted anything more than the extra warmth that they engendered by lying close.

'I wish you'd try not to annoy Frieda,' Gunther said. 'I know she can be difficult, but she's unhappy and the work she's doing is enough to grind anyone down.'

'Darling, I never could get on with those old maid types. Still, I will try. For you.'

She kissed him quickly, but Gunther did not respond. She tried to make herself relax and appear at ease because she didn't want him to enquire too deeply into the cause of her quarrel with Frieda.

Frieda had been quick to see how shaken Elsa had been by Christine's story of her search for Kurt Waldenheim. She had taunted her after Christine had left, not coming out into the open, but hinting that Elsa had been his mistress, even suggesting that she knew where he was and did not want him to be found because of what he might reveal about her.

The thing that had frightened Elsa was that it was true. Because she had been afraid she had relaxed the guard she normally set on her tongue and had answered insolently, and the animosity between the two women, usually kept beneath the surface, had spewed out in an exchange of home truths intended to wound. It had been a mistake on Elsa's part and she was annoyed with herself. The cigarette she had lit had been to calm her nerves as much as an act of defiance. She ought to have laughed off Frieda's accusations and normally she would have had the control to do it, especially if she had been able to believe that Kurt was dead or safely out of the way. But coming soon after a singularly unnerving meeting with him she had been shaken by hearing his name again from Christine, of all people. It was going to ruin all her plans if Kurt was located and talked too freely.

Their meeting had been no accident. He had sought her out, not as she had at first thought because he was still in love with her – if his strange feeling for her could be called love – but because he believed she could be of use to him. She had been appalled to discover how much he knew about her.

'I suppose it was inevitable that you should be taken up by the Americans,' he said. 'The most naïve of our conquerors, and the richest.'

He had waylaid her in the street, coming up and talking to her quite openly.

'Your name is on their wanted list, did you know that?' she asked.

'Of course!' His thin eyebrows rose in exaggerated surprise. 'But you won't denounce me, Elsa. You have too much to lose by admitting that you were the mistress of a so-called war criminal.'

'If I explained that I was forced by circumstances . . .' she began desperately.

'I've no doubt you'd make it sound most touching,' he interrupted her. 'All the same, it would tarnish the image a bit, wouldn't it? No, I don't think you'll give me away. On the contrary, I think you'll help me.'

'I can't believe there is anything I could possibly do that would help you.'

When he told her what he wanted she was panic-stricken. She was to get on intimate terms with a certain Colonel Blake Tickener.

'You know him already,' Kurt had said. 'Oh, yes, you do! Useless to deny it, Elsa. Now you are going to get to know him a great deal better. You won't be the first German girl he's laid. For someone of your talents it should be easy.'

'What are you going to do to him?'

'Don't worry, it's no part of our plan to harm him. I want some information, possibly the loan of his keys for a few hours, access to some files. Once we've got what we want you can drop him.'

'You say "our" and "we" – who are you?'

He looked at her with scorn. 'We are the same as we have always been. Do you imagine we've given up? Our great Leader is dead, but the cause remains the same. We will rise again, stronger than ever.'

His black eyes glittered, a flush of colour rose in his bony face.

'You're mad,' Elsa whispered.

'Mad, am I?' He caught hold of her arm and she winced as his thin fingers bit into the flesh. 'You'll find out how mad I am if you betray me. If I'm taken there are others who will know who to blame. You'll never be safe again, Elsa.'

It had been his fanaticism that had frightened her, his total conviction that the Nazi Party would come back into power. Reason told her that it was impossible, but reason had nothing to do with Kurt's blind faith. She believed him when he said he had friends who would deal with her if she denounced him.

She began to understand the reason behind what Kurt wanted her to do when she got to know Colonel Tickener better. He was in charge of information on Nazi war criminals. He was thirty-eight and unmarried, a great bull of a man who appeared at first sight to have more muscle than brain, but this did not do justice to his natural shrewdness. He liked women and Elsa did not think it would be difficult to arouse his interest, but this was far from saying that it would be easy to lead him into indiscretion. On the contrary, she judged that he might become suspicious if she tried to rush him into a more intimate relationship. Not that there were not young women in Berlin ready and anxious to fall into bed for the sake of food and warmth and a few of life's necessities, but Elsa had acquired the reputation of being someone rather special.

It was already several weeks since Kurt had approached her. He knew that her friendship with the Colonel had progressed and they were seeing a lot of one another. She only hoped that he wouldn't start getting impatient because a new and dazzling prospect had begun to open up for Elsa. Colonel Tickener seemed to take her far more seriously than the other men she teased and kept on a string. Suppose she could persuade him to marry her?

It would mean getting rid of Gunther, which would be a pity in some ways, but she couldn't go on living a life of abject poverty for very much longer: something would have to change, and she doubted whether it would be Gunther's circumstances. If she could marry Blake, go and live in America, leave the tired old world of Europe behind . . . she was breathless with anticipation as she thought about it.

It occurred to her now, lying in Gunther's arms, slowly losing the chill that had seemed to strike into her very bones when she first got into bed, that she might have been too hasty in warning Christine against trying to find Kurt. She ought to have encouraged her. If the British took him it would suit Elsa very well indeed.

Gunther was still awake. He was not restless, but she could sense a tension in him that would not allow him to relax. Because she, too, was wakeful and her mind centred on Christine, Elsa said: 'We must try to arrange for you to be at home next time your English mistress calls, darling. I think she was disappointed at not seeing you.'

'Don't call her that,' Gunther said.

'Your mistress? Wasn't she?'

He answered obliquely. 'It was a very long time ago.'

'I think she remembers. Why else should she take so much trouble to find you? Such a pity she didn't tell us when to expect her again.'

Because he was tired and off guard Gunther replied carelessly. 'She's leaving Berlin in the morning.'

Elsa was more alert than he was. 'And how do you know that, darling? She didn't tell us.'

'I saw her as she was leaving.'

'Really? And then it took you an hour and a half to walk up the stairs?'

'I walked back with her and we had a drink together,' Gunther said.

'And you weren't going to tell us about it? What a naughty boy!'

'It was nothing. There was such an atmosphere when I walked in that I decided not to mention it.'

'I'll believe you – this time,' Elsa decided. She sounded more amused than annoyed. 'What did you talk about all that long time?'

'She told me about her husband.'

'Yes, of course; she's a widow. So *dangerous*! I shall have to keep an eye on you, darling.'

Gunther moved restlessly, taking his arm from underneath her. 'Don't talk like that. Tell me, Elsa, if I had been wounded, left helpless and tied to a wheelchair, would you have stayed with me?'

Whatever Elsa's faults, hypocrisy was not one of them. She thought it over, but in the end she answered with stark honesty.

'Such a ghastly prospect. I don't know – it isn't exactly *me*, is it? I think I would have waved you a quiet farewell.'

It was the answer he had expected and he respected her for making no pretence, but he couldn't help letting his mind dwell on a girl who would have been staunch no matter what it cost her.

'Why do you ask?' Elsa said. 'Is that what happened to Christine's husband?'

'So she told me.'

'What a lovely confidential talk you had! I feel almost jealous.'

'Don't be silly. I doubt whether I'll ever see her again.'

He said it in an offhand way, as if it was of no importance, but it did matter, that he had said goodbye to Christine that evening. He lay on his back, open-eyed in the darkness, with his wife cuddled up against him, and admitted to himself that it was just as well that he and Christine couldn't go on meeting. The attraction she still held for him was dangerous. Elsa, in her better moments, was still a warm little bundle of joy, but Christine was something special. No longer an untried girl, but a woman who had faced danger and tragedy and had matured in a way that made her twice as desirable as she had been before the war. Beautiful, too. He was still dwelling on the recollection of the lovely line of her jaw and the way her hair lifted away from her temples when the grinding fatigue of his day overcame him and he fell asleep.

Chapter Fifteen

At the beginning of February, some three weeks after Christine's departure from Berlin, an elderly man collapsed in the street at the feet of two British military policemen. Although he was too weak to stand he did not lose consciousness and as they bent over him he whispered in English: 'I am Professor Gregoire Bernhardt. Please to inform your Scientific Department . . .' His voice trailed away and his eyes closed.

His body was emaciated and his feet were raw under the rags in which he had swathed them, but after rest and medical attention he was able to tell his story.

He was a scientist, an eminent mathematician and an authority on radio waves. Until the last few months of the war he had been held in high regard, but early in 1945 he had had the misfortune to bring Hitler's anger down on him because, as he said: 'I could not perform miracles.'

Since he claimed to be an expert in radar the team for which Christine was working was contacted.

'Gregoire Bernhardt!' one scientist exclaimed. 'I certainly do know him! We corresponded regularly before the war. I'll come to Berlin to see him.'

Christine, supervising the production of the part of the report that was already in preparation, was called in to see the scientist.

'Sit down, Section Officer,' he said. 'I've got a job for you. If you agree, that is. There's a man in hospital in Berlin who's probably got more useful information locked up in his brain than all the other people we've interviewed put together. I'm going to see him tomorrow. This is a very confidential assignment, of course. He's walked away from the Russians in order to give the benefit of his knowledge to us. I don't want it to leak out that we've got him in our hands, certainly not to the Russians and preferably . . .' He hesitated.

'Not even to our friends?' Christine supplied, smiling.

'You've got it. We'll share what we know later, but I want a chance to assess it first. You do shorthand and typing and you speak German. Will you come with me and do all the notes on my talks?'

Christine smiled again. She liked this clever little man and enjoyed his enthusiasm. 'I'm supposed to be at your disposal,' she pointed out. 'All you have to do is give me an order. I have to obey – whether I want to or not.'

'I'd rather have a keen volunteer,' he said.

'You have one.'

Because they had been given an office close to his in the administrative building in Wilmersdorf one of the first people she met when she returned to Berlin was Major Dawson. She did not expect him to recognize her, but he stopped her in the corridor and asked: 'Section Officer Telford, isn't it? Tell me, did you ever – in spite of the good advice I gave you – find out anything more about Kurt Waldenheim?'

'I came across somebody who used to know him,' she admitted.

'But no clue to his present whereabouts?'

'You told me not to ask,' she pointed out. She tried to remember exactly what had been said when she mentioned the name. 'There was an atmosphere,' she said slowly. 'But I didn't want to take it further because it was a little awkward. The person who knew him was the wife of . . . of a friend of mine from before the war.'

'I think I'll take the name and address,' Major Dawson said. He noticed her worried look and added: 'No need to be embarrassed. I'm not asking you to inform on your friends. I merely want to follow up a possible lead on a particularly vile criminal.'

She gave him the information he wanted, but she was unhappy about it. Kurt Waldenheim might be all the Major said, but it was repugnant to think that Gunther's wife might be involved in unpleasantness because Christine had talked about a conversation between them.

For the first few days Christine was not particularly busy and no-one knew what to do with her. She was on a special assignment; she could not be used for any other work; she had a status that was almost civilian, although she was still nominally subject to military discipline. It was a boring situation and it left her with too much time to think. To think, and to look out of the window.

She was doing just that one day when a tall, familiar figure in an old *Luftwaffe* overcoat walked quickly down the street. Christine moved nearer to the window to make sure she wasn't mistaken, but it was Gunther and he was coming into the building. It ought not to have surprised her; she knew that he was, as Frieda had said, 'collaborating with the British', but the realization that they were actually in the same building jolted her. She hadn't meant to see him again, but now that he was here, so close, she had to try and speak to him.

She left the office she shared with her superior and almost ran along the corridor. As she approached the main entrance she slowed down, ashamed of her undignified haste. As she had expected, Gunther was still there. It took time to go through the formalities, stating one's business, producing identification, and being passed on to the right person.

She managed to say, with just the right degree of surprise: 'Gunther! How nice to see you.'

He didn't look at all pleased. In fact, he was frowning as he said: 'I thought you had left Berlin.'

'I had to come back. How are you?'

'I am well.' He glanced back, out of the door he had just come through. 'If you are going out you should wear your coat. It is raining.'

'I'm not going out.' Christine realized that she could produce no excuse for being in the entrance hall. Her colour deepened as she admitted: 'I saw you from the window and ran down to say hello.'

To her relief he laughed. 'So! You are as impulsive as ever, Christine. I must not stop. Already I am late for a meeting to discuss some return of public transport. You see how important this is?'

'Yes. Of course,' Christine said.

She smiled brilliantly to hide her disappointment. She had time on her hands, but Gunther was busy. She respected him for the way he was trying to help his people, but it did not stop her feeling like a child who had been dismissed.

'Give my best wishes to your mother,' she said.

He nodded, and she wandered back to her office, disconsolate and annoyed with herself.

An hour later there was a tap on her door. The smart young Corporal who opened it said: 'Herr Hofmeyer to see you, ma'am.'

Behind him, Gunther caught her eye and gave her a tiny wink. Suddenly he looked exactly like the mischievous boy she had known in Kitzbühel when they had first met.

She tried to look as if she had been expecting him, but after the Corporal had left she shook her head at him.

'After the meeting I have endured I must refresh myself by talking to someone sensible,' Gunther explained. 'Oh these bureaucrats! They are well-meaning, but they . . .'

'Bumble?' Christine suggested.

He considered it. 'It is not a word I know, but it sounds good,' he agreed. 'Yes, they say bumble, bumble and nothing is *done*. Now, tell me what brings you back to Berlin.'

Christine looked at him and bit her lip. 'I . . .'

'You must not tell me?' It didn't please him, but he passed it off with a shrug. 'To me it does not look as if you are working very hard.'

'Not at the moment,' she admitted. 'Tell me more about what you are doing.'

He gave her a graphic account of the meeting he had sat in on that morning. He made it sound funny, but she understood and sympathized with his frustration.

'We must begin to help ourselves, not rely on former enemies to prop us up,' he concluded.

Half an hour had gone by. Gunther stood up and buttoned his overcoat.

'I believe it is necessary for me to have an escort down to the front hall,' he said.

'I'll come with you,' Christine said.

'To be shown out by such a high-ranking officer, that is indeed an honour.'

The teasing look was back on his face. They went down the corridor laughing and Christine returned to her desk after she had seen him off feeling completely contented. It was all right. She had seen him and the sky had not fallen in. They were friends. He was still one of the most attractive men she would ever meet, but she would be sensible about it.

Twenty-four hours later the hunger to see him again was so intense that she hardly knew how to bear it. She went over and over their conversation. Had there been anything about it to show that he had the same feeling towards her? No, nothing. Only that sense of comradeship that seemed to spring up between them every time they met. Only the strangely rested look he had had when he left her, as if he had indeed been refreshed by their talk.

He was so near. She could, if she chose, go and visit him in his home. But there was not the same ease between them when his mother and sister were there. And his wife.

At that point Christine halted her train of thought. He was married and, as far as she could judge, happily married. She must stop thinking about him.

He came back the following day. As it happened, her superior was in the room when her telephone rang and she took the message that Herr Hofmeyer was enquiring for her.

'I'll come down,' she said. She glanced at the scientist, but he was too engrossed to notice her reaction to this simple message.

Gunther was in as much of a hurry as he had been on the first morning.

'I am not here today for a meeting, but with a message for you from my mother. She has three dolls ready for you. Is it possible for you to call on her to collect them?'

'Yes, of course. Three! She must have been working hard. I'll call round . . .' she hesitated.

'During the daytime,' Gunther said deliberately. The way he said it made Christine look up into his face, searching to see if she had understood correctly the emphasis behind his words.

Their eyes met and Gunther added: 'She is very much alone

during the day. She will be glad of a visitor then. And it is better so.'

Christine nodded, unable to speak.

With his eyes fixed on her face Gunther said: 'It is not that I don't want to see you.'

She managed a small movement of her lips that was almost a smile.

Almost under his breath, Gunther said: 'Christine, go back to England.'

They turned away from one another and parted without saying goodbye.

She went the next morning, having secured absentminded permission to make herself scarce for an hour or two. There was an American jeep with a bored-looking driver in it parked outside the dilapidated apartment house. He gave Christine a sketchy salute and a slow, admiring inspection which sent her up the stairs with heightened colour. She found both Gunther's mother and his wife at home, but Elsa was about to leave for work with a large American she introduced as Colonel Tickener. He had called for her apparently, and had sat down for a cup of coffee which was also his gift while she finished getting ready.

'How fortunate, there is still some coffee left,' Frau Hofmeyer said. She was flushed with pleasure at this sudden influx of visitors and at being able to offer them some refreshment.

'We thought you'd left Berlin,' Elsa remarked.

'Yes, I had to come back unexpectedly,' Christine said.

Elsa switched to the English she was now able to speak with a fair degree of fluency.

'I'm glad because I wanted to speak to you,' she said. 'Come with me while I put on my coat.'

Frau Hofmeyer looked puzzled at this exchange she couldn't understand and the Colonel said: 'Don't be over-long with your secrets, girls. I'm a busy man.'

Elsa touched his arm as she passed him and smiled with an intimacy that Christine found distasteful. She took Christine along the corridor and into the bedroom. The windows were boarded over and the room was very dark and crowded with furniture.

'We had to put everything from the rooms that were damaged into the ones that survived,' Elsa remarked.

She manoeuvred her way round a chair to open a cupboard door and took out a fur jacket and hat.

'Frieda wanted me to sell these,' she said. 'But I'm glad I didn't, now that it's no longer necessary.'

Christine, pressed up against the big double bed Elsa shared with Gunther, said a little desperately: 'You wanted to talk to me?'

'I've discovered where Kurt Waldenheim is living.' Elsa paused, peering through the gloom to see what effect this would have on Christine.

'I thought you were against me trying to get in touch with him?' Christine asked.

'I'll give you the address. You must decide for yourself what use you make of it,' Elsa said. She didn't want to be more explicit than that, but she added: 'As long as I'm not brought into it.'

Surely this English girl would have the sense to understand what she was hinting at? Elsa wanted Kurt out of the way. He had been in touch with her twice in the last three weeks and each time he had been more impatient. He had jeered at her, saying that it had not taken her that long in the past to get a man into bed with her and he had not believed the excuses she had given him.

Not that Elsa had been wasting her time. On the contrary, she was engaged in what, from her point of view, was likely to prove a most profitable campaign. Blake Tickener wanted her, but Elsa, playing her fish with skill, had not so far granted him anything but a few kisses. Encouraging him to call at the Hofmeyers' flat was all part of her scheme. He must be made to see that Elsa was something different. Very delicately she was edging him towards a picture of her as an aristocrat who had married a war hero from a lower social scale and was finding in peacetime that they were not compatible. She was keeping him well away from Gunther, partly because she had an uneasy feeling that if the two men did meet they might like one another in the strange way that all Gunther's former enemies seemed to like him, and also because she was afraid

Gunther might start to suspect her, and if her ploy failed then she would have to hold on to him and make do with what she had.

The one thing she did not want was for Kurt to grow desperate and carry out his threat of revealing their past liaison. If it had been one isolated incident she thought she could have persuaded Gunther to be understanding about it; she was not sure that he would overlook a sustained affair. He knew her too well; he would guess that no matter how she might protest now, she had found excitement in conquering Kurt, and he would be less tolerant towards her than he was at present.

As for Blake, she had worked hard at the romantic image she had built up for him in the hope of persuading him that they were so much in love with one another that marriage was the only solution. Her reading of him suggested that to Blake black was black and white was white; either she was a good little anti-Nazi and a faithful wife or she was a criminal and a whore. She believed that any hint of an affair with an SS officer would drive him away in disgust.

After Elsa had gone Frau Hofmeyer brought out the three dolls to show Christine. Somehow she had contrived to make two dressed in peasant costume and a clown with bright red hair, a black button nose and wide satin trousers.

'They're absolutely delightful!' Christine exclaimed. 'The girls will be thrilled. Are you bored with making them or would you be prepared to do more if anyone was interested?'

'It's a great pleasure to me to be able to earn some money,' Frau Hofmeyer said.

All the same she was embarrassed when Christine brought out her wallet. She looked away and Christine tactfully put the money down on a ledge on the old-fashioned wooden dresser, saying nothing.

'How is Frieda?' she asked, more out of politeness than out of real interest.

Frau Hofmeyer sighed. 'Poor Frieda. She is not suited to the work she's doing. The women she works with are rough and they know why she is with them. They taunt her. She is very unhappy.'

She went to the dresser and opened one of the drawers.

'I came across these old photographs the other day.'

She did not add that they had been in a silver frame which Frieda was trying to sell or barter. She held them out to Christine. 'You would hardly believe it was the same girl.'

And Christine, looking at the picture of the bright-faced child with flaxen braids wound round her head, had to admit that she would never have known her for the bitter woman Frieda had become.

There was another child in one of the photographs, a little boy, sturdy and smiling.

'Is this Gunther?' she asked.

'Yes. What a little rascal he was!' She sat with the photographs in her hand and a look of bewilderment on her face. 'That was in the happy times, before all this trouble started. By the time Frieda grew up her father was dead, the Nazis were in power and she had joined the Party. She and Gunther never agreed about that. There were arguments, quarrels even. My poor Frieda, my poor little girl. Everyone thinks her hard, but I know, I know. She suffers. Inside herself where it hurts the most.'

Christine left soon after that.

'Have you come on your own?' Frau Hofmeyer asked. She looked worried, knowing that her son had felt strongly about Christine's wilful disregard for her own safety.

'I've arranged for a car to pick me up,' Christine said. 'He'll be waiting for me now.'

She felt worried and dissatisfied. She had called at a time when she could be almost certain that Gunther would not be at home, knowing that he was right in asking that of her, and yet she knew now that, against all reason, she had been hoping for a sight of him. And, quite apart from that disappointment, she was in a quandary about the news Elsa had given her about Kurt.

It seemed that Elsa wanted to inform on him, but in an indirect way. Major Dawson would be glad to know where to find him. All Christine had to do was to pass on the address. No doubt Kurt would get what he deserved, but that was a long way from the spirit in which she had set out to look for him.

The car was there and Christine climbed in. 'Are you busy?' she asked the driver.

'Not particularly, Section Officer,' he replied. 'Why? Do you want to go somewhere else before we return to HQ.'

'I'd like to go and look up a man one of my brothers knew,' Christine said. 'Everyone keeps telling me I ought not to go around on my own and this man was a Nazi. In fact, he seems to have been an odious character. All the same, I feel that I owe it to Jimmy to go and see him. Come with me, Corporal, and wait while I make enquiries at the address I've been given.'

With the comfortable conviction that an ex-Desert Rat Corporal ought to be sufficient bodyguard to satisfy even Major Dawson, Christine gave him the address.

They were almost there when an Army jeep hurtled round the corner ahead of them, tyres screaming. The Corporal swore and swerved to avoid it.

'Madman!' he said, slowing down to get himself back on the right side of the road.

As he spoke another jeep followed the first, driven with even greater recklessness. The car was in its path. Christine closed her eyes. There was a crash and when she had recovered sufficiently to look the second jeep had mounted the pavement and hit a wall. No-one seemed to be hurt, but the jeep was out of action. The driver and a Military Policeman leaped out.

'Get after that jeep, Corporal,' the MP ordered. 'Sorry, Section Officer, we'll have to commandeer your transport. We were rounding up black marketeers in the Tiergarten and the crafty devils pinched one of our jeeps.'

Christine barely had time to scramble clear before the car was on its way. She looked after it ruefully, knowing only too well that the Corporal who had been chauffeuring her was delighted at the chance of something more like active service. It was a terrible bore, just when she had made up her mind to go in search of Kurt Waldenheim. She was nearly on his doorstep. It seemed a feeble thing to do, to walk away. What could possibly happen to her at eleven o'clock in the morning in a well-populated area?

It went against all the orders they had been given about dealings with Germans, particularly those known to have been Nazis, but Christine's understanding of the possible danger had been blunted by her contact with Gunther's family. Even Frieda was just another girl who might as easily have lived in England or America and waved the national flag with more than customary fervour. Although she knew that a different class of Nazi thugs existed, Christine had not come face to face with any of them. She knew about the concentration camps, the massacre of the Jews, the brutal, meaningless executions, but it was all words to her. The only victims she had seen were the German people themselves and however much they might have brought their punishment down upon themselves she still felt compassion for the sufferings of the women and children and the exhausted, beaten men.

With this picture in her mind of a defeated enemy, Christine picked her way over the broken ground and fallen masonry towards the cellar where Kurt was supposed to be living. She paused once and asked a small boy: 'No 52?'

He cupped his hand hopefully: 'Cigarette?'

She shook her head, but she kept a few sweets in her pocket for just such moments as this and she took them out and dropped them into his open palm. He did not look particularly impressed, but he pointed to a place where some broken steps led down into what had once been the basement of a fine house and then he darted away, his head turned back towards her to see if she followed his directions.

The man who looked out was not, as she had hoped it might be, Kurt Waldenheim himself, but a strange looking individual who had once been fat and had suddenly become thin, so that the loose skin lay in folds along what had once been fleshy jowls. He had pale blue eyes which seemed unaccustomed to the light. His thick, pale-lashed lids blinked rapidly as he looked at her. He did not speak and Christine, speaking very slowly and carefully because she had doubts about his intelligence, said: 'I am looking for Kurt Waldenheim. Is he here?'

The blinking increased in rapidity. The man glanced over

his shoulder and then shook his head and would have closed the door if Christine had not held it open with her foot.

'Have I got the right address?' she asked. 'Number 52 Hildenburger Strasse?'

'Yes,' he said, and it seemed as if he spoke with the greatest reluctance.

'Then this is where I was told I would find Herr Waldenheim,' Christine said firmly. She was becoming more and more sure that the man was weak in the head. 'If he isn't here, where can I find him?'

'Don't know. Never heard of him. Go away,' the man said in short, staccato phrases.

'I have a message for him,' Christine persisted. She hesitated for a moment and then added: 'An offer of help.'

The man's expression changed. He was still suspicious, but he stopped trying to push the door shut.

'You . . . help *us*?' he said.

'If I can,' Christine said.

He thought about it and then he said: 'I'll ask. Wait here.'

He pushed her foot away with his own and shut the door in her face; she heard the key turn on the other side. She waited, shivering in the cold February wind. She wished she hadn't come.

She had a feeling of being watched, but although she looked round she failed to see the peephole through which Kurt was inspecting her. He had no idea who she was, but she appeared to be alone and defenceless and he was in the mood to gamble. He nodded to the doorkeeper and Hans went back and unlocked the door again.

'He's here,' he said. 'You can come in.'

She followed him, stumbling in the gloomy light on the uneven surface of a short passage which smelt damp. He opened a door and there was a room in front of her. The place was a positive rabbit warren, a whole network of basement rooms underneath the ruined mansions. This room was dark and unfurnished and she had the impression that it was merely an ante-chamber to something else beyond. She could see a line of light underneath a door opening out of it and she thought she could hear voices.

305

A figure she could hardly make out on the far side of the room struck a match and lit a candle. She saw his face clearly as the match flared and knew that she had found Kurt Waldenheim. Of course he was older than he had been in the newspaper photograph Jimmy had carried in his wallet, but it was the same face, thin, pallid, with arching eyebrows and the skin pulled tight over high cheekbones. He was wearing a thick, dark sweater and black trousers and until he had lit the candle his dark-clad figure had merged into the shadows.

He placed the candle on a broken shelf on the far wall and said: 'Who sent you here?'

'I came . . . because of my brother,' Christine said. It was not an answer to his question and she was not surprised when his voice sharpened.

'What's your name?'

'Christine Telford. It was Christine Brookfield. You have met both my brothers – Michael and Jimmy.'

'Brookfield? I know no-one of that name.'

Christine undid her overcoat and felt in the pocket of her jacket for the newspaper cutting. Without saying a word she held it out to Kurt. He took it and stood by the candle reading the account of his meeting with Michael. When he had finished he crumpled the piece of paper in his fist in a futile gesture of annoyance.

'I remember. It was the other one – the boy – who said he would come and find me after the war.'

'He said that when we'd won the war he would give you help if you needed it. Jimmy was killed, so I've come in his place.'

Kurt laughed, but there was sharp annoyance in his voice as he said: 'I seem to have made a mistake. That wasn't the sort of help I thought you meant when Hans gave me your message. Still . . .' He looked her over thoughtfully, '. . . you may yet be useful. You haven't told me how you found me.'

By this time every nerve in Christine's body was screaming to her that she should not have come. This man was dangerous, just as everyone had insisted. There was a sinister aura about him and about this network of cellars and the people who seemed to be living there. She thought of Elsa, Gunther's wife, who had given her the address and she did not feel disposed to tell Kurt who had passed on the information to her.

'I asked around and eventually came across someone who knew you,' she said.

'His name?'

'I've forgotten.'

Kurt came closer to her. 'I think you're lying,' he said. 'Very few people know my whereabouts. I'd like to know who betrayed me.'

'It was someone in our Intelligence Section,' Christine said.

Kurt laughed again. 'Now I'm quite sure you're lying. If the British Army knew where to find me they wouldn't send a nervous girl but a party of soldiers with guns. I won't press you for an answer just now. As I've said, you may turn out to be useful. I must ask for instructions. Wait here.'

He opened the other door into a well-lit room and Christine was left in the empty cellar with only the candle and a few chinks of daylight through a grating in the ceiling to show her where she was. As soon as the door had closed behind Kurt she took the candle and made for the exit into the passage. The door opened, but Hans was standing outside.

'I'm leaving,' Christine said firmly.

He shook his head. 'No,' he said.

There was no hope of getting past him in the narrow passageway. 'Get out of my way,' Christine said furiously.

'No.'

He put a massive hand against her chest and pushed. Christine staggered backwards, almost losing her balance. The candle in her hand shook violently, sending strange shadows leaping over the walls. Hans slammed the door and she was back in the empty room knowing for certain now that she was a prisoner.

It was still almost impossible for her to believe that anyone was going to be so foolish as to mistreat an officer in the British forces, especially a woman. Surely they didn't believe they could get away with it, and what could they possibly hope to gain? When Kurt came back to her she was more angry than frightened.

'Since you are obviously not going to accept my offer of help in the spirit in which it was meant I've decided to go away and forget all about you,' she said.

He ignored that. 'Come this way,' he said.

'I told you, I would like to go now.'

'Please, don't put me to the trouble of forcing you to do as you're told.'

'Don't you dare threaten me!'

Kurt gave what sounded like a weary sigh. Without replying he took the candle out of her hand and thrust it towards her face. The heat of the flame seared her cheek. Christine gasped and stepped back.

'You see?' Kurt said. 'Now, follow me.'

Stumbling slightly, one hand surreptitiously touching the scorched place on her face, Christine went with him into the lighted room next door.

There were half a dozen men in it and at one end there was a long table. On the wall was a flag, red and black and white, with the swastika sprawling across it; on the opposite wall was a large picture of Hitler.

One of the men got up and went to sit behind the table.

'You speak German?' he asked.

'Yes,' Christine said. She looked round, absorbing the meaning of the symbols which surrounded her. 'Who are you?'

'We are the remnants of a once great organization. We were, we thought, safe in this hideaway. It would interest us very much to know how you came to locate our friend Kurt.'

'I've already told him. I got the address from Major Dawson of our Intelligence Section.'

'You're lying. I'd like to see your papers.'

'I have no intention of showing them to you.'

'You keep them in your breast pocket, I suppose? I can offer you a choice of volunteers to come and take them off you.'

With shaking hands Christine took out her identification papers and handed them over.

'Section Officer Christine Laura Telford. Tell me again the story you told Kurt.'

Stumblingly Christine went through the story of Michael's mission to the United States, his meeting with Kurt, Jimmy's challenge.

The man looked at Kurt. 'You corroborate this?'

'Yes, Herr Oberst.'

'A curious story. The British are undoubtedly mad. I'm inclined to believe she's speaking the truth, except about the way she discovered your whereabouts, Kurt. You might perhaps examine your own conscience about that. There's been an indiscretion, I think.'

There was a menace behind these flat words which made Christine's blood freeze in her veins. She glanced at Kurt and was not surprised to see him lick his dry lips.

'There's one possibility,' he said. 'Elsa Obermann – General Obermann's daughter – I recruited her to get information out of the Americans.'

'The daughter of a traitor. Your judgment seems to have been at fault. Do you have a hold over her?'

'She was my mistress. She doesn't want it known.'

'And you told her where you were to be found?'

Kurt hesitated. 'Not the address. I think I may have given away the locality. She's capable of following me to find out where I went.'

'A resourceful young woman. A pity she is not to be trusted.' He turned to Christine. 'Elsa Obermann gave you the address?'

'I don't know anyone called Elsa Obermann,' Christine said truthfully.

'She's married to Gunther Hofmeyer, the *Luftwaffe* pilot,' Kurt intervened.

'Perhaps you know someone called Elsa Hofmeyer?' the Colonel suggested to Christine. 'No? What a faulty memory you have. However, it's of no immediate importance. What we have to consider is how we can make use of you.'

He sat back in his chair and looked at Christine thoughtfully. She tried to control her breathing, praying that they would not sense her fear.

The Colonel spoke to Kurt: 'Do you have a knife?'

He pulled out a glittering blade and held it up. The Colonel nodded.

'Her identity card and a lock of hair should be enough to start with,' he said. 'It will be interesting to see what value the British place on the life of one of their women officers.'

Christine stood like a rock while Kurt hacked through the strands of hair.

'You won't get away with this,' she said, but she knew that it was a futile threat.

When Christine did not report for work that afternoon her superior was mildly annoyed. The scientist recollected giving her leave to make herself scarce for the morning, but nothing had been said about the afternoon. At four o'clock he decided to give up waiting.

He met Major Dawson in the corridor and grumbled to him. 'I've got reams of notes, packed full of interesting stuff and that girl has let me down. I brought her with me because I thought she was reliable, but she's been out all day and hasn't come back.'

'Where did she go?' the Major asked.

'To visit some German friends, I believe.'

'The Hofmeyers. I know about her friendship with them.' He was frowning.

'I suppose she's all right,' the scientist said uneasily, as if the idea had only just occurred to him.

'I'll follow it up,' Major Dawson said. 'I wish you'd reported it earlier. I don't like to hear of one of our girls being missing, especially one as independent as Section Officer Telford. I've already told her that she shouldn't walk about the streets alone.'

'In broad daylight,' the little scientist protested feebly. 'And she told me there was transport laid on to bring her back.'

'Then she ought to be here,' Major Dawson said. He glanced out of the window. It was already dark. 'I'll see if I can trace the driver who was collecting her.'

The result of his enquiries did not please him.

'Damn fool driver joined in a chase after some black marketeers, got into a punch-up and was knocked out. Too woozy now to remember anything. Only one thing for it, I'll have to call on the Hofmeyers myself. I'd like to have a word with them. Christine told me they once knew a man I'd be very glad to get hold of.'

Only the three women were at home when Major Dawson arrived at the apartment. As soon as she heard his errand Frieda shrugged her shoulders. 'I wasn't here this morning,' she said. 'I didn't even know she'd called.'

Elsa sat still and kept quiet. Nothing could have happened to Christine, she told herself. And even if it had, it couldn't be as a result of the information she had given her. Major Dawson looked at her enquiringly.

'I left for work soon after Christine arrived,' she said. 'Colonel Tickener had called for me.' She hoped that name would impress him. 'I thought she meant to make only a short visit.'

'She stayed a few minutes more talking to me,' Frau Hofmeyer admitted. Her fingers pleated her cotton apron nervously. 'She collected some rag dolls I'd made and I showed her some photographs of my children when they were younger. She's a sweet girl, so friendly and kind to us. I thought when she left here that she meant to go back to her own people.'

It all sounded very innocent. All the same, Major Dawson took the precaution of looking round the apartment. It was very much the same as a lot of other Berlin flats he had had to search, with its makeshift arrangements for cooking and heating, the broken windows, the fallen ceilings, the battered furniture.

'If any of you recollect anything that Section Officer Telford said which might show that she meant to call anywhere else on her way back to HQ, please get in touch with me,' he said before he left. 'I'm beginning to be extremely worried about her.'

He reached the door and then turned and said, as if it were an afterthought: 'By the way, which of you knows Kurt Waldenheim?'

He did not miss the way Elsa jumped. 'I . . . knew him,' she said.

'Where is he now?'

'We're not in touch.'

'Are you sure? You didn't tell Christine Telford where she could find him?'

311

She shook her head, terrified now that there was some connection between Kurt and Christine's disappearance.

'I told her that he was dangerous, that she shouldn't try to find him.'

'I told her the same thing,' Major Dawson said. 'But she's a headstrong young woman. I wouldn't put it past her to ignore both our warnings if she knew where he was.'

He waited, but no-one said anything and he went away with a fairly strong suspicion on his mind that Elsa knew more than she was saying.

When Gunther arrived home the first thing he heard was that a British Major had called and Christine had disappeared.

'What can have happened to her? That nice, kind girl,' Frau Hofmeyer worried.

'She may have returned by now,' Frieda said, but with no great conviction.

Frau Hofmeyer had a sudden thought. 'Elsa, you were alone with her. Did she say anything about calling on anyone else besides us?'

Elsa shook her head, just as she had for Major Dawson. She knew that Gunther was looking at her. She gave him one frightened glance and looked away.

'Why did you take her into the bedroom?' Frau Hofmeyer persisted.

'I wanted to ask her to get me a lipstick.'

'Was that a secret?' Frieda enquired.

'Colonel Tickener was here. I didn't want to ask her in front of him.'

'I would have thought he would have been the best person to ask for cosmetics. He keeps you well supplied with everything else you want.'

'I thought a girl would understand better.'

'It sounds strange to me,' Frieda said. 'Are you quite sure you didn't do what that British officer suggested – give her the address of your SS friend?'

'Of course not!' Her fear made Elsa's voice shrill.

'I don't understand this. What SS friend and why should Christine want his address?' Gunther asked.

'Hauptmann Kurt Waldenheim,' Frieda said. 'He appears to have been remarkably kind to Elsa at one time.'

'I never quite understood,' Frau Hofmeyer said apologetically. 'You told me that he was a friend of the family helping you to deal with your father's affairs, Elsa, but to Fräulein Brookfield – I mean Frau Telford – you said he interrogated you and let you go after the Generals' Plot against Hitler.'

'My father committed suicide. The Gestapo didn't want that known. Kurt was, in his way, good to me, but he's a dangerous man. Christine wanted to get in touch with him – some stupid story about her brother having promised to look him up after the war – but I wasn't able to help her.'

There was a short silence and then Gunther said: 'I'd like to talk to you. Come with me.'

She looked mutinous, but she followed him into their bedroom. Gunther leaned against the wall at the end of the bed and after a moment's hesitation, Elsa curled up at the foot.

'You seem to be very friendly with this American Colonel,' Gunther said unexpectedly. 'Does he normally call to take you to work?'

It was not what Elsa had expected and there was surprise in her voice as she answered.

'No. It was something quite out of the ordinary. He brought us a present of some coffee.'

'Kind of him. What have you given him?'

'Nothing! It's not my fault that he finds me attractive.'

'What about this fellow Waldenheim – who was also kind to you?'

Elsa's head drooped. 'I never dared tell you about that.'

'Tell me now.'

'I knew him long before I met you. He always wanted me. After my father's death he came and threatened me. There was only one way of keeping him quiet. I went to bed with him.'

'I see.'

He was silent for so long that Elsa peered through the gloom to try and discover what he was thinking, but she couldn't see his face clearly.

At last he said: 'It doesn't seem particularly important. So much has happened. I wish you'd told me sooner. Has he bothered you recently?'

She did not want to answer, but Gunther said in the same reasonable way: 'Tell me, Elsa. No matter how foolish you've been I'll try to protect you. The only thing I couldn't forgive would be if you put another girl in danger and then did nothing to save her.'

'I couldn't tell the British officer,' Elsa whispered. 'I *couldn't*! I did give her Kurt's address. I meant her to pass it on to the authorities. She can't have gone there herself. She wouldn't be so stupid, would she?'

'I think she may have done just that. In which case, God knows what may have happened. Waldenheim must be desperate. Why did he get in touch with you again?'

Elsa's mind worked swiftly. There was no need to reveal Kurt's plan to implicate her in removing evidence from the American files. 'For the same reason as before,' she said.

'You had no reason to be frightened of him once the war was over.'

She said nothing and Gunther asked, with difficulty: 'Did you . . . ?'

'No! Not since that awful time when you were away and I was so frightened.'

She began to cry, and tears did not come easily to Elsa. Gunther moved to the bottom of the bed and put his arm round her.

'Don't cry, my dear. I can understand why you didn't tell the English Major what you'd done. I don't know that I want him, or anyone else, to know what happened. Tell me where I can find Waldenheim and I'll go and see if I can discover what's happened to Christine.'

'You can't do that!' Elsa exclaimed, appalled.

'Why not?' Gunther laughed suddenly. 'Until a few months ago I was a serving officer and a tough one. Kurt has been polishing his arse on a chair all through the war. I can take him apart limb by limb. I'll teach him to blackmail my wife into committing adultery.'

'He may not be alone,' Elsa said. She felt as if she could

hardly breathe. Her fingers dug into Gunther's arm, nervously kneading into the hard muscle. It was true, what he said about being tough, but he would be no match for the organization she suspected Kurt had joined.

'I'll face that when I find him. Tell me where to go.'

She was still reluctant, but Gunther said with the firmness that had often forced her into doing what he wanted: 'So far little time has been lost since the Major let us know that Christine was missing, but we must do something *now*.'

She gave him the information he needed, but she was frightened, more frightened than she dared to admit. She did not go back into the kitchen after he had left. She stayed, huddled at the foot of the bed, shivering with cold and fear, waiting for him to come back.

Gunther did not particularly want to analyse his feelings as he put on his coat and prepared to go out. He was anxious about Christine, far more than he had any right to be. The thing he was reluctant to face was a faint, uncontrollable disgust at the role Elsa had played. He had got the impression that she had given in to Kurt's sexual demands only once and he had spoken the truth when he said he didn't regard it as particularly important. Knowing the revenge that had been taken on the families of those implicated in the Generals' Plot he saw all too clearly the dilemma she had faced. But she ought to have told him. Above all, she should have told him when the little worm came crawling round threatening her a second time. Gunther had few illusions about Elsa, and he was growing increasingly uneasy about her relations with her American friends, but he had thought that she trusted him sufficiently to tell him when anything was troubling her. It puzzled him, that omission. It hurt, too. She was his wife; she ought to have known that he would protect her.

He did not place too much importance on her insistence that Kurt was dangerous since he was thinking of him as a solitary survivor who had managed to escape the net that had trapped most of his kind, but it did occur to him that Waldenheim, unlike himself, might still be armed. Before he left the flat he went into the kitchen and took out from the cutlery drawer a small, sharp knife.

315

His mother's only comment, as she looked up and saw that he was wearing his overcoat, was: 'You're not going out again, are you, Gunther?'

'I must,' he said briefly.

Frieda said nothing, but she followed him out into the hallway.

'If Kurt Waldenheim has taken your English friend as a hostage, he won't give her up easily,' she said. 'Are you planning to use that knife on him?'

'Probably not. I thought it might be as well to have something to threaten him with.'

'You'd better keep it hidden. It'll get you into trouble if the police pick you up.'

'I've put it up my sleeve.'

Before he opened the door she said, as if the words were dragged out of her: 'Gunther, you have heard of the Werewolves, haven't you?'

'The Werewolves?' The incredulity in his voice brought a small, sour smile to her lips. Of course he had heard of the Werewolves, the organization dedicated to carrying on the fight, the fanatics who believed that they could still bring back the past and rule Germany again.

'Here – in the middle of Berlin?' he asked.

'They exist. I don't know whether Kurt is connected with them or not, but be careful.'

It was enough to make him more cautious than he might otherwise have been as he approached Number 52 Hildenburger Strasse. It was very dark. There were no street lights, nothing but some charcoal braziers at irregular intervals and a few homeless people huddled round them. Their faces, illuminated by the red glow, turned towards Gunther as he went past.

Like Christine, he paused and looked round the vast desert of rubble, uncertain where to go, but he had known the street in former days and he was able to locate Number 52 without asking for assistance from any of the dark figures clustered round the braziers, a thing he found he was reluctant to do. Why? They were his fellow Germans, only more unfortunate than he had been. Deliberately, he made himself walk back. They looked at him sullenly without speaking.

'Did any of you see a young woman here earlier today going into Number 52?' he asked.

He sensed a movement of withdrawal. Something about his question had disturbed them. One of the men spoke.

'What's it worth?'

'A couple of cigarettes.'

This brought a stir of interest and the man said: 'I saw her.'

'Was she about middle height, brown hair, wearing a green coat?'

'That's right.'

'I'm sorry, my friend, that's not the girl I'm looking for.'

The man muttered angrily and someone gave a jeering laugh. He kicked against the brazier and a little flame sprang up, illuminating the group. There was a woman with a little girl in her arms. The child was clutching a doll, a clown with wide satin trousers and red woolly hair. Gunther put out his hand and touched it.

'Where did you get that, sweetheart?'

'Found it.'

'Where?'

The child pointed vaguely into the darkness. 'Over there.'

'Can you show me the place?'

She nodded and struggled to get out of her mother's arms, but the woman said: 'Leave the kid alone, can't you? I don't know what you're after, but we don't want anything to do with it.'

'Five cigarettes,' Gunther said.

She hesitated and then shrugged. 'All right. Come on, Heidi, show the gentleman where you found the doll.'

The broken ground was the child's playground. She knew exactly where she was leading them in spite of the darkness.

'You're not going to take the doll away, are you?' the woman asked. 'First thing she's ever had to play with.'

'No, she can keep it. Where's she gone?'

'Watch your step, there's a hole just here.'

The little girl, surefooted as a goat, had scrambled over a

broken wall and jumped down into what must once have been an area in front of a basement entrance.

'This is where I got my clown,' she said. She patted the ground with her hand and Gunther heard a small metallic clatter. There was a grating of some sort. He struck a match and saw it. An aperture about thirty centimetres across and ten centimetres deep made of pierced metal which had corroded so that it swung loose. Big enough for Christine to have reached up and pushed a doll through.

'Can I see your clown again, sweetheart?' Gunther asked.

He drew them away from the hole and took the doll from the reluctant child. He knew he was not mistaken, it was the one his mother had sewn; there couldn't be another like it in the whole of Berlin. His fingers searched it and he cursed the lack of light which made it impossible to see what he was doing. He found what he was hoping for inside the wide satin trousers. A brief note, scribbled on a small sheet of lined paper torn from a notebook. He struck another match to read it. It was in German and it said:

'I am a British woman officer. My name is Christine Telford. I am being held a prisoner at 52 Hildenburg Strasse. Please contact Major Dawson at the British HQ in Wilmersdorf.'

The match began to burn Gunther's fingers and he dropped it hurriedly. He stood for a moment in the darkness, moved to a curious feeling of pride at the resourcefulness and obstinate courage that had inspired Christine's attempt to outwit her captors.

'What about my cigarettes?' the woman asked. She sounded nervous.

'Do you know anything about the people in Number 52?' Gunther asked.

'No. Don't want to. Funny lot. Only a couple of them ever come out, but there's more than that down there. There'd be room for all of us if they'd let us in, but they keep it locked up like a prison.'

It was a prison. As Gunther found the cigarettes and handed them over his mind was trying to grapple with the problem of getting Christine out.

'Do something for me,' he said abruptly. 'Take this note

and give it to the first British military patrol you see. You're sure to find one on the Kurfürstendamm.'

'All that way,' she grumbled.

'It's not so far.'

He pressed the crumpled scrap of paper into her hand. She took it and began to walk away.

'Don't let me down,' Gunther called after her, but she did not reply. 'There could be something in it for you,' he said desperately. 'I'll try to find you somewhere to live.'

Her receding footsteps paused. 'All right,' she called back over her shoulder.

It was only half past six. People were still going home from work. He looked over his shoulder and saw an Army jeep coming along the road. He ran towards it, shouting and waving his arm, but in haste he forgot to watch where he was going. He stumbled over a pile of fallen bricks, lost his balance and went sprawling. By the time he had picked himself up the jeep was out of sight.

Cursing his clumsiness Gunther limped back to the place where the child had found the doll. He thought he heard something behind him and turned quickly, but it was only the loose stones he had dislodged, trickling down the slope. He knelt down and tried to peer into the grating. It was difficult because it was so close to the ground. Was Christine down there? It was impossible to tell.

He bent closer. The grill was loose and it might be possible to prise it out of the brickwork. It was far too small for him to get through, but if Christine was there it would make it easier for them to talk.

He pressed his lips close to the metal and said in a low, penetrating whisper: 'Christine? Are you there?'

Below him in the darkness he heard someone move and then a whisper answered him. 'Yes. Who is it? Is it Gunther?'

'Yes. I'm going to loosen this grating, take away a few bricks and try to make a hole large enough for you to get through.'

He was not at all sure that that would be possible, but he took out his knife and began to chip away at the mortar. Again he thought he heard something behind him and turned his head, but saw nothing. He went back to work, but before he

could make any real impression something struck him a
stunning blow on the head and he toppled forward unconscious. The knife slid out of his slack hand, caught for a
moment on the grill and then fell through the hole he had
made into the dark cellar below.

Back at the brazier the woman with the child straightened out
the scrap of paper and held it sideways to the glow to read
what it said.

'What you got there, Lilli?' someone asked.

She held it out. 'That man wanted me to give it to the
Tommies,' she said.

Two or three of them crowded round to read it. 'Could
mean trouble,' another woman said. They handed the paper
back to her. It was her problem, not theirs. She held it in her
hand for a moment, then she crumpled it up and dropped it
into the brazier. The fire flared briefly, flames licking at the
paper, and then it was gone.

In Wilmersdorf Major Dawson was reading a message from
Christine's captors:

'As you will see from the enclosed, we are holding one of
your women officers. We are prepared to exchange her for
three of our own nationals held prisoner by you: Helmut
Feldman, Wilhelm Beiderhof and Dieter Johannes.'

'Three of the highest-ranking Nazis we've got,' Major
Dawson exclaimed. 'They're lucky not to have been executed.'

He read on:

'You will signal your agreement by hoisting a white flag
over the British HQ at Wilmersdorf at eight o'clock tomorrow
morning. Instructions for the exchange of prisoners will be
given later.'

' "Instructions".' Major Dawson muttered angrily.
'Damned nerve.'

There was an identity card with the note. Christine's face
looked up at him, younger than he remembered her, softer
and less experienced. A scrap of paper was wrapped round

something soft: a few strands of hair. On the paper was
written: 'Tomorrow a finger, the next day an ear.'

Chapter Sixteen

When Gunther came to he was in a dark room, lying on the floor, but his head was supported on something soft and warm. He stirred and Christine's voice said: 'Gunther, can you hear me?'

He struggled to sit up, but she pressed his head down into her lap again. 'Keep still.'

His head was still singing. He felt cautiously and located the place where something had struck him. There was a massive bump which throbbed when he touched it and he thought that the skin was broken.

'How long have I been out?' he asked.

'About ten minutes.'

He grunted, surprised that so little time had passed.

'How did you know I was here?' Christine asked.

'Elsa gave me the address.'

'She warned me not to come. I should have listened to her. Now I've got us both into terrible danger. What do you think they mean to do, Gunther? What do they want?'

He succeeded in sitting up. 'I expect they'll try to exchange you for someone they want out of prison. No need for you to worry too much, Christine, my dear. You're a great deal more valuable alive and unharmed than you would be damaged.'

'And you?'

It took him a moment to find a reply to that. He was expendable. Who cared whether Gunther Hofmeyer got home safely?

'They will probably throw me in also for good measure,' he said cheerfully.

The door opened and a shaft of light fell across the floor.

Hans and Kurt came in. Hans stood by the door, but Kurt came over to look at his two prisoners.

'Gunther Hofmeyer,' he said. 'So you're the man Elsa married. Interesting, to meet you like this.'

Gunther leaned back against the wall, closed his eyes and groaned. Kurt laughed.

Believing that Gunther was really suffering, Christine spoke hurriedly to divert Kurt's attention.

'Do you mean to starve us?' she asked. 'I've been here for hours and I'm ravenous.'

'You will be given food, but not if you speak to me in that insolent way. It is in my power to do just what you said – to starve you. Keep that in mind. You'll find that your German friend has more respect for me.' He stood over Gunther. 'On your feet, Hofmeyer.'

Very slowly, Gunther stood up. He was pleased to find that he was half a head taller than Kurt.

'I suppose that little traitor, Elsa, gave you this address. What a wife you've got, Hofmeyer! Half the American Army must have had her by now. Don't you care? Or do you keep your eyes closed and accept the favours she brings you?'

Gunther leaned his shoulders against the wall and said nothing. It took a superhuman effort, but he knew better than to involve himself in this sort of argument with Kurt. He knew his type – eager to get the last ounce of satisfaction out of his position of power. The most frustrating thing he could do was refuse to reply to Kurt's taunts.

'Answer me when I speak to you!' Kurt's voice was shrill. Gunther pressed his lips together and maintained his silence.

A voice spoke from the doorway. 'Kurt! Give the prisoners their food and come away.'

Kurt turned round. It was the Colonel who had interviewed Christine when she had arrived.

'Yes, Herr Oberst,' he replied automatically. 'Do you think it's wise to keep them together?'

'What choice have we? It's the only undamaged room we have, apart from our sleeping quarters. By morning we'll know whether the British are going to give us what we want.'

He did not move from the open doorway, but his next

question was addressed to Christine: 'Are you right-handed or left-handed?'

'Right-handed,' she answered. 'Why?'

'I'll be kind to you. The first finger we remove will be from your left hand.'

Christine drew a deep breath. Gunther could feel her trembling, but she managed to keep her voice steady as she replied: 'You've almost succeeded in taking away my appetite.'

The Colonel laughed quietly. 'You're not without courage. Perhaps you don't believe I'll do it.'

'No, I don't,' Christine said. 'You'll give an order and you'll watch while someone else uses the knife.'

'Quite true,' he said. 'Kurt is right – you are insolent.'

Another man in their uniform of dark sweater and trousers came in carrying a loaded tray. Gunther glanced round and calculated the chances of making a break for it. Kurt, Hans, the officer by the door, the man carrying the food. Not a hope, not when he had to get Christine away too and had not had an opportunity of planning an escape with her. He slid down and sat with his back against the wall once more.

'You'll sit down when I tell you to,' Kurt said.

'My head hurts,' Gunther muttered, a complaining whine in his voice.

'Leave him alone,' the Colonel said. 'Put the tray down on the floor and come away.'

After the door had been locked behind them, Christine knelt down by his side.

'Is it very bad?' she asked.

'I've got a headache, but it won't kill me. I'm sorry about the unheroic act, but I want them to despise me.'

'Is there any hope of our getting out?'

'Ask me after I've had something to eat. Your message was found – clever girl – and I've asked a woman to pass it on to the British.'

As he spoke he had a sudden sickening qualm. He ought to have gone himself. He dismissed the thought – too late to regret it now.

'Just the same I think we'll have to try to make a break for it,' he said. 'I had a knife, but like a fool I lost it.'

324

'I've got it,' Christine interrupted him. 'It fell through the grating and I hid it in that corner.'

'Good girl! That could be a great help. The trouble is, I've no idea of the layout of the place.'

'It's all very derelict, but there's a door on our left which gives on to a passage and that leads to the outer door. The door in front of us which Kurt and the others came through leads into an inner room. I had the impression that there were other rooms beyond that, but I haven't seen them. Gunther, they've got swastikas and pictures of Hitler on the walls in there.'

'Fools! Idiots!' He broke off, suppressing his useless anger. 'An unguarded passage leading to the street door? That doesn't sound very likely.'

'The one called Hans was there when I tried to walk away.'

Gunther finished off the last of the bread and soup, then he began to move restlessly round the room. By the door he paused and asked: 'Does the passage go on past this room?'

'Yes. There's a turning to the left which leads to a horrible little lavatory.'

'Any windows?'

'One, but it was boarded over.'

Gunther went back to her. 'The important thing is to lull their suspicions. I'm a fool who's had a nasty blow on the head and is completely cowed. You're a woman and afraid.'

'That's true enough,' Christine said with a shaky laugh.

'Come and sit by me. If anyone comes back to collect the tray pretend to be crying.'

It was the surly Hans who came back for the tray. 'What's the matter with her?' he asked.

'She's upset. What do you expect?'

'If I had my way we'd treat her the same as the Russians treated our women. She's not bad looking. Once the colonel's finished with her I might ask if I can have her.'

Gunther's fingers clenched so hard on Christine's arm that she knew it would be bruised, but he said nothing. There was a laugh from the open door.

'You aren't living up to your *Luftwaffe* reputation,' Kurt

325

said. 'I quite thought that if I sent Hans in to you alone, you would try to overcome him. I'm disappointed.'

'I'm not such a fool,' Gunther said in a sullen mutter.

'I suppose you've had all the fight taken out of you since you surrendered to the enemy. How I despise you and your kind! Some of us haven't given up. We continue the fight and will until our day comes again.'

He got no reply and he turned away. 'Come, Hans, leave them alone.'

The door slammed to again.

Christine and Gunther sat side by side, leaning against the wall. It was cold and the bricks felt damp behind them. Christine dug her hands into the pockets of her overcoat and shivered.

'Cold?'

'A little. Frightened, too. They cut off some of my hair. Will he really do what he said about my finger?'

'You'll be out of here long before that.'

'Perhaps. I don't even know what they'll ask for, in exchange for me.'

'Release of some Nazi prisoners probably.'

'What good will that do them?'

'No good at all. It's nothing but an illusion. They think if they have some of their former leaders back they'll be able to seize power again.'

'But surely they won't be able to live in this country?'

'No. Abroad. South America probably. They've got money there. If they can get their hands on it they can use it – to finance plots, buy arms, God knows what.'

'I was too stubborn to take the advice that was given to me,' Chrstine said in a low voice. 'I'm ashamed of the trouble I've caused.'

'So you should be, you silly girl.' His voice was more gentle than his words. 'You must stop shaking, Christine. Here, come inside my coat.'

He undid his overcoat and held it open, she crept up close against him and he wrapped it round her.

'Better?'

'Yes, thank you.'

It was more than the warmth of his body that comforted her. It was his nearness and the feeling of familiarity. A sense of belonging.

'I don't even know why you were looking for Waldenheim,' Gunther said.

'Because of Jimmy.'

She began to tell him the story and he encouraged her to talk. Anything to take her mind off what might be going to happen to her in the morning.

'He was killed,' Christine concluded. 'He was so young, Gunther. Such a wicked waste! So near the end of the war.'

'When did it happen?'

'On a raid over Hamburg at the end of March.'

She felt his slight, involuntary withdrawal and mistook the reason for it.

'I know what you are thinking. We all knew the raids were heavy, but it's only since I've been over here and seen the results that I've asked myself whether they really did what they were intended to do – destroy military targets.'

'The damage was fearful,' Gunther said. 'No use blaming anyone now. We showed you the way and you followed where we led. London was badly hit. Coventry, Liverpool, Portsmouth, Southampton, all the other towns.'

'None of them was as bad as Hamburg – or Berlin.'

'Some of the damage was the result of the bombardment.'

'Are you ever going to be able to rebuild it?'

'Yes. If I have to do it brick by brick with my own hands it will be rebuilt.'

Christine had relaxed in the circle of his arm. He could tell she was smiling from the sound of her voice.

'I hope you'll be one of the architects who helps to plan it.'

'That is my ambition.'

They talked on, about their experiences during the years that had separated them, their hopes for the future. It was a strange interlude. To both of them there gradually came the realization that there was no-one else to whom they could talk so readily, no-one else with the same instinctive sympathy.

At last Gunther said: 'When you get out of this, they'll send you back to England.'

327

Christine moved her head slowly against his arm, acknowledging the truth of what he said. She realized that they had reached a point when they both wanted to say something about what was between them, and yet what was there to say? It was Gunther who spoke and when he said the words she knew that they had been inevitable from the day she had gone to his home and their eyes had met across the crowded kitchen.

He moved his head so that his lips brushed against her forehead. 'I love you.'

Christine stirred in his arms. 'I love you, too.'

They sat perfectly still until Gunther said: 'There's no future for us.'

'No,' Christine said.

'I can't desert Elsa. She's not always wise, perhaps not always faithful, but she is still my wife and, though she doesn't realize it, she needs me. But even without that . . . too much has happened.'

He stopped and Christine said: 'I was never able to think of you as my enemy.'

'Your family would never accept me. Not after everything that has been done in the last six years.'

'I went against my family once because of you; I could do it again. If you were free, I know I would try to argue against you.'

'But I'm not free. You do see that I have a duty to Elsa?'

'Yes, I know what you are saying is right. But you do love me?'

There was something desperate in the way she asked it and an answering despair in his reply: 'Dear God, yes! Beyond all reason. I would give anything to be able to call you mine.'

Christine moved closer against him. 'In other circumstances . . .' she said.

He managed a shaken laugh. 'Yes, indeed, in other circumstances we would make love and find joy in one another, however temporary it might be. But not here, not now.'

'No. You know, I thought I could see you just as a friend. It wasn't until that night at the café that I suddenly realized how much I loved you still.'

'I knew, almost as soon as I set eyes on you again. You were different, and yet you were the same. So beautiful, and so self-willed! It made me want to shout with joy, the way you went your own way in spite of all the regulations and good advice you were given.'

'Look where it's landed us.'

'Forget it for the moment, my love, my heart's dearest.'

In the cold darkness they kissed, fumbling a little in the awkwardness of their heavy winter clothing, seeking for such solace as they could find in the small contact they could allow themselves.

At last Gunther drew back. He pulled Christine's head down against his shoulder. 'No more. Be still now, my love. Let me hold you and keep you warm while I try to think of a way of getting you out of this prison my countrymen have put you in.'

Elsa was roused from the torpor into which she had fallen by Frieda coming to find her.

'Your American colonel is here,' she said. She sounded hostile, as she always did when she spoke of Elsa's American friends.

Elsa got up from the bed and pulled a comb through her hair, but nothing could disguise her pallor or the look of strain on her face, so different from the smiling appearance she usually showed to Blake Tickener.

'Honey, we've got trouble,' he said without preamble. 'The British have been on to me to see if I can put some pressure on you to get the information they want. They've had a note asking for three Nazi prisoners in exchange for Christine Telford. You told Major Dawson earlier that you didn't know where to find Kurt Waldenheim, but that's not true, is it? You were mighty friendly with him at one time, spent three days with him at the Kaiser Hotel after your father's death, met him there on various occasions after that.'

'You *knew*?' Elsa whispered.

'Sure.' He paused and added with an apologetic air: 'I guess I must seem like a heel, but I have to keep a pretty close watch on the people who associate with me and my boys. It's been real nice knowing you, Elsa, don't get me wrong, but I had information on you right from the start and I always had it in mind that you might still be connected with Waldenheim and could lead me to him.'

'Kurt wanted to make use of me, but I resisted it,' Elsa said. She spoke in a dull voice. All her bright dreams of a new life in America were evaporating.

She tilted her chin and smiled with lips that trembled. 'How clever you've been. I almost persuaded myself that you really cared for me.'

'You'd get under any man's skin. I guess that's over now. But before I go, you've got to tell me where to find Waldenheim and his pals.'

'I've told Gunther. He's gone there!'

'Christ! That's all we needed! I suppose they've got him holed up, too. Come on, Elsa, the address.'

She gave it to him and he said, genuinely startled: 'Right in the heart of Berlin? And we never suspected!'

He paused on his way out. 'I'll do my best to get your husband back in one piece,' he said with an embarrassment that finally destroyed all Elsa's hopes of a future with him.

The long hours Gunther spent with Christine in their prison convinced him that the woman outside had not passed on Christine's message. They would have to make an attempt to rescue themselves.

He knew by the weight of Christine's body leaning against him and her regular breathing that she had managed to go to sleep. He was still wide awake himself, stiff and cold, acutely aware of holding the woman he loved in his arms. He tried to tell himself that the feeling that had reawakened in him for Christine would die once she had gone back to England, but he knew that it wasn't true. No matter what he succeeded in doing with his life, there would always be a regret at the back of his mind, a feeling of loss.

He moved cautiously, easing his cramped limbs, and Christine stirred and muttered.

'Wake up,' he said in a low voice.

She sat up, not knowing for a moment where she was or

why she felt at the same time so uncomfortable and so much at peace, and then she remembered: she was with Gunther, but they were being held prisoner. Above their heads a faint glimmer of moonlight showed through the broken grating.

'Get up and move about,' Gunther said in the same quiet voice. 'Don't make the slightest noise, but try to ease the stiffness. We may need to move fast.'

'Do you have a plan?'

'Of sorts. First, we must get out of this room.'

'Can you pick locks?'

'No, but I can undo screws.'

He caught hold of her hand and led over to the door which opened on to the passage. 'Feel.'

She felt where he directed her hand. The hinges were secured by metal plates to the door itself.

Gunther chuckled softly. 'This place wasn't built to be a prison,' he said. 'It isn't necessary to unlock the door if I can take it off its hinges.'

The screws were old and rusty and it took longer than he had hoped to get them to turn with the improvised tools he had to work with. The knife was too pointed. In the end he managed with a small coin. There were three screws in the bracket at the top and three in the one at the bottom. By the time the sixth screw was loosened Christine was shivering with nerves. It fell to the floor with a tiny clatter and she held her breath.

Gunther lifted the door. There was a creak. In the faint glimmer of moonlight she could see that there was a gap.

Gunther spoke with his lips close to her ear. 'Go through and feel your way along the wall to the lavatory.'

She squeezed through the opening. In the passageway it was pitch dark. Somewhere on her left she could hear someone snoring: Hans, presumably, sleeping by the outer door. She turned to the right, feeling with her hand for the wall, and guided herself along it until she came to the turning which led to the wretched little toilet. She could hear Gunther following close behind her.

They both squeezed into the tiny room and Gunther bolted the door behind them.

Again there was a little light from the moon shining between the boards which closed the window space. He tried gently to shake them, but they had been well nailed down.

'What I need is some sort of lever,' he said.

'There was an old brush propped up in the corner,' Christine said. 'Would that help?'

She felt around until she found it. The brush had a long, narrow handle of hard wood.

Gunther manoeuvred it under one of the boards and began to work it to and fro. When the end of the board came loose with a splintering rush he staggered back against Christine. 'Sorry!'

'Someone will hear us,' Christine said.

The second board came away more easily.

'That's a big enough hole for you to get through,' he said. 'Come on, up you go, and I'll help you through.'

'I'm not going without you.'

'Stop arguing! Get through and then help me by kicking in the last board.'

She had to take off her coat, but with Gunther's help she got through the gap. She cast one triumphant look around at the empty landscape, all cold bars of moonlight and dark shadows, and then gave the last board a hard kick.

It was just giving way when there was a noise of running footsteps in the passageway below and then someone tried the door of the lavatory.

'They're in here!' a voice shouted.

'How the hell did they get out?' That was Kurt's voice. 'Hans, force the door!'

There was nothing to hold the lavatory door but the flimsiest of bolts. A couple of charges from Hans' hefty shoulders and it gave way. Gunther was on the lavatory seat, climbing through the opening, when Hans came through in a rush. Gunther kicked hard and caught Hans in the face. He staggered backwards against Kurt, but Kurt recovered quickly and sprang forward.

Gunther was through the hole and scrambling to his feet. 'Run!' he called urgently to Christine.

Kurt followed him. Thin and agile, he scrambled through

and out into the open, and he was feeling for the gun at his waist. Gunther had his knife in his hand. He struck out, slicing into Kurt's arm. Kurt let his gun drop, but he sprang forward and the two men grappled together in silent and deadly combat. Gunther still held the knife in his clenched fist. He struck upwards into Kurt's body. He knew from the way it slid into the soft flesh that he had found a vulnerable spot. Kurt gave a choking scream and fell back.

Gunther turned and ran in the direction he thought Christine had chosen, stumbling awkwardly over the broken ground.

A dazzling light suddenly illuminated the whole area.

'Stand where you are!' a voice commanded.

Gunther slowed. Just ahead of him he could see Christine. She turned her head and saw him and held out her hand. Very slowly, he went and joined her and together, hand in hand, they waited for the captain who came towards them.

'Both of you out?' he asked. 'Good! In that case, we can move in and take the lot of them.'

It was a successful little mopping up operation, but they failed in one important objective. They captured all the men inside the cellar, but they didn't even know that they had overlooked the one outside.

Kurt, doubled up and clutching his stomach, had rolled into the cover of an overhanging wall when the searchlights had lit up the area. There, in a recess like a shelf, he curled up and lay still while heavy feet pounded over his head. There was a lot of noise, some shooting. When the action died down and the prisoners had been taken away, he was still there.

Gunther and Christine took it for granted that he had been captured with the others. They were both preoccupied with the thought that they were being separated without having another moment alone with one another. They looked at each other blankly when Gunther was told that he would be taken home and Christine would be given a bed at the Army HQ for the rest of the night. They were surrounded by people, there was nothing they could say.

Christine held out her hand and Gunther took it in his . He stood holding it for a moment and then dropped it and turned away.

His mother, usually so undemonstrative, wept and put her arms round him when he walked in unharmed. Even Frieda allowed herself to look profoundly thankful.

'The thought of something happening to you after all we've survived was more than I could bear,' she said.

Elsa, strangely pale and subdued, clung to him in a way that bore out what he had said about her dependence on him, but when she tried to make love to him he put her away from him gently.

She accepted the rebuff, believing that he was too exhausted by his experiences to welcome her advances, but in her mind she had decided that she would have to make a fresh start with Gunther; he would have to become attached to her with the fervour he had shown in their early days.

Kurt stayed in his hole all night. When he crawled out the next morning the blood from his wound had soaked into his dark sweater and congealed. He knew that if he moved carelessly it would start the bleeding again, but he also knew that he had to get away from the basement.

He was unsteady on his feet and his head was swimming from loss of blood and the beginnings of fever, but the Berliners were accustomed to the sight of haggard men who walked the streets aimlessly and muttered to themselves as they staggered by. He had enough sense to conceal the gun he still carried beneath his sweater and nothing else about him aroused interest.

He had only one thought in his head: that he had been betrayed. All his friends had been taken. He was alone in the world. That little bitch Elsa had given him away.

'I loved her,' he said out loud and a man passing by gave him a curious look, not unsympathetic. It was a familiar situation: some poor devil had come home and found that his wife was dead or, just as likely, had taken up with someone else.

The street tilted crazily as Kurt stumbled along it. The ruined buildings swayed above him, impossibly tall, rearing up into the early morning sky. He had no conscious destination, but inexorably his wandering footsteps took him towards the Hofmeyers' apartment.

Inside, Elsa was using the long, anxious night they had spent as an excuse for not going to work. She couldn't make up her mind whether the job she had filled so satisfactorily was still open to her or not. Colonel Tickener had not said in so many words that she wouldn't be wanted again, but he had said goodbye very definitely and without the stimulus of her pursuit of him she felt no great interest in it. On the other hand, the money she brought in was a welcome addition to their income. She decided to wait until the following day and then to turn up as if nothing had happened and see what sort of reception she got.

Kurt found himself a place amongst the broken walls of the building opposite and waited. He saw Gunther go out and then Frieda. That meant only the old woman and Elsa were in the flat. He must see Elsa. For a moment he couldn't remember why and then it came back to him: she had betrayed him and the Führer. In his crazed imagination he began to believe that he had come straight from the Führerbunker and that it was because of Elsa that Hitler was dead.

He was still trying to make up his mind what form his revenge should take when Frau Hofmeyer came out with a shopping bag over her arm. Kurt hesitated no longer. He crossed the road, ignoring the shouted abuse from an Army car which nearly ran him down, entered the dilapidated building and began, very slowly, to climb the stairs.

When Elsa answered the door the breath caught in her throat in horror at his appearance. The skull-like look he had always had was accentuated by his extreme pallor and the way his eyes seemed to have sunk back in their sockets. He was muttering to himself and at first it seemed as if he did not know who she was. Then his eyes focused and he spoke loudly and with precision.

'Traitor! Murderess! You killed the greatest man the world has ever known!'

She backed away from him and he followed her. His strange eyes glittered, there was a smell of blood about him, he looked like death. A thin trickle of fresh blood began to run down his arm and dripped from the fingers of his useless left hand. With his other hand he felt beneath his jersey and pulled out a gun.

'No!' Elsa whispered. 'No, Kurt. It wasn't me. It was that English girl and Gunther. Not me, Kurt, not me!'

He did not hear her. There was a noise like great waves breaking inside his head, a noise like the crashing acclamation that had greeted the Führer at the great rallies of the past: '*Sieg Heil! Sieg Heil! Sieg Heil!*'

Kurt drew himself upright. '*Heil* Hitler!' he said, and shot her through the heart.

Chapter Seventeen

Christine was sent back to England immediately after her rescue, although, as she explained to her mother, she would have to return within a few weeks.

'I have to give evidence at the trial,' she said briefly.

'Darling, you must have had the most terrible time,' Barbara exclaimed. 'Now, when the war is over – at least in Europe – I did think you would be safe. That's what comes of treating Germans like friends. I wasn't at all happy when you said you'd located the Hofmeyers again. I knew it would lead to trouble.'

'Worse trouble for them,' Christine said quietly. 'Gunther's wife has been murdered.'

'What a terrible, terrible thing. Oh dear, will it never end?'

'When people like Kurt and his kind have been exterminated perhaps.'

Barbara glanced at her uneasily. Christine troubled her. She was too quiet. The look of suffering she had worn in the past was back again.

'It must have been strange, seeing them all again,' she said.

'Very strange.'

'I expect they'd changed a lot?'

Christine looked at her mother with a faint smile.

'Gunther was older, as I am too,' she said. 'I still love him and he loves me.'

It was not at all what Barbara wanted to hear.

'But . . . he married someone else,' she said feebly.

'So did I. If Larry had lived, if I had never seen Gunther again, I suppose I would have forgotten him. But Larry is dead and Gunther and I have met once more and I know now that what Larry always suspected was true: he was secondbest

337

for me. I did love him, but it wasn't the same. Not the feeling of total belonging, the way I love Gunther.'

'What are you going to do?' Barbara asked, defeated by Christine's quiet certainty.

'I don't know. I'm thankful that I'm being given the chance to go back to Germany at least once more. I must talk to Gunther. He may never want to see me again. If he wanted me, I would marry him.'

'You must be out of your mind,' Barbara said with complete conviction.

It might perhaps have comforted her if she had known that Gunther was equally adamant about the impossibility of any future together for himself and Christine. It was a thought that didn't even come to him in the first weeks that followed the horror of Elsa's death. The whimpering, mindless thing that had once been Kurt Waldenheim had had to be forcibly detached from the corpse of the woman he had killed, the only person he had ever loved. Now he was in an insane asylum and never likely to see the outside world again.

Gunther grieved for Elsa. He had loved her without illusion for what she was, a pleasure-loving, sensual animal. She had not been at her best since his return, but he understood her weaknesses and he sympathized with her more than she had ever known. Elsa was a flower that needed the sunshine and when the clouds loomed she sought where she could for the light she craved.

He went through the drawers of her clothes and found the nylon stockings she had hidden from him and smiled and sighed as the delicate things drifted from his hands. Poor Elsa. Wicked, delightful, laughing Elsa. Every man's idea of the perfect mistress, but never intended to be a staid wife and mother. He remembered with anguish that he had turned away from her on their last night together when she had sought his love and he blamed himself for not giving her that brief pleasure before her life was ended. He hardly thought of Christine and when he did it was as someone with whom he might once have made a life, but who was now lost to him.

Only one thing lightened the load of unhappiness he carried around with him in the weeks following Elsa's death. The news

338

had got through to Willy Neumann in Lübars and he came to Berlin to visit Frieda, bringing little Anna with him.

It was not the first time he had called on them, always a little diffidently and always with the excuse of bringing a present from the farm. This time it was a leg of pork, which sent Frau Hofmeyer into ecstasies.

'We killed the pig and I knew it would be welcome,' Willy said awkwardly.

'You've heard what's happened here since your last visit?' Frieda asked.

'Yes, that's why I came. If you and your mother wanted to get away you'd be welcome at the farm.'

'I have to go to work,' Frieda said automatically, but she was touched by his thought for them.

'Anna would like you to come,' Willy persisted. 'You'd like that, wouldn't you, Anna, if Auntie Frieda came and lived with us?'

Anna made a determined effort and clambered up onto Frieda's lap. 'Yes,' she said. 'Love Auntie F'ieda.'

Frieda's arms closed round her and she bent her head to hide her emotion.

'What we'd really like, Anna and me, would be if you'd come permanently,' Willy said.

She looked up at him wildly, not believing she had understood what he was saying. Willy cast a look of appeal at Frau Hofmeyer and she suddenly realized what was happening and went and took Anna from Frieda.

'You come with me, Anna, and I'll see what we can find for you to play with,' she said, carrying the child out of the room.

'You don't mean it,' Frieda muttered.

'Yes, I do,' Willy said. Now that they were alone he became more assured. 'I know I'm not good enough for you, but I thought you might at least think it over. Anna's fond of you and so am I. I respect you. You work hard and it's not work you've been used to and yet you don't complain. I've heard what you did, bringing those girls back from Czechoslovakia against orders, and I admire you for it.'

'I was a member of the Party.'

'Put that behind you. There's plenty of others who've got

339

things to forget. I fought in the *Wehrmacht*, but now I'm a farmer – only in a small way, I admit, but it's satisfying, working your own land. I've moved into a house of my own, a bit of a ruin, but I'm doing it up in my spare time. I could offer a roof over your heads to you and your mother. What do you say?'

Frieda put her hands over her eyes and shook her head.

'If that means no then I'm sorry,' Willy said.

Frieda let her hands drop in a gesture of despair. 'I don't know what to say.'

'Come and stay on the farm and think about it for a few weeks,' he suggested. 'No point in making up your mind until you know if you'd like the life – and if you could put up with sharing a house with me.'

'You're a good man,' Frieda said with conviction.

'Then come and give it a trial. Bring your mother, too. I'd like her to see what I'm offering you.'

He could see that she was wavering and he went and stood closer to her.

'It'll work out, you'll see,' he said.

He bent over her and kissed her, awkwardly and a little roughly. When he straightened up they looked at one another, surprised that it should have been so pleasant. Frieda began to smile.

'You'll come,' Willy said.

'Yes, I'll come, and if you still feel the same when it's time for me to go then you can ask me again.'

Frau Hofmeyer, torn between a feeling that she ought to stay with her son and a desire to see the place that looked as if it might become her daughter's home, was easily persuaded that she owed it to Frieda to go with her.

'I can look after myself for a few weeks,' Gunther said.

He meant what he said, but it was a dismal, lonely business, coming home each night to an empty flat and scraping around for something to eat before he climbed into bed. It wasn't easy to be there alone in the place where Elsa had been killed, and his thoughts were not happy ones. There seemed every likelihood that his mother and sister would move permanently to the farm at Lübars. He would be glad for them if they did.

Anything would be preferable to living in the desert Berlin had become.

The trial came as a relief, even though the details of it were distasteful. The evidence Gunther and Christine were to give related only to part of the case against the men who had been taken that night, who were indicted on charges far more damning than the short imprisonment of one man and one girl.

She was still in uniform when he saw her again, very trim, her hair neatly rolled at the back under her hat, her belt pulled in a little more tightly and her skirt shortened an inch more than the regulations allowed. She looked across the room and smiled at him and something inside him relaxed: Christine was back.

She gave her evidence in a clear voice, not allowing any emotion to intrude, and Gunther followed her and spoke briefly of his own part in their capture. He was surprised by the warmth with which he was congratulated on their escape, since he didn't think he had made a great success of it. Harder to bear were the words of condolence about the death of his wife. Her past association with Kurt was not mentioned. There seemed to be a tacit agreement to treat the shooting as an act of revenge against Gunther.

When it was over Gunther hesitated. It was impossible to walk away without even speaking to Christine.

She came up to him. 'I'm glad it's over,' she said. 'Gunther, I've been waiting to see you. My dear, I'm so sorry about Elsa.'

'Thank you. It's been . . . a difficult time. Poor girl, she didn't deserve to die like that.'

There seemed to be nothing more to say. Gunther cast round in his mind and said at random: 'I think Frieda is getting married.'

'No! Who to?'

'The father of the little girl she rescued off the street.'

'Give her my good wishes.'

'Yes, I will – when I see her again. She and my mother are staying with Willy at the moment. He's got a small farm near Lübars.'

Again they fell silent and once more it was Gunther who broke the silence.

'When do you go back to England?'

'The day after tomorrow. I'm to be demobilized next week. After that . . . I don't quite know what I'll do.'

They looked at one another, desperate for something more to say that would delay their parting a little longer.

'Take me to that bar, please, where we went before, and buy me some wine,' Christine said abruptly.

'It's out of your way.'

'Does that matter?'

'Christine, we ought to be sensible and part now.'

She shook her head and he gave in to the temptation to be with her a short time longer.

They made their way to the café, walking side by side with steps that matched, not talking but glad to be together. It was March now and there was a hint of spring in the air. Berlin was still desolate, but the streets were tidier than they had been, there was a hint of order in the chaos.

They sat at the same marble-topped table with glasses of red wine in front of them which they scarcely touched.

'We must face the truth,' Gunther said desperately. 'Your life is in England and mine is in Germany. I can't ask you to be my wife.'

'If you did, I would accept,' Christine said. There was a drop of wine spilt on the white-topped table. It looked like blood. She moved her finger over it to make it disappear.

'Too much has happened.' Gunther picked up his glass and swallowed half his wine. '*Liebchen*, I have to tell you this: the night your brother Jimmy was wounded I was in the air, defending Hamburg. I could be the one who killed him. I don't know, we will never know, but it could have happened. I fought over England. I could have been responsible for your husband's death, for Michael's injuries. With all that between us could we ever hope to live together in happiness?'

'I think we could. But if you don't agree with me there's no more to be said.'

'Drink your wine.'

'I'm trying to make it last.'

342

She tried to smile, but her lips trembled and Gunther reached out and laid his hand over hers with something like a groan.

'I'm sorry,' Christine said. 'I was all right until you called me "*Liebchen*". That brought back so much. Do you remember . . .'

'Don't! Don't ask me if I remember what it was like before the war. Of course I do. But we can't go back. We are two different people.'

'Who love one another.'

'Please, *Liebchen*, don't make it more difficult for me.'

'I'm *trying* to make it difficult,' Christine said. She was openly crying now, the tears running unchecked down her face. 'Please, Gunther, can't we have one more time together?'

'No. It would be wrong for me to involve you more deeply. It seems I must be strong for both of us. Drink up your wine, Christine, say goodbye, and go.'

She picked up her glass with a hand that shook. 'Forgive me. I forgot for a moment that it's only a few weeks since you lost your wife. I'm being selfish and insensitive.'

'It's not that,' he said quickly. 'Christine, for God's sake let us talk about something else.'

'Yes,' she agreed quickly, responding to the desperation in his voice. 'Tell me what you are going to do with your life now.'

It took him a moment to answer her, but when he did he said: 'I think that at last I may be able to take up the profession I always wanted. There's an opening in a new department which is planning the rebuilding of Berlin.'

'I'm glad about that. I like to think of you rebuilding, doing something to help get your country back on its feet.'

'My wonderful Christine, my dear, dear girl. Not many people would be so forgiving when they have lost so much. Now tell me what you are going to do so that I can imagine you sometimes.'

'I'll have to get a job. I trained as a secretary and was good at it. I speak German, which may be an asset. I think I'll apply for a post with the civil side of the British Control Commission.'

His head jerked up. 'No!'

'Why not? It would be a good career for me.'

'But you'll be *here*, almost on my doorstep.'

'Why not?' she repeated. 'Can't you bear to have me living in the same country as you?'

'No, I can't.' Gunther stood up, his chair scraping along the floor. 'It would be more than I could stand, knowing you were here, trying to avoid you, always expecting to see you whenever I turned a corner. You can't torture me like that.'

Christine's tears had dried and she was smiling. 'Perhaps we ought to talk it over somewhere more private. It's only ten minutes' walk to your flat.'

Gunther sat down again, shaking his head helplessly. 'I daren't be alone with you. While we are surrounded by people I can keep my head and do what I know is right. It isn't easy, wanting you so much, and knowing that you want me, but it's not the answer, Christine, you know it's not.'

'The only thing I know is that I love you and you're sending me away.'

'I must. This is a sad, defeated country. It will be years before we are back on our feet again and even longer before the world forgives us for the crimes that were committed in our name. To join yourself to me would be to cut yourself off from your own people. You come from a happy family. They love you, but would they forgive you?'

'My own family would. Larry's parents – no, they wouldn't understand. I would have to accept that.'

'I understand how they feel.'

'But you personally, you weren't guilty.'

'I was. Yes, Christine, just once before we sink back into complacency let me say it out loud: we were all guilty. Looking back, I am sickened by the way I held my tongue when I should have spoken against what I knew to be wrong.'

'You were a boy!'

'Old enough. I shut my eyes, turned my head away, persuaded myself that it was none of my business – and that attitude led to concentration camps, to people falling into the hands of fanatics like Kurt.'

'I honour you for admitting responsibility, but you do

344

realize, don't you, that you're punishing me because you feel guilty?'

It brought him up short and he said, with less assurance than before: 'I didn't think of it like that.'

He looked up and met her eyes, anxiously fixed on his face, and smiled. 'You argue very cleverly, but it won't do.'

'The stupid thing is, if I were the man and you were the girl no-one would oppose us – at least not seriously. There are already love affairs between British and American soldiers and German girls and some of them will marry.'

'To the victor the spoils. The girls will go off and live in more comfort than they would enjoy in Germany, but if we were to marry you would be doing very badly for yourself. You belong on the winning side and I am one of the losers.'

'I read something the other day,' Christine said slowly. 'Mr Chamberlain hasn't been very well regarded in England since the Munich Crisis, but he said something which struck me as being very wise: "In war there are no winners, only losers." England is tired and shabby and poor. It's going to be nearly as hard for us to recover as it is for you.'

'But you still have your self-respect.' He spoke in a very low voice and he would not look at her.

He put his hands round his wine glass and sat with his head bent, looking down at the table, while Christine watched him in baffled despair. He was no longer a boy, but a man with a will stronger than her own. He believed it would be wrong to strengthen the tie between them, while her own belief was that it was wrong to deny the love they felt for one another. She was sure that she was right, but she was beginning to be afraid that he would not yield.

'You'll marry again,' she said.

'Possibly. And you, too.'

'I suppose so. And both of us will be cheating.'

Her voice was bitter and Gunther frowned. There was something in what she said. He would marry one day, for companionship, for a settled home life and a family, but he wouldn't be able to offer to any woman the depth of feeling he had for Christine. During the weeks since they had last met it had seemed obvious that they must live separate lives. He realized now that he had spent a lot of time thinking how damnably it was going to hurt him, but he had always told himself that it was for Christine's good. The pain it would cause her was something he hadn't taken into consideration.

'The only thing I want is your happiness,' he said.

'My happiness is in being with you.' She smiled, a painful, resigned smile. 'I'm not going to shake you, am I? Then you're right, we must say goodbye quickly.'

She picked up her glass and held it up to the light. 'To your future happiness, Gunther.'

'And to yours,' he answered automatically.

Christine got to her feet. 'Don't come with me. It's early; I shan't run into any trouble. Did you know that "goodbye" is a shortened version of "God be with you"? I can't think of anything else to say.'

Gunther stood and watched her go. It hurt more than he would have believed possible. He sat down again, knowing that he must let her get away, out of sight, otherwise he would not be able to stop himself from running after her.

He heard a squeal of brakes, a scream, a lot of confused shouting. He flung open the door of the café and rushed out into the street.

There was a jeep slewed across the street, a knot of people. Someone was bending over a girl in Air Force blue who was lying on the ground. Gunther pushed aside the people, frantic to get to her. He dropped on his knees beside her just as Christine began to struggle to sit up. There was a graze on her cheek and her cap had fallen off. She looked dazed and as if she might burst into tears, but she was not seriously hurt. She looked at Gunther and then stretched out a hand to him. He took it and held it tightly, unable to speak, not knowing that he was chalk white nor that there were new lines deeply etched on his face.

'Jeepers, ma'am,' the American driver exclaimed. 'I thought you were a goner. What possessed you to walk out into the street like that?'

'I was . . . thinking of something else,' Christine said.

With Gunther's help she got to her feet, but she was glad to have his support and had to lean against him.

346

'You look real shook up. Can I drop you somewhere? Some place where you can go and get cleaned up?' the American asked.

'She will come home with me,' Gunther said.

Christine closed her eyes and rested her head against his shoulder.

'Well, OK, I guess I can take both of you . . . if that's what you want, ma'am?' He looked doubtfully at the pair of them. The guy who had spoken was a Kraut and the girl was a British WAAF. It was a strange combination, but when Christine said: 'Yes, that's what I want,' he shrugged his shoulders and fitted them into the jeep and drove them to the address they gave.

Gunther put his arm round Christine to help her up the stairs to the flat and, even though it wasn't necessary, she leaned against him for the joy of being close to him. He took her into the kitchen and made her sit down while he bathed her grazed cheek with gentle fingers. Apart from that, and a lot of dust on her uniform, she was unhurt.

'I didn't know where I was going or what I was doing,' she said, by way of excuse.

Gunther turned away to empty the bowl of water. 'My heart stopped,' he said with his back to her. 'In that moment I knew that you were right and I was wrong. All the arguments I used were true, every one of them, and they all count for nothing beside one fact: I can't live without you.'

She moved round the table to his side and he took her in his arms. They kissed as if they would never stop, swaying where they stood as the soft, incessant engagement of their lips ebbed and flowed, until at last Gunther pulled her even closer and spoke with his lips against her hair.

'I knew it would be like this. I knew I would be lost if I touched you. *Liebling*, my heart's delight, it is beyond bearing. I must love you, now, before I am broken in pieces.'

He took her by the hand and led her to the room he had so recently shared with Elsa, glad now that he had cleared out all trace of her. All her clothes and cosmetics had gone, and not even the faintest whisper of her perfume remained. All the surplus furniture had been taken to the house Willy was

347

renovating and the room was stripped to its bare essentials, a bed and a cupboard and a chest of drawers, and nothing but his own few clothes.

He turned her to face him, but his fingers fumbled over the unfamiliar fastenings of her uniform.

'So many buttons,' he grumbled under his breath.

Christine pushed his hands away. 'Let me, I'm used to it,' she said.

She moved away from him, to the other side of the bed, and began to undress quickly. Gunther stood and watched her and then, suddenly realizing that she was ahead of him, followed her example, tossing his own clothes to the floor with an abandon that made Christine smile as she remembered the younger, impulsive Gunther.

When they were both naked they stood, looking at one another in the dim light that filtered through the boarded windows.

Christine lifted her head proudly, knowing that her body was beautiful, glad to be able to offer him her round, firm breasts, her slim waist, her flat belly, the voluptuous curve of her hips, the fine texture of her skin.

'You are more beautiful even than I remember you,' Gunther said unsteadily.

Christine put one knee on the bed and held out her arms to him. He moved forward and pulled her towards him. She felt the long shudder that ran through him as her smooth body moved against his.

'You will not find me patient,' he said. 'Not this time.'

'I'm ready,' Christine said. 'My dear love. Don't try to spare me. This is my doing and I want it as badly as you do.'

They were older and more experienced than they had been the last time they had made love in that same room, but nothing else had changed. In spite of all the years between and all the deep unhappiness, they knew one another as intimately as if they had never been parted. As soon as Gunther entered her Christine thought: 'Yes! This is what it was like. This is Gunther. I know him, I have always known him. He is mine and I am his and nothing, ever, is going to separate us again.' And then all thought was swept away in a

348

tide of passion that carried them beyond themselves to a place where it seemed that love could never end.

They were too dazed to speak when it was over. Gunther's lips brushed against Christine's cheek and she moved her head on the pillow, mutely acknowledging the meaning of that slight gesture. Darkness had fallen. They were alone in a world which had been created just for them, warm and contented and slack with satisfied desire.

They whispered love words to one another, laughing quietly as they began to come back into themselves.

'Can you stay all night?' Gunther asked.

'My dear, I can't. If I'm not back in reasonable time Major Dawson will send out another search party for me.'

'But you need not go yet, not yet.'

'A little longer,' she said. Her hand moved over his broad shoulders. 'How magnificent you are. I am so proud that you love me.'

'As I am proud of you, *Liebling*. You were right, we can't turn our backs on our love. Somehow, some time, you must be my wife. It will not be easy. I have given you all the reasons against it and they will be repeated by all your friends and family, but if we are steadfast we will wear down the opposition.'

'As I wore down yours,' Christine said.

'Mm . . . I am a little suspicious about that. Almost I could believe that you paid that American to knock you down.'

'No, I had completely given up. Strange, just when I thought I was defeated, I suddenly won you over.'

'And England was victorious once again. But that was a war I was glad to lose.' He raised himself on his elbow and looked down at her. She could hardly see his face, but she knew he was smiling. 'Will you fight one more battle with me, my most beautiful enemy, before I set you free and send you home?'

She reached up and put her arms round his neck, pulling him down to kiss him. 'I have no defences against you. All my frontiers are open, now and always.'

'There is a promise I would like to make to you,' Gunther said. 'Now, while our love is new, before the world has broken in on it and said it is not possible. I will always love you; we will be man and wife; we will live together in kindness and by our example we will help to build a happier future.'

'I will always love you,' Christine repeated after him, as if it were a marriage vow. 'I will be your wife. No matter what happens, I will stand firm and together we will make a new world, a better world for our children to live in.'